Sebb Argo & Dion Yorkie
Heart-Struck

MEDIA
PUBLISHING
HOUSE

First edition

ISBN: 978-1-0693690-0-0

Editing by Connor Welter
Cover art by Nitish Bhardwaj

to the fireflies that glow even on the darkest of nights, hold on to that light.

Contents

Acknowledgments

Before anyone else, we'd like to thank the SebasDion family for your unwavering support and for giving us the freedom to create art in all forms. For over nine years, you have been on this journey with us, fueling our passion for storytelling. Thank you for embarking on this adventure with us.

We began writing this book at the same time we started planning our wedding, and this novel wouldn't be what it is today without the love and encouragement of our besties. Special thanks to our groomsgays and groomsgirls—your kind and humorous hearts inspire us to live life always spreading light. Thank you for the moments that shaped characters and storylines that will live on in our hearts forever. Your love and support mean the world to us.

To our parents—thank you for raising two passionate souls who can't go a day without creating. Your unconditional support and love mean everything. Thank you for always picking up our calls and for being our home, no matter how far we are.

To our grandmas, thank you for being such a strong and inspiring force in our lives. Thank you for sharing happiness everywhere you go. We'll always love you.

To Danny, the best man, thank you for being the Mary-Kate to my Ashley, the Jamie Lee to my Lindsay. From day one, you've been our number one supporter, always cheering on every idea and project. Thank you for your endless love and guidance.

A huge thank you to our bestie Nitish from nb Art Studio for the most amazing cover art. You are one of the most talented artists in the world! You captured the gay superheroes with perky butts *perfectly*.

Throughout our career, we've always found our way back to working with another one of our incredibly talented besties, Taylor Holm. Thank you, Tayrontoo, for crafting stunning visuals to promote this book. Your eye for futuristic aesthetics belongs to the year 2073!

To our editor, Connor Welter—your insightful notes and observations helped strengthen our story in ways we couldn't have imagined. Thank you for taking the time to dive into this project with us.

And last but not least, thank you, dear reader. Whether you pre-ordered this book, picked it up randomly, or bought it because it looked fabulous, we are incredibly grateful for your support. We are living in a critical moment when governments and people in power are attempting to erase the LGBTQ+ community. Now more than ever, we invite you to be visible, claim your voice, and fight! Hold on to that light inside of you.

If you enjoy this book, we'd love for you to review or rate it wherever you can!

1

now boarding

I t is a popular belief that lightning never strikes in the same place twice. Over the ages people all around the world have talked about this natural occurrence as if it is an extraordinary canon event. A one in a billion chance of it ever happening. However, this belief is nothing but a myth. Lightning is likely to strike in the same spot hundreds, probably thousands of times. The Empire State building, for example, used to be hit around 23 times every year. That was before the year 2055 remodel where the New York city council partnered with RainforesTec to add 31 extra floors. Since 2055, the empire state building has been hit around 89 times per year. Nothing special about it. Having two separate lightning strikes in the exact same place at the exact same time however? That is a canon event able to change the course of where the world is heading.

Sidric

"I'm going to miss you so much," Sidric's mom whispers in his ear as she hugs him goodbye. The floral and citrus notes of her perfume fill his lungs, leaving behind a magnetic pull between them as she pulls away. Sidric knows he will see his parents in exactly one week but every time he says goodbye to them he can't help but feel like he is slowly departing his childhood. One flight at a time, he waves the innocent boy with sparks in his eyes goodbye.

"I'll be back soon ma," he chuckles as he grabs his bags and hugs his dad goodbye. The year is 2073, and he is attending his fifth OnlineCon, a convention where virtual reality meets real life. At least that's how the website describes it. Attendees expect to see their favorite VR creators, gamers and lifestyle content creators all in one room. Sidric only goes to meet up with the friends he's made from the first year he attended. It used to be a place where fans could meet their idols, get free merch and celebrate being unique. They would have all kinds of people come from all around the world. It's the place where Sidric first felt comfortable with being gay. He had made so many friends and connected with so many people that he finally felt like he had found a community where he belonged. Lately, however, the convention had lost its magic making it feel more like a dentist convention. RainforesTec had purchased the rights to the convention. That meant less color, less queerness and way more business talks about how RainforesTec is changing the world *for the better*.

Speaker Announcement
FLIGHT NUMBER AM1307 TO LOS ANGELES NEW GATE IS GATE 89

Of course, Sidric's gate is the one on the opposite side of terminal 2. Sidric rushes through the goodbyes and starts speed walking towards his flight. He looks back and waves as he sees his mother failing in an attempt to hold back her tears. She always does this. No matter if it is a weekend trip or if he is flying off to college for the semester. He smiles one last time as if to say, "I'm always with you mom," and runs for the gate. He's one of those airport people who like to be at their gate hours before boarding, so right now, he is panicking. He passes security seamlessly, puts his headphones in, and hits play on 1989, *Taylor's Version*, of course. The gate is packed with travelers waiting to board the flight to the city of angels. So many different stories, dreams, and journeys waiting to fly. The air in the airport feels cold and sterile, somehow, all airports Sidric has been to have the same scent. On his left, he sees a young kid holding a doll. They are wearing a pink dress, pink shoes and pink socks. It feels like whoever dressed them is for sure trying to make a statement about their child. The kid has a shaved head, their eyes are red and puffy. Sidric starts to wonder what is the story behind this kid's sadness, he takes little encounters like this and creates scenarios all the time. He loves people-watching, imagining the stories lurking amongst everyone that crosses his eye line. He spots a doctor traveling last minute because his wife is going into labor, a lawyer sitting by the bar who just lost the biggest case in his life against a robotic lawyer so he is drinking his sorrows away and now this little kid. They look around seven years old. Next to them sitting is a slender tall woman wearing a pair of smartglasses. She is having a conversation with someone on the other side. Her hand gestures make it look like she is playing with some sticky gum on her fingers. Sidric pauses his music and tries to listen in on the conversation. He snaps a photo of the woman and sends it to his friend Naya.

SIDRIC
  -She's giving Slenderman in Drag but less fabulous..

NAYA
  -dead… not the SmartGlasses. I can see her brain rotting already.
  -When does your flight land? I just checked into the hotel.. WE

GOT GOODIE BAGS!

SIDRIC
  -Oh shitt! I land at 6:45pm. See you soon!

Naya is the first friend he made at OnlineCon back when they were only 16 years old. It was Sidric's first year attending the convention and also his first year being out of the closet. For registration day, he had picked out this cute shirt with a cat puking a rainbow paired with an old pair of jeans given by his fashion forward brother (who two years later also came out as gay!). The whole outfit was not what a conventional straight masculine guy would wear so it was a big step for Sidric. He was just starting to experiment with his looks and was stepping out of his comfort zone. However, as soon as he arrived to check into the hotel everything blurred. His heart started racing and he felt a giant knot in his stomach. He rushed to the bathroom and hid for what felt like 3 hours but in reality was probably 5 minutes.

Naya barged in singing an indie band song. Sidric was startled as this was the men's bathroom and she seemed quite unbothered. She saw Sidric hyperventilating in the corner and said, "nice shirt cat boy." Her dark brown eyes stared right at him.

Sidric tried to hide his panic attack and quickly replied, "Thanks."

Naya stared at him for a few seconds realizing he was about to burst into tears and gave him a quick pat on the head. "I don't know what's going on but you probably shouldn't be sitting down on this floor. It's nasty."

Sidric quickly stood up. He splashed some water on his face and explained how he had just come out and he didn't want to be judged by everyone for being *too gay*. Every queer person goes through this stage. The stage after finally coming out when the judgy assholes say fake positive things like, *"I accept you for being gay cause at least you're not THAT kind of gay,"* as they point to an extremely flamboyant human. Inherently putting queer-identifying individuals into a box labeled "backhanded compliments." A concept that peeked through every corner of Sidric's thoughts.

"Well, I think your outfit is decadent. The mix of tones in the cat's puke reminds me of a true art piece and I don't mean no AI shit, something Picasso would have painted," Naya said as she inspected the shirt up close. She pulled out a small tin of lavender glitter from her cross-body bag and stuck two fingers in it. "Forget about the haters and own it!" she said as she traced her glitter-covered fingers on his cheek. Sidric looked in the reflection and stared at both Naya and himself.

"What's your name?" Sidric chuckled.

"Naya, what about you cat boy?"

"I'm Sidric."

Speaker Announcement
FLIGHT NUMBER AM1307 TO LOS ANGELES NOW BOARDING

Sidric grabs his bag and heads towards the line. In front of him, the slenderman suit woman takes a step forward holding the shaved head kid's hand in a tight grip. The kid has tears rolling down the side of their face. As the flight begins to board the kid's cry grows louder.

"I want to go home!" they scream.

The suit woman quickly tightens her grip on the kids arm, adjusts their sweatshirt and smartwatch, and moves forward. Something about these two people set off flags in Sidric's mind. Maybe something serious is going on or maybe it's just his tendency of creating storylines for strangers while he's bored.

2

ciTy of stRangers

Deux

"Looking for love in the city of angels, you will need luck in this city of strangers," Deux writes in his lyric book while he waits for his suitcase at the luggage pick up. He inspects every single detail of Los Angeles International Airport: the mismatched tiles with cracks that reflect the sunlight in the most cinematic way possible, the palm trees sticking out and peeking through the windows, welcoming every lost soul ready to find themselves. It is all exactly as he imagines. His whole life, he has dreamed of coming here— something inside him has always felt the need to be here. The salt air, the smell of dust, and the scent of dreams all hit him at once, and he knows flying all the way from Toronto was the right decision. This trip is his first trip all alone, of course, his grandma has decided to tag along at the last minute but all the plans he has at OnlineCon are just for him.

Deux is a featured guest at OnlineCon this year, he is part of the LGBTQ+ speakers. It feels good to have OnlineCon recognize all his years creating content online. Deux first grew a fan base after posting his coming-out video and since then he has been focusing on spreading positivity in the LGBTQ+ community. He posts new videos every week touching on all gay experiences one could imagine. He found a community that listens and relates to everything he has to say, a stark contrast to his small hometown. There, he always feels like a firefly among people content to be nothing more than fruit flies. He has dreams to chase and is not going to let anything get in his way.

Ever since he began sharing his life online, it started as a way to combat boredom and find a creative outlet. But now, a few years later, a sense of responsibility has taken hold of him. Deux feels a duty to use his platform to speak out and represent the LGBTQ+ community. Lately, the world seems to be regressing, with new laws targeting queer individuals, an alarming rise in hate crimes, and a pervasive sense of division. It only fuels his determination to inspire other queer youth to embrace their authentic selves and live their truth. Being in Los Angeles, about to be recognized for what he does, fills him with a sense of pride he has never felt before.

"Deux please tell the cab driver to stop at a liquor store before we get to the hotel, Grandma needs her wine," Grandma says snapping Deux back into reality.

She watches as Deux and the driver struggle to fit all the luggage into the car. For a small trip, they surely packed a lot. Four checked bags and 3 carry-ons. Deux smiles at Grandma and exchanges looks with the driver making sure he hears her. Grandma is the only person Deux would allow to crash his trip. Since Deux came out, she always tried to see things from his point of view. Likewise, whenever she can't, she is always quick to ask questions and learn about how she can do better. It brings a small tear to his eyes thinking of how lucky he is to share this experience with her. He admires her wisdom, if he ever needs advice she knows exactly what to say and which wine to pair the advice with. Boy problems go with red wine, getting fired for being too much went great with rosé, and celebrating his first 1,000 subscriber milestone was definitely a white wine moment. It is one of her many superpowers. The drive to the hotel gives Deux some time to ground himself and take in everything he has only seen in photographs. His body tingles with excitement as they drive past the Hollywood sign. What he hadn't seen in the photos was the RainforesTec logo now accompanying the sign in the bottom corner. Drones fly in the distance dropping off packages from one location to the next.

At the hotel Deux opens up his welcome package with the same excitement he had opening up his Santa Claus presents when he was nine. The only difference is that instead of it being a stuffed Grinch plush toy, it is his special guest pass, weekend itinerary, and VIP party pass. He stares at the package for a moment. He grabs his Grinch plush toy and places him next to the welcome package, sharing a small milestone with his most prized possession. He starts unpacking the rest of his bags while Grandma pours herself a big glass of white wine. Miley Cyrus plays in the background. Suddenly, there is a knock on the door. Grandma jumps out of the mid-century love seat and opens the door.

"Just one second," she says in a nice proper tone, "it's for you Deux, looks important!" she whispers.

A middle-aged woman dressed in all gray is standing outside of the room, she has long blond almost silver-like hair pulled back in a slick ponytail. She is wearing the new RainforesTec SmartGlasses. She has a small box decorated with rainbow wrapping paper in her hands.

"Ah you must be Deux! We are so happy to welcome you to OnlineCon!"

"Wow thanks!" Deux replies, "I am so excited to be here, it's my first time attending so I'm honestly expecting the unexpected," His voice is one octave lower than usual. A quirk of him that happens often whenever he first meets someone. In reality, it is a form of defense mechanism he learned after years of being bullied in middle school. Deux' voice has always had range, he loved singing since he was a kid and was not shy about it. One of the first videos he ever posted was a cover of "Defying Gravity" in which he, to no surprise, hit all the right notes. Unfortunately, as soon as he posted the video Shane Bryant, one of his middle school nemesis, shared it with the whole class. They all made fun of how high-pitched his voice was and would blast it down the hallways. Middle school kids will find anything to make the different kid an outcast. Up to this day, he still forces himself to have a lower voice around people he doesn't know or doesn't feel completely safe with.

"You should expect the best time ever. You'll be shocked, there isn't a single moment to rest," she smiles back, "Here, we wanted to personally gift you our new RainforesTec PrideTime smartwatch. Specifically designed for LGBTQ+ creators like yourself. It's coming out in stores next month!"

www.rainforestec.com/PrideTime-SmartWatch

The PrideTime Smartwatch is a vibrant celebration of individuality and inclusivity. Designed to honor the LGBTQ+ community and its allies, this smartwatch features a dynamic color-shifting display that transitions through the full spectrum of the rainbow throughout the day. Both subtle and striking, this one-of-a-kind feature lets you wear your pride on your wrist with style and elegance.

Powered by RainforesTec's revolutionary Micro-Puncture Technology, the PrideTime Smartwatch goes beyond traditional wearables. Its discreet and painless sensors deliver unmatched accuracy in health monitoring, offering insights into your body's vital functions.

Now that's a mouthful... Deux thinks to himself.

"Thank you," he says.

"Additionally, there is a welcome mixer tonight to promote the pre-launch of the new smartwatch we would love to have you wear it at the event," She hands Deux an envelope with the party details.

"Awesome! I'll be there," he awkwardly spurts out. Deux doesn't have much experience being social with strangers. He knows attending OnlineCon is going to force him to put himself out there—to talk to other people rather than just his camera. He is ready to push himself to be social, or at least he is trying to convince himself that he is.

He closes the door behind him and takes a deep breath. "Grandma, I got a free watch!" Deux shows the shiny box.

Grandma takes one look at the box and chuckles. "What's new with this one? Does it read your mind? Will it fill up my glass whenever it's empty?" She laughs, raising her wine glass.

She was born before RainforesTec took over all technology in the world and has witnessed its evolution from a humble tech startup to the giant it is today. Nowadays, it's impossible to go anywhere without encountering at least one RainforesTec product. She's always cautioning Deux and his siblings against becoming too reliant on technology. "You should at least be able to survive a day without any of these toys," she constantly says.

Deux carefully unwraps the colorful gift, taking care not to rip the rainbow-patterned wrapping paper, and slides the watch onto his wrist. As he adjusts the strap, he feels it vibrate and tighten automatically. The screen lights up, projecting a 4D hologram of a spinning rainbow wheel with the word "calibrating." While it loads, Deux turns his attention to picking out an outfit for the party. He pulls out a pair of black jeans and a black T-shirt—his go-to look.

Grandma immediately yells from the sofa, "Too basic Luv! This is *Los Angeles*! We didn't come all this way for you to wear the same things you wear back home." She turns the TV on and puts the Midnights News channel on. The only channel she trusts to get her news from and probably the last broadcasting channel not owned by RainforesTec. "It is always midnight somewhere!" She chants at the same time as the channel's host.

He goes back to his suitcase to look again. Even though he's packed way more than he needs, he still feels like he has nothing to wear. After putting looks together for thirty minutes he decides to go with a shiny shimmering button-up and a pair of light-washed jeans. It is the perfect mix of fancy and, *"Oh I just threw this on."* He proceeds to do his makeup, just a light base and contour. With the California heat, it will all be melted by the end of the night. Minutes later, after applying, adding too much, washing out, and reapplying his eyebrow tint he puts his shoes on, kisses Grandma goodbye, and heads out the door. The event has sent over a car to pick him up and take him to the party. He loves being treated like a celebrity. He imagines this is what Meryl Streep must have felt like. Meryl Streep and *Mamma Mia!* are staple names in Deux' family. They watch all her movies at least twice a year. Thanks to the movie *Mamma Mia!,* Deux discovered his love for musicals and all things artistic. He would recreate all the musical numbers with his sister Atlanta. Of course, he would play Meryl's character and his sister would switch between the daughter and one of the aunts. If Deux had it his way, he'd play every role. They would stay up until 5 am dancing and chanting the tunes around the basement. That was usually when his mom and dad would wake up from all the noise and send them straight to bed.

After spending so much time online and having a platform to express everything he wanted, he feels like his own small version of Meryl Streep—and that is everything. A sleek black car pulls up to pick him up. He hops in, and the driver greets him with a cheerful, "Hi, Mr. Yates! Let's get you to the party."

Shit, I love this.

3

fiveloko dAte

Sidric

O nce Sidric's flight lands he rushes his way out of the plane and through customs. It's always interesting trying to explain to the border cyborg-patrol officers what OnlineCon is. It doesn't even matter that RainforesTec literally coded their artificial intelligence software; they're always clueless about anything going on outside of the airport. After a few intruding questions and the all-too-familiar racist remarks about Mexicans from the robot, Sid is good to go. He grabs his documents, dragging them on the desk slightly to add a bit of sass to his *"Thank you"* and walks away. He heads to baggage claim to grab his purple suitcase and struggles pulling it towards the ride app pickup spot. License plate DS0709 pulls in. Sidric takes all of his energy into getting the suitcase in the trunk and immediately feels a drop of sweat forming on his forehead. *Sweet LA heat doing me dirty.* As he opens the door he jumps back in shock. He looks around the car and then peaks into both the front seats. There is no driver in the car. *This must be one of those famous RainforesTec driverless cabs.* Still an uncomfortable reality to Sidric, he prays to Taylor Swift, Madonna, and Tina Turner that he gets to the hotel safe and sound.

A man's voice coming from the radio interrupts his prayers, "If you are fastened in and all set say: Go!"

"*Go?*" Sidric asks, unsure if he actually wants to. The car's engine roars to life, and within seconds, it accelerates to full speed. Sidric grips the passenger door handle as tightly as he can, feeling sweat drip onto the fancy Italian leather seats.

He arrives at the hotel, and just as he's about to knock on the door, Naya greets him, holding a wicker welcome basket filled with Sidric's favorite things. There are a few packs of Sour Patch Kids, flaming hot Cheetos, a pair of socks with little llamas on them, and three cans of Sidric's favorite drink which happens to be illegal in almost every state in America, Gold FiveLoko.

"Oh my god! Naya!" Sidric screams out in the highest pitch possible, "What a way to welcome your biggest hater!" He teases her as he opens his arms to hug her.

She puts the basket down and goes in for the hug. She is wearing a blue oversized shirt with paint splatters all over, black pants with polka dots and her long black hair pinned up into two space buns. Her fashion choices reflect exactly what goes on in her mind. She's never afraid of how she looks because at the end of the day, she is always rocking it.

Sidric grabs the basket and immediately goes towards the Gold FiveLoko. "I still don't know what the fifth ingredient is in this drink but it is exactly what I need after a long flight," Sidric says as he pops one open and takes a sip. The gold drink lightly burns his throat while going down. They just recently released this new edition with a secret fifth ingredient meant to make you even more Loko than before. Hence, the name FiveLoko.

"I still don't know how you drink these. They're illegal for a reason bestie," Naya says while going through her bag. She pulls out a huge tequila bottle and places it on the table. "I, on the other hand, am loyal to my one true love, Jose Cuervo." She kisses the bottle and pops it open.

"So what are we doing tonight? Stealing goodie bags from registration? Finding a sugar daddy?" Sidric asks.

"Well, while you were flying here I was in the lobby getting to work. I got talking to this famous singer, she just hit 10 million followers. I told her I was a manager looking for new clients," she says while mixing some tequila with dollar-store lemonade. Naya has a way of socializing with anyone. She has a sixth sense of knowing how to get to people's hearts and how to connect with them by saying the right thing at the right time. "She was so interested in working with me that she invited me to a VIP party tonight! It's a pre-launch event so we can expect free stuff. Of course, I had to ask if I could bring my talented assistant and she agreed and put both of us on the list. VIP MAWMA!"

"Shut up! At what time does it start?"

"8 pm sharp. But we can be fashionably late. I am a world-renowned manager after all."

"Perfect, let's get ready and then hit the welcome show before the party," Sidric says while chugging the last of his first can of FiveLoko.

"I mean, I am ready," Naya chuckles, pointing to her colorful outfit. "But you're more than welcome to fix yourself up. I won't be having any assistants looking like they just got beat up by Satan himself."

Sidric laughs and zips open his suitcase. He tosses out a pair of black cargo pants and a white crop top to go with it. He takes a brisk shower, shaves his stubble, and plucks his eyebrows. Every day, he thanks his Latino ancestors for his thick, full eyebrows—even if he has to pluck a few stray hairs now and then. He gets dressed and applies a bit of makeup to cover up some pimples and shaving irritation, finishing it all in under twenty minutes. When he senses Naya getting impatient, he calls out for her to prepare two tequila shots for him while he grabs his necklaces and bracelets. Finally, he puts on his sun-stone crystals, ready to bring all the good vibes to the party.

Dressed and ready to serve Diva-Three-Thousand, the pair swings open the doors to the main convention hall, their eyes immediately lighting up. The atmosphere is electric as they walk through the large hallway towards the theater. People all around talking loudly about new RainforesTec gadgets coming out and greeting friends from last year's event. Large posters hang from the ceilings almost 4 meters high showcasing a few of their recent developments.

Sidric can't help but feel out of place as he looks around. Something feels off about the event this year, he can't quite put his finger on it. He turns to Naya, who seems equally excited as everyone else, and says, "This all seems too good to be true, doesn't it?"

Naya looks at him, raising an eyebrow, "What do you mean?"

"I don't know," Sidric replies, "It's just... everything seems so sponsored, so perfect."

Previous years at OnlineCon were filled with outlandish inventions and unforgettable community events. One highlight was the famous Cowffee Shop, where a dozen cyborg cows produced the best matcha lattes known to mankind. Equally iconic was the TrampoThon, held on opening night, one of the most popular parties at the event. Every attendee was given a pair of TrampoShoes—shoes with trampoline soles that allowed effortless jumps nearly seven feet high. These unique experiences were what brought the magic to OnlineCon.

This year, however, a sleek VR stand occupies the spot where the Cowffee Shop once stood. It offers attendees a virtual tour of the RainforesTec headquarters—a very different vibe, but one reflective of the changing times.

As they make their way into the theater, Sidric notices several of

RainforesTec's top executives milling about. They all have the same slicked-back hair and smooth, mysterious demeanor, Sidric gets a chill in the back of his neck. He recognizes the same slenderman lady from the airport.

The theater is packed with people, all ready to hear the welcome speech from RainforesTec's CEO, Jacques P. Bizous. Sidric and Naya take their seats near the back of the room, and the lights dim as an ominous beat plays. The CEO takes the stage rolling in on a hoverboard just a few inches above the ground. The crowd goes wild.

Jacques Bizous is a tall, imposing figure, with piercing gray eyes and a commanding presence. His robust torso looks unproportionate to his thin long legs. He begins his speech by raising his arms and taking in everyone's cheers. "Think about all the billion ways your life has improved thanks to RainforesTec in the few recent years!" The crowd cheers even louder.

"Nobody is doing it like us that's for sure. Today people can use our RainforesTec SmartGlasses to do virtually anything you can think of. Immersing yourself into your favorite scary movie to performing open heart surgery. We are limitless," The man is good with his words since moments after he dives in Sidric has forgotten all about his previous worries.

"You heard about our recent trials on muscle technology. Ninety-nine percent of the paralyzed subjects can now fully walk! Rain-foresTec is doing it for everyone out there."

Sidric and Naya cheer extremely loud as Bizous starts announcing the lineup for this year's special guests. Bizous closes his inaugural speech by promising a future that no one can even dream of as six cyborgs march onto the stage shooting free t-shirts at the crowd. Sid and Naya spend the following hour captivated by all the music performances and free gifts.

Deux

The SmartWatch Pre-Launch mixer is in an indoor go-kart racing track called K1-Speed, just a few minutes away from the hotel. Deux arrives at the party just as everyone else is arriving. He takes a deep breath before going in and gives himself a quick pep-talk. *You are happy and you are confident. You are a star, Deux!*

Loud music blasting through the doors and people in racing suits dancing around the entrance push Deux to be in the moment. He walks in and is welcomed by a woman on stilts holding a tray of appetizers: cheeseburger taquitos and pepperoni sushi rolls. He grabs a taquito and as he bites it his mouth is filled with emotions. *This cheeseburger taquito is what dreams are made of.*

Inside, there are two huge race tracks where people are lining up to drive the go-karts. Around the first track, tables full of food and welcome bags pack the front corner. He peeks into the bags to see the new Pride SmartWatch and a few merch items. *I guess they really want them out there.*

He walks towards the bathroom to pretend like he has somewhere to go. As he approaches the entrance he bumps into THE Nate and Andre. This queer power couple has built an audience of almost 1 million followers by showing off their remodeling skills. They are so good at transforming places that it is rumored that they are hired to remodel the new wing of a popular hotel chain that rhymes with Milton. Due to NDA's signed they are not at liberty to confirm or deny.

"Deux! Hey! I follow all your socials! I'm Nate. This is Andre," Nate joyfully says as he reaches out for a hug. His warmness catches Deux off guard. Through all the years he has been online he has only met people who were complete assholes to him, so this is a nice surprise. Nate is about 5'6, with loud red hair and deep blue eyes. Andre is about the same height as Deux, and his eyes give off the same energy as those of a newborn cat.

"Hi, nice to meet you both. I've seen your remodeling series. What you do is pure talent!" as Deux says this he impresses himself with how easy words are coming out of his mouth.

"Oh, honey, you haven't seen anything yet. Wait until our new series comes out. You're going to—" Nate is cut off by Andre, who elbows him.

"Nate... NDA... *remember?*" Andre whispers a bit too loud, "Hi Deux. How's your OnlineCon going?"

"Sorry I've been having lots of these free drinks," Nate says as he sips on a canned white wine, "Not the best quality wine to be honest."

"No worries. It's going great, loving all the free stuff," Deux says pointing to the smartwatch, "I'm excited to see what else they have planned this weekend."

"These things get wild! It's so fun," Andre says as he waves down a drone carrying tiny shot glasses, "To a crazy night!" He hands Deux and Nate a shot.

Conversation and shots keep flowing. Twenty minutes and four more canned wines later the three of them are already planning a wine-tasting trip across the entirety of Europe.

Sidric

On the other side of the party, Sidric and Naya are pulling into the event's entrance. They get out of the cab and fix each other's outfits. Naya brushes the lint off Sidric's pants smacking his butt. Sidric blows on the feathers of Naya's extravagant coat she added on last minute, as they giggle at how stupid they both look.

"Wait, let me hide this," Sidric whispers pulling out his last FiveLoko can. He shoves it into a bush right next to the entrance, hoping nobody steals it. To secure, he shuffles some leafs on top of it. "Perfect, be back soon baby," he blows some air kisses.

"I think we should get you some help Sid."

They both laugh and prance into the party enjoying how stupidly carefree they feel whenever they are together. The laughter grows into excitement as they pass the doors and get their VIP passes. "Act like you belong, honey, let's get crazy," Naya cackles.

The DJ starts to play some early Britney Spears. It's always so easy to get people dancing once you have some Britney on. Sidric and Naya dance their way towards the bar. Bumping into strangers and grabbing some taquitos, they fit right in. They pass a group of drunk girls in line for the photo booth. These uptight box blondes try to give Sidric and Naya dirty looks, but the moment Naya notices, she *accidentally* bumps into one of them and spills her drink all over the tallest blonde's dress.

"Instant Karma!" they say to each other at the same time. They have had an inside joke about karma ever since Sidric showed Naya Taylor Swift's iconic *Midnights* album. Naya claims to be a T Swift hater but thanks to that album she was able to get over her fuckboy ex-boyfriend. They couldn't be more the same.

The girls share looks and groans amongst each other and suddenly one girl hushes them and whispers in a sweet southern accent, "Y'all be nice she's the new it-manager. Travis was just telling me about her."

Sidric and Naya overhear her and immediately run away cackling.

"We need to get you a website stat," Sidric laughs.

Drones fly past them with trays full of deliciously smelling snacks. Naya's nose follows the scent trail.

As they get closer to the bar, by some twist of fate, Sidric's eyes meet Deux's for the very first time. Though they are strangers, Sidric recognizes those eyes. Flashback to a few months ago—Sid was supposed to be studying for his finals but ended up procrastinating by watching videos of hot guys in *Spiderman* suits. He claims it was just his feed acting up, but secretly, he more than enjoyed it. When the video ended, he was recommended another: a cute guy talking about how coming out had changed his life. Sid clicked on it and instantly developed a crush on him. He didn't even really pay attention to the content, captivated only by the guy's hazel eyes. Moments later, his roommate walked in, and he quickly closed all the tabs, pretending to be doing homework.

Up until this moment at the party, he had forgotten all about the mystery video boy. But now, seeing those hazel eyes in person, up close, he knows it was him. *This is the mystery video boy.* Time seems to slow as their eyes lock, exchanging a million unspoken words per second. A connection is made.

After a few seconds, Deux keeps walking, pulled by Nate and Andre towards the free merch table. He looks back only to see Sidric's eyes looking right back. He turns quickly feeling the intrigue of lust. Two simple words come to his mind as he admires his brown warm sight. *Timeless perfection.* He forces himself to stop staring. The last thing he wants to appear like is a creepy stalker. He follows his new friends towards the merch section and tries to distract himself by picking out some free sunglasses. Deux is always down to meet new guys, he loves meeting cute guys actually. However, he never knows how to make the first move. He'd rather have cute guys come to him and then he can take over.

Back by the bar, Sidric grabs Naya's arm and squeezes it tightly.

"Naya, I've been struck," Sidric says as he stares into imaginary cupids flying all around him. He pretends to faint into her arms.

"Struck by what? A bus? I always knew you were missing some neurons," she sassily replies pushing him away from her. She is very strong for someone who is 5'5.

"No, I'm serious, I've seen that guy before. I need to meet him. I

21

need to know his name."

"What guy? Where did you see him? *Grindr?*"

"I saw him online, I think he makes videos," Sidric says, "Would it be creepy if I go introduce myself?"

"I mean, if he makes videos just go and ask for a photo, pretend you're a fan. Or don't pretend since you actually are a fan," Naya's planning wheels start turning as she sips more canned wine, "Or...I could also do my manager bit, and say I want to sign him. He'd be on my roster in minutes."

"Naya... you are not an actual manager. You have no roster. I think I'll ask for a photo and then go from there," Sidric pulls Naya towards the merch booth, "and you'll take the photo."

Deux

Deux sees Sidric making his way towards him. With every step Sidric takes closer to him he feels his heart beat a bit faster. His hands getting sweaty and his breath rising. He turns around and tries to keep up with what Andre and Nate are chatting about. *It's all in my head, this gorgeous tanned brown-haired boy is not walking toward me.* His thoughts are abruptly interrupted by a tap on his shoulder. Deux turns around to see him standing right in front of him. *The mystery boy.*

Sidric

"Hi!" Sidric quickly adjusts his volume, "uhm...I love your videos, could I get a photo with you?" Only Naya can tell his voice is cracking and his hands are shaking. Deux is a bit taller than him. He didn't realize there was such a height difference until he got close to him.

"Hey, yes of course! What's your name?" Deux says opening his arm for Sidric to get under. Sidric wraps his arm around Deux's waist.

They both smile at Naya snapping the photo. Deux smells like good cologne, the one you get samples from at department stores but never actually bother to spend good money on.

Deux

Deux's hand rests on top of Sidric's shoulder, while his other hand unknowingly goes for a peace sign. He regrets it as soon as he puts it up. He is going to let this action consume his thoughts for the rest of the night. *Who even does peace signs anymore?!*

"Yass! work it! You two look good together. OH, my," Naya chants as she snaps away.

"I'm Sidric," he says turning back to look at him, "Nice to meet you." He smiles.

He has an archangel smile. The type of smile that is contagious and can brighten anyone's mood. In seconds, his smile somehow makes Deux forget about the whole peace sign panic attack.

Deux forces himself to say something after staring at him for a few seconds consumed by his beauty and his really nice teeth. "I'm Deux. This is Nate and Andre!" He points towards the design gays. They both smile and wave.

"So you're the manager everyone's talking about!" Nate says, "I'm sure you've heard about us, we are huge online."

"Yes, it's me—the only manager you'll ever need." She extends both hands to greet them at the same time. "I'm pretty selective about my clients and aim to provide nothing but the highest quality services."

"We're going to be great friends, I can already tell," Nate chuckles pointing at her.

Naya smiles and leads them outside to talk 'business.' After all the intense eye contact makes it clear to all three that Sidric and Deux want some time alone.

"What brings you to OnlineCon?" Deux asks, "Do you make videos too?"

"I do but not as good as yours," he chuckles, "I've just been coming every year for so long. Mainly just to meet with old friends. Like Naya, she's my bestie."

"I was going to say I suspect she's not an actual manager," Deux smirks at him, "Don't worry, I'll let Andre and Nate believe she is for a while. They deserve it after getting me wine-drunk tonight. This canned wine shit is disgusting by the way."

They both awkwardly laugh.

"We'll if you are tired of wine, I have something better for you," Sidric says, with a devilish smile. Deux likes that look. He catches himself getting lost in thought on how many things he would do for that smile.

"Do you like FiveLokos?" Sidric asks.

"What on earth is a FiveLoko?" a hint of a British accent comes out. He gets his accents mixed whenever he is in stressful situations. "Sounds like a bad idea," *back to American Deux.*

"Oh it is, it's a bad idea in the most beautiful electrifying poetic way. Trust me. I hid one outside."

"I trust you," Deux says winking at him. Sid melts a little inside. He has a soft spot for whenever a guy winks at him, mainly because he does not know how to close only one eye and make it sexy. The way Deux did it was probably the most charming wink he'd ever seen.

"Lead the way!" Deux smiles.

Sidric walks him to the front door, near the bushes where he hid his FiveLoko. He's always eager to convert people into his FiveLoko obsession—which, he realizes, sounds a bit cult-like. But if he had to join a cult, it would definitely be a FiveLoko cult. He reaches down and almost trips into the bushes. Just before his face hits the ground, his arm instinctively reaches back for Deux's hand. Deux tenses but grabs his hand in return.

"Sorry about that," Sidric stands back up with a FiveLoko in his hand and a bit of foliage in his hair. Deux still holding his hand. They both look down and at the same time pull their palms apart.

"Do you want to take a walk? It's getting kind of stuffy in there," Sidric says, shaking his hair to clear out the leaves. He surprises himself at how smooth he sounds, considering his insides are going hectic after holding Deux's hand.

They proceed to walk down the street from the party, the music muffles as they get further away from the venue. It's a calm night in contrast to all the chaos going on back there. A line of street lamps flicker their way down the boulevard.

"So, your videos, what are they about?" Deux asks.

"A little bit of everything, honestly. I just do it for fun—to get in touch with my creative side, I guess. I don't have a ton of followers like you, though."

"That's fine, maybe we can film a video together. I can help you get some more," Deux says, hoping to secure another day where he can see Sidric again. Every second that goes by he just wants to know more about Sidric. He is as captivated by Sidric as he was when he watched the Grinch for the very first time.

They find a bench at the end of the street, overlooking the ocean. Sidric's heart can hardly catch a break as they sit down. He loves flirting and making out with new boys, but Deux makes him feel as if he's never done any of this before. Sidric reaches for the FiveLoko can and pops it open.

"Okay get ready," he says, bringing the can close to Deux's mouth, "here comes the best drink you'll ever have."

Deux swallows a bit of the gold translucent liquid. He winces as the drink stings his throat. He gasps for air, wiping some tears away from his eyes.

"How do you drink this?! That is poison!" he cries out laughing.

"How dare you?! This is fine cuisine. Only the best," Sidric says, sipping some more unbothered and places the can in between their two bodies.

"So, Canada, what is it like?" Sidric asks, breaking away the silence.

"It's cold most of the year but it's nice. My family moved there when I was 7 from the UK," he says, followed by a big gulp of FiveLoko, "What about you?"

"Wait you're British?" Sidric eyes him up and down, he's always had a thing for British boys, "Show me your accent."

They both laugh and Deux gives his best British accent. Sitting on that bench, everything else in the world is paused, there is no OnlineCon, no parties and no worries. Only two strangers turning the pages from each other's stories.

Deux thinks about how the only thing in between them right now is that small can of FiveLoko. He wishes nothing more than to kick it out of the way and taste the FiveLoko directly from Sidric's lips. He aches to feel his breathing against his, to trace the maps that lead to his hidden treasures. This is a once-in-a-lifetime connection he feels.

As the night wears on, they continue downing FiveLoko, with Deux slowly but surely developing a like for the drink. With each passing sip, he finds himself drawn to its unique flavor, wondering if perhaps he is growing accustomed to the mysterious fifth ingredient. Or maybe it is the alcohol coursing through his veins, loosening his inhibitions and making it easier for him to swallow the potent concoction. Regardless, he continues to drink, enjoying the sensation of the cold can in his hand, the warm buzz in his head and the butterflies all around.

Sidric

The clock strikes 2:30 am, probably the most romantic time if you study all of Taylor Swift's songs. Sidric feels this as well. He watches Deux talk about his life back home and all he can focus on is his lips. How soft they look. He has kissed a few boys before, he considers himself to be well-experienced. However, Deux's lips intrigue him in a way that no other lips have before. He tries to read Deux's face as if it is a thousand page novel written in a lost tongue. He wants to get lost in every page, every sentence, word for word. His lips are thin, but they have plumpness to them that is enticing. As he speaks they stretch wide and when he laughs they curve up in just the slightest bit. Sid studies every hill, valley, and crease. The thought of tasting him consumes him, to feel him so close that they could feel each other's heartbeats. He inches closer little by little. Seconds stretching into eternities. Deux's words slow down, his attention drawn to how close Sidric is now. Deux shuts his eyes and leans in to kiss him.

As their lips touch for the first time Sidric's mind spirals into override. He loses himself in Deux, only to be found by Deux's heartbeat. Kiss after kiss, they become more acquainted by the words they couldn't speak. Deux has a heated approach to kissing, his lips take charge of the situation. Whereas, Sidric submits to him and follows his lead. Deux's stubble scratches the top of his lip. He tastes like mint leaves and the sweetness of the drinks he's been drinking all night long. Sidric instinctively moves his hand to place it around Deux's body.

As he makes his way up he spills the rest of the FiveLoko all over Deux, soaking his pants and his brand-new Smartwatch in a sea of gold liquid. The Smartwatch immediately begins to malfunction and indicates an abnormal increase in heart rate. They are too preoccupied to notice the constant beeping coming from the device.

99 bpm. 104 bpm. 109 bpm. 116 bpm. 126 bpm. 146 bpm. 178 bpm.

Sidric moves to sit on top of Deux's legs, and Deux instinctively wraps his arms around Sidric's waist. The scent of the ocean breeze surrounds them, keeping them close together. His hands grip the back of Sidric's hair, gradually pulling lower as Sid arches his back, inviting him to go even further. Sidric teasingly moves back and forth, tempting Deux with the anticipation of what is to come. The intensity of their connection generates electric shocks throughout their bodies, but it's only when they share another kiss that they realize the true source of the electricity. Sidric gasps as he kisses Deux again, and a bolt of electricity surges through their bodies, illuminating the area around them with a burst of light.

Sidric pulls away to see Deux's hair full of static lifting above his head. He reaches his hand up to feel his hair doing the same thing. Deux's wrist glimmering and crackling with sparks from the SmartWatch malfunctioning.

"Uhm, Deux? I think your wrist is on fire!" Sidric exclaims.

"Oh shit," Deux curses out as he scrambles to his feet, frantically shaking his arm around like a bird, "What do i do?!"

"Take it off!" Sidric points to the faulty watch.

Together, they attempt to remove the watch, receiving electric jolts every time they touch it. After a few failed tries they finally manage to take it off.

"And that's why my grandma doesn't trust modern technology," Deux laughs, pointing to the SmartWatch about to combust.

"For real, I feel like we need to sue Jacques Bizous, get all his RainforesTec money," Sidric says, half-jokingly. He grabs the remaining FiveLoko and pours it on top of the SmartWatch expecting the combustion to die down. Instead, it only reignites it once again.

There is a quick awkward laugh and then silence with the thought of how they were on the brink of hooking up still fresh in their minds. Breaking the silence, Deux speaks up.

"Should we head back? I think my grandma might go crazy if I don't get back soon," he suggests.

They ride back together in the same cab, their knees touching a precise 23 times, according to Sidric's count. Deux, however, counts 25. Though they both yearn for another kiss, neither dares to ask for it, at least not tonight. The elevator ride up to their respective hotel rooms is a torturous affair, with tension building by the second. After what seems like an eternity, the doors finally open on the 14th floor.

"This is me," Sidric sighs. "Will I see you tomorrow?"

"Absolutely," Deux responds, flashing a playful wink.

As Sidric exits the elevator, he's left reeling from the effect of that wink. *Damn, he's been struck.*

4

sparks fly

Sidric

The following morning, Sidric wakes around eight o'clock. His body refuses to succumb to the drowsiness that comes with a hangover; he always manages to wake up early after a night of drinking. Although a slight headache creeps into his consciousness, his thoughts are consumed with the memory of last night's kisses. He's been fixated on Deux's lips since he left, and can hardly wait to feel their touch once more. As he trace's back his midnight hookup, a surge of electricity courses through his body. Every inch of his skin erupts in goosebumps, electrified by a wave of intense energy. He's wide awake now, fully alert and focused on the potential for another thrilling encounter with Deux.

Last night when he first got back he filled in Naya on his secret make-out session. She was ecstatic, turns out her, Andre and Nate had made bets on what was going to happen between them. Naya had bet on them hooking up.

"No more FiveLoko for me," Naya groans, as she rolls over.

"Come on, it's not that bad!" Sidric insists, rising from his bed and beginning to prepare for the day ahead. The headache he'd been starting to feel had faded. He feels as alive as if he'd just drank 5 espresso shots. "We have a long day ahead of us," he seizes the hairdryer and expertly styles his hair, a craft he's honed over half his life.

"Did you make any plans with your new boo?" Naya asks, holding two cold cans of coke against her eyes.

"Actually, no, I didn't even get his number." Sidric regretfully points out.

"What the hell we gonna do now?" Naya grumbles.

"Well, obviously, we have to find him. Then I'll charm him again, get his number, and hopefully get one more kiss." Just the thought of kissing Deux again sends a flutter of butterflies through Sidric's stomach. He closes his eyes and imagines Deux's hands exploring every inch of his body, the parts he's kept hidden from everyone else. As his mind wanders, the hairdryer begins to smoke, sending sparks flying from the electricity socket. The sparks continue to travel along the chord and all around the hairdryer.

"Uh, lover boy, you're about to set your hair on fire." Naya warns him. The smell of burning hair fills the room as Sidric quickly unplugs the hairdryer.

"Shit, shit, shit," he whisper-screams, tossing it into the sink. He turns on the tap, diffusing the fire. "And that's why I never use cheap hotel hairdryers. I can't believe I forgot my good one at home."

"Alright, let me get up and shower," Naya stretches, but suddenly feels the aftermath of yesterday's taquitos coming back up. "Oh no—" She runs to the bathroom.

Deux

Unlike Sidric, Deux usually sleeps in after a night out. It's a family tradition to sleep in, order takeout, and lounge around on weekends. But today, he's different. Throughout the night, he's been jolted awake

31

by electric shocks from his bed sheets. As he wakes up at 8:25 am, another electric shock ripples through his body. He wonders if it's the hotel's bed sheets being extra static or just the memories of last night's kiss that have him feeling so electrified. He slips out of bed, careful not to disturb his slumbering grandma, and shuffles towards the bathroom. Once inside, he cranks the shower handle and steps beneath the warm, cascading water. As he lathers soap across his body, he notices small spots of golden skin discoloration around the area where his Smartwatch once sat. He gently rubs his fingers over the speckles, studying them in confusion. After completing his shower, he dries off and finds some gauze in his grandmother's medicine kit, which he uses to cover the peculiar marks. Despite his focus on the task at hand, his mind keeps drifting to the memory of his intimate 2 am make-out session with Sidric. If only he had asked for his number or social media details.

Deux's schedule includes a panel at four o'clock, the "Queer-time Q&A" discussion moderated by beauty guru Jazmina Chere. He's a bit apprehensive, given that it's his first time on a panel, but takes comfort in the fact that his new friends Nate and Andre will be joining him. As he walks backstage, he attempts to stay centered and calm to avoid any potential panic attacks in front of the audience.

"Andre! Nate! It's good to see you guys," Deux says, as Andre embraces him in a warm hug.

"How was your night?" Andre inquires, his expression curious.

Nate interjects with a sly grin, "Did y'all bite each other's corn dogs? I have twenty bucks riding on it."

Deux looks bewildered, "What? Bite a corn dog? What are you talking about?"

"We made a bet with Naya," Nate explains, "I said nothing would happen, she said y'all would kiss, and Andre...well, he said y'all would 'bite each other's corn dogs.' I have no idea where he came up with that phrase."

"Well, there was no corn dog biting, unfortunately. But there was lots of kissing."

"Ugh, we owe her $20. So.. Are you ready for the panel?"

"Yes, I'm pumped!" he forces a smile. If he keeps repeating how excited and prepared he is, he hopes he'll trick himself into quelling his nerves. Unfortunately, it isn't working. Deux was a confident public speaker as a child, but high school was a turning point. Throughout his first year of high school, the bullying had become so unbearable for him that skipping school seemed like the only way to avoid his tormentors. Ironically, these same guys pretended it was all jokes once Deux gained recognition online, but he saw through their facade. Although he's grown more self-assured over time, he still has moments where he feels like the insecure boy he once was, mocked by his peers. He inhales deeply, surveys his surroundings, and begins to feel better. *You got this, it's just answering easy questions.*

Sidric

Meanwhile, Sidric and Naya comb the entire convention center, determined to locate Deux. They discover that he's scheduled to participate in a panel in Diamond Hall, but despite their best efforts, they're unable to locate the correct room.

"Stay focused, Naya! We're on the hunt for Diamond Hall," he yells over the clamor of the bustling convention center.

Naya's lungs burn as they sprint through the maze of corridors. They run through several meet and greet rooms popping their head in and realizing it's the wrong one time after time.

"I think I see it! Diamond!" she gasps, on the brink of exhaustion. Running has never been her forte.

They reach the entrance to the hall just as Deux is being questioned by the panel leader. Unfortunately, they are too late to know what the question is.

Deux

"Well, now that you mention it…" Deux begins to respond, but his attention is suddenly diverted to the crowd. As his gaze locks onto Sidric's, his heart begins to race and his palms become sweaty. He's been doing well up until this point, but the sight of the handsome boy who captured his heart last night pushes him over the edge. Flashes of Sid's body on top of his flood his thoughts.

Sidric waves and smiles, mouthing the words, "You got this." This simple gesture sends Deux into a frenzy, and beads of sweat start trickling down his forehead.

Suddenly, the speakers and spotlights begin to malfunction, flashing and sparkling erratically. The panel leader apologizes for the technical difficulties, but most people can't hear him over the intermittent feedback from the microphone. A high-pitched static sound echoes through the hall. Nate looks down at Deux's hand gripping the mic, and gasps as sparks fly from it. Deux doesn't feel anything, but he can sense something is off from Nate's reaction. He throws the microphone down in confusion, unsure of what's happening as the electricity in the room intensifies and his heart rate increases.

The lights go completely out, and the only remaining illumination comes from the backup emergency lights. Panic sets in as the fire alarm blares and sprinklers burst from the ceiling, drenching the crowd. Deux is left bewildered, as the sparks and electrical mayhem engulf the room.

"Please remain calm and exit the premises in an orderly fashion," the panelist instructs the crowd, who completely ignores her and rushes out as fast as possible.

"Deux, this way," Nate beckons, leading him through a back exit. Sidric and Naya trail closely behind.

"Good morning, boys," Naya greets them, her hand extended, anticipating payment for a lost bet. She shoots a sly grin towards Deux. "Deux, how you doing tiger?"

"Hey!" Deux responds, feeling giddy like a schoolboy with a crush. He can't help but keep his gaze fixed on Sidric, the fire alarm chaos forgotten.

"That was a bit wild. You'd think RainforesTec, being a tech company, would have proper plugs for their speakers," Andre grumbles. His lack of awareness often requires Nate to explain things to him. Deux finds this a trustworthy quality.

"Deux how's your hand though? That thing nearly exploded," Andre takes his hand and inspects it.

Deux's eyes dart to Sidric, who meets his gaze with a slight puzzled look. The corners of Deux lips purse into his teeth as if trying to solve an unsolvable math equation.

None of this adds up. Deux thinks. *Could our connection be so intense that it disrupts the electromagnetic waves? I don't even know what electromagnetic waves are but it sounds correct. If I need to kiss him again to see if these "electromagnetic waves" act up, I am more than willing to do so. I just really need to kiss him again.*

"Uhmm... It burns a little but I think I'll be fine," Deux lies, and pulls his hand away. Until he knows what is going on he isn't going to let others think he is an outcast. "I don't know about you but I'm starving! Should we go get some food?"

"Yes, please! I'm craving chicken," Andre chimes in enthusiastically, his eyebrows arching high with excitement.

"You're always in the mood for chicken, babe," Nate remarks, giving Andre's shoulder a playful nudge.

5

i make what hard?

The whole squad heads to Olive Garden, a sanctuary for forgetting almost electrocuting yourself with a microphone, while relishing in the joy of unlimited breadsticks. Nate opts for a classic Linguine Alfredo, while Andre gets adventurous with the chicken risotto that has an interesting smell. Naya, Deux and Sidric all get the Tour of Italy, a dish that could satisfy an entire basketball team. Sidric sits in between Naya and Deux. They all chat about their day, and exchange gossip about other creators. Sidric blushes when the topic shifts to their kiss the night before, which Deux finds charming. He can't help but notice their knees grazing each other several times throughout the meal, each touch lasting longer than the last. At one point, they both reach for the same breadstick, and their hands touch again, causing another electric shock. They pull away and gaze at each other, feeling the electricity in the air. Naya picks up on the awkward pause and fills the silence.

"If y'all won't have it, I will." She snatches the last breadstick with a dramatic flair, her fingers curling around it like it was a prize. She takes a bite, then grimaces, holding it at arm's length as if it's personally offended her. "Ugh, burnt. Guess I'll be asking for more."

"Anyways, Did you guys hear about Quinton Lanes?" Nate murmurs as he leans in, the rest of the group leans in as well. "He's known as one of the biggest queer creators, right? Well, this morning he posted a video saying he is "coming out" as straight and how he will be deleting all of his LGBTQ+ content. He says it does not reflect who he is and what his values are anymore."

The group stares in shock.

"This is the fourth popular creator to do a stunt like this in the past month," Deux sighs, "first it was Sue Sparkle saying 'she no longer believes lesbianism is for her', then Stephen and Brandon break up and go full on priests who hate the gays, and now Quinton?! What is going on?"

"It's so awful," Andre says, while he chews the last bite of his chicken risotto, "and the truth is people are getting so hateful online."

"Yeah! The amount of hate comments we get now in comparison to last year is astonishing. Back then we would report them and they would be gone. But now? Nothing. Interestingly, a lot of these accounts used to be fans but now suddenly they hate us?" Nate says as he pulls up his phone with screenshots.

Deux swipes through the phone reading hundreds of horrible comments holding back tears. Not from sadness but from anger. He's tired of seeing things get worse for queer people and no one doing anything about it.

@heidiho- this is why gays deserve no rights
@camera.draws- they should play this video at conversion therapy
@ko.ssio- this justifies all hate crimes

"It makes my heart hurt anytime something like this happens," Naya murmurs, "wasn't Quinton at OnlineCon? I feel like I saw him at the hotel lobby yesterday."

"Yes! He was even supposed to be in our panel today but he didn't even show. He posted that video early in the morning and left to go back home. I just hope he is okay," Nate says, concern lacing in his voice.

Deux empathizes with Nate's pain. LGBTQ+ people in this world have no choice but to be strong in the face of adversity. It's painful to witness that strength waver, and to see beautiful hearts buckle under hate. *Something is not right.* However, he finds comfort in the little group he has formed around the table. Just yesterday, he arrived in LA not knowing anyone, but now he has friends he feels safe with. He gazes at Sidric and smiles, feeling mesmerized by his natural beauty. Even eating chicken Parmesan looks sexy when Sidric does it.

"Need a separate table, you two?" Andre howls in his thick British accent.

After gorging on all-you-can-eat breadsticks, they all head back to the hotel. Naya goes to Andre and Nate's room, making up an excuse that they want to show Naya their outfits for tonight's event, but really, they want to give Deux and Sidric some alone time.

"Want to come to my room and film some videos? I think my grandma is out at the mall," Deux suggests, winking at Sidric.

Deux notices the look in Sidric's eyes. "Oh naughty boy, not that type of videos!" he exclaims.

Sidric

As they walk towards Deux's room, their hands brush against each other every few seconds. The hotel halls seem to pull them closer together, and neither stops it from happening. Sidric wishes he had the courage to make the first move, to continue where they left off last night. He craves Deux's touch, his kisses, and the feeling of his breathing on his neck. *If it wasn't for that stupid watch exploding we'd already been past third base.*

"We've arrived," Deux points to a yellow door with the number 2907 on it. He enters the room and calls out for his grandma, just in case she returned early from the mall. The coast is clear.

"I'm beginning to wonder if this Grandma of yours is real," Sidric jokes. "You're not going to have me end up on a RainFlix docuseries, are you?"

"I don't think that's what's written in the stars for us," he says, sending a lustful chill up Sidric's body. "Don't worry, you'll meet her one day," Deux laughs.

Sidric walks in, taking in the simple room that looks similar to his and Naya's. Yet, it has one noticeable difference - Deux. Amid the blue and gray carpets, neatly folded white sheets, and dark wood furniture, there are little hints of Deux everywhere. The room smells of Deux's cologne. Two books about music theory and one about lyric writing sit on the bedside table, along with a plush Grinch on the twin bed to the left. Sidric marvels at how much he's learned about Deux in just a few seconds and aches to know more.

Deux sees the books and picks them up, flipping through them. "These are new," he says, chuckling. "Classic grandma. I've had these on my wish-list for months, I think she picked them up for me earlier today."

Sidric sits back and appreciates Deux's smile. A warm feeling rushes through him as he realizes how much that small act from Deux's grandma means to him. Suddenly, the lights above the beds flicker.

"What's going on?" Deux points at them. "Either the hotel isn't paying its electricity bill on time, or do we just have bad luck today?"

"Well, we're alone in your room, so I don't see that as too bad luck," Sidric smirks at him.

"You're so nonchalant," Deux teases Sidric, and they both laugh. Deux starts setting up the camera for their video collab, which is about growing up being gay, something people can relate to.

"Okay, it's ready. You can sit here next to me, and we'll just start talking. No pressure or anything. Whatever feels natural, just say it."

Sidric's mind starts racing. *What if I choke up and can't speak? I'm not an unprofessional fan-girl who doesn't know what to do when they call action. I know what being gay is like, but what if my mind trips me out and I say the complete opposite? I don't want to get canceled over a stupid mistake. I just have to relax, breathe and open up. Be yourself.*

Fear starts to build up in Sidric's eyes. Deux reaches out and takes Sidric's hand.

"Hey," he says softly, "we don't have to do this if you're not comfortable. We can do something else, like a fun challenge or just hang out."

As their eyes meet, Sidric feels a wave of relief wash over him. It's as if Deux can read his mind and understand his fears. He squeezes Deux's hand and smiles. For a moment, everything else fades away, and all that matters is the warmth of their small embrace.

Sidric takes a deep breath and looks down at his feet for a moment. He finally looks up and meets Deux's gaze. "It's not that I don't want to do this," he says, "it's just that I've never really talked about what it was like for me with anyone. I have this amazing life full of people who love and accept me now, but when I first came out, it wasn't like that at all. My parents took some time to accept that I was bisexual. They would ask if I just didn't want to choose to be fully gay instead, as if being bi wasn't a real thing. They even sent me to therapy to 'figure things out.' The therapist we found turned out to be a dumb idiot who didn't even believe bisexuality was real."

He pauses for a moment, taking a deep breath before continuing. "I feel bad talking about all of this because it's not like that anymore, and

I don't want to get pity from people for something that's in the past. I think people would just be annoyed to hear me say I had a rough time, like I'm ungrateful for all the love and support I have now."

Deux places a hand on Sidric's shoulder, his touch grounding. "Look at me," he says, and Sidric meets his gaze. "It's okay to feel how you feel. Your past experiences are valid, and you don't have to minimize them just because things are better now. You don't owe anyone anything." Deux's words hit Sidric in all the right places, making him feel seen and understood. "You went through a tough time, and it's okay to acknowledge that and talk about it. It's not about seeking pity, it's about being honest and vulnerable. And don't worry about what others might think. There are probably a lot of people out there who can relate to what you went through and need to hear someone else talk about it to know they're not alone."

Deux notices the pain lurking behind Sidric's warm sunset eyes, all too familiar with the feeling. "It's not fair," Deux says, "they want you to be yourself, but only as much as they're comfortable with. But you deserve to be your whole self, every part, no matter what anyone else thinks."

He leans in closer, almost whisper distance from Sidric. Immediately, he pulls away and lays down on the bed.

"Ugh, you make it so hard," Deux groans.

"I make what hard?" Sidric asks, hoping for clarification. His eyes wide open.

"You make it hard not to want to kiss you."

Sidric's heart jumps at the admission.

"I mean... you can if you want to."

Deux scrambles back onto the bed. Sidric watches his lips, drawn to them like a magnet, anticipation curling in his chest. When Deux leans in, his breath brushes against Sidric's skin, and the world seems to hold its breath with them. As their lips meet, they both know there's no turning back. Tender touching turns into wrist grasping, and Deux somehow knows all the places Sidric likes to be touched. He's only waiting for Sid to give the signal that he wants more. Sidric pushes Deux onto his back and straddles him. He touches Deux's body, tracing constellations from each freckle to the other. A hum of energy—real or imagined—crackles between them, sending shivers that make them draw closer rather than pull away.

Deux's hand grabs Sidric's butt, Sidric confidently smirks knowing his Latinx genes have blessed him with an amazing ass. He is ready to release everything he feels for Deux.

Before they know it two pairs of briefs are crumpled on the floor next to the bed and they are fully exposed to one another. Sidric kisses his body, going lower after each kiss. He feels Deux grow inside his mouth, and Deux lets him be in control while he squeezes the comforter into his fists. Sidric comes up again and makes out with Deux, mixing both tastes in their mouths. The twin bed creaks and squeaks, creating a synchronized chorus with their breathing. Electrifying volts bounce between their bodies. Deux turns Sidric around and continues to kiss the back of his neck. The feeling of Deux's breath behind him drives Sidric mad; he wants Deux inside him. As Sidric arches his back, Deux enters his body, and they become one.

They've both done this before, but nothing has ever felt like this— every touch, every breath, every shared glance ignites something entirely new. It's as if the universe rewrites itself in this moment, making it the one they've been waiting for all along. Sidric moves back as Deux pushes forward, hands clasping for each other, begging to keep going. Small whispers between each other here and there, Deux asks if it feels good and Sidric demands it harder. As they reach the top, ignoring the unstoppable shocks being sent from one body to the other, they both hold hands and look into each other's eyes, connected like never before.

6

stars aNd Satellites

Deux

Deux wakes up with the scent of Sidric's hair filling his senses. He loves the smell, he catches a hint of red fruit shampoo mixed with sandalwood cologne. He nuzzles his face against the back of Sidric's head and takes in a deep breath. It feels so natural to be cuddling him like this. Sidric stirs awake and turns to look at him. It's incredible how they've only known each other for a day, but they're already so deeply enamored with each other that time seems to stand still when they're together.

"If only you lived in Canada, Sid, I would take you out on sushi dates all the time," Deux says, smiling at him.

"I love sushi," Sidric replies, gazing deeply into his hazel eyes. In the sunset light, they look like two galaxies brimming with life. "I'll come visit you one day, you can take me to your favorite sushi place."

"I don't just want a visit," Deux confesses, "I want to see you every day. I want to hang out with you all the time. In a non-creepy way. As long as you want to hang out with me too, then whenever you need space I would give you space and then afterwards hang out again."

44

Shit, I'm rambling.

Sidric chuckles and gives him a quick peck on the lips. They lay in silence, lost in their own thoughts. Deux can feel Sidric's heart pounding against his chest as they cuddle. This romance with Sidric is different from anything he has ever experienced before. He knows that tomorrow is going to be hard when they part ways, but he's trying his best to live in the moment and enjoy every last minute with Sidric.

Deux remembers a time when he was younger and would fill his math notebooks with hearts around his crush's initials. Back then, he was committed to finding the one. But as he got older, he became jaded by the disappointments of love and forced himself to give up on his fantasies. He didn't want to be the guy who pined after someone who was going to leave him when things got hard.

However, being with Sidric has rekindled that spark in him. He feels like he's living in a romance movie, and he never wants it to end. He knows that they both have to return to their respective countries tomorrow, but for now, he has this moment.

"We should probably clean up before my grandma shows up out of nowhere," Deux breaks the silence, "she has a habit of walking into rooms unannounced."

"Do you see my underwear anywhere?" Sidric gets up from the bed, and Deux can't help but stare at him. He's mesmerized by Sidric's beauty from all angles. Sidric has the best body Deux has ever seen, and he has the sweetest peach he's ever tasted.

They scramble to get dressed, anticipating Grandma walking in at any moment. Sidric reaches for his hoodie, but before he can put it on, he offers it to Deux.

"Here," he says, "so you can remember me when it gets cold in Canada."

It's a big step for Sidric, who values his oversized hoodies more than anything. But at this moment, he doesn't care. He wants Deux to remember him. He wants him to think about their time together for as long as possible. This way he will have physical proof of their two-day romance. And he knows that he'll be doing the same, cherishing every moment they spent together.

They head upstairs to Nate and Andre's room, after Deux receives a message about a new VIP party Naya got them invited to. "She's fucking crazy. I'm obsessed with her," Deux finishes reading Nate's message out loud.

"I'm glad they're getting along. I feel bad I ditched her for a hook up," Sidric chuckles.

"A hook up?" Deux gives him a playful push against the elevator wall. "Is that all I am to you?"

The tension between them is still just as fresh as the first instant they met. Sid gasps in surprise as Deux grabs both of his hands and holds them above his head. Sidric leans in and kisses him once more.

"Maybe. Maybe not," he attempts at flirting with him, which he does quite successfully to his surprise.

There's a sudden stop in the elevator, the lights go out and come back on after a few seconds. As soon as the doors open up they both quickly jump out.

"I do not risk it with elevators," Sidric laughs, hiding his panic.

Sidric

They walk down to the Dorothea suite, the second largest room in the hotel after the presidential suite. "Shit, they're *fancy* fancy," Sidric whispers, as Deux knocks on the door.

"Darlings!" Nate opens the door, "Come in! We're toasting to Naya for getting us VIP party tickets!" He hands them each a champagne

46

flute.

Naya and Andre are standing at the end of the room by the balcony admiring the sunset. As they walk in, Sidric is losing his mind. The grand foyer unfolds before him, revealing three separate hallways and a spacious main room. It's the largest hotel room he's ever seen, with marble floors stretching as far as the eye can see and extravagant fresh flower arrangements adorning every accent table.

"Listen, I was born to be a manager. It's a gift that keeps on giving!" Naya declares, downing the contents of her flute in one go. "Sid, they have to give you a tour of the room. There's even a bowling alley in here."

"This way, darlings," Nate beckons, leading them past a full kitchen equipped with two ovens and an espresso ice cream maker. Sidric's mouth waters at the sight.

"How did you guys manage to book this room? Isn't it incredibly expensive?" Deux inquires, taking in the kitchen's lavish amenities.

"We... we're not paying for it," Andre chuckles. "Can I spill the beans, Nate?"

"Andre, N...D...A...," Nate chides in a loud whisper before ushering them into a small room-sized refrigerator with a silver door. Surprisingly, all of them fit comfortably standing inside.

"Is this safe?" Sidric asks, a shiver running down his spine as he steps inside.

"I think so, just don't close the door completely," Nate assures him, "So, here's the tea. We got contacted by none other than Jacques Bizous himself. He sent us a proposal for a launch campaign for a new product. I'm assuming he really wants to work with us since he gave us this room for free, and we haven't even signed the deal yet!"

"We're definitely signing, though. It's good money," Andre adds with a smile.

"The gays slaying the game!" Deux cheers, pulling everyone into a group hug. "Congrats, you two!"

Naya takes over the music to start off the night, she plays some all time classics then moves on to weird remixes she has found over the years. They're all sitting around the balcony enjoying the warm breeze.

"Also, more tea. Quinton Lanes started dating a girl?! Did you see that?" Nate sassily says, while sipping more champagne.

"That fast huh? It's been just a few hours since he said he was straight," Sidric sighs.

"Seems like you can't trust any gay these days."

They clink their glasses together.

Minutes later all five of them are squishing into an autopilot car.

"Amount of passengers exceeded," the car's speakers blurts out, as they try to find a way to sit comfortably.

"Shut up!" Naya drunkenly yells out, "Sidric you sit on Deux's laps, Andre sit on me and Nate you can sit in between Sidric and Andre," she orders out.

They all drunkenly follow along until the autopilot fails to recognize the extra passengers. Within 20 minutes they reach the VIP party just as Naya starts losing sensation in her legs from having Andre's weight on top of her.

They struggle to get out of the car onto the busy streets of Los Angeles. The streetlights dimly light their heroic exit as Naya finally gets up. They each take a minute to find their balance and fix their outfits to appear a bit more sober than they actually are. The cars speeding by create an energetic flow of air bringing them a little back to sobriety.

Guiding the group with a confident stride, Naya retrieves her phone and begins scanning each member's face, ensuring they're all registered for the party. "Your face is your ticket. Don't lose it," she quips, a playful grin dancing across her lips. Her words are met with chuckles and nods of agreement from the others as they fall into step behind her.

Approaching the venue, the vibrant glow of neon lights spills onto the sidewalk, casting an iridescent sheen over the bustling crowd. A crimson carpet unfurls beside the front door, stretching roughly six meters in length. It's a stark contrast to the drab concrete pavement, signalling the threshold to a world of excitement and intrigue.

Standing sentinel by the entrance, a towering security guard commands attention. His imposing figure looms at an impressive 6'5", a formidable presence against the backdrop of flashing lights and pulsing music. Adorned with the latest model of RainVision X glasses, he exudes an aura of authority and vigilance.

www.rainforestec.com/RainVisionX

The new RainVision X glasses, equipped with state-of-the-art X-Ray capabilities, have become ubiquitous among security personnel, from bouncers to airport officials and law enforcement. With the ability to detect concealed weapons with unparalleled precision, they serve as a potent deterrent against potential threats.

Naya confidently strides toward the guard, bypassing the line of eager concertgoers. "We have VIP entry," she announces with assurance.

The guard's low voice rumbles as he instructs them to scan their faces. They form an organized line, with Naya leading the way followed by Nate and Andre, leaving Sidric and Deux at the rear. A jolt of electricity shoots through Sidric as Deux's hand accidentally brushes against his own. Reacting instinctively, Sidric sizes Deux's hand, a silent gesture of reassurance amidst the bustling crowd.

Naya steps forward to scan her face, greeted by the welcoming green light. With a confident stride, she enters the venue, leaving the others to follow suit. Andre leans in to give Nate a quick peck on the lips before Nate scans his face and prepares to enter. But just as he's about to cross the threshold, the guard abruptly blocks their path.

"You four are going to need to go somewhere else," the guard declares sternly, his tone leaving no room for argument.

Andre's voice rises in protest. "What? But the light went green! We all have tickets," he scans his face getting a green light as well.

"I don't care. I decide who comes in and none of you *are* coming in tonight. Only women and men. Nothing in between."

"Woah," Deux walks forward, "That was offensive in so many ways. Just because we're gay doesn't mean we're not men, and even if we were non-binary, we should still be allowed in, you asshole."

"This is bullshit! It's not fair!" Naya says from behind his back.

"You want out with these fags? Then leave," he shoves her out of the venue.

As tensions escalate, Sidric feels his pulse quicken. Normally composed, he finds himself on the brink of unleashing his fiery Latino temper in the face of such ignorance and discrimination.

"Excuse you?!" He yells out from the back. "I'm going to have to ask you to repeat yourself just once more cause I think I misheard you, tough guy."

Deux stands in silence right behind him. He never expected tiny Sidric to be so fiery, but he likes it.

"Listen, you four were making out. Being gross out here in front of me. I can tell you're all pretty wasted so I'm letting you go home without calling the cops."

"Calling the cops?! Over what?! Holding hands? Call them." Sidric gets up in his face. Naya, Nate, Andre, and Deux all back him up.

The rest of the people in line are all staring at what is going on. A few voices from the crowd break out in their support. A few others, do the opposite.

"If you don't back off in 2 seconds you will be sorry," the guard huffs.

"What are you going to do about it?" Sidric walks a step closer, the champagne from earlier definitely making him feel a bit braver.

Within seconds the guard races his left fist and aims it straight at Sidric's eye. Immediately, Sidric's whole body tenses up and he feels a high-voltage shock go all around ending in his face. The guard's fist slams against Sidric's face but somehow Sidric remains unfazed. On impact, the guard snaps backward against the wall. The group all look at each other confused.

"We need to get out of here now." Deux pulls Sidric by the hand and runs away from the venue. With Nate, Andre, and Naya in tow, they make a hasty retreat from the venue, leaving the chaos behind them.

Exhilarated the squad makes their way back to the hotel. Champagne leads each new celebration chant Naya and Andre come up with.

"IncrediSid, IncrediSid! Incredibly Incredible!" they sing out the open windows.

"The way you took that punch!" Nate's laughter fills the air, punctuated by a genuine concern. "How's your head feeling, by the way, babes?"

Sidric chuckles, his voice tinged with a hint of disbelief, " Honestly, I think the alcohol blocked my pain detectors, 'cause I feel perfectly fine!"

As they arrive at the hotel, a sense of camaraderie envelops them, weaving through the night air like a comforting embrace. They navigate their way to the rooftop, their steps charged by excitement and the thrill of clandestine adventure. With practiced ease, they wedge a brick under the door to prevent it from locking, securing their impromptu gathering spot.

Settling in, they form a circle, their voices rising and falling in a symphony of conversation. Topics shift rapidly, a whirlwind of ideas and opinions swirling around them. Against the backdrop of the city skyline, bathed in the soft glow of moonlight, they find solace in each other's company.

Sidric's gaze sweeps over the group, his heart swelling with a sense of belonging. In a world that often feels cold and unforgiving, this crew of weirdos has become his refuge, a sanctuary where he can be his true self without fear of judgment or rejection. For him, it's a reminder that acceptance and love can be found in the most unexpected of places.

"Hey, you want to go find somewhere to talk?" Deux whispers in Sidric's ear, creating chills all around his neck.

"I'm down," Sidric replies, attempting to sound as cool as possible.

As they make their way out of the hotel lobby, Deux and Sidric walk hand in hand around the parking lot, searching for the perfect spot where they can continue their conversation without any distractions. They wander around the rows of parked cars, feeling the warm night all around.

Finally, they find a secluded corner between a red pickup truck and a blue car. They sit down on the pavement, their backs resting against the side of the cars, and face each other with a look of excitement and curiosity. The glow of electric car chargers illuminates their faces ever so slightly.

Deux and Sidric share stories and laughs, discovering more about each other's passions, dreams, and fears. For a moment, they forget about the impending goodbye that awaits them tomorrow. They only focus on the present, savoring every moment they have together before the night ends.

Deux looks up and admires the beautiful stars, sparkling at different speeds. "I love the night skies here, they're so majestic," he remarks.

"Not to ruin the moment," Sidric interjects, "but those aren't stars.

They are RainforesTec's satellites. He gaslit everyone into thinking his satellites would be a solution to the light pollution. There's thousands up there."

"Shit, I feel lied to," Deux whispers.

Sidric laughs. "You have to come see the ones in Savannah," he says, "Those have actual stars! I sneak onto the rooftop of my dorm every chance I get. It's the perfect time to pause life."

"I'll have to come see it someday," Deux says, reaching out to grab Sidric's hand. As soon as their fingertips touch, another electric shock runs through them.

"Okay, so…are we going to talk about this? One time, I get it, but all these shocks, power outages, things getting set on fire. Not to sound over-dramatic but I literally did not feel the security guard punching me. All I felt was electricity all around my body. What the hell is going on?"

"I know, it's weird," Deux admits, "When I was on stage, I swear the power outage started when I saw you walking in the room. I started panicking. It's like we have some kind of connection or something."

Sidric's mind races. *Deux got panicked when he saw me? This beautiful boy is crushing on me? The crush is mutual then! It's usually just me having a crush on someone and it never being reciprocated. Mark the date!*

"I mean, I was panicking from public speaking," Deux's face goes red. "And then you walked in, it was all just so messy. A blur."

Sidric can't help but smile, feeling butterflies in his stomach. He's already imagining their future together. *We should definitely plan a wedding in Mexico, no one does weddings like Mexico.*

"Hello? Sid," Deux waves his palm in front of Sidric's eyes, snapping him back to reality.

"Shit, sorry. I was thinking. It all leads back to when we were… uhm… making out and your watch exploded. That's when I first felt the shocks," Sidric explains, trying to make sense of the strange

53

occurrences.

Deux's eyes widen, realization dawning on him. "Oh my god. I remember feeling a shock too, but I thought it was just static electricity from our lips rubbing or something."

They sit quietly for a moment, letting it all sink in. The hum of the car chargers fills the space. Something powerful and unexplainable happening between them.

"Do you think it's just the electrons leaving our bodies? From the burnt watch? I mean, RainforesTec should not launch those watches if they're just randomly going to get set on fire if you spill on them," Sidric says, frowning.

"Agreed! I figured they'd at least be waterproof. But yes, I think it must be our bodies getting rid of the excess charge. I'm not really good at science, but I think it's almost out of our systems based on how much friction we just experienced back in my room," Deux chuckles.

Sidric feels Deux squeeze his hand and lean in close enough that he can feel his warm breath on his cheek. "That was an electrifying moment," Deux whispers as he kisses Sidric's neck, causing another shock.

"Shit, that one hurt. I'm used to people biting me but not shocking me, Deux."

They both laugh until the screech of a car breaks the moment.

"Sidric Alvarado," a commanding robotic voice blares, "You are being detained for assaulting a security personnel."

Metallic stomps echo as a figure emerges from the car, moving toward them.

"You can't take him!" Deux yells. "He did nothing wrong—the bouncer tried to punch him!"

"Move aside," the robocop commands, shoving Deux away as it closes in on Sidric.

I'm fucked. This is it. Goodbye life.

"Listen, it wasn't just him! I helped assault the officer. Take me in as well," Deux commands the robot's attention.

The robocop turns around and seizes Deux's hands with his long metallic arms, immediately, two extra arms pop out from the sides of the robocop. He uses the extra two to seize Sidric's hands.

"Deux Yates and Sidric Alvarado. You have the right to remain silent. Anything you say can and will be used against you in a court of law. You have the right to an attorney. If you cannot afford an attorney, a robo-attorney will be provided to you."

What started as their first date ends with them behind bars.

Deux

"Grandma," Deux warily says through the phone, "there's been a slight hiccup. We're in the police station."

After two minutes of back and forth, he hangs up the phone and then gets escorted back to the waiting cell by an old human police officer. He has complete grey hair and a matching mustache. Deux enters the cell and sits next to Sidric against a yellow brick wall.

"How mad was she?" Sidric asks.

"I think she was a bit drunk because she started laughing and asked for details about what we did. She's always been a rebel."

"That's good. Hopefully, we can get out of this one." Sidric sighs.

Deux notices Sidric's hands trembling.

"You're not good at getting in trouble are you?" He asks placing a hand on top of his.

"The worst I've ever done is run past a stop sign and that gave me panic attacks for a month," he chuckles.

"Don't worry, the Yates have plenty of experience with getting into trouble and getting out of it," Deux assures him, "So tell me more about you, I feel like I know nothing about you but at the same time know exactly who you are."

He looked straight into Sidric's eyes. Somehow making Sidric feel more vulnerable than before.

"Okay, so I was born in Mexico and lived there my whole life until I moved for college in Savannah. I'm studying film and photography right now but my passion is any type of art to be honest. I turn 22 in September which means I am a Virgo, so you're lucky to be in my presence," he nudges him, "What about you? Do you miss the UK?"

"I don't really remember that much. I've always wanted to go back but I have never had the chance."

"Oh my god! We should go backpacking! I'm into it." Sidric falls into Deux's distraction plan.

Deux admires Sidric's hopefulness for their future together, but he isn't sure if he's ready to commit to a long-distance relationship just yet. He wants to keep Sidric in his life but he likes to take caution with new relationships. As he thinks about the possibilities the future holds for them, Deux can't help but smile. *How am I falling for this boy while we're inside of a jail cell?*

Suddenly, Sidric asks him a question, "Wait so how old are you?"

"I just turned 22 in April," Deux responds.

Sidric jokes, "Good, I don't hook up with guys younger than me. I like the experience they offer."

Deux chuckles and teases, "Are you sure you don't have a little British in you? Your banter is UK level."

Sidric feigns ignorance, "What the hell is banter? Are you talking about my ass?"

Deux laughs and replies, "No, but your butt is on another level too."

"Thank you, I know," Sidric smirks, "But no, I don't have any little British in me. I mean, I had a big British in me a few hours ago, but I don't think that's what you meant."

Deux can't help but groan, "Oh my god, I hate you." they both laugh.

"Yates, Alvarado. You're free to go," the old cop yells out as he opens the gates.

They run out of the cell and see Christa, Deux's grandmother, standing in the waiting room in full glam.

"Grandma! You saved us!" Deux yells as he hugs her.

"Ma'am, thank you so much. I was about to have a massive panic attack." Sidric politely says, trying to hide how emotional he actually is.

"I'm no Ma'am," Christa says, "call me grandma!" She pulls Sidric in for a hug.

They walk out of the station and walk into a 24-hour diner right next door. Grandma orders three tequila shots as soon as they get seated.

"I don't think we carry tequila but let me see what I can find," the waitress smiles.

"Sorry if I ruined your night grandma," Deux says, "you look like you were somewhere fancy."

"Nonsense! I got dolled up to come get you guys out. I've been through this a couple times. These cops can never resist a dolled-up grandma," she jokes as she flips her hair.

"Dolled up Glam-Ma!" Sidric adds, "I love the hair!"

"Thank you," she plays with the ends. "That cop back there loved it as well! Took some flirting but I managed to get you two out with no issue. He even promised to come buy me a drink when he clocks out."

"Glam-Ma!" Deux laughs out loud "That is amazing. I owe you big time."

The waitress comes back with three tequila shots on her tray. "Gary, our cook, had a secret stash he was willing to share," she winks at grandma as she places them down.

"Listen boys, tequila is the best for when life tries to kick you down but fails," she says, grabbing a shot. "A kind heart and a smile will always win!" She sings out flashing her pearly whites.

Eventually, after plenty of jokes and chatter, Christa sends them home before her date arrives.

The stars or satellites above twinkle with hope in a sea of darkness, casting a romantic aura over Deux and Sidric as they walk to their hotel, savoring their final moments together. Although dreaded goodbyes loom, neither wants to be the first to say it. Deux's flight departs at 8 am the following morning, leaving him just a few precious minutes with Sidric.

Desperately, Deux slips his arm around Sidric, resting his head on top of Sidric's head. Sidric, too, longs to freeze the moment, thinking to himself that if the world ended now, he wouldn't regret how he spent his last moments.

"I'm going to miss you, Deux," Sidric sighs.

"I'll miss you too, but we'll stay in touch. I promise."

They reach Sidric's floor and both get out of the elevator. They stand looking at each other, neither dares to say goodbye.

Sidric gazes at Deux with a wistful expression. "Can I have one last kiss before you go?"

Deux leans in, giving him a small peck on the lips.

"That's not enough," Sidric whispers, "I need a real kiss."

Deux grins, leaning in again for a deep, passionate kiss. The electric chemistry between them only gets stronger as they lock lips, both souls cherishing each moment.

One last kiss becomes two, and then three, neither willing to let go. But eventually, they must part, reluctantly saying their goodbyes and promising to keep in touch.

Back in his room, Deux messages Sidric.

DEUX

-Hey Sidric, this is my number! Save it for whenever you need anyone to drink a FiveLoko with you.

SIDRIC
-Who is this? I gave my number to soooo many hot brit guys this weekend.

DEUX
-HA HA

SIDRIC
-I'm kidding khbfns I'm going to take you up on that offer ;)

DEUX
-I *really like yo-*
delete delete delete

DEUX
-I will see you soon! xxx
send

7

electRIc touch

Deux

U pon returning home, Deux experiences a bittersweet feeling that lingers. While he was homesick during his trip, as soon as his flight landed in Toronto, he missed LA, his new friends, and most of all, Sidric. He pushes these emotions aside and heads to the kitchen to share his travel stories with his parents. They are both cuddled up on the couch, engrossed in an old slasher movie. His mom is fast asleep, cradled in his dad's arms. In the kitchen, his sister, Atlanta, is making some popcorn with grandma.

"How was your trip, kiddo?" his dad asks, not taking his eyes off the TV where a high school cheerleader is being attacked by a masked killer. Deux sees it as a poetic metaphor of life stabbing away all the possibilities of love by keeping Sidric so far away from him. However, he decides against telling his parents about Sidric, as things are still sensitive when it comes to his dating life. Their awkward dinner with his first boyfriend, Jonas, still haunts him. There was meatball sauce, red wine, and a white tablecloth that now looks more like a tie-dye DIY project.

"Let's see," Deux responds, "I met a lot of other creators, filmed a couple of things, and grandma had lots of wine. It was great!"

"Hey!" Grandma yells as she walks into the room, "I had sufficient wine." She winks at him.

Throughout the years, Deux's relationship with his dad has improved significantly. He now shows a genuine interest in Deux's life, his social media career, and how he's doing in general. When Deux first came out, started creating videos, and becoming more vocal on his queerness, his family was hesitant to support him. But after many uncomfortable conversations and education, things have progressed a lot.

"Good to hear. I look forward to you making millions and buying me a Porsche," his dad teases, "none of that electric crap though. Have you seen those videos online? This one car locked its driver in and sped away instead of parking. That's insane, son!" His dad is prone to falling into internet rabbit holes that feed his conspiracy theories, and these videos have been popping up everywhere.

"I saw that! A poor old lady almost got run over!" Atlanta walks into the family room with a big bowl of cheddar popcorn in her hands, "Hey Deux!" She hugs him tightly.

As Deux's hands wrap around his sister he catches glimmers of the golden stains on his arm. *Not this.*

"I'm going to lie down for a bit, I'm so tired from the flight," Deux nervously says and runs upstairs.

Just as he shuts the door to his bedroom, it swings immediately back open nearly knocking him down. His sister strides into the room immediately after. "Catch me up first though," she laughs while eating some popcorn, "How were the parties?"

Deux quickly hides his wrists in his hoodie's pockets. "Oh you know, average parties. Lots of free stuff."

"Did you get any RainVision X? I want those for my birthday. I heard they have an intense metal detector, so my friends and I wanna go to the beach and find all the forgotten treasures," she says, clapping her hands excitedly .

"No, they didn't have those. But… I did meet a guy," he says, smiling at her. She has been a constant presence in his dating life. If she doesn't approve of the guys he dates then that's a red flag.

"A guy?!" Atlanta squeals out, "I need details. Name. Age. Sign. Everything."

"So his name is Sidric. He's 21, I think he's a Virgo and he's from Mexico but goes to college in the states."

"Okay, okay. Virgo and Aries. A fiery coupling but it can work out," Atlanta attentively ponders, "and he's older than you."

"Only by a year. I told him I was 22 though."

"You lied to him already!"

"Well, we drank FiveLokos I didn't want to go to jail!" Deux laughs out, "And we kissed a little."

"Oh my god! Deux's in love!" she teases, "Well I need to meet this Sidric. I need to feel the vibes."

"Okay I will let you know when I next talk to him," he chuckles. Talking about Sidric makes him forget all about the gold stains. The thought comes back in his mind and he jumps up from his bed.

"Anyways I'm going to take a shower. I still have airplane bacteria all over me, I feel gross."

He starts the shower and waits some minutes for the water to heat. His house is a full house, his three siblings, both parents and grandma all share two bathrooms. Snatching one bathroom for a long hot shower is rare. The room fills up with steam, signaling it's time to get rid of these golden speckles. He first grabs his sister's fancy soap and tries to scrub them away, no luck. He follows scraping with his loofah, again, nothing. He grabs his brother's body wash and scrapes even harder, almost irritating his skin. The bathroom door swings open, and Deux's older brother Luna rushes in.

"Sorry bro, I need to pee badly."

Deux remains absorbed in examining the golden speckles on his skin, barely acknowledging Luna's presence.

"Just make it quick," he mutters distractedly, his eyes fixated on the odd markings.

After a few moments, the toilet flushes and immediately the water in the shower suddenly turns boiling, causing Deux to scream in shock. As he jumps back from the frigid stream, bright volts of gold burst from his palms, shooting towards the ceiling and the light fixtures. Startled, he stumbles and tangles himself in the shower curtain, bringing it down with him as he falls. In an instant, the bathroom is plunged into total darkness.

Luna calls out an apology from outside the door, his voice muffled by the sound of the still-running shower. Deux lies on the ground, bewildered and disoriented, trying to process what just happened. Slowly, he realizes that there are small, glowing sparkles emanating from the golden spots on his arm. He brings his arm closer to his face to examine them more closely.

Suddenly, an electric wave of energy surges from one of the spots toward Deux's finger. He pulls back, startled, but then watches in amazement as the wave follows the movement of his finger. He tentatively presses his finger to one of the spots again, and a huge wave of energy ripples through his body, causing him to jerk and twist uncontrollably. As he separates his hand from the skin, the wave travels around the room, causing the light bulbs to flicker to life.

Deux stands up, bewildered but exhilarated by what he's just experienced. Something inside him has awakened, something that feels powerful and mysterious. As he towels himself off and gets dressed, he wonders what other strange and incredible abilities might lie dormant within him, waiting to be unleashed.

He has no idea what he just witnessed, but he's certain that he almost died. He turns off the shower and drags his exhausted body towards his room, collapsing onto his bed. Closing his eyes, he hopes that a nap will fix everything.

Two hours later, Deux wakes up from a dream where he's about to kiss Sidric, his sheets twisted around his body. It's 12 a.m., and normally he'd go back to sleep, but his mind is racing. He's lowkey having an emotional meltdown and highkey on the verge of dying from anxiety. Every inch of his body feels like it's being jolted by electric shocks. He feels like he's not in control at all, which makes him wonder if anyone is ever really in control of their own bodies.

The bathroom blackout has confirmed what he has been avoiding all weekend long. Something strange is going on, and it's not just his body getting rid of the smartwatch malfunction debris. This feels like something bigger, something he's less than qualified to deal with. On top of that, flashbacks of Sidric's body keep popping up in his head making it extremely hard for him to relax.

Deux grabs his laptop and does what any 20-year-old does best: he goes online to self-diagnose. The thing about self-diagnosing, though, is that it gets a lot harder when you have no clue what's actually going on. He searches for anything related to electric malfunctions and smartwatches, but nothing seems to match. According to his findings, his body could shut down at any moment. His nails and teeth might fall out first, followed by the growth of a third nipple on his forehead. These scenarios sound impossible, but to a hypochondriac like Deux, they all seem frighteningly plausible.

As he spends the next 30 minutes researching, his dream replays in his mind on an endless loop. He needs someone to talk to—someone who might understand what he's going through. But he hesitates. How can he explain what's happening to him without sounding like a lunatic? With a heavy sigh, he closes his laptop, the weight of loneliness pressing down on him more than ever. *What if I'm infected with some kind of strange virus? What if my body is being taken over by an alien parasite? I've seen how this ends and it's not pretty.* The more he thinks about it, the more he starts to panic. He paces back and forth across his room, his heart pounding in his chest. He takes a few deep breaths to steady himself before reaching for his phone. It's around 10 pm in California, Sidric is probably hanging out with everyone. He types out a quick message, his fingers trembling slightly.

DEUX-
Heyy! Sorry to text out of nowhere.. Do you have a minute to chat ab-
　DELETE *DELETE* *DELETE*

He throws his phone across the room, where it lands on a pile of sheet music. Deux slumps against the wall, his heart pounding with conflicting emotions. He's barely known Sidric for two days, yet he feels an undeniable pull toward him. The way Sidric looked at him, the way his touch lingered on Deux's arm—it felt like a connection that transcended words. Still, the last thing Deux wants is to come across as desperate. He wants to seem chill, like he can totally wait at least 24 hours before texting Sidric again.

But at this moment, with his body seemingly malfunctioning and no explanation in sight, Deux feels a sense of urgency that he can't ignore. He can't risk waiting any longer to text Sidric.

He picks up his phone again, his fingers shaking as he types out a message. He debates whether to be straightforward and tell Sidric everything or to play it cool and just ask if they can talk. In the end, he decides to just text and see what comes out.

DEUX-
  -Hey Sid! Miss yo-
  DELETE

DEUX
  -HEYYY!
  DELETE

DEUX
  -hey! Hows the last day going? Should've changed my flight to
tomorrow.
  SEND

It's a nice, chill way to start the conversation, but he can't help feeling
a little anxious about it. All he wants to do is tell Sidric how much
he misses him and how he's pretty sure he's overdosing on electricity,
but he knows he needs to ease his way in. So he waits. And waits. And
keeps waiting. Five minutes feel like an eternity as Deux paces back
and forth across his room.

Finally, his phone vibrates, and Deux jumps towards it like an
American football player catching the ball at the last minute.

It's Sidric.

SIDRIC
  -Hi Deux! It's been good. We went to Disney today! Rode the
zero-gravity coaster. Naya puked a bit afterwards.

He's attached a photo of himself, smiling and wearing Mickey Mouse
ears. Deux traces his face on the screen with his finger, unable to help

the smile that spreads across his own face. It's a reminder that the past two days really did happen and that he didn't just dream them.

SIDRIC
   -Wish you were here though :(

Deux startles at the notification, realizing he's still staring at Sidric's photo. He starts typing back.

DEUX
   -How are you so cute?!
   -Whenever you get home, do you wanna chat maybe? I need to talk to you about something, nothing bad so don't worry.

Sidric responds quickly.

SIDRIC
   -Sure! We're just grabbing some food. Naya convinced everyone to do some edibles and go to Olive Garden as a goodbye dinner. I might be STUFFED tonight...
   -by the food... Not a person.

Deux laughs out loud at Sidric's joke.

DEUX
   -Omg hahaha now I really wish I was there so I could get stuffed and stuff–
   DELETE *DELETE* *DELETE*

He's not sure what the limit is on how dirty he can get through texts with someone he likes but just met. Deux overthinks every letter and punctuation in his texts, but he loves that Sidric shares the same banter and humor as him. It's a big turn-on, especially after hooking up with Canadian guys who didn't know what banter was. Deux decides to be playful and flirty, keeping Sidric wanting more.

DEUX
  -That works with me! Let me know when you're free.
  -and omg I wish I was there.. Yes it better just be by food ;)

He can feel the weight of his emotions and the uncertainty of his future bearing down on him. He knows he needs to find a way to calm himself down, so he locks his phone and takes a few calming breaths.

He looks around his room, searching for something to distract him. His eyes land on his laptop sitting on his bedside table. He reaches for it and opens it up, the soft glow of the screen illuminates his face.

Without hesitation, he navigates to his favorite website. He takes a minute to find his favorite video. He clicks on the *Mamma Mia!* movie, a spark of excitement building inside him. As the film begins, he's instantly transported to a world of ocean waves, starry skies, and Amanda Seyfried's beautiful voice serenading him with 'I Have a Dream.'

Deux closes his eyes and takes a deep breath in, letting the music wash over him. He can feel his heart rate slowing down, and his thoughts become more focused. As the movie progresses, he finds himself humming along to the songs, and even tapping his feet to the beat. All of his worries seem to fade away as he becomes more and more immersed in the movie.

He knows that everything will be alright, thanks to Meryl Streep and Amanda Seyfried.

8

stoned at olive Garden

Sidric
Moments before Deux's text.

"I promise it's not from my strong bag of gummies," Naya winks as she passes a fuzzy peach gummy to Sidric. "These are only 10 milligrams each. You'll feel good and buzzy."

Sidric takes the edible and pops it into his mouth without hesitation. If he's ever going to try edibles, it has to be with Naya. She's a self-proclaimed connoisseur of all things weed-related, and he trusts her implicitly. She passes more fuzzy peaches to Andre and Nate, and they all hang out by the hotel pool to celebrate their last day in LA. Despite the chilly weather, Nate and Andre cuddle up on one chaise, while Naya wraps herself up with hotel towels. Sidric wishes Deux was here so he could be in his arms instead of wearing an oversized hoodie to keep warm. Cuddles from a cute boy are always the best resource to keep someone warm.

"These are good!" Andre yells as he pops two more into his mouth.

"Babes, maybe take it easy. We don't want you to pass out on your pasta," Nate says, taking the bag away from him.

"I'm scared. I've never been high before. How long until it kicks in?" Sidric asks nervously.

"About 45 minutes. It'll probably hit once we get to the restaurant. I'll call the taxi now," Naya says, as she puts five fuzzies in her mouth. "If y'all start panicking or anything, let mama know. I'll be your guide."

The next 45 minutes feel like an eternity in the awkward taxi ride to Olive Garden. The driver's playlist is an odd mix of country music and opera that's grating on their nerves. The gummies are slowly taking effect, and they're all beginning to feel a little light-headed. Sidric's hands are clammy, and he can't stop fidgeting.

"Naya," he whispers loudly, "I think it's hitting."

"Yeah, it's supposed to," Naya says with a chuckle. "Just relax and enjoy the ride."

Sidric takes a deep breath and starts rubbing his hands together, trying to ground himself. He doesn't want to spiral out of control during his first high. Finally, the driver pulls into the parking lot, and the lights go on to signal their arrival.

"Don't forget anything. Once I'm gone, what's left behind is mine," the driver says with a groan. They all exchange glances, wondering if he's joking or not.

"Thank you," Naya says, tossing a twenty in his direction.

"I might need some help getting out, besties," Andre calls out from the backseat. "I fear my legs have become paper straws."

"Andre! I told you not to take too many gummies!" Nate yells as he gets out of the car. "Oh, wait, I think I'm paper straws too." He collapses onto the ground, leaving Naya and Sidric bursting out laughing.

"Mama's got this," Naya says, psyching herself up. "Excuse us, sir, we're celebrating their wedding anniversary. Sidric, make sure we didn't leave anything behind in the car, please." Naya helps both of the stoned guys get back on their feet, and they all stumble toward the restaurant entrance.

Sidric starts looking around the back of the car, and as soon as his hands cross his eyesight, his heart drops. A gold stain is splattered across his whole left hand, and a few speckles are on the right. He reaches out to touch the big spot on the left and immediately shocks himself. Thoughts sprint through his mind, each one chasing the next, colliding, overlapping, and leaving him breathless. *No more electric shock please.* He cries out in his mind. He takes his hoodie off and wraps it around both his hands. He slams the car door and heads straight to the restaurant.

"I'll see you guys inside! I- uh- I need to shit ASAP!" he blurts out.

"Okay, Sid, TMI bestie!" Naya replies with Andre hanging from her shoulder as she picks up Nate. "Oh lord, why are gays such lightweights?" she whispers to herself.

Sidric barges in and looks around for the toilet. The hostess looks him up and down and starts speaking before he can sneak his way in.

"How many in your party?" she rudely asks.

"It's four. Name is Sidric," he tries to say calmly. "I'm just gonna use the bathroom real quick." He points towards the bathroom with his hands still wrapped. As he lifts his hands up, sparks come right through the shirt.

"Sorry I forgot to turn my taser off" He cries out running towards the toilet.

He rushes into the room, quickly locking the door behind him. The tungsten lights cast an eerie glow throughout the room, and Italian music plays softly in the background. His eyes scan the walls adorned with fake Italian paintings, the warped perspective making him feel like he's stepped into a scene from a horror movie. It's the perfect setting for a marijuana-induced panic attack.

With trembling hands, he unwraps the tightly wound fabric, each movement slow and deliberate. His pulse quickens with every passing thought, anxiety coiling in the pit of his stomach like a restless serpent.

"It's just the edibles," he murmurs to himself, his voice barely a whisper as he tries to calm his racing mind. "You don't have an abnormal gold rash growing on your hands. It's just glitter from the party two nights ago." But the reassurance rings hollow, drowned out by the relentless drumbeat of panic.

He squeezes his eyes shut, forcing himself to take deep, steady breaths. When he opens them again, a wave of dread crashes over him, just as crushing as the day he couldn't get tickets to the Taylor Swift concert, as he stares down at his hands.

"Oh crap, please don't let it be an STI," he pleads silently, his mind spiraling into a vortex of fear and uncertainty.

With a trembling hand, he peels back the fabric to reveal what lies beneath. His breath catches in his throat as he beholds the gold stains tattooed on his skin, "Oh shit! It's real!" he cries out, his voice one octave higher cracking with desperation.

Frantically, he lunges for the sink, the rush of water drowning out the sound of his escalating panic. He scrubs at his hands with desperate fervor, the harsh friction a desperate attempt to erase the evidence of his affliction.

Just as he's on the brink of a breakdown, a series of urgent knocks echoes through the room, jolting him from his frenzied trance. Someone outside is trying to push open the door, their persistence a stark reminder of the precariousness of his situation

"Just a minute!" he calls out.

"It's just me!" Naya calls back. "We're seated at the table now. You good?"

"Yes, just trying to get this off!" Sidric replies, trying to calm himself down.

"Get what off?" Naya yells from the other side of the door. "I'm coming in."

"No!" Sidric yells, throwing his hands up. Two tiny electric bolts come out of his hands, splitting the mirror with a sharp crack right down the middle. "I mean wiping! Just wiping! I'll be out in a minute!"

"Okay… I'll order you a tour of Italy."

Sidric stares in horror back and forth between the broken reflection and his golden stained hands. The Italian music still plays in the background, filling up the dead silence. He grabs his phone and, without even thinking about it, video-calls Deux. After a few rings, Deux picks up.

"Hey! Sorry to call you out of nowhere," Sidric apologizes, hearing the music coming from Deux's phone. "Wait, is that 'Dancing Queen'? Are you watching *Mamma Mia!*?"

"Hey!" Deux pauses the movie. "Yes, sorry, I had to take my mind off some things. '*Mamma Mia!*' always does the trick."

"I feel that. I think I'm in need of some *Mamma Mia!* distraction right about now."

"Why? What's wrong? Don't tell me you're tripping in an Olive Garden bathroom," Deux says inspecting the background paired with the Italian music.

"You don't understand. We took these edibles, and Naya said they weren't strong, and everything was going great, but then we got to the restaurant, and I looked down, and there were stains all over me. I was freaking out, and my heart has been beating like 190 miles per hour ever since."

Deux's eyes open wide as he watches Sidric's panicked expression. He can see the worry etched on his face, the furrow of his brow and the way he bites his lip nervously.

"Then I'm trying to rub these golden stains away and fucking flashes keep coming out of my hands. I think I might be dying, Deux, so please remember me as the hot guy you hooked up with in LA with an amazing ass," Sidric says, his voice trembling with fear.

Deux's heart drops. "Wait, what?"

"Okay, maybe it's not an amazing ass, but just promise me you'll remember me, yes?"

"No, that's not it. You do have an amazing bum. Show me the golden stains. Did actual lightning bolts come out of your hands?"

"Okay, but don't freak out because I'm pretty sure I'm losing it as we speak," Sidric says, as he pulls up his hands towards the front-facing camera. The gold in his skin shimmers through Deux's phone, casting a warm glow across his face.

"Holy shit," Deux whispers, "Holy. Shit."

"I know. It's bad. And I..."

Sidric goes down another spiral, not even taking a second to breathe in between words. Somehow he moves from topic to topic and is now in despair about how he thinks global warming is ruining the lives of polar bears, tears forming in his eyes.

"Sid, listen to me," Deux speaks loud and clear, trying to get his attention. "Firstly, I know the polar bears need our help, and that will be at the top of our list as soon as you're not high, okay?"

Sidric nods, wiping tears away from his eyes.

"Secondly, you might not be alone in this."

Sidric's eyes question what he means.

"I was taking a shower earlier today and found some gold stains on my hands as well. They won't come off at all. I tried everything." He shows the marks on his skin. Sidric stares in shock.

"Oh Lord, is it an STI?! Is that why you wanted to talk ?! How am I going to find meds in this country?! They don't have healthcare! It's so messed up how-"

"Sid!" Deux gets his attention. "Breathe. I don't think there's an STI out there that gives you golden marks and lightning bolts."

"Lightning bolts?! Is that what we're calling them?" Sidric's heart starts slowing down. Just by talking to Deux, he feels safe.

"Listen, what we're going to do is I'm going to go do some research online, see what I can find. You are going to go eat some delicious pasta and breadsticks. Forget about this for tonight. It's your last night in LA, so enjoy it, and tomorrow morning I'll call you with answers, and we'll have this all fixed."

Deux isn't sure about any of this, but he knows it's pointless going over it all right now. The boy is locked in an Olive Garden bathroom; it's not really the best place to figure things out. "If anything happens, just call me. I'll be here."

After ending the call with Deux, Sidric takes a deep breath and tries to compose himself. His heart is still racing from their conversation, and he can feel his body humming with energy. He splashes some water on his face to cool down, avoiding looking at his reflection in the cracked mirror. He puts on his hoodie, pulling the sleeves over his hands so that nobody can see them shaking.

As he heads back to the table, Naya waves him over, and he can see the food spread out before him. Caesar salad, linguine Alfredo, chicken Parmesan, lasagna – all his favorite dishes, all lined up and ready to be devoured. Sidric's stomach growls with hunger, he can't wait to dig in.

For the first few minutes after the food arrives, there is no con-versation, just the sound of forks and knives scraping against plates. Sidric's mind is focused solely on the food; he's never been this hungry before. He devours his meal with relish, savoring every bite. Despite the bathroom incident earlier, Sidric feels relaxed and happy in the company of his friends.

The waiter arrives with a massive plate of calamari, and Nate eagerly reaches out to grab it. Naya watches with a mix of fascination and horror as the plate is placed on the table.

"I'll have some of that!" Andre exclaims, spooning a generous portion onto his pasta.

Sidric, who has never tried calamari before, serves himself a small helping and takes a bite. He closes his eyes in ecstasy.

"This is so delicious I might cry," he says.

"I know, right? I love calamari!" Nate exclaims, his excitement palpable.

"CALAMARI!" Andre chants, waving his fork in the air. "Everyone say it, it's fun!"

"CALAMARI!!" Nate and Sidric chant in unison as they continue eating.

Naya watches, her stomach churning with unease. She can't keep the truth to herself any longer.

"Okay, I can't keep it in anymore," she says, drawing everyone's attention. "I stopped having calamari a while ago…"

Nate and Andre pause, still chewing, while Sidric looks up with interest. "Okay?" Nate asks.

"I stopped having it because I read this thing that says most restaurants do not use actual calamari for their calamari," Naya continues.

"What do they use instead?" Sidric asks, his brow furrowed. "Is it like imitation crab?"

"I don't know," Andre says, inspecting a piece before biting into it. "It doesn't really taste like crab, it tastes like—"

"PIG ANUS!" Naya interrupts, her voice rising. "It's pig anus," she whispers.

Andre chokes on his food and spits it out, while the others stare at the calamari with a mixture of disgust and disbelief.

"Is it bad that I kind of want to keep eating it, though?" Nate asks.

"I mean, the crispiness is pretty good," Andre says, trying another piece.

"If you add some sauce, you probably can't taste the anus of it all," Sidric adds, trying to lighten the mood.

All three of them turn to Naya, waiting for her approval, their eyes pleading for her to reassure them that they haven't just eaten pig anus.

"Listen, I've never been the type of person to keep the gays away from some anus. Bon Appetite." She pushes the plate towards them. They all crack out laughing.

They finish eating their delicious meal and ask the server for the bills. The server looks happy that they're finally leaving. They all share a ride back to their hotel. Nate passes out in the front seat after eating twice his weight in pasta, in the back Naya and Andre debate how it could've been actual calamari that they ate today, and Sidric stares out the window trying not to think about the electricity forming in his fingertips. He takes a deep breath, trying to calm his nerves as he feels his body vibrate with shocks in and out.

Once they reach the hotel, Sidric and Naya say goodbye to Nate and Andre and head upstairs to start packing their stuff. Sidric begins folding his clothes, which cover eighty percent of the hotel room's floor. His mind races through every memory made this past weekend, mainly focusing on how often he felt the electric shocks right after kissing Deux. He tries to think of anything he could have missed, knowing that it wasn't just a random reaction, there was something more.

Naya notices he's way too quiet and asks, "Hey Sid, you good? Is the edible still in your system?"

"Uhm.. no... well, a bit yes. But also there's something that has been going on, and I don't know how to explain it or what to do about it."

"What do you mean? Did you hook up with someone else? I need details!"

"No! Only Deux!" Sidric yells back, "But something happened the first night we kissed. I spilled FiveLoko all over his new watch-"

"Oh, it's fine Sidric. Those things come with a warranty. Also, I'm sure he didn't mind since he kept hanging out with you. Also, he looked very into you, so-"

"It's not about the warranty, though. Wait, you think he's really into me? Like on a scale of 1-10."

"I'd say 13 bestie," Naya says with a smile.

Sidric can't help but smile too.

"Anyways, what is it about then?" Naya asks.

"When I spilled the FiveLoko, we both got a bit electrocuted. I thought we were fine, but in the last days I have felt electric bolts, jolts and shocks all over my body. And then today, this happened." He pulls out his hands in front of Naya's face, revealing the gold shimmering stains.

She inspects them with a shocked look. Naya usually knows everything about everything, she's a walking random facts book. This time, however, she's speechless. Seconds of silence pass by, making the room feel dense.

"Wait, so the hair dryer exploding... you think that was you?" she asks.

"Maybe. I still don't know what the fuck is happening, honestly. I do think it could have been me. It randomly comes and goes."

"Okay," she says, staring at Sidric with a million thoughts coming in at once. She walks closer to him and slowly reaches her hand towards his chest.

"Let me know what you feel." She rubs her thumb against her index finger and then squeezes and pulls Sidric's left nipple as hard as she can.

"AH! What are you doing?!" Sidric screams in pain as a bolt of electricity surges toward his chest. The charge quickly jumps to Naya's hand.

"HOLY—! You weren't lying," Naya exclaims, pulling her hand back, her body tingling with the shock. Her hair stands on end from the static. "I'm officially flabbergasted," she sighs.

"Imagine how I feel," he whispers.

9

ctrl

Deux

Days after OnlineCon Sidric and Deux's communication reaches an all-time high. They text each other constantly throughout the day, updating each other on every little thing. Sidric finds himself grinning at the sound of his phone buzzing, knowing it's probably Deux. He has memorized his phone number just by how many times he has seen it pop on his screen. Their conversations now range from what they're doing at the moment to their childhood stories. They've become each other's support system, the one person they can count on to always be there to listen.

As their bond grows stronger, Deux can't help but wonder when Sidric will bring up the electric shocks incident. He tries to hint at it a couple of times, but each time he does, Sid's tone changes, and the phones start to glitch. Deux takes that as a sign to change the topic.

Despite never discussing the incident, they've already learned so much about each other. Deux discovers Sidric's various doomsday scenarios—none of which ever actually happen—and how he categorizes everything by Taylor Swift eras. In turn, Deux shares numerous snippets from his journals with Sidric. He frequently encourages Sidric to start journaling, explaining how it has helped him manage his anxiety. Sidric says he will start soon, but he never actually does.

One Sunday afternoon, Deux lies down on his bed editing a video he had just filmed. Earlier that day, he attended a pride event in the mall parking lot. People were raising awareness of the anti-trans laws being put in high schools all around Canada. Apparently, even in 2073 people are still obsessed with what bathroom people shit in. Towards the end of the event, Deux got a bunch of attendees together and led them into the mall to pass out signs that said "love is human" and other inspirational self-love quotes. A social experiment video about sharing love. In big cities like New York or Los Angeles, these things happen all the time but in small towns like Deux's it is seen as the town's gossip of the week, news travels fast there. Everyone at the mall stared and most of them reacted negatively tossing the paper into the trash seconds later. Not because they were directly homophobic but because they looked down on anything different, anything standing out. The point of the video was to show people's reactions to queer individuals claiming their space.

As he adds some background music and adjusts the lighting in the last shot, his younger brother Austin bursts into his room, munching on a bag of cheese-Os.

"Hey D, what you up to?" Austin plops down on Deux's bed.

"Just editing a video," Deux replies, barely glancing up from his work.

"Oh, is it the one you filmed at the mall today?"

"Yeah, it's a social experiment-"

"The whole town knows, D," Austin interrupts. "It's cool that you're out and proud and doing your online stuff, but remember that your whole family lives in this town too."

Deux looks at Austin, confused. "Okay, what about it?"

"What you do in private is your business, but what you do in public has consequences. You don't have to shove it down everybody's throat." Austin pulls out his smartwatch and shows a recording someone got of him going around the mall passing out papers. "Maybe this was a bit much. Don't ya think?"

Austin gets up and walks out, slamming the door behind him. Deux clenches every muscle in his body and slams his back on his bed. His brother's reaction triggers his biggest fear. Deux wanted to show how people react to queer individuals claiming their space in public. He had hoped to spark a conversation and make a positive impact, but it seems that no matter how loudly you scream for acceptance, some people will never give you the respect you deserve.

Deux looks back at his computer screen and contemplates whether he should upload the video. He remembers the negative reactions of people at the mall, but he also knows that it's important to stand up for what he believes in. He decides to upload the video, hoping it will resonate with someone out there who might need a message of self-love and acceptance. Not everyone is going to like him and that is okay. If asking for acceptance makes people uncomfortable then maybe they deserve to feel uncomfortable, even if it's his own brother.

Deux's heart beats hard on his chest, bringing to light hurt and confusion. His brother and best friend of all his life just came into his room and essentially shat on who he was, giving him terms and conditions for how to be himself. He used to never be like this; they used to share secrets all the time. He was the first person Deux came out to. A while back, when they were in 11th and 10th grade, they were both watching TV one night, and Deux felt a panic attack coming on. Austin could tell something was bothering him all night since he kept fidgeting his legs. He turned to look at Deux and saw tears coming down from his eyes.

"What's up, D?" he placed his hand on his shoulder. "You want to talk about anything?"

When Deux felt his palm touch him, it was like a trigger setting everything free. He started bawling. Austin knew what was up.

"Are you gay?" he asked, no negative connotations or tones attached to that question.

"I'm bisexual," Deux silently cried out.

Austin pulled him into a hug, "Listen bro, I love you no matter what. I am proud of you for being who you are."

What happened to that boy? Did all the homophobic celebrities get into his head? Was it that easy to brainwash him? His eyes water as he closes down his laptop, trying not to let the hurt get to him. But the pain keeps getting stronger and stronger. The lights in his room start flickering on and off, and he feels an electricity within him that's stronger than ever before.

He quickly grabs a bag and packs his journal, some pens and a music theory book. He needs to get out of the house. As he walks down the hall towards the front door, all the lights he passes flicker. The electricity within him feels like it's growing out of control. Deux quickly runs out of the house before his family can blame him for the flickering lights. He crosses the street and turns left towards Oakwood Park. He speeds up once he's close to the park, running through a red light seconds before it turns green. The sound of tires scratching the pavement fills the air as a car slams its brakes inches away from hitting Deux. He jumps up in the air, startled, and places both hands on the front of the car to prevent it from hitting him. The car's alarm turns on at the same time as its windshield wipers and lights. He looks at the driver and then back at his hands. *This is getting out of control.*

"You okay boy?" The driver screams out over the noise. He tries to turn off his car, but it's pointless; the car has a mind of its own.

Deux runs through the park's entrance and does not stop. He knows the park like he knows Meryl Streep's monologues. He comes here every time he needs a break from the world, and today he needs that break more than ever. He walks up and down a few hills until he finds his favorite tree. A gigantic oak tree sits right by a small lake. He climbs up the tree, just like he has done since he was 7. He gets all the way to the top in seconds, sits on a thick branch, and closes his eyes.

He remembers the first time he climbed up this tree. It was a warm summer day, and he had just gotten in a fight with his best friend Silvy. They were hanging out by the lake, and she blasted water over some fireflies, almost killing them. His heart was filled with pain seeing their lights go out from the suffering. Back then, he thought these were the forest's fairies. He didn't talk to Silvy for a whole day. He climbed up the tree that day and vowed to always protect nature.

Thinking back on that day fills him with a bittersweet feeling. Life has gotten so much harder. And now, he has a new concern. Tired of not feeling in control of his body, he inspects his palms, where he feels constant electric jolts. *If it's not going away, there must be a way to control it.* He focuses and rubs his palms together, breathing in and out. A golden orb forms around his palms. He pulls them apart, and the electricity disappears. He tries again, breathing in and out, focusing on his hands. Nothing happens.

Frustrated and defeated, he cracks his knuckles one by one. Trying to understand why his body is producing insane amounts of electricity isn't something any twenty-year-old should have to figure out—only he and Sidric are. *Sidric.* Just the thought of him brings the electricity surging back, like a thunderstorm breaking through the clouds. He retraces their conversations, the sound of Sidric's laugh beside him, the moment their lips touched for the first time. Opening his eyes, he sees electric bolts dancing between his fingers, jumping from one to the other. He's doing it. With cautious excitement, he plays around, bouncing the bolts back and forth—little balls of light flying around him. He can't believe what he's seeing.

The sun begins to set, casting half the park into shadow beneath the towering trees. He takes a deep breath, the earthy scent of oak and faint echoes of childhood memories filling his lungs. Across from the tree he's sitting under, a streetlamp flickers to life. Fixing his gaze on it, he stretches out his hands, focusing intently. He closes his eyes and whispers Sidric's name.

In an instant, the light leaves the streetlamp, traveling toward him like a shiny tennis ball tossed across the air. It reaches his hands in a matter of seconds, surging into his body. The sensation is familiar, the same electric shocks he felt in Los Angeles, but this time, he's in control.

He keeps thinking about his breathing, his mind set on Sidric. He pushes open his right hand towards the same streetlamp. Light gets shot towards the bulb, and it lights up again. He smiles, feeling exhilarated. *I'm doing it!* He has control over his powers now. But with this newfound control, he also feels a responsibility he never imagined.

"Shit," he whispers, "this is neat."

Deux spends hours sitting atop the oak tree, his focus never breaking as he continues to play with the electric bolts jumping between his fingers. As he gazes out at the park, he spots a cluster of fireflies hovering over the small lake, and he feels a surge of protectiveness towards the tiny creatures.

With a determined look on his face, Deux points his hands towards the fireflies. He focuses on the electric energy, imagining it as a bright, glowing ball of light. Slowly, he begins to move his hands towards the fireflies, guiding the ball of light towards them. At first, the fireflies seem to shy away, but then they start to fly towards him. The ball of light grows bigger and brighter as it draws nearer, and Deux can feel the electricity pulsing through his body.

With a sudden burst of energy, the ball of light shoots towards the fireflies, breaking into multiple tiny sparkles. Deux watches in amazement as the fireflies start to flicker and fly around his sparkles, dancing through the night.

Deux's heart is racing with excitement as he recalls his successful attempt at controlling the electricity surging through his body. He feels a sense of accomplishment knowing that he can finally harness his powers. As he walks down the street towards his house, he can't help but think about the possibilities of what he can do now.

He reaches his house and walks past his brother's room, shooting a quick middle finger towards his door. Deux jumps onto his bed, still feeling the adrenaline from his experience in the park. He takes out his phone and begins to research RainforesTec, the company that produced the smartwatch that caused the incident. He is determined to get to the root of the problem and figure out how to fix it.

He texts Sidric.

DEUX
-Heyy! You up?

Within seconds Sidric texts back, it is hard for him to play it cool.

SIDRIC
-Hey :) yes, just organizing my Taylor Swift vinyl collection.

DEUX
-You have a TSwift vinyl collection? Please show me.

Sidric sends over a photo of him with all of Taylor Swift albums up on the wall behind him.

SIDRIC

-It is always so hard because I have 44 of her albums but my wall only has room for 10 so I have to keep switching every now and then. Also, we should go to her next tour! She's 86 years old but trust me the show she gives is out of this world!

-Anyways, how was your day?

Deux smiles at his phone. He loves how Sidric will just ramble on about Taylor Swift.

DEUX

-Okay. its a date!

-It was actually okay then bad then good. Long story short, I think I got the shocks under control for a second.

Within seconds, his phone rings and Sidric is on the other end of the line, practically bursting with questions.

"Okay tell me everything. Was it just now? How did you do it? Did anybody help you out? I think I've gotten a bit better at handling it, but I still get electrocuted every time I shower. Have you showered yet? How did you feel?" Sidric's words tumble out in a flurry.

Deux chuckles at Sid's excitement. "Sid, breathe. So, I was upset at my brother for being a complete asshole, so I needed some time alone. I went to a park near my house and just focused on everything going on inside."

"Shit, what did your brother do?" Sidric's concern is palpable.

"It's not important. What's important is now I know how to handle these powers."

"Okay, what made you keep it all under control? Also, powers? Is that what we're calling them?" Sidric's curiosity is insatiable.

Deux hesitates, wondering whether or not to tell Sidric that thinking about his lips, smile, and eyes helped him control his powers. He doesn't want to come across as a complete stalker or creep.

"I just focused on my breathing and tried to clear my head," he lies, "And yes, I have to show you what I can do. I feel like a whole ass vampire wizard right now."

"Ugh, I'm jealous. I can't clear my head. I'm always going a million thoughts a minute."

"I believe that," Deux teases.

"Also, vampire wizard? That's not a thing, Deux. There are vampires and there are wizards, but not both."

"How would you know, Sidric? Have you met any wizards before? Or vampires? Exactly."

Deux's cheeks start hurting from smiling.

"Anyways, I did some research on RainforesTec. I fell down a rabbit hole and found out there are a lot of issues with some of their watches, but no one has had the same thing as us," Deux explains.

Sidric sighs on the other end, listening intently.

"However, there's a RainforesTec Summit happening in a couple weeks, and I figured we could go and ask around. Someone might be able to help us out."

"That sounds like a good idea!" Sidric says, "it's right before my classes start again, so we could make it a whole undercover vacation. Let me look at ticket prices."

"Sick! I'll figure out how to get us in," Deux says confidently.

"Now all I have to do before we leave is not electrocute anyone I know. We got this," Sidric jokes.

"Try to bring your mind to memories that bring you joy and peace. Whenever you feel like things are getting out of control, just give yourself some time to clear your mind. Also, you can call me anytime. I'll help you, Sid."

"Thanks, Deux. If I was going to become a radioactive human

with electric powers, I wouldn't want to be with anybody else," Sidric laughs.

"What are you doing for the rest of the night?" Deux asks.

"Not much. I was going to watch Ma and pass out," Sidric replies.

"Ma? Is it that stupid slasher movie with Octavia Spencer?" Deux jokes.

"Excuse you! Ma is an iconic, underrated piece of art. Octavia Spencer brought what was missing in this world. I'm still so pissed they didn't make part two."

"Part two? Doesn't she die at the end?" Deux questions.

"Well, the house burns down, but the viewer doesn't really know if she dies or not. Imagine, she survives the fire, and then part two is called... MaMa! Get it?" Sidric chuckles.

They both start laughing.

"Okay, what about MaMa Mia?! a Musical?" Deux says.

"Yes! You *get* it! or Mavatar? Mapocalypse!? The options are endless!"

Deux was worried that the sparks he felt for Sidric would be gone once there were a million miles in between them, but it is the complete opposite. The sparks have turned into a wildfire.

"Fine, you've convinced me. I'll watch it with you. Turn your video on," Deux says.

"One sec," Sidric replies.

Deux hears him moving around: the water faucet running and then shutting off, the sound of bristles brushing against teeth, a quick spritz of what must be cologne. Finally, the camera turns on.

"Hey, cutie!" Deux says the moment Sidric's face appears on screen. "Did you just get ready for me?"

Sidric's face goes fully red.

They watch 'Ma,' constantly pausing it because either Sidric is explaining a fun fact about a scene, or they are both uncontrollably laughing. After the movie ends, they stay on the phone for three more hours talking about everything you talk about with someone you like at 3 a.m. They keep chatting until Sidric falls asleep. Deux admires how peaceful Sidric looks and touches the screen as if it was his face.

"Goodnight, Sid," Deux says as he turns off his lights.

Deux places his phone gently on the bedside table, the screen illuminating the room with a soft glow. He lies back on his pillow, staring up at the ceiling, his mind still filled with the sound of Sidric's voice and the warmth of their conversation.

As he drifts off to sleep, Deux can't help but replay the moments they shared on the phone. The way Sidric laughed at his jokes, the genuine interest he showed in Deux's life, the way he made Deux feel seen and heard—it all makes Deux's heart swell with affection.

Lying there in the darkness, Deux wonders how he got so lucky to have someone like Sidric in his life. It's not easy being in a long-distance relationship, but moments like these make it all worth it. The connection they have transcends the physical distance between them, as if their souls are intertwined despite being miles apart.

In his dreams, Deux envisions the day they will finally be together, holding each other's hands, exploring new places, and creating memories that aren't confined to video calls and text messages. He closes his eyes, feeling the weight of their connection still pounding in his heart, and whispers softly into the darkness, "Goodnight, Sid," once again as if the words could somehow reach across the distance and find their way to Sidric's dreams.

With thoughts of Sidric swirling in his mind, Deux falls into a peaceful slumber, knowing that tomorrow will bring a new day filled with hope, love, and the anticipation of their next conversation.

10

witH friends like TheSe

Sidric

"Sidric! We have to leave in 10 minutes!" his mom calls out from the other side of the door.

It's 7 a.m., the start of another school break, and as usual, Sidric's mom is sticking to her routine. Every vacation, she takes both him and his brother to get blood tests done. With her sons living away from home most of the year, this is her way of staying in control—keeping tabs on their health and ensuring everything is in order.

Crap, that's today. What are my results going to be like? If anything alarming comes up, that will only make my mom have a major freak out and forbid me to see Deux ever again. She'll lock me up in my room and never let me out. It'll be worse than Romeo and Juliet.

A flicker of uncertainty crosses Sidric's face as he contemplates the implications. Would his body's electrical anomalies even register on a standard blood test? The very notion makes him question the nature of his existence. Perhaps his blood is no longer the familiar crimson hue. Perhaps it's transformed, attached to the crackling energy that courses through his veins.

Determined to find answers, Sidric swings his legs out of bed and hurries to his bathroom. With a steady hand, he pricks his fingertip with a sewing needle, the brief pinch of pain a stark reminder of reality. A small red droplet wells up, confirming at least one certainty amidst the unpredictability swirling around him. He allows himself to relax a bit knowing his blood will look normal.

He puts on an oversized hoodie and gym shorts, he brushes his teeth, puts on a bit of makeup foundation on top of the golden stains on his arms, and heads downstairs to meet his mom and brother already waiting for him in the car. He takes this as an opportunity to mention his upcoming trip to Washington.

"Hey ma, I was thinking of doing a trip in a few weeks," he casually says as he puts his seat belt on.

"Where are you going now? Who else is going? For how long?" All her questions come in at once. Sidric's eyes go wild looking around for answers, he questions telling his mom about Deux. Is it too soon to talk about him to his family? How would he describe him? Boyfriend? Hookup? The relationship is still extremely fresh. His superstitious self fears that by talking about him he will be jinxing any possible romantic relationship with Deux.

"Naya, obviously," he lies, "and this new friend we made at OnlineCon. His name is Deux. We're going to a RainforesTec conference—they're launching new products."

"Deux?!" Damon cuts in, his tone dripping with classic sibling rivalry. "Is he the guy you've been nonstop talking to? Is he your *new special friend*?"

"What? No. He's just a friend. We're all very interested in their new tech advancements."

"It's all good with me, just make sure to tell your dad about it. Maybe avoid telling him it's a RainforesTec convention though. You know how much he hates Jacques Bizous," Sid's mom says as she swerves the car almost running through a red light.

Sidric's dad, Lenny, despised RainforesTec ever since he got a smart-massage bot from them. The first day he tried it the robot malfunctioned and nearly choked him to death. He called, messaged and even went to the Mexican RainforesTec headquarters but was never able to talk to a human who could help him get a refund. He destroyed the robot and swore to never buy any RainforesTec gadgets again. Once you are in Lenny's blacklist, you are blocked forever.

As they arrive at the clinic, the sound of Sidric's knuckles cracking breaks through the podcast his mom is listening to. Damon notices Sid's nervousness through the rear view mirror. Usually, Sidric talks nonstop, cracking jokes or filling Damon in on the latest pop-culture drama. They get dropped off at the front door of the medical clinic.

"Go in while I look for parking!" their mom yells out from the front seat.

In the waiting room, posters lined on the walls advertise all the different tests you can get done. Today, Sidric and Damon are doing a blood sample and a full body scan. These full-body scans were introduced recently and are everyone's new obsession. They can identify any disease, virus or infection within seconds. Sidric's head starts spinning on the possibilities of the scan identifying him as a radioactive anomaly and the doctors sending him into an evil lab where the government can do tests on him. He is completely lost in his head.

"Are you good Sid?" Damon's deep brown eyes looking right at him, able to read every emotion.

"Yeah, it's just been a couple of stressful weeks," he admits, his voice tinged with weariness as he attempts to ground himself in the present moment.

Damon's older brother instincts kick in, his voice laced with concern and affection. "You don't have to worry about these tests; you know

93

it doesn't hurt. And it's not like they're going to find anything bad. Unless you've been doing drugs. Is that why you're so jittery?" His words are laced with a blend of teasing and genuine concern, a testament to the bond between them.

Sidric shakes his head, a nervous laugh escaping his lips. "No! It's not that. I—" He hesitates, grappling with the weight of his confession. "Okay. Deux and I are kind of—somewhat dating. And we had some things go down in LA that we have to get some answers to, which is why we're going to Washington."

A knowing smile spreads across Damon's face, his suspicions confirmed. "I knew it! You have literally been keeping me up every night with your little phone calls! Sid!" He envelops his brother in a tight embrace, genuine happiness radiating from him. "I'm so happy for you!"

The moment of celebration is interrupted by the nurse's call, drawing their attention back to the present. "Sidric and Damon Alvarado, Examination Room 2A," she announces, prompting Sidric to tense up involuntarily. In his state of nerves, he inadvertently sends a surge of electricity toward Damon, who recoils with a mixture of surprise and amusement.

"What the hell! You just shocked me!" Damon exclaims, laughter bubbling up from within him despite the unexpected jolt.

The testing room is sterile and clinical, resembling a typical doctor's office, but with extreme advanced technology. At its center stands a towering glass tube, its sleek surface gleaming under the bright lights. Damon steps forward, his movements hesitant as he approaches the imposing structure.

Sidric watches as Damon steps into the glass tube, exuding confidence that Sidric can only envy. A shiver runs down Damon's spine, though he hides it well, standing still within the sleek, cylindrical confines. Above him, a slender robotic arm descends from the ceiling, its metallic fingers curling delicately, hovering over Damon's forearm.

Sidric tenses as the arm lightly pierces Damon's skin, extracting a syringe full of dark crimson blood. The process is swift and precise, almost eerily so, and Damon doesn't even flinch. Sidric's eyes follow the translucent tube carrying the blood away, unable to look away from the unsettling yet fascinating sight.

The robotic arm retracts into the ceiling with a soft hum, and three glowing blue lights suddenly ignite, encircling Damon. The faint hum of scanning energy fills the room as the lights pass over his body, casting an ethereal glow over his features. Sidric's hands grip the edge of his chair as he watches, his heart pounding harder with every second.

When the scan finishes, Damon steps out, exhaling a calm breath that seems to dissipate all tension. His eyes meet Sidric's as he flashes an encouraging smile. "See? It's not that scary, Sid. You've got this!"

Sidric swallows hard, forcing a shaky nod. *If Damon can handle it, so can I... right?*

Sidric repeats as many Taylor Swift lyrics as he can think of before stepping into the sleek glass tube. The air crackles with anticipation as he settles into position, his pulse quickening with each passing moment.Within seconds, the robotic arm whirs to life, its precise movements extracting Sidric's blood with a clinical efficiency that borders on unnerving.

As the arm retreats, carrying its maroon cargo, the room plunges into an eerie silence punctuated only by the soft hum of machinery. Lights flicker to life, casting ethereal shadows across the chamber. Sidric feels a sense of dread creeping over him, making it hard to breathe.

Then, as if triggered by some unseen force, a surge of energy courses through Sidric's veins, setting every nerve ablaze with an electric intensity. It's as though he's been thrust into the eye of a storm, the calm before the inevitable chaos. He is immediately taken back to the Olive Garden bathroom fiasco.

A torrent of sensations overwhelms him, washing over him in a dizzying wave. His vision swims, blurred by a golden haze that dances before his eyes. It's a sensation like to being caught in the grip of a fever dream, a surreal landscape of light and shadow.

And then, with a deafening crack, the glass encasing the tube shatters, shards of shimmering fragments scattering like stars across the void. The room erupts into chaos as alarms blare and emergency lights flicker to life, bathing the scene in an eerie red glow.

"EMERGENCY EVACUATION IN PROGRESS. Please find the nearest exit."

A commanding voice sounds all around the building.

In a flash, the squeaky-clean room plunges into chaos, the whole building freaking out under the pressure. Sidric stands frozen like a deer in headlights, his heart racing as his brain scrambles to process the absolute disaster unfolding around him.

As the dust settles and silence descends once more, Sidric is left to grapple with the enormity of what he has unleashed.

"Oh my god! Sid! Are you okay?!" Damon's voice rings with genuine concern as he springs into action, scrambling over the remnants of the tube to reach his brother. With a determined pull, he hauls Sidric out of the wreckage, his protective instincts kicking into high gear. "We are so suing this place," he declares, his anger simmering beneath the surface as he surveys the damage.

Together, they make a hasty exit from the building, the adrenaline still coursing through Sidric's veins as he tries to process what just transpired. His mind whirls with a mixture of shock and disbelief, the memory of the malfunctioning machinery replaying in his mind like a broken record.

But despite the crisis, a nagging doubt gnaws at Sidric's conscience. Deep down, he knows that it wasn't entirely the machinery's fault. Sidric feels agitation building within, a gut instinct telling him that there may be more to the situation than meets the eye.

Outside the imposing building, their mother's frantic gaze scans the bustling crowd, her worry etched deep into her furrowed brow. She weaves through the crowds of people exiting the building, her heart pounding with fear and apprehension.

As their eyes meet, relief floods her features, and she rushes toward them, enveloping them in a tight embrace. "What happened? I was about to go in, but suddenly the alarms went off," she asks, her voice trembling with concern.

Sidric exchanges a glance with Damon, silently urging him to explain the situation delicately, praying that it doesn't involve revealing his radioactive abilities. With a rush of words, Damon blurts out, his voice laced with a mixture of fear and indignation.

"Their scanning machine malfunctioned, Mom! It nearly killed Sid!" The words spill out in a rush, carrying the weight of the terrifying ordeal they had just experienced. "We're never coming back here," he adds emphatically, his resolve firm and unwavering.

Hours after the chaos at the testing center, Sidric stands in front of his full-length mirror, examining his outfit. He's decided to go out clubbing with his friends tonight to take his mind off of this whole radioactiveness. However, he can't shake the feeling that something's missing. It's not that he doesn't have the right clothes or that he hasn't been able to drink FiveLoko since that OnlineCon party; it's the fact that Deux isn't here. He wishes nothing more than to be able to spend another night with him. He knows that he would help him figure out this powers situation and get it all under control.

Even though Sidric and Deux are basically living on opposite sides of the planet, they've somehow built a bond that feels solid and unbreakable. Their days are a nonstop loop of phone calls, where they overshare every little detail about their lives—whether it's Deux showing off his cool new tricks or Sidric forcing Deux to binge-watch his favorite movies like some kind of cinematic hostage situation.

Sure, their relationship isn't exactly the romantic dream Sidric imagined, where they'd actually get to, you know, be in the same room. But the thought of seeing Deux in person soon keeps him going. In just a few weeks, he'll finally get to hug him, feel his warmth, and maybe even confirm that Deux is not, in fact, a figment of his imagination.

Long-distance relationships are basically a crash course in patience and bad Wi-Fi connections, but Sidric knows it's all worth it. The second they're reunited, every awkward video call and missed time zone will feel like a small price to pay for the chance to be with the person who makes his heart skip a beat. Love might be tough, but for Sidric, it's also totally worth the struggle.

Sidric runs his fingers through his hair, trying to tame the wild curls that refuse to stay in place. He's trying to style his hair differently, it's a new era for him. He grabs some makeup foundation and builds it up over his golden stains trying to make them blend into his skin. He's used to this process after doing it every day for the past week. He knows Deux would laugh if he saw him right now, and the thought brings a smile to his face. He grabs his phone off his nightstand and checks for any messages from Deux, but there's nothing new. Sometimes he can't help but wonder if he's putting all his love into a relationship that may never be more than a long-distance affair. He worries that he's giving too much of himself to someone who may not feel the same way about him. *Are we dating? Are we pen-pals? Boyfriends?* He usually hates labels but right now a label on what they are would be extremely helpful.

The doubts begin to build up in his mind, and he feels his hands tremble with electricity as he tries to calm himself down. He takes a deep breath and reminds himself of the moments he's shared with Deux, the late-night phone calls, the virtual movie nights, the little moments of intimacy they've managed to create despite the distance between them.

Sidric recognizes that the feelings he has for Deux are real, but the fear of rejection or of being hurt is overwhelming. He tries to push those negative thoughts aside as he finishes getting ready, reminding himself that he deserves to be happy, to experience love, and that he shouldn't let his fears hold him back. A quick snap of light comes out of his finger and towards the lightbulb over the bathroom mirror cracking it into little pieces. That is the third bulb this week he's broken. He sighs and cleans up the mess.

He snaps a quick photo and sends it to Deux.

SIDRIC

-Ready for the night! Also just popped another lightbulb.

Deux's reply comes quickly, accompanied by a photo of himself in a leather jacket and jeans.

DEUX

-You look hot! I'm going out too, just heading to have some pre-party margs with Silvy.

He smiles down at his phone and heads out. On the car ride to the club, he thinks about last night's conversation with Deux. He was telling Deux about the club he was going to and Deux almost hinted at becoming official.

"I don't want you going and kissing other guys," Deux said.

"Are you going to kiss other guys?" Sidric asked back.

"No, I won't but you shouldn't either okay?"

"I mean, we haven't determined if we're exclusive or anything. Aren't we just talking?" he tried to play it cool. "What does it mean? Are we like dating?" Sidric asked, hinting at wanting to be something more.

"We're not dating, for now," Deux replied, "For now, okay?" he winked through his camera.

Even though that conversation made him think things could develop more in the future Sidric still feels anxious about it. He is not a patient person, when he wants something he goes for it and expects results immediately. Them not being able to see each other makes it a million times harder since he can't fully see how Deux feels about him. It's hard for Sidric to not be in full control for once.

He arrives at his friend Trey's house and they take a few shots while he tells them all about Deux, all except for the electric powers of course. He usually sees his friends from Mexico a few times per year so every time they see each other is a monumental *chisme* party. *Chisme* is the Spanish word for gossiping, its always better when it's *chisme*. His friend Lara pours three Mezcal shots and passes them around.

"I know you don't do Mezcal but it's a special occasion Sid, the double B's are back!" She cheers out.

The double B's was their nickname back in high school. All three of them snuck into a junior year party once and after a lot of jager bombs, they started calling themselves the Boss Bitches, double B's for short. Now, the nickname stuck.

"To the double B's!" Trey raises his glass spilling a bit over the coffee table. They clink their glasses together and take the shot.

Sidric struggles holding it in. He grabs a handful of limes and squeezes them in his mouth. "That was rough," he cries out, shaking some Tajin chilli flakes in his mouth. "Never doing it again."

"Okay tell us more about this guy. Is he nice? Should we trust him?" Lara says, her breath smelling like a full tequila bottle.

"He's very nice and trustworthy. I don't know, from the short time I've known him I can tell he has such a kind heart. The way he puts literally everyone else before himself. He literally brought his grandma to his first solo trip. He's just something else." Sidric finds himself smiling, staring at the empty shot glass.

"You are so in love Sid!" Lara yells out. "My goal of the night is to find a Mexican Deux."

"I want a Mexican woman Deux!" Trey jokes out.

As they head out the door, Sidric can't help but feel a little jealous of his friends. They'll be dancing and flirting with strangers all night looking for their own Mexican Deux, meanwhile he'll be thinking about the real Deux.

In the club they play all the good songs, lots of Beyonce mixed in with other divas and the occasional male rapper. All three of them form a triangle in the middle of the dance floor protecting Lara from any creep trying to do anything sketchy. Even in the year 2073 most straight men still struggle to understand what consent is.

"Boss Bitches?!" Lara screams out through the music. "They added a photo booth!" She points towards the back of the room where flashing lights are coming out from behind a curtain.

They walk in a triangle formation towards the booth. Sidric feels the alcohol sneaking into his system. He wonders what Deux is up to right now. *Is he also feeling the alcohol? Is he out dancing?*

They get into the booth and take three photos. One where they all smile, one candid where they pretend to laugh, and the final one where they scream out, "Boss Bitches" out loud. The flashing lights blinds them for a second as they wait for their photos to print. Suddenly, Lara feels a stranger's hand squeezing her butt from behind. She jumps up and turns around quickly to see a scrawny boy with a mustache smirking at her. Another man thinking he can just do whatever he wants because he is that, a man. Sidric and Trey see it all happen. Trey rushes to check in on Lara and make sure she is okay.

"I'm fine," Lara breathes out, "so fucking disgusting."

"I'll be back," Sidric says, his sight still set on 'mustache man'.

"Sidric no, I don't want to cause any trouble," Lara says after being attacked.

Sidric sikes himself up as he walks towards the guy. *This creep is about to get the zapping of a lifetime.* The 'mustache man' is turned around now getting in line to order a drink.

"Hey!" he yells out calling him to turn around.

"Hey buddy! Yo, your friend is mad hot," he yells back grabbing Sidric's hand for a high five.

Sidric holds onto his hand and pulls him closer. "You just sexually assaulted her. Touching people without their consent is assault—just a quick reminder." As he speaks, he feels his frustration channeling into the palm of his hand. He releases it in a sudden shock, making the guy's whole body tremble. "Don't ever touch another woman again, creep."

He lets go as tiny electric bolts still travel through the creep's body. He turns around and smiles at his two friends proudly staring back at him. Sidric has no idea how he just did that but he feels a warmness rush through his whole body. For the first time, his powers didn't destroy anything, in fact, they helped him. If he could go and electrocute every other creep in this club he would. He gets back to his friends and Trey immediately says, "Okay that calls for some... SHOTS!"

The bartender places a tray of shots in front of them, the colorful liquids enticing them to indulge in the moment. Sidric takes a deep breath, ready to let go of his worries and embrace the night ahead.

"To the double B's!," Sidric says, his voice filled with conviction, as he clinks his shot glass against Trey's and Lara's. They raise their glasses in unison, the clinking sound blending seamlessly with the pulsating music.

One shot turns into thirteen and suddenly Sidric is seeing double double B's. His head is fuzzy with a mix of tequila, vodka and what they thought was gin but was actually whisky. Sidric heads to the washroom and goes into the first door that opens. He can feel the whole room spinning around him. He kneels down and holds on to the walls.

"Oh shit," he whispers to himself seconds before he projectile vomits half of the drinks he just had all over the toilet. He chuckles. No matter how sick he is, projectile vomit will always make him laugh. There's something so cartoon-y and camp about it. He drunkenly grabs his phone and calls himself a car to take him home. He is too drunk to be surrounded by straights when he could be in bed talking to Deux.

As Sidric stumbles out of the club, the cool night air hits his face, momentarily sobering him up. He clutches his phone tightly, eagerly awaiting the arrival of his ride. His mind swirls with a mixture of alcohol-induced dizziness and a longing for the warmth of his conversations with Deux. He says goodbye to Lara and Trey hugging them tightly and thanks them for such a good night.

As the car pulls up to the curb, Sidric clumsily climbs into the backseat, struggling to give the driver his home address. The drive feels like a blur, the city lights passing by in a hazy kaleidoscope. His head hangs from the window as he takes in all the beauty from Mexico. Before he moved away he never really appreciated how magical this city is. But now he is fully mesmerized by it. His thoughts drift back to Deux, and he wishes he could teleport him here, so he could share this magic with him. He longs to take Deux to his favorite childhood restaurant where they make the best Chilaquiles, or to take him on a stroll downtown on a Sunday morning where the air feels the freshest ever. He wants to share why he is who he is with him.

Finally, they arrive at his house. Sidric stumbles out of the car, fumbling with his keys before managing to unlock the front door. He slumps against the wall, momentarily gathering his balance, as he ascends the stairs to his room trying to be as quiet as possible to not wake his parents up.

Once inside his room, he kicks off his shoes, leaving a trail of discarded items in his wake. His mind is still spinning from the drinks, his body heavy with exhaustion and the weight of missing Deux. He craves the solace of their late-night conversations, the sound of Deux's voice soothing his restless soul.

Sidric collapses onto his bed, the room spinning around him. He reaches for his phone, feeling a mixture of excitement and yearning as he taps on Deux's contact. He hopes that, despite the late hour, Deux will be awake and willing to talk.

The phone rings, each passing second stretching into eternity. Sidric's heart races, his fingertips drumming nervously on the mattress. Just as he begins to lose hope, the call connects.

"Deux," Sidric says, his voice filled with a mixture of drunkenness and longing.

There's a pause on the other end, and then Deux's voice breaks through the static. "Sidric? Are you okay?"

Sidric's lips curl into a tipsy smile. "Yeah, why wouldn't I be?" he replies, the relief evident in his voice.

The familiar sound of Deux's laughter fills the airwaves, instantly calming Sidric's racing thoughts. "Well, it's nearly 4 am. I thought you were in trouble or something. How was your night my drunk boy?" The world outside his rooms fades away as he becomes fully immersed in their conversation. The distance between them may be vast, but at this moment, it feels insignificant.

"Pretty good. I snapped a creep for being... well a creep and then took some shots. Then puked in the bathroom. An eventful night overall. How about you?"

"Jesus, not as eventful. Why was he a creep?" Deux chuckles. "We had a lot of wine though. Silvy and I had a scary movie marathon. I need you here to cuddle me and protect me from the ghosts."

"Ooh! I love scary movies. I want to be in your arms keeping all those scary demons away. I miss you Deux. This long-distance shit is hard."

"I know, but we get to see each other soon. You'll be in my arms in no time." He tries to make Sid feel better but deep down he hates how long he has to wait to hold him again. "What's your favorite scary movie?"

As they exchange stories and share their deepest thoughts, Sidric's mind drifts away from the effects of alcohol, finding solace in the connection he shares with Deux. The night may have taken an unexpected turn, but in the presence of Deux's voice, everything feels right.

Wrapped in the comforting embrace of their conversation, Sidric gradually drifts off to sleep, his phone still pressed against his ear.

"Goodnight, Deux," Sidric whispers, right before passing out.

"Goodnight, Sid," Deux replies. Letting the alcohol do the talking, he adds, "I love you."

Suddenly, Sidric is wide awake. Silence fills the room, stretching into what feels like an eternity.

"What?" Sidric asks, his voice breaking the tension.

"Oh. That wasn't for you. That was for my friend. She's... sleeping next to me." Deux's voice is frantic, panic creeping into every word. "Talk soon, Sid." He abruptly hangs up.

11

dancing with our hands tied

Deux

A t ten a.m., Deux wakes up to the familiar sound of Silvy's snoring. Despite trying every home remedy known to Dionysus, the Greek god of wine himself, nothing ever stops Silvy's symphonic snores. He gives her a nudge with his elbow and even pinches her nose for good measure. She shifts, rolls over, and finally quiets down. Watching her blissfully unaware state makes Deux chuckle, which immediately triggers a pounding headache.

Hangovers usually have Deux in a chokehold for the entire day. Armed with a pint of salted caramel ice cream and a party nut mix, he's officially declared hangovers as DNDs: DO NOTHING DAYS. At least now, he doesn't have to spend his DNDs alone. Last night's conversation with Sid wasn't just a hazy, alcohol-fueled dream—it was real.

His breathing starts picking up the pace as he remembers the words coming out of his mouth. *I love you. Why did I say that?!* It was no secret he always felt invincible after drinking a bit of liquid courage, but in this case, feeling invincible was far more dangerous than his

DANCING WITH OUR HANDS TIED

electric touch. Somehow, the sinister confidence and downright slick motivation he projected when drunk could not only be uninhibited, but out of control. *Was it too soon to say those three words?* Even if it wasn't, he hung up on Sid immediately. He didn't even get the chance to see how he would react. *Drunk Deux needs to be stopped.*

He rushes to the bathroom to wet his face. The cold water splashes over his eyes bringing him back to reality. He looks in the mirror and notices golden sparkles surrounding his hazel eyes. Every day seems like it is harder to keep these powers a secret. He knows if word got out his whole life would be turned upside down. No more freedom, no more doing what he loves, and most importantly, no more Sidric. Suddenly he thinks the headache from drinking, though horrendously brutal, is nothing compared to the sounds of billions expecting him to do something with his powers, to make the right call, at the right moment, in the right way, in the right cadence, without hurting anyone.

He yanks a towel from the shelf messing up the rest of the neatly organized towels and screams into it as hard as he can. He proceeds to dry his face and heads back into the room.

"Are you good Deux?" Silvy asks groggily, completely out of it as she prepares her morning dose of the self-proclaimed Silvy Special, Clamato juice with celery on it, a coffee, and a few puffs of her flavored vape. Today's flavor is grilled cheese. Silvy eyes him up and down as she smokes some vaporized sandwich.

"Oh did I wake you up? I'm sorry," Deux replies, "I think I'm just going to sleep for the next few years. Wake me up if they ever make a sequel to the Grinch." He jumps back in bed and puts his pillow on top of his face.

Silvy stares at Deux in amazement. She's long been accustomed to his theatrics; after all, he brings the kind of melodrama every small-town girl secretly craves. Having been in each other's lives since they were nine years old, Silvy knows Deux better than anyone. She's witnessed firsthand the immense pressure and disregard people have piled on him over the years. She's seen how it closed him off from the world, and in a way, she understands him better because of it.

In a town like Hornbridge, finding someone like Silvy or Deux is rare—almost impossible. They've always had each other, and they know, without a doubt, that they always will.

"I think you need some sushi," Silvy says.

Within minutes, they arrive at their favorite all-you-can-eat sushi spot, *The Roll'n Stones.* A bionic waiter guides them to their regular booth, though not before Silvy spends a solid ten minutes passionately explaining why sitting anywhere else would ruin the entire vibe of their meal.

"Thank you so much again," Deux says with an exaggerated smile, staring into the soulless eyes of the metallic waiter. "I know these robots are designed to have no feelings, but I'm 100% sure this one hates us."

"Right? I get the same vibe," Silvy says, eyeing the robot with suspicion. "And it's always this same rude one. Still wearing the friendship bracelet I gave him when I tried to flirt my way to a discount. I really thought we had something special."

Silvy notices Deux's lack of reaction and narrows her eyes. "Okay, spill. Are you down because of last night?" She leans closer, locking eyes with him. "Oh, *Sid! I love you!*" she teases, making exaggerated kissy noises.

"Oh, you heard that?" Deux's face starts warming up revealing a cherry-red blush.

"I was right next to you. I would be worried if I didn't hear that. Why did you make it so awkward though?" Silvy says as she places the order on a tablet.

"I don't know! I don't know how I feel, to be quite honest. I really like Sid. I might even actually..." Deux hesitates, the words feeling heavier in sobriety, "...love him." He finds it hard to admit feelings that his drunk self had worn so freely on his sleeve. "But what if it's too soon? Or what if he doesn't say it back? And I definitely don't want our first 'I love you' to be over the phone after we've both been drinking. I want it to be romantic—straight out of a Taylor Swift song. That's what he deserves."

"I mean..." Silvy's eyes widen, signaling that Deux has already answered his own question. "It's obvious you love him if you care about it this much. You want to paint him like one of your French girls, and that's valid. Honestly, I would too."

"What?" Deux eyes screaming confusion.

"Titanic? You can't tell me you don't know that one!" Silvy's voice trails. She has an immense knowledge of movies and an impeccable delivery when it comes to being a natural comic. She can apply a movie quote to any situation. If only she had a quote last night when Deux almost fucked everything up. Deux could really use her wippy quick witty charm when he got all tongue-tied with Sid.

The bionic waiter glides in smoothly, placing a plate loaded with an assortment of sushi rolls on the table. "Remember. Finish what you order or pay the price," it intones in its monotone robotic voice before rolling away.

"*Hasta la vista, baby,*" Silvy whispers with a smirk. The robot pauses mid-glide for a few seconds, as if processing her comment, then resumes its journey back to the kitchen.

As Silvy stuffs her face with imitation crab, she tries her best to cheer Deux up, adopting her trademark '*I refuse to be stressed*' attitude.

"Listen, you've got two options," she says between bites. "You can either pretend nothing happened and hope he was too drunk to remember, or you can just confront it head-on and admit how you feel. Sure, it won't be the big romantic gesture you dreamed of, but so what? Life isn't about those over-the-top moments. It's about the small, ordinary ones that remind you it's the real deal."

"Okay, that was surprisingly profound," Deux says, gulping down a sip of soda. "I think I'll—"

"Two dragon rolls, seven spring rolls, four egg rolls, three California rolls, and one Mexican roll," a robotic voice interrupts. The bionic waiter stretches out its four arms, carefully stacking plates onto their already crowded table.

"I forgot we ordered all this," Silvy says, sighing as her eyes widen. Plates of sushi battle for space on the tiny table. "You've got to start helping, kid. I can't eat all this on my own."

Deux glances at the robot, its unyielding gaze locked on it like a silent enforcer of its earlier warning. *Finish what you order or pay the price.* The stakes feel higher as they pick up their chopsticks, savoring each piece under the robot's watchful stare.

The metallic eyes of the bionic waiter seem to intensify, silently urging them to conclude their feast. However, Deux and Silvy share a conspiratorial smirk. The bionic waiters may be vigilant, but they've mastered the art of outwitting them. As they exchange glances, a silent understanding passes between them – a testament to their well-practiced routine.

Both Deux and Silvy possess bags with false bottoms, a subtle rebellion against the stringent rules of the establishment. The extra slices of sushi find a clandestine refuge within these secret compartments. It's a game, a delicate dance between diners and vigilant robots. A game they've played before, always emerging victorious in their silent rebellion.

"I think we cracked the code to life," Silvy jokes.

"I think I need some hot tea," Deux says laughing all bloated.

"You and me. We make a great team," Silvy smirks.

Once the sushi is gone from the plates, the robot zooms back to the table to cash them out. Silvy takes that as her queue to go to the toilet.

"I'll pay queen," Deux offers.

As the bionic waiter starts printing the receipts from its mouth, it begins to glitch. His head spins 360 degrees.

"GRRRRRRR- system malfunc- GRRRRR- ERROR IN HOST"

Deux looks at it as if he is experiencing an exorcism. Suddenly, a paper receipt gets spat out. Deux catches it in the air and stares at it.

DEUX WE KNOW.........9.13
ABOUT UR POWERS.........3.19
KEEP LOW PROFILE............9.23
KEEP THEM UNDER.........3.49
CONTROL.........8.04
RT IS EVIL............1.53

Shocks run through his whole body. His eyes widen as he re-reads the note. A million questions flood his mind. *Who knows about my powers? RT is evil? Who is RT?!* The robot snaps back into reality.

"Cash or card?" It sassily asks.

He folds the note up into his pocket and pays the bill. He adds that to his growing list of things to worry about.

Hours later, Deux wakes up from a needed sushi coma, feeling stressed about the note but a bit more grounded about Sidric. *Life is not about the big romantic gestures; it is about all those small ordinary moments that remind you it's real life.* Silvy's words linger in his mind. Every minute that goes by where Deux isn't messaging Sidric could be a minute too late. He decides to tackle this task before he tackles the ominous panic-inducing receipt. Suddenly, he knows what to do.

Deux

-Hey Sid! Are you free in 30 minutes? Also, do you have a VR headset?

Sidric

-Hi! Yes and Yes! I just have to find it haha my room is such a mess right now. Why?

Deux

-Can't say. But meet me in 30.

******

"Hey Sid! It's me!" Deux waves over at an avatar that looks like a cartoon version of Sidric. Shaggy brown hair, big brown eyes, and a white shimmering smile. "It's like you're here with me! But not really."

"Hey Deux! I had to update my avatar, haven't used this headset since I was in middle school. You do not want to see what I used to look like then."

"Ugh, now I need to see it."

They stand face to face, their avatars existing in a shared virtual space that mirrors the distance between them in reality, spanning thousands of miles. The simulated room, a rooftop garden overlooking the Eiffel Tower, bathes them in the virtual glow of Parisian magic.

Deux admires the setting, appreciating the effort put into creating the digital marvel. "You did a good job setting this up!" he remarks, looking around the picturesque scene. "Why Paris, though?"

"It's always felt like a magical place to me, even though I've never been," Sidric explains.

"I'll take you there, my short baby boy," Deux promises with a teasing grin.

"I'm literally a few inches shorter than you; you're not that tall," Sidric chuckles, the banter lightening the atmosphere.

"Sure thing, shorty."

"I hate you!" Sidric laughs and nudges Deux. Surprisingly, as Sidric's hand goes through Deux's avatar, they both feel tiny shocks running through them. The advanced VR technology allows for sensations to be felt between avatars, but this experience feels different, the electric tingles send chills through their bodies.

"Ugh, the things I want to do with you, Sidric," Deux whispers, his virtual tone filled with desire.

"Woah, now this I'd pay to see in real life," Sidric quips.

"Just come over to my place; my parents are gone for the night," Deux suggests.

"You know, I love it when you talk virtual reality to me," Sidric jokes.

Deux leans in for a kiss in the game, the virtual sensation tingling on Sidric's lips, reminiscent of their first encounters.

"I'm coming over right now," Sidric says gleefully.

"Okay, I don't want to stop the fun, but we have to leave this room," Deux says, manipulating the virtual environment. Lights flash around them, transforming their surroundings into a fantastical world. Whimsical greenery falls like confetti, waterfalls materialize, and mountains with cliffside lakes form around them. In the distance, cheers rumble out from a stadium. Sidric steps forward, immersing himself in this virtual wonderland. Deux pulls him by the hand and leads him towards the entrance of the stadium. They enter the stadium and two AI avatars hand them two light-up bracelets.

Sidric looks back at Deux in disbelief. "What are we going to see?!"

"Just wait" Deux laughs, adjusting his bracelet on his wrist.

As they approach the stage Sidric recognizes the backdrop from a video he'd seen from 40 years ago. "There's no way you recreated the Eras Tour," he squeals.

Deux points toward the stage and mouths, 'Look.' When Sidric does, he spots a Taylor Swift-like avatar coming out from the ground performing her hit song 'Cruel Summer'.

"Shut up! How did you do this?!" Sidric exclaims, awe and delight evident in his expression.

"I know my way around VR design," Deux says, winking at him. Even in virtual reality, that wink weakens Sidric's knees.

"You really did all this just so we could go on a virtual date?" Sidric asks, genuinely touched.

"I did this to show you that anything is possible. I know you doubt our relationship sometimes, and I guess I needed to make sure you knew that every day can be as dazzling and beautiful as you are. Everyday can be an Eras tour for you."

"You're the best! How did you manage to do all this hungover?" Sidric jokes, playfully trying to steer the conversation back to the events of the previous night.

"I had lots of sushi," Deux replies with a smirk, swiftly changing the topic. He debates telling him about the ominous receipt but decides to tell him in person so he can be there for Sidric if he has a massive panic attack. "Which reminds me. Dinner is served."

"What do you mean?" Sidric questions as the scent of freshly made pizza fills his lungs. "Where is that coming from?! Don't play with me with pizza."

"You're a goof. Open your bedroom door," Deux instructs.

Sidric removes his headset, and as he opens the door, his brother Damon stands there, holding a pizza box. The aroma of the pizza wafts through the room, signaling a delightful surprise orchestrated by Deux.

"I guess this is for you Sid." He hands it over. "I had a slice as payment." He walks off yelling, "Enjoy your cyber sex!"

Sid's cheeks flush with warmth. "You're on a whole other level of incredible, Deux," he exclaims, the joy evident in his laughter.

Deux grins, a twinkle of pride in his eyes. "Yeah, I figured you'd appreciate this more than me filling a truck with water and pretending we were on a yacht date. The concept of VR rooms has some kinks to be worked out, but hey, remember those rooms people used to pay to get locked in for an hour? I'm a visionary, Sid. I am."

They settle onto the artificial grass, immersing themselves in the simulated concert while indulging in slices of pizza. Sidric feels his heart pulsating with affection for Deux, three little words ready to be set free sit on the tip of his tongue, waiting for the right moment.

The digital rendition of Taylor Swift continues her performance moving on to the acoustic section, she picks up a guitar and "You Are In Love" starts playing prompting Sidric to stand up. "Dance with me?" he offers, extending his hand toward Deux.

Deux reaches out, his hand meeting Sidric's, and a cascade of sparks ignites, a testament to the unique connection their powers have forged. Despite being miles apart in different countries, the sensation of each other's touch remains vivid.

"I don't know how to dance," Deux confesses, inching closer to Sid.

"That's okay, neither do I. We'll figure it out," Sid reassures him.

"Together," they say simultaneously, their voices merging in a whispered promise.

Embarking on the dance floor, their initial moves are awkward, but with each attempted step, they synchronize. The world around them fades away, leaving only the two of them in a shared moment of intimacy. The chorus of the song becomes a rhythm for their impromptu dance, a harmonious blend of uncertainty and discovery.

12

better thAn RevengE

Sidric

S idric is used to tossing and turning until 3 a.m.. However, he
wasn't always like that, the quiet of the night used to cradle
him gently into slumber. His nightly ritual of a strict 7-step
skincare routine was always followed by a peaceful drift into dreams.
Sometimes, his mind would wander into whimsical fantasies featuring
his latest crush, but never had it been an impediment to his rest.

Yet, ever since meeting Deux, sleep has become an elusive mistress.
For the past three nights, Sidric finds himself stuck in a relentless
cycle of wakefulness, his mind a whirlwind of thoughts and emotions.
Each night, he lies awake, haunted by the memory of their last kiss,
the echo of Deux's laughter reverberating through his mind, and the
anticipation of their next encounter.

The hopeless romantic within him resurfaces with a vengeance,
weaving a web of longing and desire that entangles his heart. Sidric is
powerless to resist, his thoughts consumed by visions of Deux and the
intoxicating allure he exudes. Their video calls are now even more
regular since Deux teaches Sidric more things about how to control

their powers. Sidric attempts to retain as much information as he can but every time the camera is pointed at Deux's face all he can think about is how handsome he is. With their Washington DC trip coming up soon Sidric forces himself to test out a few tricks whenever he can.

All these thoughts swirl through Sidric's mind as he finishes another set on the fly machine at the gym. His focus on Deux is abruptly interrupted when he spots a familiar figure—greasy hair, smudged face—walking across the gym floor.

It's Jake Muskinson, Sidric's old high school nemesis, the guy who never missed an opportunity to make his life miserable.

Sidric watches as Jake strides toward the treadmills. Without warning, Jake steps over Sidric's foot, his shoulder brushing past Sidric's arm.

"Move it faggot," Jake mutters under his breath, just loud enough for Sidric to hear.

Sidric tries to keep his cool for a few seconds but alternately decides to put his powers to the test. Using the adrenaline of the three espresso shots he took as pre-workout and the anger he currently feels towards this troll, he channels his powers onto the treadmill. Focusing on the machine, he breathes deeply and moves his fingers around attempting to release some energy. The treadmill speeds up within milliseconds to 30 mph. The bully flies all the way to the floor, landing right by a couple of girls using the step climber. They both laugh out loud. Immediately, Sidric runs into the locker room to make sure nobody blames him for that incident even though there is no way to prove it. He finds it easier to control his powers when there is a strong emotion behind it, like hatred for an old bully. Otherwise, it can all feel overwhelming to him.

That night he calls Deux to tell him all about it.

"You should've seen it, Deux! He was lying on the ground for like three seconds then his face went all red. I swear I could see a few tears," Sid finishes telling his story.

Deux laughs along but then starts lecturing Sidric about how he should not use his powers in a negative way.

"Don't you love *Spiderman?*" he asks Sid, "What does his uncle always say? With great power comes great responsibility Sid. No matter how much that asshole deserves it, you are better than that. Karma will get him."

"I guess you're right," Sid groans.

With every day that goes by Sidric realizes how otherworldly Deux is. The way his heart always looks to do right by everyone inspires him to do the same, maybe he doesn't need to be thinking of how to get revenge on all of his enemies.

"But you have to admit, sometimes people do deserve a little payback. It's healthy to put your foot down and draw the line."

Deux

The next day, exactly 2027.25 miles away from Sidric, Deux's morality is put to the test. He is sitting in his living room looking back at the few photos he took with Sidric in California. Cozied up on a green soft couch sipping on a large iced mango avocado smoothie. His brother Austin slams down next to him. After their argument a few days ago the house has felt extremely tense. Deux's family talked to him privately about it but they refrained from calling Austin out. His parents constantly make excuses for him: "He's under a lot of pressure at work, he didn't mean any offense by it." Deux knows Austin is far too stubborn to ever admit when he's wrong. Whenever someone calls him out, he explodes in anger, refusing to take accountability. Like every other time, Deux decides it's best to ignore him and move on.

"Who's that?" Austin asks, peeking into Deux's screen.

"That's Sidric, I met him on my trip he-"

"Hmmmm, interesting," Austin interrupts, his tone buzzing with judgment—judgier than Judge Judy herself.

"What's interesting?" Deux can tell where this is going but he needs to hear what he has to say.

"It's just that, you, for example, don't seem gay. But this guy—you can tell he's gay. No offense," Austin says, a snarky chuckle following his words.

Deux feels his eyes roll so hard that they practically do a full 360. "Why would I be offended if he *'looks'* gay to you, Austin? Being gay isn't a bad thing."

"That's not what I mean. Don't freak out on me. It's just my opinion." The gaslighting begins. Deux recognizes this pattern and chooses to leave before Austin starts spitting more ignorant remarks.

"Have a good one Austin." Deux stands up taking deep breaths.

"What? You're not gonna watch the game with us? It's the final!" Austin yells out, syncing his smartwatch to the screen.

Sometimes, people do deserve a little payback. It's healthy to put your foot down and draw the line. Sidric's voice echoes through Deux's mind, the words syncing perfectly with the rhythm of his heartbeat. He wants to take the high road, brush off what Austin said, and move on. But a little payback? That might just bring his anger down a notch.

What bothers Deux the most isn't even Austin's ignorant comment—it's that he tried to come for Sidric. He doesn't know Sidric, hasn't spoken a word to him, and yet he's already hating. The thought fuels Deux's frustration as he storms to his room, his hands tingling with energy. Tiny shocks ripple through his body, each one pushing him closer to a single, electrifying focus: *payback.*

He inhales deeply, drawing in the electricity around him like a magnet. First, the lights in his room flicker out. Then, the entire second floor plunges into darkness. Just as the soccer match is about to kick off downstairs, the whole house goes black—no electricity, no game, no escape.

A loud scream echoes from the living room, and a satisfied smirk spreads across Deux's face.

"Mom! Fix it now!" Austin whines. "It's the *finals*! This isn't fair!"

Deux leans back on his bed, his smirk growing. Karma works quickly when it's paired with a little electric nudge. And thanks to it, Austin never gets to watch his team lose spectacularly in the finals.

******

"I told you!" Sidric's laughs out loud at the retelling of the events, "sometimes you have to be a little cheeky."

"It was all practice for me. I wanted to see how far my powers could go." Deux jokes, his eyes fixated on Sidric's smile on the screen.

"But thank you for sticking up for me. I honestly don't understand straight people sometimes, they are more obsessed with the gays than gays themselves. It's always the same thing."

"I know, and usually my brother isn't one of those idiots, but lately he has been such an asshole. I hope he comes back to his senses soon."

They keep chatting, their conversation bouncing from topic to topic, when suddenly Deux remembers the ominous note from the sushi restaurant. As Sidric excitedly shares his latest theory about why he thinks Taylor Swift is about to drop a new album, Deux starts rifling through a pile of dirty laundry.

After digging through a couple of pairs of jeans, he finally finds the note, crumpled and forgotten in a pocket. He stares at it for a moment, debating whether to bring it up. He hesitates—part of him wants to keep it to himself for now—but he knows Sidric will find out sooner or later.

"Sid, I have something to tell you," Deux sighs, his voice heavy.

"Sounds serious. What is it?" Sidric's voice is quieter than usual, laced with concern.

"Someone knows about us—about our powers." Deux explains the situation with the note.

"Shit, shit, shitty shiitake mushrooms *shit*! Are we being watched?! I *knew* there were hidden cameras everywhere. This is more serious than we thought, Deux!"

"Sid, breathe," Deux interjects firmly. "I'll bring the note to DC. We'll figure out the truth there. Plus, I'll teach you more tips to control these powers. We need to be ready."

As the first light of dawn filters through Deux's window, casting a soft, golden glow across his face, a wave of calm washes over Sidric on the other end of the line.

"Okay," Sidric exhales deeply. "I'll try to relax."

"Sid," Deux says, his voice softening, "I never thought I could feel this close to someone who's so far away."

A smile spreads across Sidric's face, the same sentiment blooming in his own heart. "Me neither. But I'm glad we found each other."

"I can't wait to see you," Sidric whispers, the anticipation of their reunion lighting a spark within him.

"Neither can I," Deux replies, his voice filled with quiet, heartfelt longing.

13

don't do anytHing stUpid

Sidric

It's 10 p.m., and Sidric is leaving for the airport at 3 a.m. tomorrow. His empty suitcases lie open in the middle of his room as he tears through his closet, trying to find the perfect outfits. When he first met Deux, his outfits were cute, but not *let's-make-out* cute. This time, he wants everything to be planned out. He starts throwing clothes from the closet toward the suitcase, frustration bubbling up as nothing feels right. Finally, he lets out a small scream.

The lights in his room flicker.

Shit, breathe, Sid. Breaaaathe.

He inhales deeply, and the lights settle back to normal.

Over the past week, Sidric has caused four blackouts in his neighborhood. He's been trying to master the breathing and mind-clearing techniques Deux taught him, but so far, he's nowhere near professional. Glancing at the mirror, he notices his hair sticking up in every direction, frizzed and pointing upward like a lightning rod. He rolls his eyes and tries to fix the hair disaster.

There's a knock on the door, and his mom walks in holding a first aid kit. "Te traje esto. It has all the medicines you could need and more. Are you going to be safe?" she asks, her face lined with worry.

"I'm not sure, ma. Maybe I'll do some drugs, shave my head, and get a tattoo," Sidric responds sarcastically. His mom is not amused.

"Qué chistosito. I'm serious, mijo. You never know who's out there trying to harm you." She pulls him into a tight embrace before handing over the first aid kit.

Sidric sighs as she leaves, turning back to the chaos of his room. He's still struggling to decide which outfits to pack when his phone buzzes. It's Naya calling from San Francisco.

"Hey, Sid! You're going to want to kiss me after this," she announces confidently.

"I *always* want to kiss you, you know that," Sidric replies with a laugh. "What's up? I'm dying over here trying to pack for D.C."

"Well, you know the amazing manager I am," she says, smirking. "One of my connections in L.A. is a RainforesTec community consultant. I messaged her yesterday and asked for backstage access for my clients. Check your email." She winks at the camera, a triumphant grin on her face.

Sidric quickly checks his email, and his face lights up with excitement. "Oh my god! You didn't! This is amazing! It'll give us so much freedom at the convention. Thank you! We really need to get some answers."

"Anything for my most electric gays," Naya replies with a playful smirk. "But seriously, be careful. Don't get arrested without me."

"I wish you were coming with us. I'll catch you up on everything that happens. Also, I'll definitely catch you up if we make out again," Sidric jokes with a mischievous grin.

"Please do! I might actually quit my job soon. I'm so over my boss—he's such a rat," Naya says with a dramatic eye roll. "Now, go pack, and don't forget your PrEP and Doxy!" she teases before ending the call.

Sidric tosses his phone onto the bed and turns his attention back to packing, making sure to include the first aid kit his mom gave him, the PrEP and Doxy as well. As he throws in another pair of jeans, his mind wanders to that night Deux drunkenly said, "I love you." He wonders if Deux will say it again during this trip, this time sober.

Sidric can feel himself falling harder for Deux, and the thought both excites and terrifies him. He shakes his head, trying to push away the doubt. *Am I setting myself up for heartbreak?*

But then he remembers Deux's smile, his laugh, the way he makes him feel like the most important person in the world. *Whatever happens, it'll be worth it,* Sidric tells himself, zipping up his suitcase with determination.

******

Once his flight lands, he finds a bathroom and takes his time freshening up, making sure he looks his best for Deux. He brushes his teeth and uses mouthwash to get rid of any remaining airplane breath. He fixes his hair and splashes some water on his face to wake himself up. After making sure everything is in place, he sprays a small amount of cologne in the air and walks through it. With a newfound confidence, he heads towards baggage claim to meet Deux.

What am I supposed to do? Do I shake his hand? Go in for a hug? How long should the hug be?

He pulls out his phone and starts typing.

SIDRIC
-Hi, sorry this old lady was taking forever to get off the plane. Almost at baggage claim 7

DEUX-
    -Perfect, I'll see you there xx

In a perfect world, Deux would be waiting by the baggage claim with his back facing the escalators. Sidric imagines himself coming down from behind and confidently calling his name. But, reality is far from perfect. As Sidric arrives at the baggage claim, he sees his bag going around the rail, but no sign of Deux. As he rushes down the stairs to get his bag before it disappears, he misses a step and slips, falling hard on his bum. He winces in pain and tries to get up quickly, hoping no one sees him. But the sharp pain shooting through his back makes it difficult to move.

"Sidric! That's not how you're supposed to go down the escalators," a familiar voice yells from behind him. He turns around slowly, and immediately wants to black out. It's Deux, looking flawless as ever, coming down the stairs. His dark curls rest softly on his forehead, rosy cheeks just rosy enough to be noticeable. He's wearing a dark green button-up shirt accentuating his muscular shoulders and dark blue shorts exposing his toned legs. Sidric tries to catch his breath and hide his embarrassment, but it's too much for him to control.

"Here, I got you," Deux says, putting his hand out for him as soon as he gets to the bottom of the stairs. Sidric takes his hand and feels the electricity that was once there coming back, except this time he's not surprised by it.

"Deux! Hi! I was just sitting down waiting for you," Sidric blushes.

"Sure, I didn't just see you eat shit," Deux laughs and pulls him in for a hug. "I missed you, Sid!"

Hug it is. Sidric's heart starts beating three times faster.

"I missed you too! Let me get my bag, and I'll call a car to the hotel."

*****

125

The ride to the hotel is short but heavy with an unfamiliar weight. After weeks of longing, of craving closeness through flickering screens and pixelated video calls, they are finally in the same place at the same time. Yet, instead of the effortless flow of their late-night messages and whispered confessions through phone speakers, there's a pause, a hesitation—an invisible distance despite their bodies being inches apart.

They fill the silence with small talk, polite laughter, stolen glances. The driver chats casually, blissfully unaware of the storm between them. Sidric and Deux exchange flirty looks, but there's an underlying tension, like they are trying to bridge a gap they hadn't expected to be there.

Knees touch. Skin brushes against skin. It should feel exhilarating, but Sidric is too aware of it, of the sheer reality of it. The whole time he was in Mexico, he had worried about controlling his powers—about whether his emotions would manifest in unpredictable ways. But now, sitting beside Deux, he feels something even stranger. It's as if Deux's presence puts him back in control of his own body.

Shouldn't I be freaking out? If I am so in love with him why do I feel so calm? Sidric overthinks every second. For so long, Deux had existed to him as a voice, a digital presence, a perfect silhouette on a glowing screen. Now he's real—warmth and breath and weight next to him. The shift is unsettling. Sidric wonders if Deux feels it too. If his heartbeat is steady for all the wrong reasons. If he expected the space between them to be filled with an instant, magnetic pull, only to find it tangled in unspoken uncertainties.

He swallows, shifting slightly, knees still pressed together. He needs to break this strange limbo, to reclaim the ease they once had. Because if they've already fallen for each other in one world, shouldn't they be able to do it again in this one?

After checking into the hotel and going up ten floors squished in a tiny elevator, they finally get to their room. Sidric taps the card and pushes open the door for Deux.

"Hmm, they gave us a room with only one bed," Deux turns looking back at Sid who fakes a shocked face.

"What? I literally asked for the two-bed room. Should I go say something?"

"No, don't worry. I'm down for cuddles," he winks at him.

There it is. Sid feels a jolt travel through his whole body.

Not that long has gone by since he last saw Deux, but it's all coming at him at once. The winks, the looks, the light touching, the sandalwood scent of his cologne. It's making him extremely thirsty to be with him, to feel his body touching his. He tries to keep his chill vibes and walks into the room.

"It's pretty nice. I like the view," Deux nods, closing the door behind them. "I think I'm gonna take a shower—I feel gross from the plane," he says, setting his things on the nightstand.

"I'll take one too. I need to get cute," Sidric replies.

Deux glances at him, a small smirk forming. "What do you mean? You're already cute," he says, holding Sidric's gaze. "You can join me if you want."

A rush of excitement runs through Sidric at Deux's suggestion. "Uhm... yeah. I'm down. Let me grab my stuff. I'll meet you in there."

Deux walks into the bathroom and turns on the water. Through the half-open door, Sidric can see him taking off his clothes. His shirt falls to the floor, followed by his shorts. Sidric feels his blood pumping as grey underwear flies towards the door.

"Are you coming?!" Deux yells from inside the shower.

"Coming!" Sidric takes a deep breath, then another, before making his way to the bathroom.

As he steps inside, a thick layer of steam fills the air, clinging to the mirrors and curling around his skin. Through the mist, he sees Deux standing under the stream of water, his silhouette softened by the haze.

Sidric moves closer, his heartbeat quickening. At the sound of his approach, Deux turns, his eyes locking onto Sidric's.

"Hi," Deux says, pulling him into a kiss.

"Hi," Sidric chuckles back as they keep kissing.

They both feel each other grow. Deux's hands trace Sidric's arms, leading to the golden spots. He places his palm against his as they both admire the patterns their new skin marks create. Deux follows his palms towards Sidric's back and towards his butt. He squeezes as he kisses lower and lower every time.

After being on his knees for a while, he rises and gently turns Sidric to face the opposite direction. Pressing him against the wall, he takes control, his breath warm against the back of Sidric's neck, sending static through his skin despite the water cascading over them. As he moves, Sidric feels his body charged with electricity.

Deux holds Sidric's hand against the wall and feels him squeeze every time he moves his hips forward. Minutes later, Sidric's sight starts to go dark.

"I think I'm gonna faint," Sidric sighs, gripping the wall for support. The thick steam in the room makes it nearly impossible to breathe properly. Seconds later, his body goes limp, weightless. Just as he's about to collapse, Deux catches him.

Deux carries him effortlessly out of the bathroom and places him on top of the bed. Both of their bodies are dripping from the shower.

"Here, drink this," Deux says, handing him a glass water bottle.

"Oh shit, is this from the mini bar?" Sidric takes a sip, slowly regaining his senses. "This is gonna cost a fortune," he sighs.

"I'll pay for it, don't worry," Deux laughs. "You scared me! I thought I killed you."

"I mean, your D is pretty bomb, but it's not big enough to kill me,"

Sidric teases and pulls him onto the bed with him. "Can you remind me what we were doing though?"

Deux leans on top of him in between his legs and whispers in his ear, "I got you."

******

After turning the once tidy room into a mess, with bed sheets scattered everywhere except on the bed, they both lie looking into each other's eyes. Sidric tries to catch his breath after what he can only describe as a religious experience.

"That was…" Deux sighs, his eyes drifting up to the ceiling. "I'm speechless."

"I knew it was going to be good, but I never expected all of that," Sidric says.

Deux's stomach growls, agreeing that the energy was well spent. "Let's order some pizza," Deux chuckles.

The phone rings exactly 22 minutes later. Sidric picks up the phone, and a robotic voice immediately answers.

"I'm outside. Please open the door."

"Ew," Sidric whispers, goosebumps crawling up his skin at the creepy voice. He hangs up and opens the door to find a short robot with four long arms holding a pizza box on top of its head. He yanks it from its hands, but the robot holds it tighter and says, "Don't forget to tip!"

"This is wild!" Sidric yells. "Why do we have to tip robots now?"

Deux laughs from inside the room.

He taps on the screen that expands on its face, and it starts printing a receipt. Sidric pulls it out, grabs the pizza, and slams the door in the robot's face.

"Let us eat!" Sidric sings out, tossing the pizza box onto the bed.

"Finally! I'm starving," Deux sits up eagerly. "How much did you tip?" He grabs the receipt from the top of the box. He squeals, making Sidric jump.

"What? Did I tip too much?!" Sidric yells, his eyes open widely.

"It's them! They know we're here!" Deux shows Sidric the receipt, revealing a note just like the one he previously received. Sidric inspects it closely, reading it over and over again.

YALL DONT.........2.11
DO ANYTHING STUPID.........2.22
STAY AWAY FROM...........4.99
RAINFORESTEC.........6.44
WE ARE WORKING.........3.57
BTS @ HQ..........1.99

"Why do they want us to stay away from RainforesTec? What are they hiding?" Sidric questions. "There's probably hundreds of RainforesTec secret agents all around the hotel waiting for us to show our electric powers." His breathing starts to pick up.

"Sid, these notes are creepy as hell but they seem to be on our side. They just don't want us to *do anything stupid*," Deux replies, grabbing a slice of pepperoni and M&Ms pizza. "We're still going to the conference tomorrow, though. I need answers, and if anything, these notes only make me want to go more."

Sidric smiles at Deux's contrarian nature. "I'm in. But while we wait, maybe we can eat some pizza, then hop in the shower again?"

"I don't know. You almost died on me earlier," he teases, "but I could be persuaded."

They both smile and cheers with their pizza slices.

14

you're on your own, kid

*** Sidric ***

At seven in the morning, Sidric's alarm goes off. It's the first day they're attending RainforesTec Summit, so Sid wants to make sure they get as much time to snoop around as needed. He wakes up in Deux's arms. Sid holds his ear close to Deux's chest, hearing his heart beating. He hears something weird, the regular *boom boom boom* mixed with static. They both had gotten so carried away between reconnecting, Sidric almost fainting, and the weird note that Deux didn't even get to show Sid how to control his powers.

Sidric quietly moves around the room, packing his backpack with the essentials he'll need for the day. Headphones, chapstick, Sour Patch Kids, and his wallet. He checks his phone for any messages or emails, making sure he's caught up on any important updates. As he finishes up, he turns to see Deux still sleeping soundly in the bed. He smiles, enjoying the peacefulness of the moment before he has to face the busy day ahead.

Careful not to disturb Deux, Sidric tiptoes to the bathroom to get ready. He takes a quick shower, using Deux's shampoo and conditioner, enjoying the citrus fragrance that remains in his hair. He then blow-dries his hair and styles it neatly. He puts on a pair of dress pants and a white shirt, ensuring everything is professional-looking and wrinkle-free. He checks himself in the mirror, feeling confident in his appearance.

Sidric goes to the small kitchen area of their hotel room and starts brewing some green tea. The water begins to boil, and he pours it into a cup. He sips the hot tea, enjoying the refreshing taste as he waits for Deux to wake up.

"Oh god, it's seven? Why so early you sleep demon?" He groans half asleep.

"We need lots of time. Also, you have to teach me how to control these powers, I don't want to *do anything stupid.* We're already being watched the last thing we need is more attention."

"Ugh, I'll get up in 5."

After an hour of Deux hitting snooze on his alarm, Sidric watches him finally get up and fix the bed. They sit facing each other, and Deux places his hand on Sidric's chest.

"Shit, your heart is beating so fast," Deux observes.

"Sorry," Sidric struggles to find words. "I'm just nervous about this whole thing."

"That's okay," Deux reassures him. "It's actually better if you're nervous or anxious. When you feel strong emotions, it's when the powers will manifest the most because your body doesn't know what to do with all of it. It needs to push it out somehow. You just have to hop on top of it and control it."

"You mean hop on top of it and ride it?" Sidric chuckles. "I'm kidding, but I think it sounds easier said than done. How do you just hop on it? What should I do?"

"Listen, it has taken me lots of practice, but you will get there. You have to listen to your body, clear your mind, and focus on something that makes you feel grounded. Something that makes you feel good inside."

Sidric closes his eyes and tries to follow Deux's advice. *Hot Cheetos and FiveLoko.* Nothing happens. He tries once again, breathing in and out, clearing his mind. *Taylor Swift just released a new album. I got front-row tickets to her new tour. She's inviting me on stage!* Suddenly, lights start flashing in the room, and Deux gasps. Then it all stops.

"What were you focusing on? That kind of worked," Deux says.

"I was thinking of a Taylor Swift concert. It's dumb; I can't do it," Sidric replies, falling back on the bed. "Maybe it will all go away if I ignore it."

"Trust me, it won't," Deux says, shaking his head. "But don't get annoyed. Try again, but this time think of this instead." He leans in and kisses Sidric's lips just once.

Sidric's eyes open wide, and he tries again, focusing on Deux's kiss. He feels it all building up inside of him. Closing his eyes again, he starts thinking of the previous night, how magical it all was, all the kissing and fooling around. He opens his palms, and there it is: tiny lightning bolts jumping from one finger to the other.

"You're doing it!" Deux chants in joy. "Keep going! Now focus and send it all towards the bedside lamp. Turn it on."

Sid half-opens his right eye and sees the lightning bolts. He can feel all the electricity in his body pointing towards his hands. He looks up at Deux, smiling, and Deux smiles back. Sid plays around with the bolts in his hands like a kid playing with a bubble stick.

"Wait," Sid stops for a second and looks at Deux straight in his eyes. "So, when you were back home figuring this whole thing out, what did you think about to get gain control?"

Deux hesitates for a moment but then decides to jump all in and tell the truth. "I was thinking about kissing you, Sid," he starts to blush. "I tried everything and nothing was working, but when I started thinking about our time together, when I pictured your smile, it was as if I had always been in control. It felt so natural because of you."

Sid's eyes start to water a little, his throat feeling like there's a rock stuck inside of it. Nobody has ever connected with him this much in the past. Sidric would always end things before they even got close to this. He jumps towards Deux's arms and hugs him tight. Deux places his arms around him and pulls his face up. They start making out, bolts flying all around the room.

After a few minutes, they break apart, panting. Sid is looking at Deux with a newfound appreciation. "I never knew," he whispers.

"Knew what?"

"That kissing could be such a powerful tool for control," Sid says, still slightly in awe.

"Well, when you kiss me, it's not just about control, it's about love," Deux says, looking into Sid's eyes. He takes a deep breath in. "I am falling in love with you Sidric."

Sid leans in and kisses Deux again, feeling the electricity flowing through his body. They pull apart, grinning like fools. "I am falling in love with you too Deux," Sid replies.

They stare at each other, the whole world could be on fire right now but neither of them would notice. "So what's the plan now? What are we looking for at the summit?" Sidric breaks the silence.

Deux shrugs. "Well, obviously, we won't find any answers about our powers in any public places. We're going to need to snoop around—a lot. Befriend workers, find documents, anything. Also, we need to be on the lookout for anything sus. If we know anything, it's that RainforesTec is hiding something. The creepy notes we got confirm that. For now, let's practice using our powers so we don't have any accidents."

Sid nods, feeling a sense of purpose for the first time in a long time.

With Deux by his side, he knows he can do anything.

******

They arrive at the summit and realize this is nothing like OnlineCon, there is no hint of color anywhere. The sleek glass and steel structure seems to reflect their own nervousness back at them. They are about to go undercover for the firs time and find out what RainforesTec is hiding. *Are we the first people to get superhuman abilities from malfunctions with their products? Why did the note say RainforesTec was evil? Be brave, Sid.* He sighs.

The large convention center is full of people in suits walking from room to room. Faint elevator music fills in the silence as they walk towards security. There's one guard behind the desk robotically checking multiple screens. A second guard stands imposingly by the metal detector. They line up behind a couple of old men who look like clones of each other. Deux walks by past the metal detector seamlessly, he waits on the other side for Sidric. Sidric takes a deep breath and walks through it extremely fast.

Not even a second goes by, and the security guard calls him back.

"Excuse me," he raises his voice at Sidric. Sidric immediately feels his heart drop. "Can I take a look at your badges?"

"Oh, sure. Badges," Sidric says, handing over his event badge. He suppresses his shakiness as best as possible.

"You two are not supposed to be here," he says as he starts whispering something into his smartwatch. His left hand pressed against an earpiece in his left ear. "Please step aside and let the others go in."

Sidric and Deux exchange looks. Sweat starts forming on Sid's forehead and suddenly a third security guard pops up behind them.

"Would you mind taking them to Hall A, Shonda?" The guard yells out at the new guard.

"What's Hall A? We didn't do anything wrong!" Sid cries out trying to keep his composure.

"Relax, boy. Hall A is the VIP entrance. You are VIP guests aren't you?" Shonda says as she reads out, "Mr. Helbig? Is that you?"

Sidric quickly remembers his pseudonym for today's mission, and Deux jumps in. "Yes! Oh, perfect. Sorry, my friend isn't feeling well today," he says, "hungover," he mouths to the guard.

Sidric exhales, silently thanking Deux for his incredible improv skills.

Deux and Sidric nod goodbye to the guard and walk through the doors of Hall A, trying to blend in with the crowd of executives and industry leaders. They both wear sleek suits and fake name badges.

"Mr. Helbig and Mr. Hart have entered the summit," Deux whispers, high-fiving Sidric's index finger with his index finger.

Sidric takes note of the various displays and booths set up by RainforesTec's partners and vendors. The noise level is high, with people talking and laughing, making it difficult to hear anything specific.

Suddenly a familiar voice yells out Deux's name. They both turn around abruptly.

"Deux! Hi! So nice to meet you in person! I've been following you for so long," Meli Nora, a twenty-year-old video-game streamer with millions of followers, walks up to them. She is the only one in the room not wearing office clothes. In contrast, she is wearing a pink flowy dress and high heels. Deux recognizes her from one of her old videos where she did the Chapstick Challenge with her ex-girlfriend.

"Hi, Meli! I didn't expect you to know who I was. Nice to meet you," Deux replies politely, subtly hiding his badge with the fake name.

"I didn't," she responds bluntly. "Well, I did after my manager showed me your socials. I just signed with RainforesTec Management, so they've been showing me everyone's stats, details, etc." She eyes Sidric up and down as she speaks. "And who are you? Gerald Helbig?" she asks, reading his badge.

"Hi, uhm—yes, I'm Gerald. I brought Deux here to get a behind-the-scenes look at the new gadgets."

"Okay, anyway, we should totally grab a drink, Deux!" she says, winking as she reaches out for his arm. "I'm sure all of this is pretty boring to you."

Sidric gets the feeling she won't leave until Deux goes with her. At least if he does, maybe they can get some intel on the management.

"I mean, you were interested in signing with RainforesTec, weren't you, Deux? Why don't you two grab a drink and chat about it while I handle some business stuff?" Sidric says, shooting Deux *the look.*

Deux immediately mouths, *WTF NO.*

Sidric counters with a firm *Trust me.*

"Loves it, babes," she coos, pulling Deux by the arm out of the hall. "Bye, Geraldine."

"Bitch," he mutters under his breath.

"What was that, Hun?"

"Quiche! I smelled quiche on your breath. Delicious. I'm gonna look for some. Bye now." Sidric disappears into the crowd.

Meli pauses for a moment, eyes narrowing slightly. Then, with a subtle flick of her wrist, she discreetly checks her breath against her palm, her expression unreadable.

Sid tries to blend in as he watches Deux and Meli walk out of the room. His heart races as he scans the area for anything suspicious—anything that could lead him to some answers. He moves carefully, eavesdropping on people's conversations and politely nodding when he makes awkward eye contact. His eyes land on the bar. *I guess it's five o'clock somewhere.* He walks over and orders a vodka soda with a lime—not because he wants to drink it, but because holding a glass will help him blend in with all the other people holding various alcoholic beverages. Also, maybe a bit of liquid courage will give him the bravery to do this alone. He takes a sip and immediately winces at the lack of sweetness.

The robo-bartender smirks at Sidric's reaction. "Not a vodka soda guy, huh?" The robotic voice surprises him.

Sidric forces a casual shrug. "Just… not what I was expecting." He takes another sip, trying to suppress another wince.

He leans against the bar, scanning the crowd again. Executives in tailored suits clink glasses, laughing a little too loudly. Engineers animatedly discuss specs on the latest tech, their hands moving in quick gestures. He watches as security guards weave through the room, their gazes sharp and calculating.

Suddenly, someone catches his attention. He turns to see a bald man pacing at the back of the room, speaking in hushed tones on his phone. *I'm intrigued.* Out of everyone in the room, this bald man definitely looks like he's up to no good. Curiosity gets the better of Sidric, and he discreetly makes his way closer to the man, trying to eavesdrop on his conversation.

"…the test subject is showing promising results. We'll need to run a few more trials before we can move on to the next phase," the bald man says, his voice low and urgent.

Sidric's heart races as he tries to piece together the meaning behind the man's words. *What test subject? What kind of trials? And why is it so urgent?* He tries to remember all the important details so he can fill Deux in.

"I'll send over the latest report. I'm telling you Project Gamma will be approved by the PrideTime Smartwatch release."

PrideTime Smartwatch. Wait, that's the one that shocked Deux! Sidric stays hidden behind a RainforesTec promotional screen, keeping a close eye on the man. The words 'Project Gamma' echo in his mind building even more questions. But there's something more than just curiosity driving him now. It's like a gut feeling, something telling him that he *has* to follow the bald guy. He can't explain it, but he knows it's important. It's a rush of urgency, like everything's about to change, and he's not about to let this chance slip away.

The bald man sneaks his way out of the room, his footsteps tapping against the polished floor. Sidric tries to keep up, his heart pounding with anticipation. The man takes a sharp left, and Sidric waits a few seconds before following. He watches as the bald man disappears into an unmarked door, and without a second thought, Sidric slips inside behind him.

The room looks like any other hotel conference room—boring walls and red carpet all around. The lights are dim, allowing Sidric to hide behind a tall plant and watch as the bald man opens a briefcase and pulls out a laptop. Sidric hears his fingertips tapping rapidly on the keys. His legs start to ache from crouching, but he has a feeling whatever the man is typing could hold the answers they need.

"Hi," his ominous voice fills up the entire room, "The report has been sent. Let Mr. Bizous know that we will send an updated report on the other subjects soon."

Sidric can hear the voice on the phone but he can't make out what they are saying.

"Yes, Nate and Andre." The bald man replies. "Great. See you then.

Sidric's stomach starts bouncing inside of him. Hearing the names of his friends come out of this scary man makes his whole body feel dizzy.

"I just got confirmation he's with Meli Nora," he says.

MELI NORA?! Deux is with Meli Nora! I need to get him out of there NOW!

He ducks lower as the bald man exits the room.

Sidric makes his way out of the room, scanning the area for any sign of the bald man. He's gone, no trace of where he could have run off to. Sidric pauses for a second, then rushes off to find Deux. Whatever it is that is going on he needs to be as far away from Meli Nora as possible. He can't wait to tell him everything he's just learned. But as the events replay in his mind, he realizes he still has more questions than answers. One thing's for sure, though: the bald man is involved.

He arrives back at the main hall, scanning the crowd. No sign of Deux or Meli anywhere. Sidric takes out his phone and tries to call Deux. The call fails to connect. *Shitty ass service.*

Sidric runs into the lobby and spots Deux and Meli standing inside a glass elevator, ascending slowly. He tracks the elevator's movement as it rises, watching it stop at the twenty-fifth floor. He gives himself a small mental high-five for catching that. Navigating through the crowd of suited men is no easy feat, but he finally reaches the twenty-fifth floor. He's faced with two large corridors, each leading in opposite directions. He pauses for a moment, considering which way they might have gone. He looks left, then right, then left again. His heart beating out of his chest.

Shit. Now what? Sidric pulls at his white dress shirt sleeves, trying to strategize his next move. Suddenly, something inside him shifts. The noise around him dulls, and all he can hear are faint murmurs coming from every direction. He jumps back, scanning the area, expecting someone to be near. But there's no one. The murmurs swirl around him, and he can't pinpoint their source. He covers his ears, then starts walking toward the corridor on the left. The closer he gets to the first door, the louder the murmurs grow. He focuses all his attention on the door, and suddenly, the voices begin to merge into one. A low, raspy voice echoes from the other side.

"Listen, you need to stop before we close the deal," the voice says.

Sidric is stunned by how clearly he can hear it from the other side. It doesn't feel normal—it's probably one of his new powers. Door by door, he walks, eavesdropping on what's going on inside each room.

He hears someone singing in the shower, the faint murmur of a news station from a TV, and a cellphone conversation between a man and his grandma.

"Can I help you?" an actual close by voice comes out from behind him.

He quickly turns his back to the door he's been listening in on. "Oh no, uh, Luisa," he reads the name from her name tag, "I have numeric memory loss. I couldn't remember my room number, so I left some music playing to hear it from the outside."

Sidric is really good at lying except when he's put under pressure. On occasions like this one he tends to make up extreme stories that not even a five-year-old would believe. Shockingly, she believes him.

"Okay sure Hun," she nods half smiling. "Keep at it." She carries on pushing the cleaning cart.

The murmurs come back as he tries to focus on Deux's voice. Seconds go by as he walks towards the end of the hall and suddenly there it is. He hears Deux's nervous laughter. He recognizes it from the first time they were about to kiss.

It's this one! He jumps in excitement. Room 2515.

He places his hand on top of the door-key scanner and focuses. The jolts vibrate all through out his body and towards his left hand.

The door swings wide open.

Sidric, his mind still reeling from his newfound powers, bursts into the room. Just as his eyes land on Deux and Meli, his breath catches in his throat.

They're tangled together, lips locked in a kiss, their bodies pressed so close Sidric can practically feel the heat between them. Everything inside him stills. He wasn't ready for this. Not like this. For a moment, it's as if the world stops turning. Sidric's thoughts rush through him— confusion, hurt, disbelief. Just when he thought there might actually be something between him and Deux, something real... he sees the truth. Deux doesn't want him, he doesn't love him. He only cares about figuring out why they have powers.

Sidric's heart sinks, a deep ache settling within him. He can't help but feel a profound sense of loss. The trust he had placed in Deux, the bond they had forged through all of this mess and shared experiences, now feels shattered. His lips are drained of all color.

Without a word, Sidric turns on his heel, tears welling up in his eyes. He can't bear to witness the sight any longer. His footsteps echo through the empty hallway as he runs away, desperate to escape the pain that now consumes him.

"Wait Sid!" Deux's voice echoes through the halls.

As he flees, Sidric barely registers the cleaning lady, Luisa, standing by the room. She watches him with concern and empathy etched across her face.

Sidric's pace quickens, his mind racing with a maelstrom of emotions. He runs blindly through the corridors and down the stairs, the tears streaming down his face. His heartache feels all-encompassing, a relentless ache that threatens to engulf him. Without noticing he has gone down twenty-five sets of stairs.

Unaware of his surroundings, Sidric suddenly finds himself outside the convention hall, disoriented and filled with an overwhelming urge to escape. He runs aimlessly through the crowded city streets, his breath ragged and his heart pounding in his chest. With each step, the weight of betrayal presses down on him, crushing his spirit.

Exhausted and overwhelmed, Sidric stumbles into a serene park, tucked away from the chaos of the city. Seeking solace, he collapses against the sturdy trunk of a tree, trembling as he surrenders to the weight of his emotions. Before him stretches a tranquil view of a glistening lake, its calm surface reflecting the turmoil within his heart.

As sobs wrack his body, Sidric feels a pain deeper than anything he's ever known. It eclipses every previous heartbreak, gripping him with an intensity that leaves him gasping for air. Tears stream down his face, tracing a path of anguish and confusion.

In this vulnerable moment, Sidric confronts a profound sense of isolation. Alone in an unfamiliar city, with no support or familiar faces to turn to, he feels more trapped than ever. The weight of this realization intensifies his despair, amplifying the crushing sense of being lost within his own existence.

His mind swirls with unanswered questions and uncertainties. *Was he lying to me the whole time? Do I pack up everything and go home? Will I live forever alone with these radioactive powers?* The hurricane of emotions ravages his mind.

In the midst of his despair, Sidric feels his phone vibrate in his back pocket—a shocking reminder of the world he's desperately trying to escape. With a mix of hesitation and defiance, he glances at the screen and sees Deux's name flashing across it. The temptation to answer, to seek some form of explanation or closure, tugs at his wounded heart.

But then a surge of defiance and self-preservation wells within him. He swallows hard, realizing that answering the call would only prolong his agony. With a determined resolve, he ignores it and powers off his phone, cutting off the outside world and giving himself a brief respite from the chaos surrounding him.

In the stillness of the park, Sidric sits alone, enveloped by the weight of his emotions. The world continues to move around him, unaware of his turmoil. And as he gazes out at the tranquil lake, he knows that, eventually, he'll have to return to the hotel and face Deux.

15

loMl

S un starts to set, painting the whole park in orange tones. Sidric looks up, the warm glow shining on his face making him for a small second forget about his broken heart. He takes a deep breath and pushes himself up from the ground. A numbness travels across his whole body, like a gray wave rushing in taking away all of the color inside of his soul. He starts walking trying to find his way back to the hotel without needing to turn his phone on. He knows that once he does it will take seconds for him to reach out to Deux and demand an explanation. But he doesn't need an explanation for what he saw. Deux and Meli were there, standing right in front of him kissing quite passionately. Why on earth would Deux agree to go up to her room even after she was such a bitch to Sidric?

Clouds move fast over his head turning the beautiful sunset into a cloudy night.

The memory of Deux and Meli's betrayal replays over and over in Sidric's mind, like a haunting black-and-white film that refuses to end. Of course, the soundtrack of this film is 'loml,' one of Taylor Swift's saddest songs, its melancholic notes amplifying the ache in his chest. Shivers run down his spine as he recalls Meli's twisted smile when he burst into the room. It's as if she knew exactly how much she was crushing his heart, her expression a silent triumph over his pain.

Suddenly, he remembers every single guy that has hurt him before. Starting all the way back to kindergarten, Sidric's mind retraces the painful memories of past heartbreaks. Each moment of hurt and betrayal resurfaces, intertwining with the fresh wounds inflicted by Deux. It's as if a floodgate of suppressed emotions has burst open, overwhelming him with a tsunami of pain.

He recalls the childhood friend who turned on him when he tried to hold his hand, mocking him for being different—only for that same friend to later come out as gay. Then there was the teenage crush, whose indifference shattered his heart. And the countless others who took advantage of his kindness, leaving scars that still linger.

Sidric's heartache becomes a mosaic of past wounds, interwoven with the present. The weight of all those memories crushes him, threatening to drown him in a sea of despair. The realization hits him—this pattern of heartbreak has haunted him for most of his life. He falls too fast. He jumps off planes with no parachute.

Amidst the anguish, a spark of resilience ignites within Sidric. He refuses to let the pain define him. He realizes that he has the power to break this cycle, to rise above the torment and forge a new path. He can figure out this RainforesTec situation on his own. So what if he thought he found the one. So what if he was already working on cute nicknames for Deux. Love comes and goes and this time it chose to go with a quirky girl named Meli. *Let her have him.*

Who cares about all those sleepless nights talking to each other. Deux was probably just trying to get any answers he could from me.

As he takes a deep breath, Sidric acknowledges that the hurt inflicted by Deux cuts deep, almost as much as one thousand cuts. But he also recognizes that dwelling on the past will not lead to healing. Instead, he focuses on the present moment and the strength he has gained from his experiences.

The city is dark now and the streetlights start to turn on. He looks up and is immediately triggered by the light shining down on him like a spotlight. He realizes that after all this chaotic depressive energy he didn't once set off his powers. It's like he is finally in full control. The old him would have set the whole building on fire after having his heart broken. *I can do it with a broken heart.* He spots a glitching coffee shop sign going on and off. He tests himself. Shoots it with his index finger. Just like that. It is recharged and working properly.

There's an immediate change in soundtrack. Sparks fire inside of him. A warmness spreads across as he realizes he does not need Deux to protect him. Sure he loved kissing him and hugging him and holding his hand but he does not need him. He can find any other attractive boy who's tall and has curly dark hair to kiss. The world is not lacking cute boys. *Deux wasn't just a cute boy though.* Sid shakes his head trying to forget every inch of Deux's face. He catches himself retracing every conversation they had together.

With every step Sidric takes, his thoughts spin in a dizzying cyclone of emotions. Confusion overtakes him, leaving him uncertain of his true feelings. Is he entering his *Tortured Poets* era, destined to live with this hole in his heart forever? Is he in his *Red* era, where sadness and heartbreak dominate his thoughts? Or maybe he's in his *Reputation* era, craving revenge—and chic thigh-high boots? Or could he be in his *Speak Now* era, longing only for the solace of Deux's embrace?

The streets stretch before him, a maze of possibilities that mirrors the labyrinth of his conflicted heart. Sidric's mind races, grappling with the multitude of choices that beckon him from every direction.

But through the storm of emotions, one nagging question persists, adding another layer of bewilderment.

Sure, Deux is ridiculously hot and undeniably attractive but—
Sidric abruptly stops walking.
Meli is the biggest lesbian on the internet. What the hell is going on?!

16

i hAte it here

Seconds after Sidric bursts into the room.

"Meli!" Deux angrily yells out wiping his lips. "Why would you do that? I thought you were a lesbian!"

"Deux, don't be so dramatic. It was just a kiss. I had no idea your little manager would get that butt hurt," Meli says, casually fixing her hair in the mirror. "Also, I stopped being a lesbian a while ago."

"He's not my little manager, and he wasn't butt hurt. He was heartbroken," Deux says, his throat tightening mid-sentence. The image of Sidric's devastated expression flashes through his mind, a look of pure pain he never wanted to be responsible for.

"I have to go."

He gets up and heads towards the door.

"You're not going anywhere, cutie," Meli purrs, her entire demeanor shifting in an instant. Before Deux can react, she steps in front of him and shoves him onto the bed. *She's got some Hulk-like strength.*

"Not until we post a cute video of us making out."

148

"What now?!" Deux scrambles backward, inching away from her as she closes the distance. "We're not doing that. You're insane!"

"I'm contractually obligated to do it, Deux." Meli's voice is eerily calm, her strawberry lip gloss shimmering under the dim hotel lights. "It was all in my RainforesTec agreement. They said they'd find me a cutie to date. I texted my manager that you were here, and she said you should be into it. I won't get paid if we don't do it. Come on, you just have to pretend to date me for a while. We all win. You might even fall for me."

She leans in, her arms bracketing Deux against the bed. He's trapped, her breath warm against his cheek.

The words swirl in his mind like a jigsaw puzzle missing half its pieces. *Pretend to date? Why?* And then—Sue Sparkle. Quinton Lanes. Stephen. Brandon. One by one, the names flood his mind. All people who once identified as queer. All who suddenly came out as straight.

His blood runs cold. *Is RainforesTec behind this? Are they brainwashing people into being straight?!*

"But Meli," Deux yells, his voice cracking with desperation, "you're a lesbian!"

He shoves her away with a burst of instinctive panic—except this time, electricity surges from his fingertips. A sharp crack splits the air as golden sparks fly. Meli's body jolts violently, her scream lost in the electric snap. She's flung backward, crashing against the wall with a sickening thud.

The room fills with the acrid scent of burnt ozone.

Meli's eyes go wide with shock and fear as she struggles to pick herself up from the ground, her body trembling. "What the fuck just happened?!" she screams, her voice raw. Then, as if waking from a daze, her expression twists in disgust. "Why the hell was I trying to kiss you?!" She wipes her mouth furiously, spitting onto the floor like she's trying to rid herself of the moment entirely.

Deux stares at her, equally confused. Then—beep, beep, beep.
A familiar, rhythmic sound cuts through the silence. Deux's gaze
snaps to Meli's wrist. *Her smartwatch.*

"Take that off. Now!" he shouts, pointing at it.

Meli looks down, realization dawning. Without hesitation, she rips
the watch from her wrist. The moment it leaves her skin, sparks erupt
from its screen, the tiny device crackling violently before bursting
into flames.

They both take a step back, watching in horror as the watch melts
into a smoldering pile on the floor.

Meli clutches her head, her breathing unsteady. "I'm so confused.
It's like I just woke up from a nightmare... but I was never asleep."
Her eyes dart around the room as if trying to piece together reality.
"Shit. I broke up with my girlfriend. Told her I wasn't attracted to
girls anymore." Her voice wavers. "And I meant it. At least, I thought
I did."

Deux takes a cautious step forward, his mind racing. "But... you
are? You're still lesbian?" he asks carefully.

Meli snaps her head up to meet his gaze, her expression pained.
"Deux, no offense but men will never be my *type.*" She exhales sharply,
pressing her palms to her temples. "It's like someone else was living
my life, making my choices, and I had no say in it."

"Do you remember when this all started? Anything could help,"
Deux asks, his voice urgent.

Meli's eyes widen as realization dawns on her. "Yes! Right after
OnlineCon!" Her expression twists in fury. "Oh my god—ugh! I'm
going to kill Jenna!" She practically screams.

Deux blinks, caught off guard. "Who's Jenna?"

"My manager!" Meli huffs, pacing frantically. "She's the one who
kept pushing these ideas on me! Telling me I needed to find a
boyfriend, convincing me it was the best career move. That's why I

came on to you! She probably—" Meli gasps, suddenly clutching her head. "Oh my god. She's been drugging me. My mint lattes—every morning. That's how she's been making me easier to manipulate!"

"She's your new RainforesTec manager?" Deux asks.

"Yes! Oh my god, she is so fired," Meli huffs, furiously pulling out her phone. "Oh, look, she's already texting me—'Where are you? Where are you?' Up your ass, Jenna."

"Wait! Don't text her yet!" Deux blurts out.

Meli pauses, giving him a suspicious look.

Deux hesitates, debating whether to lay out his full theory about RainforesTec brainwashing people into being straight. But right now, Meli is too pissed off. The last thing they need is Meli blasting off on Jenna. Any advantage they have over RainforesTec not realizing they're onto them is worth keeping.

"Wouldn't it be better if you pretend you don't know what's going on? Just to see what other insane things she tries to make you do. Then, when the time is right, you can expose her. That's front-page news. You'd get so much attention for that." He appeals to her ego.

Meli's expression shifts from anger to intrigue. A slow smirk tugs at her lips. "Deux, I did not know you were this good at the game. I love that."

"Okay, for now, tell Jenna we're going on a date. You're going to help me find Sidric."

"Let's do it. After all, I owe you one. You tossing me against the wall literally woke me up from a blackout. I'm not sure how you... did that..." She furrows her brow in wonder. "...but it might have actually put some of my past lovers to shame." She playfully nudges his shoulder.

Deux smirks but is quickly pulled back to reality—the very real problem that the man of his dreams is out there somewhere, hurt and confused.

Deux runs out of the room followed by Meli. The image of Sidric's heartbroken expression is etched deeply in his memory. The weight of guilt and regret presses heavily upon Deux's chest as he frantically searches for Sidric. His footsteps echo through the empty corridors of the convention center, each one an echo of his remorse.

Deux's hands tremble as he fumbles for his phone, dialing Sidric's number with a mix of desperation and hope. But the ringing falls silent, met only with the cold void of unanswered calls. His heart sinks with each unanswered ring, a bitter reminder of the consequences of his actions. *He's going to hate me for the rest of his life. How can I explain to him the truth? I don't even fully comprehend the truth.*

In his frustration, Deux rakes his fingers through his tousled hair, his normally composed demeanor shattered. The air feels suffocating, and he struggles to draw in a breath. Realizing the constriction of his outfit, he hastily loosens his tie and unbuttons the top two buttons of his shirt, seeking solace in the brief relief it provides.

"Here, I have an idea," Meli says, noticing Deux's nearing panic attack.

She pulls out her phone and opens the CityViewer app.

www.rainforestec.com/CityViewer
The CitiViewer mobile and VR app, launching this summer, is a real-time live feed of hundreds of thousands of locations worldwide. Designed to bridge distances and unveil the unseen, CitiViewer grants users unfiltered access to streets, alleys, shopping malls, and beyond—offering a continuous, unblinking window into life as it unfolds.
Seamlessly integrated with an expansive network of surveillance feeds, CitiViewer redefines the boundaries of observation, turning every corner of the world into a stage. See without being

seen. Know without being known.
Powered by RainforesTec. Remember, the world is always
watching.

"Look," Meli shows him her screen, "Here he is running out of the convention center. We can just track him with all the cameras."

"That's extremely creepy. Is it new?" Deux asks, his eyebrows fruncing in horror.

"Yes! I have beta access because I'm signed to RainforesTec. Or was signed? I don't know there's lots to figure out."

Deux is drowning in the realization of just how deep RainforesTec's grip on the world really is. With every new piece of evidence, the puzzle forms a terrifying picture. One where people are unknowingly handing over their lives, their choices, their very identities to a corporation that controls more than anyone could imagine.

This is worse than I thought. Worse than when Meryl Streep lost the Oscar for The Devil Wears Prada *back in 2006.*

Deux's inner dialogue is cut short after he see's the hurt in Sidric's face as he runs away. Frantic, Deux swipes through the cameras, searching for him. Street after street, feed after feed—nothing. He and Meli rush out of the summit, the cool air doing nothing to calm the storm inside him.

His eyes scan the city, desperate for any sign of Sidric. He has to find him. He has to apologize, to explain, even if it means tearing himself open and laying every raw, vulnerable truth at Sidric's feet. The weight of his mistake crushes him. The late-night conversations, the quiet moments, the trust Sidric had given him so freely—he had thrown it all away. He had taken Sidric's heart and set it on fire.

Meli snatches the phone from his hand and takes the lead, her sharp eyes darting between the screen and the streets ahead. They turn left, right, then double back. The search becomes a dizzying maze, the city folding in around them. Deux shoves past the crowd, his pulse hammering. Sidric is out there somewhere, hurting.

And Deux won't stop until he finds him.

"He took the subway two minutes ago!" Meli shouts, excitement lacing her voice.

They race through Union Station, Deux's heart pounding with a newfound sense of hope. Maybe, just maybe, this can still be fixed.

"He got on the yellow line," Meli says, yanking Deux into the next train. "If we take this one, we can catch him at the next connection."

As they collapse onto their seats, catching their breath, Deux's gaze drifts upward to the LED screens above. An ad for RainforesTec's Brain Accelerator Program flashes across the screen. His stomach twists.

"This is really bad," he mutters.

Meli follows his stare, her face paling as realization dawns on her. "Wait... You don't think—" Her eyes widen. "The watch exploding? Brain chips?! Is that what they're doing?"

"I have no answers," Deux admits. "But after what happened to you, there has to be a connection."

"I have to call my ex—explain all this before she gets chipped or something."

They leap off the train at the next stop, sprinting toward the yellow line connection.

"He's taking the green now!" Meli screams, pivoting and bolting in the opposite direction.

As they reach the platform, Deux spots Sidric on the other side of the station, two subway lines separating them.

"Sidric!" Deux yells, but his voice is drowned out by the screeching trains pulling in from both sides.

Sidric's head snaps up, his red, tear-streaked eyes scanning the crowd.

"Sid!" Deux shouts again.

Sidric, already inside his train, locks eyes with him. But then he sees Meli standing beside Deux. His expression hardens instantly. His eyes roll, and he flips Deux off, fresh tears threatening to spill.

"No! Sid, it's not—"

"Deux!" Meli's panicked voice cuts through the chaos.

He turns just in time to see a slender woman in a black suit gripping Meli's wrist. Three men in matching suits close in, their faces obscured by sleek RainVision X glasses.

Before Deux can react, the woman snaps a smartwatch onto Meli's wrist. Sparks flicker across the screen as it activates. Meli's breath catches. She looks at Deux in horror.

Across the platform, Sidric watches, confusion morphing into alarm.

Deux barely has time to mouth one word "Help."

And then, Sidric's train speeds away.

Frantic, Deux yanks out his phone and shares his live location with Sidric. It's all he can do.

17

imgonNagetyouback

Sidric runs to the back of the train as it speeds away, his heart hammering against his ribs. Through the window, he sees the group of suits tightening their circle around Deux and Meli. *Something's not right.* His stomach twists.

Without hesitation, he pulls out his phone, fingers shaking as he tracks Deux's location. The dot moves further and further from him.

He might still be hurt about the kiss, but none of that matters at the moment. The last thing he wants is for Deux, or even Meli, to be in real danger. Sure, he'd wish for Meli to step in dog poop or have broccoli stuck in her tooth for the rest of her life, but these people looked way more dangerous than that.

It's time to put his game face on. He jumps out of the train and jogs out on to the city streets. He speedwalks as he tracks Deux's location. *Can this day get any wilder? I will rescue you Deux and then I will slap you for cheating on me. Is it considered cheating if we're not officially boyfriends?*

Determined to prove he's no damsel in distress, Sidric shoves his way through the crowd, his breath coming in sharp bursts. His Latino ancestors light a fire under his ass, pushing him forward with relentless speed.

The dot on his screen suddenly stops moving. His heart skips a beat.

With renewed urgency, he quickens his pace, strutting through the streets like he owns them. Ten minutes of power-walking later, he finally arrives at the location. His chest heaves, his pulse pounds in his ears, and the leather in his brand-new shoes is officially creased. *Great, I wont be able to return this now. Deux you're pushing it today.*

He stands outside the building—a cute Parisian café called *Le Diplomate*—his fingertips buzzing with energy. *Hmm. This would've been a cute date spot for us.*

People lounge outside, sipping wine and nibbling on small aperitifs, their laughter blending with the hum of the city. Sidric scans the crowd, searching for any sign of Deux. He moves toward the left side of the café and drops into the first empty seat he finds. Pressing his hands against the window, he cups his eyes, peering inside. A bead of sweat drips down his forehead.

And then, he spots Deux's smile.

But something's off. Deux sits across from Meli, but his usual spark is missing—his mouth is tense, his eyes dull. Sidric narrows his gaze and focuses on tuning into their conversation.

"So I literally told the girl, *I* wanted Topaz Green nails. *Not* Mint Green," Meli rants, tossing her hands dramatically.

"Wow. That's... an extremely wild story," Deux responds, his voice flat, disinterested.

He reaches for his drink, takes a sip, then glances to his right, just for a second, before quickly turning back to Meli. Then, as if on cue, he grabs Meli's hand and forces a laugh. *What?*

Sidric follows Deux's gaze and spots them, the suits. All four of them.

Two tables near the entrance. The slender woman. Her eyes locked onto Deux.

This isn't good. Think. Think. Think.

His eyes dart around the café, searching for an escape route. Then, like divine intervention from *Mother Swift*, he spots it—an emergency exit past the kitchen, tucked into the back corner.

Sidric moves fast, surfing through the outside of the cafe. He yanks the back door open, and the scent of steak frites floods his senses. *Not the time for cravings, Sid. Focus. Rescue mission.*

Inside, the kitchen is chaos. Flames leap from pans, steam hisses, a head chef barks orders in rapid-fire French. Sidric stays low, moving in the shadows until he spots a row of chef's uniforms hanging on the wall. He throws on a white coat, then tugs a black skull cap over his head. There's no clear plan—he's improvising.

Then, the glow of a fire alarm catches his eye.

Bingo.

He takes a deep breath, soaking in the energy around him like a sponge. The kitchen flickers—first a dim pulse, then total darkness. A second later, the halls and main dining room follow. His body hums with static. He reaches out, yanks the fire alarm, and—

BEEP.

A piercing siren explodes through the air.

"Arrêtez ce que vous faites!" the head chef shouts. "Turn everything off and walk out the door!" He switches to English, his French accent thick with urgency.

The kitchen staff obeys instantly, pouring past Sidric as they evacuate. Sidric pushes against the current, slipping into the restaurant.

Meli bolts for the front door.

He scans the room. No Deux.

Maybe he's in the bathroom.

Sidric spins around—

And crashes straight into Deux.

Their eyes lock. Deux inhales sharply.

"Sid!" he whispers.

"Follow me!" Sidric grabs Deux's arm, yanking him toward the back exit.

As they burst into the night air, a flicker of concern for Meli crosses Sidric's mind. *She should be fine... right?* He pushes the thought aside—he needs to talk to Deux. Alone.

They run, hand in hand, weaving through narrow streets. Sidric risks a glance at Deux, and for a split second, the sparks are back—the same ones that were there before everything got messed up.

They descend into the subway, breathless, and jump onto the first train that arrives. The doors slide shut behind them, and only then does Deux speak.

"Sid... you saved me." His voice is uneven, like he still can't believe it. "Thank you."

Sidric exhales, leaning against the train pole. "Yeah, I don't know what's going on with you and Meli, but there was no way I was leaving you with those creepy suit guys. Bad vibes. Really bad vibes."

"Shit. Meli!" Deux exclaims, pulling out his phone. "One second."

Sidric crosses his arms, rolling his eyes. "Really?"

"I swear, I'll explain everything. Just let me get them off my scent first."

He quickly types out a text to Meli.

DEUX-

Meli! So sorry I had to run out of the date. That steak gave me really bad diarrhea! You do not want to be near me right now. I really hope we can continue this later on.

Deux holds up his phone, showing Sidric the message.

159

"Kinda TMI, don't you think?" Sidric raises an eyebrow.

"I need to throw them off my trail, make her lose interest," Deux explains. His voice lowers, more serious now. "There's a lot I need to tell you, Sid."

Sidric's expression hardens. "Why don't you start by telling me why you were kissing her?" The words come out sharper than he intended.

Deux exhales, rubbing his temple. "Listen, what you saw in that hotel room—it wasn't what it looked like. Meli's been acting off ever since we ran into her. She told me her manager convinced her that if she started dating a guy, she'd make a ton of money."

Sidric frowns. "But... isn't she into girls?"

"Yes! That's the thing!" Deux throws up his hands. "She dragged me upstairs and went full Hulk trying to hook up with me. I pushed her off, and—well—I kind of electrocuted her."

Sidric blinks, then stifles a laugh. "Shit. Okay, I'm listening." He smirks, already picturing Meli with her hair standing on end like a cartoon character.

Deux leans in. "I shocked her so bad I fried her smartwatch. And the second it broke—boom. It was like she snapped out of a trance."

Sidric's eyes widen. "What do you mean she woke up?"

"She was back to herself. Like a zombie reawakening," Deux says, his voice urgent. "Confused. Questioning everything that had happened the past few weeks—like she hadn't been in control. And she was back to being queer."

Sidric stares, his stomach twisting.

"Then we went to find you, but the second I saw you, her Rain-foresTec management showed up. They slapped a new smartwatch on her wrist, and just like that, she was back—obnoxiously straight Meli. Like nothing had ever happened." Deux swallows hard. "I had to play along. I told them we were going on a date just to keep them off my back."

160

Sidric shivers. "Deux, this is *terrifying*."

"I know," Deux murmurs. "This is way bigger than we thought. Who knows how many people they've already turned? And it's not like we can just go around shocking everyone back into reality." He takes a deep breath, his fingers trembling as he reaches for Sidric's hand. "But listen to me. No matter how bad this gets, I need you to know something." His grip tightens. His voice lowers to almost a whisper. "I love you, Sidric."

Sidric's breath catches.

"I love how much light you bring into every room you walk into," Deux continues, his voice raw with emotion. "I love your sass when things don't go your way. But most of all, I love your heart, how kind it is. And I swear I will never hurt you again."

Sidric feels his world tilt. His pulse pounds in his ears as he drowns in Deux's electric gaze, the warmth of his confession wrapping around him like a current, pulling him under.

"I love you too, Deux," he whispers, "We're going to figure all this out, together."

They hold hands, fingers laced together, as Deux sends a playful electric shock through Sidric's palm.

"So Rude," Sidric mutters, suppressing a smile.

Their walk back to the hotel gives them a rare moment of peace. They chat about how bright the moon is, and Deux casually mentions he could demolish an entire pizza. Meanwhile, Sidric keeps replaying Deux's "I Love You" over and over in his mind, like a song stuck on a loop.

"Oooh! Come this way!" Deux suddenly tugs Sidric into a costume shop. His eyes sparkle with mischief. "I have a feeling we're going to need some alter-hairstyles for our alter-egos."

Gays and wigs—the ultimate combination.

Thirty minutes later, they step out of the shop, each carrying an oversized bag filled with wigs of every color and style imaginable.

"RainforesTec won't know what hit them," Deux declares, dramatically flipping on a long, fiery orange wig.

Sidric shakes his head, watching him with pure adoration. *I love this goof.*

18

deactivated

Sidric

Morning comes and the sound of rain hitting the window sill wakes Sidric up. He is intertwined inside of Deux's arms. He takes a deep breath in, Deux's natural morning scent fills his lungs. A mix of faded cologne and sweat. Cozy. Safe. *Mine.*

Sidric shifts slightly, rolling onto his side until their noses brush.

"Not yet, Sid," Deux murmurs, eyes still closed, feeling his gaze.

"Come on," Sidric whispers back, grinning. "We have a lot to do today. Going undercover to take down a corrupt tech company isn't exactly a slow morning kind of task."

Deux doesn't answer.

Sidric smirks. "I *know* what'll wake you up." His fingers trail teasingly down Deux's torso, inching lower.

Deux lets out a low chuckle. "You cheeky little—" In an instant, he flips them over, pinning Sidric beneath him.

*** Deux ***

163

After an unexpected morning delay, they finally make their way to the summit. Sidric wears a black shaggy wig and glasses and Deux wears a blonde pixie style wig. As they arrive, the skies clear, casting a warm glow over the towering glass building. Business people move briskly through the entrance, their sharp suits and determined strides.

They make their way in through the VIP entrance. Despite the pleasant summer day outside, the atmosphere inside is cold and precise. The hum of conversations is subdued, and measured. The air of formality lingers like an invisible weight, pressing down as Deux and Sidric navigate through the crowd.

Sidric scans every passing face, searching for the bald man. If anyone here had answers, it would be him. But finding one suit in a sea of them feels like searching for a single raindrop in an ocean. They speedwalk through the maze of corridors, uncertain of who—or what—they're truly looking for.

"It's Nini!" Sidric exclaims, his excitement bubbling over as he points at a girl walking toward the theater, flanked by a tight security detail.

Deux furrows his brows. "Who's that?"

Sidric gasps. "She's an iconic trans activist and makeup mogul! I own literally all of her products. Do you think it'd be bad if I asked for a photo?"

Deux gives him a pointed look. "Sid, we're on a secret mission against a bald man. We can track her down later. After we figure out what's going on, okay?"

Sidric groans, crossing his arms. "Fine."

They push forward, following the signs leading to the *RainforesTec Mobility Devices* conference room. As they approach, a disconcerting bald man in a white lab coat shoves past them without so much as a glance.

Both of them freeze. Then, simultaneously, they turn to each other. "That's him," Sidric whispers.

Without hesitation, they follow him into a panel room and slip into two open seats near the back. The chatter in the room settles, and the lights dim.

The bald man steps onto the podium.

The panel begins.

The man in the white coat begins discussing RainforesTec's latest technological advancements, his voice smooth and calculated. Beside him stands a woman with a vacant expression, her presence eerily still. Deux's gaze shifts to the sleek briefcase she clutches. Something about it feels important.

Without a word, she hands it over to the bald man, who presses a button, cueing a demo video of the newest RainforesTec smartwatch. As the sleek graphics flash across the screen, Deux's stomach drops.

He recognizes it instantly.

He nudges Sidric and points at the screen, mouthing, *That's the model that gave us this!* while clumsily gesturing to the golden marks on his skin.

Sidric chuckles under his breath. "Subtle," he whispers sarcastically.

Deux's mind races. *That briefcase. It has to hold some answers.* He pulls out his phone, opening the notes app, and types:

As soon as the bald man finishes speaking, we move closer and follow him backstage. We need to get into that briefcase. You ready?

He tilts the screen toward Sidric, who reads it quickly before glancing up. He forces a small smile, but Deux sees the panic flicker in his eyes. It reminds him of the night they got arrested—the way Sidric's hands trembled, the way fear tightened his breath.

Without hesitation, Deux reaches over and grips his hand firmly.

"Wait for my signal," he whispers.

Onstage, the bald man launches into his closing remarks.

"...So, as you've seen, the new RainforesTec smartwatch not only stabilizes mental health, supplies your body with essential vitamins, tracks your daily routine *and* the stock market—but it also tells time!"

The front row of suited men chuckle on cue.

"Thank you for your time, everyone. Don't forget to grab a gift bag on the way out."

The second the applause begins, Deux leans in.

"Let's go," he whispers.

Deux moves quickly toward the backstage entrance, taking the lead. Sidric follows closely behind. A guard steps forward, blocking their path.

"Passes?"

Before Sidric can react, Deux smoothly flashes them both, cutting off any chance of interaction.

"Don't worry, cutie. I've got you," Deux reassures him, tapping Sidric's fingertip with his own in a playful high-five.

They continue down the hall, spotting the bald man in the white lab coat heading toward a black door labeled **CONTROL ROOM**. The door clicks shut behind him.

"Shit, we can't go in now. He'll see us and call security," Sidric whispers, trying to sound composed despite the very illegal nature of their actions. "We tried, right? Let's go get some snacks."

Deux's eyes gleam with mischief. "Maybe he won't even notice us."

Sidric watches as Deux's brain works overtime, already plotting.

"Follow me," Deux says, already moving.

Sidric hurries after him, shaking his head in awe. "How are you so good at this?"

Deux's eyes land on a janitor's closet directly across from the control room they're targeting. He opens the door and gently ushers Sidric inside. The closet is pitch dark, with no visible light.

Deux's fear of the bald man is palpable. The way the shine on the man's bald head gleams with an almost razor-sharp intensity fills Deux with dread. It feels as if, at any moment, the bald man could catch them, ending their mission before they can find the truth about this tech company.

The closet is cramped, and the scent of Sidric's cologne hangs in the air, wrapping around them like an Italian citrus embrace. In this confined space, the fragrance becomes a protective cocoon, making Deux feel invincible. He turns to Sidric and closes his eyes for a brief moment. In the darkness, faint glimmers of light filter through the cracks around the door, providing just enough visibility. All Deux can focus on is the sensation of Sidric's lips against his, drawing him in like a magnetic force. He yearns to pull Sidric closer, kiss him, and forget about all the troubles that could exist. Yet, their secret mission brings him back to reality.

"The vent," Sidric whispers urgently, pointing toward the lights above.

Deux glances up, his mind racing. Just when they're about to share a romantic moment in a janitor's closet, a vent becomes their focus.

"Excellent, let's go up there."

Sidric smirks, his voice dripping with sarcastic charm. "Yay, a vent for us to squeeze through, hoping nothing goes wrong… Just another day on our heist/date."

Deux lightly presses his thumb against Sidric's lower lip, as if marking him in a secret rendezvous. He watches as Sidric's mind momentarily drifts before, with a playful glint in his eye, Sidric nibbles at Deux's thumb and flashes a mischievous grin. Then, in one fluid motion, he climbs onto a nearby shelf.

Deux rolls his eyes, fully aware of how he's completely into this boy. *There's no going back.*

Before he can dwell on it, Sidric is already balanced on Deux's solid shoulder, expertly twisting the small screws securing the vent shut. A few precise movements later, the panel comes loose.

"Here goes nothing," Sidric mutters, swinging the vent open. The deafening crash that follows takes them both by surprise. They fall silent, a sudden spike in the risk factor hanging heavily in the air. It's Sidric's first time attempting anything like this, and it only serves to stoke his desire for Deux further.

"You ready baby boy?" Deux asks in a voice that sends shivers down Sidric's spine.

"I need to calm down," Sidric admits aloud.

Deux smiles, aware that he's turning Sidric on, and it warms him from the inside. Given the current situation, he's equally nervous and excited. He longs to live in the moment with Sidric but is also apprehensive about being vulnerable and potentially endangering Sidric. Right now, the vent is their sole focus, but soon they'll have to confront everything or risk losing each other. Deux seizes Sidric by the waist. *God, you're so hot.*

He lifts him into the air. Sidric perches on the shelf, his arm and leg bracing against the wall. The real challenge lies in the strength required to pull Deux up, and Sidric is more than ready to demonstrate his capabilities. Deux may be a few inches taller and more muscular, but Sidric is filled with a newfound sense of empowerment, embracing his inner rebel as he pulls Deux up into the vent.

"A thing of true beauty," Sidric jokingly flexes his arm giving his muscle an air kiss.

"You truly are," Deux replies, their bodies brushing against each other as he slides his upper body into the vent.

Every inch of Deux's form glides against Sidric, igniting a wild, passionate desire within. If they weren't in the midst of a secret mission, their clothes would likely be strewn across the floor by now. Deux burns from the inside, his internal flames stoked with desire, yet devoid of real pain. The torment coursing through him feels like the desperate need to gasp for air after a prolonged underwater struggle.

"This way," Deux says.

To both their relief, the space isn't as suffocating as they feared. Sidric fits well enough—but the real problem is Deux. Not only does Deux have to lead in the dark tight crawl space, but every time he moves, his shoulders scrape against the metal walls, producing an obnoxious squeak. *So much for stealth.*

He pushes forward, focusing on their objective. The vent above the control room should be just ahead. He listens carefully, trying to pinpoint the bald man's exact location. The first clue? A low, gravelly hum drifting through the air—a mix between the deep vibrations of a bass guitar and the rasp of a lifelong smoker. The eerie melody echoes through the vents, leading them toward the right spot.

Deux stays focused, but he knows Sidric is right behind him, tense and silent. He doesn't need to turn around to feel the shift in Sid's energy. Sidric is still learning to control his powers, and any stray emotion could set off an unintended jolt. Deux just hopes Sid remembers everything he taught him.

After yesterday's antics Deux knows the stakes are too high to get caught. He's not only risking losing Sidric forever but losing every queer human. There's no room for error.

Not when they're dangling above potential danger.

"One hand in front of the other," Sidric whispers to himself, dragging himself along the vent.

Deux can barely hear Sidric behind him; his broad shoulders have effectively blocked most of the vent, leaving him with no choice but to push forward toward the sound of the bald man. Light filters through the slats ahead, and as he inches closer, the room below comes into view.

Peering through the vent, he spots a wall of glowing screens casting an eerie light over the mysterious man. A surge of determination courses through him. He's had enough of this cramped space—the screws have scraped against his shoulders for too long, leaving behind fresh blisters and streaks of blood.

Then, the smell hits him.

It seeps into his lungs, thick and putrid. Deux has always had a thing about bad smells—if they get too overwhelming, he starts sneezing uncontrollably. And this? This is next-level disgusting. The stench is as if three hundred rotting pizza boxes were piled up in the room. His nose twitches. The tickling sensation starts, creeping up his sinuses.

Oh no.

Not now.

Deux fights against the mounting urge to sneeze, forcing himself to focus on the screens below. One of them cycles through images of creators he recognizes. His stomach tightens when he spots Nini—the girl Sidric had just seen hours ago.

Beneath her photo, a flashing message reads: **DEACTIVATED.**

The screen flickers, shifting to another face.

Deux's breath catches in his throat. His own photograph stares back at him.

LOCATION UNKNOWN.

A chill shoots through his spine, spreading across his skin in waves of goosebumps. His body feels frozen, but his mind races. Creator after creator flashes by—faces he knows, people he's followed, admired. Then, Nate's picture appears. Then Andre's.

DEACTIVATION IN PROGRESS.

Rage bubbles inside him, hot and all-consuming. His fists clench. The smell of decay thickens, clinging to the air like an infection. Then comes the sound of a deep, guttural burp from the bald man.

The screen changes again.

Meli Nora's face appears, but it's drained of color, grayed out. A thick red banner stamped across it.

DEACTIVATED.

It all clicks. Too fast. Too much. Everything he feared is being confirmed. His mind spins, piecing together the horror unfolding before him.

And then—

His nose twitches violently.

Oh, please no. Not now.

"Oh fu—"

Deux sneezes—loud, violent, and completely disastrous. His body jolts forward, head slamming into the vent. The metal groans before the entire edge snaps loose.

Then, everything goes to hell.

Sidric yelps as his skin scrapes against the metal, momentum flinging him out of the vent. He crashes into Deux, sending them both hurtling downward.

Deux lands hard—right at the feet of the bald man. Sidric follows, smacking into a precarious stack of pizza boxes. Pepperoni slices catapult into the air, one slapping onto Sidric's face with an undignified *splat*. Both of their wigs fly off across the room.

For a moment, there's silence.

The bald man rises slowly, his dark eyes flickering between them as he processes the chaos. Then, he moves—grabbing Deux by the collar and yanking him up.

"It's you," he whispers, his voice slick with something sinister.

The scent of stale pepperoni and bitter coffee invades Deux's nose.

His anger ignites. The images of his friends, their faces flashing across those cursed screens—Nate. Andre. Meli. Their lives toyed with like they're nothing. It fuels something inside him, something electric and untamed.

A charge builds in his fingertips. Without thinking, Deux grips the man's wrist, his hold vice-like.

"Let go, you creep!" he snarls, unleashing a jolt of electricity.

The bald man jerks back, his entire body convulsing as the current rips through him. His bald head trembles with residual shocks, and the acrid scent of static fills the air.

Deux scrambles to his feet, heart hammering. From this vantage point, he sees everything.

The screens.

The data.

Every single queer creator he knows—scanned, tracked, monitored. Some of them have their heartbeats logged in real-time.

His blood runs cold.

"What is all this?!" he shouts, the weight of it all crashing into him.

The bald man steadies himself, lips curling into a knowing smirk. His voice slithers through the room, low and menacing.

"You'll regret coming here, Deux."

Sidric, still sprawled on the floor, watches in horror as the bald man reaches behind his chair, grabbing what looks like a gun.

"Deux! Look out!" he yells, pointing frantically.

In a blur of motion, Deux moves in front of Sidric, instinct taking over. His arm snaps forward, and three golden strikes explode from his palm, crackling through the air. The bald man jerks violently as the electricity courses through him, his body convulsing before he crumples to the floor.

"Oh my god. I just killed a man. I just killed a bald man," Deux gasps, eyes wide in shock.

Sidric, still chewing on a pepperoni that had previously been stuck to his face, mumbles, "You're a whole-ass human taser."

The bald man twitches, a few stray sparks flickering across his limbs. He's still breathing—barely. Struggling, he tries to push himself up.

"We need to go," Deux mutters, before sending another electric strike at the shelf above him. It collapses with a deafening crash, two massive screens toppling onto the man.

A guttural groan escapes from beneath the rubble. Then—a flicker of movement. His trembling fingers reach for his smartwatch, tapping frantically.

SECURITY BREACH 710. SECURITY BREACH 710.

Alarms wail throughout the building.

"Okay, human taser, let's go!" Sidric hisses, snatching a briefcase from beside the door. He cracks it open slightly—before freezing. His stomach drops.

"Deux... there's armed men coming for us! What do we do?"

Sidric's breathing quickens. The walls seem to close in. His vision tunnels. Every nerve in his body screams as panic takes hold, slipping through his fingers like a live wire. The lights overhead begin to glitch, screens flashing wildly—his body reacting beyond his control.

Breathe. He reminds himself. But even that simple act feels impossible.

"Come here," Deux murmurs, pulling Sidric close, his arms a firm anchor. Their lips meet, grounding Sidric in an instant. Deux's hands find his, steadying them. He turns them both toward the screens, guiding him.

"Three. Two. One."

Every light in the building blinks out.

For a breath, the world is still. Quiet. Black. The only thing visible is the soft golden glow of their hand marks, illuminating their faces in the dark.

Sidric presses his forehead against Deux's chest, listening for his heartbeat. Holding onto this one perfect moment—before the chaos resumes.

Then, they're running.

Sidric grips the briefcase in his right hand and Deux's fingers in his left. The hallway erupts into chaos, security guards closing in. Deux lashes his arm forward, sending an electric wave barreling toward them. The guards fly backward, slamming into the walls like dominoes. The entire building remains in darkness. They weave through the confusion, their glow their only guide.

Deux retraces their steps, leading them toward the main hall. The crowd evacuates sluggishly, murmuring about a "fire drill." He pushes forward, squeezing Sidric's hand three times. *We made it out.*

Sidric gets the signal, but his eyes still dart around the crowd, paranoia creeping in. Anyone could be watching. Anyone could be after them.

Finally, they burst outside.

The night air is crisp as they sprint toward a bus stop near the entrance. Just as they reach it, a bus hisses to a stop. They hop on, sliding into the back seat.

Heart pounding, Sidric turns to look at Deux. The glow on his arms has started to fade, but somehow, he looks even more alive.

"What the hell just happened?" Sidric whispers to Deux, replaying everything in his mind. "You're a badass, Deux. You saved us."

"Let's get some food. I think I'm about to faint," Deux sighs, pressing a hand over his heart.

"On it," Sidric says, pulling out his phone. "Olive Garden. We get off at the next stop and walk five minutes."

They step off the bus, and Deux's breathing gradually steadies. Sidric clutches the briefcase so tightly that his knuckles turn red. Once inside, they find a booth in the back. Deux orders a Pepsi with ice and a slice of lemon. Sidric gets the same.

"Okay, so what the heck just happened?" Sidric asks in a hushed voice. "Oh! Almost forgot—I grabbed this, by the way." He lifts the briefcase onto the table, finally relaxing his grip and stretching his fingers.

"Sid! Now who's the badass?! Let me see." Deux reaches for the briefcase, eyes gleaming with curiosity.

Sidric grins like a kid getting praised for finishing all his vegetables. He pulls out his phone, trying to play it cool—until panic flashes across his face.

"Holy crap!" he blurts out just as the waiter sets their drinks down, nearly knocking one over. The waiter rolls his eyes and walks away.

"Deux, listen to this," Sidric says, reading from his phone. "'Nini Lopez made a surprise appearance today at the RainforesTec Summit. She announced her new partnership with RainforesTec and her plans to stop covering LGBTQ+ issues on her social media accounts, stating that she aims to educate her young viewers on better ways to embrace their youth.'

He looks up, eyes wide. "You were right!"

"Show me." Deux grabs the phone and scans the article. "Okay, when we were in the vent, I saw a bunch of photos of queer creators—Nate, Andre, Nini—literally everyone. But Nini's was grayed out, and it said 'DEACTIVATED.'"

"Like what? Deactivating their gayness?" Sidric scoffs, but then a realization strikes. "Oh my God! 'Project Gamma'—this is it. They want queer people gone. Nate and Andre are next!"

Deux takes a sip of his Pepsi, trying to wrap his head around it. "I'm telling you, I saw Meli go back to herself, then she was deactivated right in front of me. Think about all the people who have suddenly 'come out' as straight lately. What if it really is all coming straight from those in control at RainforesTec? Has this been the companies end game all along?"

He swirls the ice cubes in his drink, lost in thought. "What if it's not just about erasing queer people? What if they're making everyone homophobic too?"

Sidric frowns. "Is that even possible? How could they alter someone's brain and change who they are?"

They exchange a look, one that says, this is insane... but is it really that far-fetched? RainforesTec is everywhere and has been for the past 50 years.

Deux digs through the briefcase, shuffling through mostly useless papers and receipts—until his fingers close around a phone.

"Looks like we found something," he says, holding it up.

"Quick! Put it on airplane mode!" Sidric yelps, snatching it from him. "We don't want them tracking us to an Olive Garden. I refuse to die before I get my breadsticks." He hands the phone back to Deux.

"We could just destroy it. It's useless without a passcode," Deux mutters, rubbing his temples. "Every time we get close to figuring this out, something knocks us back down."

Sidric suddenly straightens. "Wait! I might know someone who can help." He pulls out his phone and fires off a text.

SIDRIC—
Hey beech. How soon can you get to Washington? We need you.

19

mawma has landed

Naya began her 9-5 working journey at the age of 14, taking on the role of a cashier assistant at a local grocery store. Her innate talent for connecting with people quickly propelled her into a managerial position at the same store within just a year. Despite her exceptional ability to win people over, Naya grappled with restlessness and boredom, resulting in her frequently changing jobs. Over the years, she dabbled in various roles, including coffee barista, pet groomer, hair stylist, and most recently, a phone repair technician.

Sidric had heard rumors about Naya's remarkable skills in repairing phones and her excellence in hacking into secured systems. While Naya wraps up a client onboarding for her new management company, MaNaya Corp, Sidric shoots her a text. Luckily, she is now her own boss, so she promptly gives herself the week off and books a flight to Washington DC to visit her friends. She packs only the essentials and makes her way to the airport.

Sidric

After a few hours and some edibles, Naya disembarks from the plane, a large blanket draped around her and a pair of large sunglasses. Sidric and Deux eagerly await for her at the baggage claim, this time they are wearing matching green wigs to remain anonymous. As soon as they spot her descending the stairs, Naya enthusiastically proclaims, "Mawma has landed!" They rush forward to welcome her with open arms.

"I can't believe you made the trip all the way here!" Sidric exclaims, his voice full of enthusiasm. Deep down, though, he isn't surprised—Naya would fly to the moon if any of her friends needed her there.

"No problem at all! I've always wanted to see the White House. Plus, I'm a business owner now," Naya says with a proud smirk. "But more importantly, why are we sporting the green hair?"

"Oh, we have a lot to catch you up on," Deux adds, grabbing her carry-on. "Is this all you packed?"

"Yep. I'm not like you guys. As long as I have clean undies, I'm good," she laughs.

Deux calls a car to take them back to the hotel. A RainforesTec driverless cab pulls up, its sleek, silver exterior flashing the company's signature silver logo. Sidric and Deux exchange uncertain glances. Deux hesitates, hand hovering over the door handle.

Naya, oblivious to their nerves, reaches out to pull it open. "Let's go, I'm starving—"

"Wait," Deux interrupts, stopping her. "Let me just order a regular taxi instead. I'd rather not use RainforesTec's services right now." His voice wavers slightly.

"Good luck avoiding RainforesTec," Naya replies with a shrug. "Did you hear about the brain chip they're launching next fall? It's wild! Supposedly, it'll replace phones, computers, tablets—everything."

"I mean, that's absurd. Who's actually going to support a tech company selling brain chips?" Sidric laughs nervously, knowing full well that most people already would.

"I only found out from Nate and Andre. They just posted about partnering with them for the launch." Naya pulls out her phone, showing them the post. "They must be getting a fat paycheck for this."

"Shit! Sid, look at their wrists!" Deux points at the screen. "They're both wearing the Pride smartwatches!"

"Wait... have Nate and Andre come out already?" Sidric asks, suddenly uneasy.

"Come out?" Naya gives them a bewildered look. "They've been out for years. Their whole brand is being a gay remodeling couple. Also—look what I managed to get after OnlineCon!" She pulls out a brand-new smartwatch, still in its box. "Mawma's on brand with y'all!"

Sidric's eyes widen to almost his entire face. Slowly, he turns to look at Deux. They lock eyes. Horror sets in.

Without warning, Sidric lets out a sharp scream and lunges for the box. Naya yelps as they wrestle over it.

"Sid! What the hell?!"

Deux watches, stressed, as they tug back and forth. Finally, Sidric snatches the box out of her hands and hurls it across the street.

"SID! NO!" Naya screams.

She starts to run after it, but Deux holds her back.

The box bounces off the hood of a speeding car and lands on the sidewalk. Naya sighs in relief—until a family rushing to catch their flight barrels through. The youngest kid, oblivious, kicks the box straight into the street.

A shuttle bus runs over it immediately. Pieces of the smartwatch fly in all directions, some landing at their feet.

A long silence follows.

Naya stands frozen in disbelief. Deux exhales, rubbing his temple.

"Okay," Deux says finally. "There's a lot we need to fill you in on."

A cab pulls up, and to their surprise, an elderly woman—probably in her eighties—steps out to open the door for them. She's dressed in a crocheted top paired with khakis, looking more like someone's sweet grandmother than a driver.

They pile into the car and waste no time catching Naya up on everything—how they found the bald man's creepy lair, how they witnessed Nini Lopez being 'deactivated,' how they were chased through the halls, and how Deux's powers saved them.

For the first time in her life, Naya is speechless.

"So, earlier when you asked if Nate and Andre had 'come out'... you meant as straight?" she finally says, processing it all. "I guess I forgive you for trashing my first-ever smartwatch."

"Yes! It all adds up," Sidric insists. "Think about how RainforesTec has been aggressively pushing their technology, while at the same time, queer people have been vanishing—little by little. Everyone's suddenly turning into pathetic homophobes out of nowhere."

Naya glances at Sidric, then at Deux, her eyes narrowing at their hands, both covered in golden stains.

"Wait... so why did it make you two radioactive instead of straight?" she asks.

"I don't know," Deux admits. "We were making out, and then Sid spilled—"

"FIVELOKO!" Both Deux and Sidric exclaim at the same time.

Naya chuckles. "Look, I'm never one to say no, but I can't drink FiveLoko anymore—not after that music festival where I somehow ended up onstage and thought it'd be a good idea to crowd dive. Nobody caught me."

"No," Deux laughs, "we're saying we were drinking FiveLoko that night, and it spilled all over the smartwatch. It must've short-circuited and electrocuted us."

"Something in the drink must have mixed with the chips they put in the watches," Sidric adds, thinking aloud. "That has to be it. But why did I get affected too? I wasn't even wearing one."

Naya raises an eyebrow. "Sid, weren't you full-on making out with Deux at the time? It was probably like an electric current—like, you two were connected by your lips." She smirks. "That's what you get for being a hoe."

Even in the middle of a crisis, she never misses an opportunity to roast Sidric.

Then, something clicks. She leans in, staring at their arms. "Wait… FiveLoko!"

Sidric groans. "Yes, Naya, we just said that."

"No, look!" Naya points at their skin. "These aren't vitiligo or moles. It looks like… splattered drink stains. The FiveLoko didn't just shock you. It literally marked you."

They exchange glances, realizing that everything is falling into place. However, as the pieces of the puzzle fit together, they uncover even more missing elements. Sidric is deeply concerned about what lies ahead. The driver pulls up to the hotel, and just before they step out, she turns back to them and says, "Whatever is going on with you kids, don't let it dim your colors!" She winks at them.

Inside their hotel room, Naya sits cross-legged on the bed, her fingers flying over the phone's screen as she tries to hack into it. Sidric and Deux pace the room, restless. What started as a search for answers about their newfound electric powers has shifted into something bigger. Their powers are just a side effect—the real problem is RainforesTec. If they don't act fast, the company will turn everyone into straight, homophobic zombies.

"Hypothetically," Naya says, breaking the tense silence, "if someone wore the smartwatch, do we know how long it takes for it to infiltrate their brain?"

Deux shrugs. "I wore mine for at least a few hours and didn't notice anything different. If anything, I was acting extra gay—considering what we were doing." He throws a knowing glance at Sidric.

Sidric turns red.

Naya smirks but stays focused. "I wonder how long Nate and Andre have been wearing theirs. Maybe they can tell us how they feel."

Sidric unlocks his phone. "Yeah, but how do you ask someone if they still feel gay without making it weird?"

As soon as he opens Nate's profile, his eyes widen. "We have our answer!" he shouts, holding up his phone.

On the screen is a breakup announcement photo.

Dear followers and friends,

Nate and I have been together for many many years. It's made us realize that even though we thought we were in love with each other we have also been hiding parts of who we really are. We confused a good platonic friendship with love. We have decided to end this romantic relationship. We will still be in each other's lives and post together, but as friends and only that. We ask you all to take a look in the mirror and find out who you really are, make sure the media is not making you someone you are not.

However, this brings an exciting opportunity, our new partnership with RainforesTec will begin with a new webseries called "Straightening Up Our Lives!" be on the lookout for more info!

Nate & Andre

#breakup #breakingup #StraighteningUpOurLives #Only-Homies

"Okay, I know this is messed up, but the post is still giving off major twink vibes," Naya cackles. "Whoever is behind this is probably a little fruity too."

"Whatever it is, it ends now." Deux's tone is firm, his expression serious. "I'm done watching everyone around me get controlled by these trash humans. Naya, hack into that phone. Sid, go to the store and get some FiveLokos—the gold flavor. I'm getting a smartwatch. We're breaking this shit apart and figuring it out tonight."

"Gee, if only we already had a smartwatch. Oh wait! You threw it in front of a bus, Sid," Naya teases.

"Sorry, bestie," Sidric giggles.

Sidric steals a glance at Deux. There's something different about him right now—the confidence, the determination. It sends shivers down Sidric's spine, but he shakes off the feeling, refocusing.

"Okay, boss!" he teases, throwing a playful wink before heading for the door.

"Wait!" Deux grabs his arm, pulling him in for a kiss. "Be safe, baby boy."

Sidric barely manages to close the door before leaning against it, taking a deep breath. His heart pounds as he gathers himself, then heads out to get the FiveLokos.

Hours later, they all reconvene in the hotel room. Sidric returns first, finding Naya sitting on the bed, nearly done dismantling the phone. Pieces of hardware are scattered across the comforter as she methodically reassembles it.

"Hey, baby boy," she teases without looking up.

"Shut up," Sidric groans, flopping onto the bed beside her. "I almost died when he said that."

Naya smirks. "Things seem to be going well between you two. A bit fast, but you're clearly into each other."

Sidric hesitates for a moment before answering. "I know it seems fast, but... I don't know, with everything going on, it's like I've been forced to see parts of him that would usually take years to uncover. That night... something sparked. I can feel how he feels, and it's weird to explain." He sighs, running a hand through his hair.

"Gays are turning straight. FiveLoko saved your brain. I think we're past weird at this point."

Sidric lets out a small laugh but quickly grows serious again. "I'm just scared. It feels like something bad could happen at any moment—like I could lose him, or this could all get ruined. I've never had someone care about me the way he does. What if I mess it up?"

Naya pauses her work, turning to face him. "The worst part of love is knowing you can lose it. But the best part? You have it now. You have this moment. Don't waste it worrying about what's coming, there's always going to be something. Today, it's you guys being radioactive gays. Tomorrow, it'll be defeating an evil trillionaire trying to brainwash the world. And the next day? Who knows! All you can do is react, keep the people you love close, and fight for them."

Sidric sits with her words, letting them settle in. Being present has never been his strong suit; he's always thinking ahead, trying to control what comes next. But maybe, just this once, he can let himself live in the moment.

He leans his head on Naya's shoulder. "Ugh, Naya, I don't know what I'd do without you." He smirks. "In the wise words of Lizzo: 'I love you, bitch.'"

"I love you too, I guess," she replies, plugging the phone into her laptop. The screen flashes to life.

"And we are in!"

The laptop screen displays a progress bar as files download from the phone. Sidric leans in, marveling at the sheer badassery of the situation—but even more at Naya's hacking skills. Just as the progress

184

bar hits 100%, the door swings open, and Deux walks in carrying a sleek black bag embossed with a silver raincloud.

"I don't want to look at my bank account for a while," he sighs, dropping onto the bed, his knee brushing against Sid's. "But we got the latest smartwatch. How's it going here?"

"We got everything. Texts, emails, photos, videos, the whole digital diary," Naya says, eyes still on the screen. "Where do we start?"

Deux takes the laptop and clicks into the emails. He types *smartwatch* into the search bar, and thousands of results flood the screen—endless discussions on future launches and new designs. No way they're reading all that. He narrows the search: *pride + smartwatch*. Fewer results, but still not enough.

Sidric watches, sensing they're on the edge of something big, though he has no idea what. Then, like a light bulb flicking on, he snatches the laptop. "I know!" He quickly types *Project Gamma*.

Only 31 emails. *Jackpot.*

They click on the first one, sent about a month ago.

PROJECT GAMMA: TRIAL SUBJECT DEACTIVATED
Good day, Mr. Delano,

I am pleased to inform you that the latest trial subject has been successfully deactivated ahead of schedule. The subject will remain in our custody.

The final prototype is approved and ready for release. We will continue to monitor the subject and share any findings. Attached is the most recent report.

Please inform Mr. Bizous about Project Gamma's timeline update.

Best regards,
Heath Ubel
RainforesTec Labs Supervisor

Silence fills the room as they stare at the laptop screen, dread sinking in. Sidric's finger glides across the mouse pad toward the attachment labeled **Project Gamma VI.** He clicks it open—a 60-page document.

The first page displays a close-up photo of a child, no older than six or seven. Sidric scrolls down, but Naya suddenly stops him.

"Wait!" she exclaims.

Pulling out her phone, she frantically scrolls through her texts with Sidric, all the way back to the day he flew to OnlineCon. She holds her phone next to the photo on the screen. It's the same child.

"Tell me this is not the same kid!"

The flashback slams into Sidric. He remembers *everything.* The child, the creepy-suited woman, the way the kid sobbed, begging to go home. And the photo he'd sent Naya right before takeoff? The kid was looking *directly* at the camera.

"That's the kid!" Sidric points at the screen, his voice rising. "They were *literally crying* at the gate! What the fuck!"

Deux yanks the laptop closer and scrolls further. His eyes dart across the page, then he reads aloud:

"Entry 1: Subject portrays masculine characteristics. Claims to be in the wrong body. Chip has been activated and is ready for introduction."

He skips ahead.

"Entry 4: After a week of wearing the chip, the subject has begun to portray accurate feminine characteristics."

A heavy silence settles between them.

"What the *fuck,*" Deux says, voice sharp. "They're literally altering this poor kid's brain."

Sidric swallows the disgust rising in his throat. "Is there any info on the chip? How the hell are they making a *smartwatch* do this?"

Deux clicks to another section and pulls up a diagram of the smartwatch, signals extending to different parts of its hardware. He taps the screen.

"It *is* the smartwatch. But look—this says it's **Model 906.** That means there were previous models."

"Which could explain why people have been randomly coming out as straight over the years," Naya mutters. "Wouldn't be shocked if they've been testing this for a while. But my concern is—how do we get this kid out? Is this enough evidence to get the FBI involved?"

"RainforesTec *funds* the FBI," Sidric sighs. "And the cops. They literally have RoboCops on their payroll. Who the hell do we even *go* to?"

Both he and Naya turn to Deux.

Deux feels the weight of their stares. The pressure. The *urgency*. But beneath all of it, he also feels something else—something he's always believed. That none of this is coincidence. That every single thing that's happened has led them *right here.*

"Listen," Deux says, his voice steady. "'Project Gamma' was meant to stay buried. RainforesTec parades around like they're pro-LGBTQ+—they push their Pride Smartwatch, collab with queer artists, sponsor our creators. But in reality? They want us *gone.* They want to erase us completely."

Sidric's heart pounds, but Deux keeps going, his presence commanding, unwavering.

"But that's not gonna happen. Because they don't know who they're messing with."

Sidric watches as fear transforms into something else—determination. Power.

"Before I met you, Sid, I had this *feeling* I needed to go to L.A. That something big was gonna happen. And guess what? It *did.* We met, and my whole world changed. Now, we have these powers—and a reason to use them." Deux looks at both of them, eyes blazing. "Let's blow these fuckers up."

Naya stands, offering a slow clap.

"If this whole superhero thing doesn't pan out, you *definitely* have a future as an inspirational speaker. I'm tearing up, bro."

Deux smirks. "Are you guys with me?" He places his hand in the center.

Naya immediately stacks hers on top. They both look at Sidric.

Sidric's heart races. He wants to believe he's ready. But the doubt lingers—superheroes are supposed to be *strong,* supposed to be fearless. He's... just Sidric.

But then he meets Deux's gaze. Deux mouths, *you got this,* then winks.

Sidric exhales sharply. Then, he places his hand on top.

"Let's do it."

An *electric shock* bursts between their palms, sending Naya flying off the bed.

"Okay," she groans, hair frizzed up like she stuck a fork in an outlet. "No more tasing me, please."

Deux and Sidric exchange a look—and burst into laughter.

But before they can revel in their victory, the laptop *dings.*

A new window pops up. A single notification.

TRACKING IN PROGRESS.

Sidric's stomach drops. "You guys... I think they're coming."

He turns the screen. Deux's expression darkens—he slams the laptop shut.

They scramble. Shoving everything into their bags, yanking on their jackets. Less than five minutes later, they're *bolting* out the door toward the elevators.

Naya steals a glance out the window—and her breath hitches.

Black vans. Pulling into the lobby.

Naya's voice cracks. "They're here."

20

getaway caR

"It's not my day today!" Naya screams as they leap into the elevator.

Deux slams the Garage button and sends an electric jolt through the system. The elevator plummets, dropping faster than the Tower of Terror at Disney—Naya's least favorite ride.

The moment the doors slide open, she shoves her way out, hand clamped over her mouth. As soon as her feet hit the ground, she hurls.

Deux barely reacts, already sprinting ahead, the glow from his hand markings casting eerie light over the garage. He scans the rows of cars, searching for something stealable.

Nothing but RainforesTec electric cars. If we steal any of these we'll be tracked in seconds.

He pushes deeper into the garage, eyes locking onto a 1999 red Mustang parked in the back.

Perfect.

Elbow to the window. CRASH. He climbs in, rubbing his index finger against his thumb before sending a precise shock into the keyhole. The engine roars to life.

Deux whips the car around and speeds toward the elevator entrance. Sidric stumbles in first, he brings in all the bags with him. Naya barely done wiping her mouth when headlights flare behind them.

The RainforesTec vans barrel toward them. Naya jumps in the back. They're about to be rammed.

"Let's go!" Sid screams putting the seat belt on.

Deux pushes his foot down on the gas and speeds out, breaking off the exit signs on their way out of the parking lot.

The red mustang flies past traffic lights and intersections.

"Where are we going?!" Naya screams.

"Anywhere we can escape!" Deux replies, speeding through the highway. "Canada maybe? That's out of RainforesTec's jurisdiction."

"That's like nine hours away! They'll get us by then," Sid replies.

"We can hide out in a cheap motel, wait for things to die down. You guys have your wig collection," Naya says.

"Will things die down though?" Deux asks, "Also, the smartwatch launches at the end of the week. We need to stop them before then. I have an idea!"

After thirty minutes of reckless speeding, Deux glances at the rear view mirror. Finally, no RainforesTec vans in sight. He exhales, taking a sharp left turn and heading toward the airport.

In the passenger seat, Sidric stares blankly out the window, lost in thought. In the back, Naya remains silent, occasionally putting her head out the window to spit out.

Deux grips the wheel, feeling the last of his sweat dry against his palms. His breathing slows, and for the first time all day, he lets a smirk creep onto his face.

We're actually doing this. We're taking down RainforesTec. Their homophobic, transphobic empire will cease to exist.

The adrenaline rush isn't just fear anymore; it's exhilarating. He glances at Naya in the rear view, then over at Sidric beside him. Running from the law feels a little too good.

He presses the gas, sending them flying down the empty streets when suddenly a police siren wails behind them.

Red and blue lights flash.

"Shit... Shit!" Deux slaps the steering wheel. "Do I stop? Or just say *fuck it?*"

Naya twists in her seat, peering through the back window. "It's not a RoboCop, just a regular human cop. We might be able to sweet-talk him," she reasons. "Probably best not to draw more attention to ourselves."

Before Deux can respond—

BANG.

A shot fires.

The zero-speed gun locks onto their car, instantly hacking into the Mustang's system. Within seconds, the engine sputters.

Their speed drops to zero.

The Mustang jerks to a stop.

They're trapped.

Gasps of suspense escape the three runaways as they reel from the sudden turn of events. Sidric and Naya exchange wary glances, their fear reflected in each other's eyes.

Outside, the officer steps out of his car. His silhouette stretches across the pavement, his presence heavy as he approaches the immobilized Mustang with slow, deliberate steps.

"Evening, son. License and registration?" His voice is calm but firm. Dark sunglasses cover almost half of his face, making it impossible to read his expression.

"Uh, sure." Deux quickly hands over his license. "This is a rental, so I'll have to dig around for the other papers. One sec." He glances at Sidric, who immediately starts pretending to search for the documents.

"Wait—don't move!" The officer's voice sharpens slightly.

Deux freezes, his mouth going dry as his brain scrambles for an excuse. *Think, think, think.*

"No way!" The officer's tone shifts completely. "Deux?! I love your videos, man! My son just came out to us, and you really helped him. He's been showing us your content nonstop."

Deux blinks, caught completely off guard. A lump forms in his throat. It's not every day he hears that he's made an actual impact on someone's life.

"Aww, that's amazing!" He fights the tears threatening to form. "I'm really glad my videos could help, but honestly, he did all the work himself." His hands grip the steering wheel so tightly that his palms are slick with sweat.

The officer nods, his smile warm. "Yeah, he's a great kid." He pauses before glancing at the car. "Listen, I'll let you guys go. Just get that tail light fixed, okay? And slow it down, whatever you've got going on, it's not worth breaking the law."

He taps a small rainbow pin on his uniform before stepping back toward his vehicle. "Drive safe, and keep doing what you're doing."

The second his car door closes, Deux releases the wheel and turns toward Sidric and Naya.

"I almost shit myself," he exhales.

"Same, D. I'm so glad you're an online gay icon," Naya says, tapping his shoulder. "I feel like this was a sign. We *are* going to take these fuckers down."

As they drive toward the airport, a heavy silence settles over them. The weight of everything ahead—what they've uncovered, what they're about to do—presses down. With every passing minute, Deux notices the quiet stretch longer. They're all lost in their thoughts, questioning if they're strong enough to stand against RainforesTec, if they're brave enough to risk their own lives to save the world's queer population.

Sidric finally breaks the silence. "Mind if we play some tunes? I feel like we all need a little mental break." He fiddles with the car's radio. "Any requests? I haven't used one of these in forever."

Before anyone can answer, *Bitch* by Meredith Brooks blasts from the speakers.

A perfectly timed anthem for when the world is against you, and all you can do is be your fabulous self.

Sidric rolls down the window and starts singing, nudging Deux, teasing a smile from the corner of his lips. Seconds later, Deux joins him in the chorus.

"Come on, Naya!" Deux yells to the backseat as he sings out.

Seconds later, Naya belts out the end of the chorus, finally giving in.

For the next three minutes, nothing else matters. The world fades away into the sunset, leaving only their friendship, the wind in their hair, and Meredith Brooks.

As they pull into the airport parking lot, reality creeps back in. Deux switches to his serious voice, cutting the music and laying out his plan.

"Here's what we're gonna do. We find the next flight to Las Vegas."

Naya scoffs. "Really, Deux? We're in the middle of a crisis, and you wanna gamble? Maybe find some strippers?"

Deux smirks. "Vegas is where RainforesTec headquarters is. It says so on the back of the smartwatch box."

"Oh." Naya leans forward between the seats. "Okay, but what's the plan once we get there?"

"We know there are people working against RainforesTec from the inside." Deux pulls out the cryptic note they received in D.C. and hands it to her. "We find them. Team up. Sneak in. Gather more proof. And then?" He glances at Sidric. "Sid and I use our powers to blow the whole place up."

Naya raises a brow. "And we're just supposed to trust whoever wrote this weird-ass letter?"

"I think so," Sidric says. "We have to trust *something*. Follow our gut."

Deux parks the car. Naya hops out, heading toward the airport entrance with him. Sidric lingers at the trunk, pulling out their suitcases. Not even a world crisis is going to stop him from overpacking.

Deux looks back and snorts. "You're something else, Sid."

Sidric struggles under the weight of his luggage but grins. "You'll thank me when you save the world in clean underwear and deodorant."

Deux shakes his head, chuckling. "We'll save the world together."

He grabs one of the suitcases with one hand—then takes Sidric's hand with the other.

The next flight to Las Vegas is in one hour—just enough time to check their bags and get through security.

As they pass through the security checkpoint, a sharp *ding* sounds. Naya glances down reaching for the phone in her pocket, its screen now displaying an ominous orange wheel, spinning endlessly. She places it on the X-ray belt and steps through the scanner, forcing herself to act normal. Once past, Sidric suddenly bolts toward the bathroom, leaving Naya with the only chance she'll get to break away.

"Deux," she whispers, pulling him aside. She holds up the phone. "They're tracking us."

His stomach drops. "Wait—we can think of something—"

"They could be here any second." Her voice is firm, but her hands tremble. "Let me lead them away. If they think I'm with you, you'll never make it to Vegas. This way, they stay on me while you and Sid get on that plane." She takes a breath. "Just... make sure Sid gets on the plane."

Deux's throat tightens. He understands. Of course he does. It doesn't make it any easier.

Without thinking, he pulls Naya into a tight hug. "We'll see you soon. If they get close, just ditch the phone and run." He reaches into his carry-on and pulls out an orange wig, fixing it over her dark hair.

She sniffles. "Love you, Deux."

"Love you too, Naya." He meets her eyes, the weight of unspoken words between them. "Keep yourself safe, okay?"

She nods, then turns and disappears into the crowd.

A moment later, Sidric comes jogging back, looking thoroughly annoyed. "I hate cleaning robots. One of those little pervs kept trying to open the stall while I was in there." He shakes his head. "Where's Naya?"

Deux swallows hard. *What do I say? She's getting a snack? She went to the bathroom? She's running for her life?*

He exhales. "Listen, Sid… Naya had to go."

Sidric stops. "What? Go where?"

"She had the RainforesTec phone. It was being tracked. She left to buy us time to get away."

Sidric's face twists. "What?! What if they get her?!" His voice rises in panic. "Why would she just leave like that? She could've waited! We could've figured something out together."

Deux reaches for Sidric's hand, gripping it tightly. "She's going to be okay." He forces a reassuring smile. "If it were anyone else, I'd be worried. But Naya?" He shakes his head. "The world is hers."

Sidric's fingers tighten around his. He doesn't speak, but Deux can feel his worry.

And so they make their way to their flight, holding onto each other, as the world closes in.

They board the plane and settle into their seats. Deux takes the window, and Sidric slides into the middle, Naya's seat. He shifts uncomfortably before finally settling in. Deux stretches out his long legs, adjusting a few times until he finds a tolerable position.

195

As the plane begins take-off, Deux reaches for Sidric's hand, squeezing it three times. He doesn't let go until they're in the air.

"Well…" Sidric exhales, turning to Deux. "We've got a few hours to kill. Should we play a game or something?"

"I was ready to pass out until we landed, to be honest."

"Oh, come on!" Sidric nudges him. "It's our first flight together." He tilts his head, giving Deux his best puppy-dog eyes, an expression so devastatingly cute, it's nearly impossible to resist. "We could play Truth or Dare?"

Deux raises a brow. "Isn't that a drinking game?"

"I thought you'd say that." Sidric grins and reaches into his backpack, pulling out a can of FiveLoko. "The lady at security almost took it away, but I told her I needed it for my panic attacks."

Deux shakes his head with a laugh. "I cannot with you." He takes the can and pops it open. "Alright, let's see how much of a fuckboy you really are. Truth or dare?"

Sidric smirks. "Truth."

The sunlight streaming through the window frames Sid's face in a golden glow, making his brown eyes even more majestic. Deux takes a slow breath, admiring him.

"How many people have you slept with?" Deux asks, lips quirking into a teasing smile.

Sidric chuckles, taking a quick sip before answering. "Starting off strong. Maybe… six or eight? I don't really keep count." He lies, it's exactly seven. "What about you?"

Deux narrows his eyes. "That's cheating. You have to ask *truth or dare*."

Sidric rolls his eyes. "Okay, fine. Truth or dare?"

"Dare." Deux grins, something mischievous flickering behind his eyes.

"Really?" Sidric hums, pretending to think. "Okay. I dare you to chug that for five seconds… and then tell me how many people you've slept with."

Deux lets out a low laugh. "Ah, you're not playing games." He tilts his head back and chugs for the full five seconds, the rush of alcohol making his veins buzz. Wiping his mouth with the back of his hand, he exhales. "Ten to thirteen. Don't really keep count." He winks at Sidric.

"Wow," he scoffs. "And I'm the fuckboy? But I've been your best time, right?"

Deux smirks, taking another slow sip. "Maybe." He feels his body start to heat up. He forces himself to look out the window before things escalate in his pants.

Sidric grins, shifting in his seat. "Truth or dare?"

"Truth."

The alcohol is definitely kicking in. Maybe it's the altitude, maybe it's Deux's powers, but instead of feeling sluggish or out of control, he feels *good*. His whole body hums with energy, an intoxicating mix of adrenaline and euphoria.

He turns to Sidric, his gaze steady. "What do you think about dating someone who lives, I don't know… *a thousand miles away*?"

The question catches Sidric completely off guard.

His eyes widen slightly, and for a split second, Deux sees Sidric panic. He takes a slow sip, then exhales.

"Depends on *who* it was, I guess." He shoots Deux a playful, teasing grin before taking another sip of FiveLoko.

Deux chuckles, shaking his head. But the warmth in his eyes lingers. "Good to know. Good to know."

As Sidric lifts the can to finish the last drop of FiveLoko, sunlight reflects off the sticky residue on the metal, sending a sharp glare directly into Deux's eyes. He flinches, momentarily blinded. But as his vision adjusts, his breath catches in his throat.

197

Sid's hands are glowing.

Not just reflecting light—glowing. A faint, golden hue pulses beneath his skin.

Deux glances down at his own arms. The same soft glow radiates from his veins.

Heart pounding, he jerks up so fast that his head smacks against the overhead bin with a *thud*.

"Oh my God, are you good?" Sidric bursts out laughing.

"Yes, I just—" Deux glances down at his hands, flexing his fingers. "I need your help. In the bathroom. Now."

Sidric is too busy laughing at Deux's clumsiness to process what's happening. He shrugs and gets up, using the back of the seats to steady himself—until he notices the glow creeping up his wrists. He stiffens. Quickly, he shoves his hands into his pockets and follows Deux down the aisle.

Deux waits for a moment when no one is looking, then yanks open the lavatory door, shoves Sidric inside, and locks it behind them.

Sidric holds up his hands, his breath hitching. "What the fuck is going on?"

"Breathe. Let me think." Deux grips his shoulders, steadying him.

"How are you asking me to breathe right now? I just chugged half a can of FiveLoko, and I swear I can feel my heart coming out of my ears."

Deux's mind races, connecting the dots. "It's the FiveLoko." His voice is firm, certain. "Think about it. It spilled on the smartwatch, electrocuted us, and somehow gave us these powers. And now that we drank it again, we just added more of whatever made us radioactive in the first place." He exhales sharply. "We're basically supercharged right now."

Sidric blinks. "Shit, you're smart." He glances at his glowing hands. "Okay, so what do we do? Wrap our hands in paper towels or something?" He starts scanning the tiny bathroom in panic.

"No, I think we just wait. It should wear off when the FiveLoko gets out of our systems."

Sidric nods but keeps pacing in the tiny space, breathing fast. "Okay, okay, yeah, yeah... I just—fuck, I need a distraction. I can feel myself starting to freak out, and I really don't wanna set this plane on fire. Oh shit. I just said 'fire' on a plane. Am I even allowed to say that? Oh no. Bomb. That's the forbidden word, right? Oh my God, I just said that too—"

Deux shuts him up by pressing their lips together.

For a moment, Sidric freezes. Then, the tension in his body melts, his breath slowing as he sinks into the kiss. It lasts only a few seconds, but when Deux pulls away, Sidric is blinking at him, dazed.

Deux smirks. "Truth or dare?"

Sidric exhales sharply. "Uh... truth." His voice is slightly breathless.

Deux leans in, his lips brushing against Sidric's ear. "Have you ever done it on a plane?"

Sidric shakes his head.

Deux's fingers skim down his arm, teasing, eyes dark with desire. "Would you like to?"

A shiver runs down Sidric's spine.

The glow of their hands flickers like embers in the dimly lit airplane bathroom. Deux steps closer, cupping Sidric's face, his thumb tracing the curve of his jaw. Their lips hover inches apart, the tension between them electric—literal sparks dancing between their skin.

Sidric exhales shakily, closing the gap. Their mouths collide, slow at first, then hungry. His fingers find their way beneath Deux's shirt, tracing the muscles of his back before pulling the fabric over his head. Deux does the same, their movements hurried but deliberate, as if they're afraid the moment will slip away.

The turbulence rattles the plane, but neither of them care. Hands roam, breaths hitch, bodies press together in perfect sync. Every touch sends waves of static through their veins, making their skin tingle with the energy coursing between them. Sidric gets on his knees and allows Deux's hand to tell him what to do. Then they switch and as Sidric gasps for air the airplane speakers crackle to life.

SEAT BELT SIGNS HAVE BEEN TURNED ON. THERE APPEARS TO BE A THUNDER STORM UP AHEAD. WE WILL BE DIRECTED TO AN ALTERNATE ROUTE TO REACH THE DESTINATION. PLEASE REMAIN SEATED.

They freeze for a second, then burst into breathless laughter. Deux leans against the wall, running a hand through his tousled hair. Sidric, still flushed, shakes his head with a smirk.

"We should… probably get back," Sidric says between deep breaths.

Deux grins, pressing one last lingering kiss to his lips. "Yeah… probably."

They quickly gather themselves, straightening their clothes before slipping back into the aisle, shoulders bumping, cheeks warm, fingers itching to intertwine.

They plan to make their way back to their seats at different times to avoid drawing suspicion. Deux's face is flushed, his rosy cheeks betraying him by revealing what had happened just moments ago. However, both of their hands have stopped shimmering.

On his way to his seat, he passes a woman with light gray hair tied up in a bun. She gives him a knowing head shake, her lips pursed. She knows. Seconds later, Sidric walks out and accidentally bumps into the same woman. She gives him the same look.

"That was amazing," Deux sighs as he sinks into his seat.

"Now you can take a nap," Sidric smirks.

Deux makes himself comfortable, using his hoodie as a pillow against the window. He shifts a few times, trying to find a position where his legs don't feel like bent-up noodles. Just as he's about to drift off, he feels Sidric's head lean against his shoulder.

It catches him by surprise. Somehow, this small gesture—Sidric resting against him—feels far more intimate than what had just happened in the bathroom. He turns slightly, glancing down at Sidric, who already has his eyes closed.

Leaning in, Deux presses his face against Sidric's hair, feeling the warmth radiating from him. Taking care of someone is a new feeling for Deux, and so far, he loves it. He reaches out, gently clasping Sid's hand, and lets the steady vibrations of the plane lull him to sleep.

Sidric

Screams wake Sidric up. His eyes take a moment to adjust but then the plane jolts suddenly bringing him fully into the moment. Everyone in the cabin is restless as the pilot wrestles with the controls, trying desperately to keep the plane steady. Sidric shakes Deux abruptly, trying to wake him up. In the list of Sidric's biggest fears, a plane crash is number two right after losing his Taylor Swift Vinyl collection. His heart starts pounding loudly adding to the chaos.

"What is going on?" Deux wakes up

"I think the plane is going down." Sid is looking around desperately, sweat beads on his forehead.

The plane flickers in and out of power, swerving violently from side to side and lurching up and down. Overhead bins pop open, sending passengers' bags crashing onto the seats below. The gray-haired woman gets hit in the process. Oxygen masks drop as the plane begins a slow, terrifying descent.

Deux looks out his window, watching clouds rush past. Amidst

201

them, he spots two RainforesTec drones flying away.

The engines sputter, cutting in and out. The plane is plummeting.

"Sid! This is RainforesTec's doing. We have to do something," he says.

"What can we do?! We've only tased a few people! We've never powered up a whole-ass plane!" Sid tries to whisper, but between the turbulence and the panicked screams, his voice comes out loud.

"I powered up a car earlier. It can't be that different."

Deux grabs Sidric's hands and closes his eyes. "Focus on the energy, Sid."

Focus. Focus. Focus.

Sidric feels the energy building between their palms. Slowly, they pull their hands apart, and a glowing orb, crackling with golden electricity, forms in the space between them. It grows, pulsing brighter as they expand the gap.

"On three, we send it to the plane," Deux instructs.

"One."

"Two," they say in unison.

"Three."

They thrust their hands upward, sending the orb flashing toward the plane's systems—only for it to disintegrate on contact. The plane keeps falling.

"We need more power. It has to be bigger," Deux says, standing up. "We need more space between us."

Sidric feels the pressure mount. There's no more hiding, no staying subtle. If they want to keep this flight in the air, they have to go all out.

"Okay. Let's do it."

"Go all the way back," Deux directs. Then he turns to the passengers. "Everyone stay calm! We can help!"

He sprints to the front of the plane as Sidric moves toward the restrooms. Flight attendants scream at him to return to his seat. Confused passengers watch them in shock, convinced they've completely lost it.

Standing just before the cockpit, Deux rubs his hands together, focusing on his breathing. Sparks begin to flicker at his fingertips. Sidric mirrors his movements, trying to replicate the effect. He takes a deep breath, clearing his mind. He thinks back to an hour earlier, in the cramped lavatory, when Deux took charge of his body. That energy, that rush, he lets it fuel him.

Electricity crackles through his veins. Golden light ignites from both of them.

Deux concentrates, feeling the plane's inner workings, its structure, its failing energy. It's like a heartbeat—weak, irregular. He syncs with it.

"You ready, Sid?!" he yells.

The plane is eerily silent now. The panic has been replaced by disbelief. All eyes are on them.

"Uh... one sec," Sidric hesitates. But he doesn't let his doubts dull his power. "I'm ready!" he shouts.

"Follow my lead!"

Deux sends a wave of electricity straight at Sidric, who mimics his movements. The volts collide in midair, forming a brilliant golden orb. It looks like an intricate dance, but it's working. The orb expands. The plane's lights flicker. Then, with a deep, shuddering rumble, the engines roar back to life.

Deux raises his hands above his head. Sidric follows. The orb moves upward—then surges into the walls of the plane, encircling the entire structure

"We're going back up!" a young boy shouts, staring out the window.

The plane, seconds from disaster, begins to stabilize. It soars through the air once more.

The passengers erupt into cheers. Some cry. Others cling to their loved ones. The flight attendants hug each other, overwhelmed with relief.

Deux exhales, grinning. "Now, if all of you could keep this little electricity show a secret, that would be great—"

No one is listening. They're too busy celebrating.

Across the aisle, Deux spots Sidric, his face glowing with triumph. Unable to contain himself, he runs down the narrow space, lifts Sidric by the waist, and kisses him right there in the middle of the plane.

"You did it! I knew you had it in you," Deux whispers, his arms wrapped tightly around him.

"We did it," Sidric corrects, pulling him even closer.

21

two most wanted

Deux

The AirAmericana flight lands safely at Harry Reid International Airport. As the plane taxis to the gate, the pilot gives an emotional speech, expressing his gratitude that everyone is safe. He personally thanks Deux and Sidric before pulling into the parking area.

Passengers line up to exit, pausing to hug Deux and Sidric as they pass. It all feels surreal, but Deux decides to go with the flow. He chuckles at Sidric, who is clearly enjoying the attention, soaking up the moment like a celebrity.

From the window, Deux spots a swarm of press and law enforcement waiting just outside. His stomach drops. *They're onto us.*

"Sid, we can't go out," he says, nodding toward the window.

Sidric takes a quick glance, then immediately ducks under the window. "Oh my god. There are robocops everywhere."

"Follow me." Deux grabs his backpack and pulls Sidric toward the back of the plane, smiling and nodding at passengers as they pass.

Just as they near the rear exit, a high-pitched voice calls out, "Excuse me!"

They turn to see a young flight attendant rushing toward them, her dark brown eyes glistening with tears. "Thank you so much again! This was my first shift as a flight attendant... I thought it was going to be my last, too."

She clutches Deux's hand, her voice full of emotion. "If you ever need flights, discounts, anything—just let me know!"

"Actually," Deux says, flashing a hopeful smile, "we're kind of in a bit of a rut. Nobody else knows about our powers, and, well... out there, there's a crowd of cops and security. I'm pretty sure if they get their hands on us, we'll end up in some lab for the rest of our lives. Is there *any* other way out?"

Her eyes widen. "Uhm..." She tucks a loose braid behind her ear. "You *definitely* can't go through the back exit."

"Oh," Sidric says, disappointed.

"No, I mean they'd see you immediately. Wait! I have an idea." Her face lights up. "Romi! We need you in here!"

A second flight attendant pops her head out from behind the bathroom doors. "What now, Michelle?"

"They need to get out of here *without* being spotted."

Romi gasps. "Are we doing it again?!" she asks excitedly.

"Doing *what* exactly?" Sidric interjects, raising an eyebrow.

"We've done this before! Back when we both worked at Disney World, we had to sneak Chappell in and out of the park. We gave her such a makeover, no one recognized her."

"We're kind of short on materials and time, though," Michelle murmurs, pursing her lips.

"We have wigs!" Deux exclaims.

"*Perfect!*" Romi and Michelle say in unison.

Minutes later, Deux and Sidric step off the plane disguised as AirAmericana flight attendants. They each wear a fitted white button-

206

up tucked into a gray tube skirt, complete with a matching neck scarf and hat. Sidric struts effortlessly down the stairs in his heels, a blonde bob with bangs framing his face. Deux, however, stumbles slightly in his too-small heels, adjusting his black bob wig as he tugs a carry-on behind him.

They leave everything else behind, blending into the sea of people as Romi and Michelle wave from the cockpit window.

"Boys, we're gonna need some clothes from you," Romi teases the pilots with a wink.

As Deux walks past the robocops, he keeps his gaze down, focusing on not tripping. Sidric, a few steps ahead, maintains a steady pace. They weave through the mob undetected and head straight to the pickup area.

"That was *intense!*" Sidric says, wiping sweat from his forehead.

"Sweety, you've got quite a *low* voice," Deux mutters, subtly hinting at Sidric to adjust his tone and stay in character.

"Oh, right," Sidric clears his throat and raises his voice. "Where to now?"

"Romi said her uncle works at the airport. He can give us a ride. He should be here any minute."

They sit on a bench outside the gate, keeping their heads down whenever someone walks by. A few minutes later, a car pulls up, blasting old Kendrick Lamar.

"Ladies! I believe I'm here for you," the driver yells in a raspy voice.

Deux and Sidric exchange glances. Deux raises a sneaky brow, silently reassuring Sid that they can keep up the flight attendant act a little longer. *As long as I don't have to walk in these heels, I could do this all day! I mean, these legs? Made for this. But this foot pain? Absolutely not.*

"Thank you so much for the ride, sir! We had no one else to call," Deux says in his best high-pitched "air attendant" voice.

"No problem at all! Any friend of Romi's is a homie to me." The man grins, shifting gears. "Now, do you pretty ladies have accommodations already? I'd be happy to host you two, just gotta kick my wife to the sofa." He chuckles.

"Oh, we do! We're heading to the *Motel Comfort Zone,*" Sidric squeaks.

"No way! You two are headed out there? Man, I used to go back in the day. *Grady's* was an amazing drag club right in front. I'd get *turnt up!* Spent plenty of nights at that motel."

Years ago, the Nevada desert was flat and endless. Now, thanks to Jacques Bizous' relentless drilling to expand his headquarters, the landscape is a sea of shifting sand dunes stretching for miles. Deux stares out the window, noticing the emptiness, the lack of cars, the lack of buildings, the lack of *life. This is definitely not creepy at all.*

"Alright, ladies, this is it." The driver pulls up to the motel and turns back with a wink. "If you two need a man for anything, you know where to find me."

Sidric giggles as he steps out of the car.

"You are *so* easy, Sid," Deux teases.

"What?! Don't be jealous he wasn't hitting on you!"

A flurry of sand swirls through the air, dusting their skin with a delicate sting. The motel, a relic of forgotten days, stands before them in all its faded glory. Its U-shaped structure houses two floors of rooms, each facing the desolate parking lot. The walls, once vibrant in pastel hues of pink and blue, are now sun-bleached and peeling— a testament to time's relentless wear. Beneath the looming *Motel Comfort Zone* sign, a flickering *Vacancy* light blinks stubbornly, casting an eerie glow against the empty desert backdrop.

Surrounded by rolling sand dunes, the motel feels like an island adrift in an ocean of nothingness. The only other sign of life is a solitary diner across the road, its neon sign flickering weakly against the darkness. With a shared glance, Deux and Sidric head toward the shelter of the motel's entrance, eager to escape the vast, lonesome expanse that stretches behind them.

Inside the check-in office, an old TV hums with static, playing a *RainyDaze News* broadcast. A woman, probably in her late sixties, sits behind a dust-covered front desk, barely glancing up as they walk in.

"Do you have a room available?" Sidric asks. "Two nights, maybe?"

"Sure thing. Cash or card?"

Breaking News.

The news broadcast suddenly cuts in.

Flight AA269 hijacked by cyber-terrorists. The hackers attempted to bring the plane down—until RainforesTec drones arrived just in time to save the passengers.

A grainy video flickers on-screen. Deux and Sidric, their hands crackling with energy, stand at opposite ends of the plane. The footage ends just before they send power back into the aircraft.

There are no reported injuries or fatalities. However, these two dangerous hackers have escaped. They go by the names of Deux Yates and Sidric Alvarado

If spotted report to Homeland Security direct line 808. We will come back with updates.

Deux's heart sinks. *What the fuck?*

"That'll be cash," Sidric says quickly, eager to get out before the woman connects the dots.

"Crazy people out there!" she mutters, handing over a key. "Here you go, Miss."

Sidric swallows his pride and takes it.

"Do you have a phone by any chance?" Deux asks, his pulse quickening. His eyes darken, flickering red.

"We sell disposable smartphones. Ninety-five bucks apiece," she says, nodding toward a small display on the counter.

Deux pulls out the cash and buys one.

"Of course. *Of-fucking-course.* RainforesTec has to frame us as terrorists *right* after we saved all those innocent people," Deux says, following Sidric into the motel room. "No one can actually be dumb enough to fall for this, right?"

As soon as they enter, both of them rip off their wigs.

"We're not in D.C. anymore," Sidric mutters, glancing around the dimly lit room. "I can already feel the spirits of all the people who have consummated their love in this motel."

Deux barely chuckles, turning on his disposable phone and immediately searching his name. The first post that pops up is from a pop culture account, **@CravePopNews.**

After alarming footage of @DeuxYates surfaced from a flight to Las Vegas, all of his accounts have been banned. Guess his five minutes of fame are up.

Attached to the post is a screenshot of his social media profiles, all blanked out.

Account Banned.

Account Deleted.

Account has violated Terms and Conditions.

He gasps. All of his accounts are gone. His heart plummets into a sea of desperation. Every video, every song, everything he had created and shared with the world, erased. The community he had built, the safe space he had nurtured, wiped away in an instant.

"Sid," he croaks, staring at the screen. "They took everything down. Everyone is about to get brainwashed by RainforesTec, and all people will remember about me is that I'm a fucking *terrorist.*" He shoves the phone toward Sidric and collapses onto the bed. His eyes well up, drowning in the wreckage of his dreams.

"Wait—" Sidric yanks him up and moves him to a chair. "The bed looks *extremely* mysterious and used. Let's not."

Deux lets out a weak, humorless chuckle. Sidric grabs the phone, his face darkening as he reads.

"This *can't* be happening," Sidric murmurs, frustration tightening his voice. The weight of the situation presses down on both of them.

"Of course, this is what happens when *every* media outlet is owned by the same evil trillionaire." His hands clench into fists. *"What the fuck?!"* he yells, voice shaking with rage. Deux's mind spirals, his thoughts immediately turning to his family. His stomach twists as he imagines their reaction. *Would they believe the truth, or would they, too, fall for the lies?*

Fingers trembling, he types in his mom's number and initiates a video call. The screen flickers to life, and his sister's tear-streaked face appears. She's huddled in a dark closet, surrounded by coats and jackets, seeking refuge in the tiny, suffocating space.

"Deux, I'm so confused," Atlanta sobs, her voice trembling with fear and uncertainty. "Where are you?"

"Atlanta, listen to me," Deux pleads, desperation lacing his words. "It's all a lie. Sid and I stopped that flight from crashing, I swear! RainforesTec is doing some seriously shady shit. They know we're trying to stop them."

Relief flickers across Atlanta's face, but doubt lingers in her eyes. "I knew something wasn't right... but these agents showed up at the house out of nowhere. They've been here for hours." Her voice trails off as she glances toward the door, anxiety tightening her expression.

Deux's heart clenches as Atlanta slowly steps out of the closet. She tilts the camera toward the window, revealing three black RainforesTec vans parked outside. A dozen agents stand outside the house, clad in black and wearing RainVision glasses.

His blood runs cold.

"Don't trust them, Atlanta," Deux urges, his voice sharp with urgency. "Tell Mom and Dad to kick them out. We'll fix this, I pro—"

Before he can finish, the bedroom door crashes open. The screen shakes as Atlanta stumbles back, revealing their parents flanked by three imposing RainforesTec agents.

Panic seizes Deux.

"Dad! Mom! It's not true!" he cries out, his voice cracking with desperation. But his pleas fall on deaf ears. His parents' expressions are blank, their words robotic as they echo the accusations against him.

Then he sees it. His mother's smartwatch, its sleek screen flashing with biometric data. She rips the phone from Atlanta's hands, her grip tight. "You are a danger to our world, Deux! Turn yourself in now! That boy is no good for you."

His breath catches. It's happening again. RainforesTec's lies have poisoned his family, twisting their love into fear. His world crumbles in real time, slipping through his fingers like sand. His vision blurs with tears.

"Atlanta! We need to leave!" His grandmother's voice slices through the chaos.

The camera jolts as Atlanta and their grandma make a break for it. The screen goes black. Call ended.

Sidric stares at Deux, his lips parted as if searching for words—*what do you say when someone's entire world has just been ripped apart?*

Deux buries his face in his hands.

For a long moment, there's only silence.

Sidric exhales sharply and grabs the phone. He scrolls through the endless sea of headlines, death threats, and conspiracy theories. His chest tightens. *They want Deux erased.*

But then, amidst the noise, something catches his eye.

A user called @tayrontoo has posted a video. The full video. It shows everything.

The plane losing control.

Deux and Sidric springing into action.

Their powers stabilizing the aircraft.

The passengers *cheering.*

The caption reads:

Nearly died today but god bless these twinks in shining armor for saving us all! @DeuxYates @SidricAlv

The comments are a battlefield. Some calling it fake, others defending Deux and Sidric. But the truth is out there.

Sidric gently taps Deux's shoulder. "Look," he says, his voice brimming with quiet excitement. "There are people who know the truth."

Deux lifts his head, eyes swollen with emotion. On the screen, the video plays—a glimmer of hope in the wreckage of his life.

"I know this whole situation is fucked up," Sidric continues, frustration simmering beneath his words. "Seeing RainforesTec twist what we did, your family turning against you... it's all wrong. But isn't this exactly why we're fighting? It has to get fucked up before it gets better."

Deux takes a breath. Sidric's words ground him, pulling him from the abyss. A spark reignites inside him.

"We're here to take RainforesTec down," Sidric declares, his voice strong with purpose. "As long as one person is willing to stand up to these assholes, there's hope. And right now, there's two of us, Deux."

Deux blinks back tears, his heart pounding. The weight on his chest feels just a little lighter.

He sets the phone aside and looks at Sidric with raw admiration.

"I knew I loved you, but *damn*, Sidric," he breathes, a small, shaky smile forming. "I am *so* madly in love with you."

Sidric grins. "Took you long enough."

Their eyes lock, the intensity between them electric. In this moment, they aren't fugitives or victims—they are *alive.*

And then, they kiss.

Passionate. Desperate. Unbreakable.

A fire reignites between them. A promise. A battle cry.

When they finally pull away, Deux exhales and straightens up. "Okay. That was necessary."

Sidric chuckles. *"Extremely."*

Deux wipes his face and leans back. "Now... how about some snacks?"

As Sidric attempts to de-dustify the room, Deux heads downstairs to grab some food from the vending machine. He walks with his head low, trying to avoid being spotted by any stranger lurking behind the cracked doors of the dimly lit motel. The glow from the vending machine beckons him, probably the most advanced piece of technology this place has seen in decades.

He selects two vanilla cheeseburgers and two peppermint sodas, sliding in some cash. The machine dings, and within seconds, a brown paper bag pops out, neatly packed with his order. As he turns to leave, the receipt begins printing. He almost ignores it, until something catches his eye.

There, embedded within the receipt, is a message.

DEUX AND SID........0.43
DON'T LET THEM.........22.41
DESTROY YOU...........12.44
TRYING TO KEEP THEM.........3.14
FAR FROM YOU........3.44
AS LONG AS WE CAN..........4.25

A shiver runs down Deux's spine. The anonymous author of these cryptic messages is starting to feel like an eerie pen pal. But the real question is, how close are *they*? Could RainforesTec already

214

know where they are? At this point, even their underwear could have trackers on them.

He bolts upstairs.

Bursting through the door, he reads the message aloud.

Sidric listens, brow furrowed. "Okay, so... good news and bad news, right?" He takes a breath, trying to calm both himself and Deux. "Yes, these people know where we are. But *they're* trying to help us. They don't want us to feel defeated. They *want* us to keep going with our mission. Our plan. Which is... what exactly?"

Deux straightens. "Here's the finalized plan. I've been thinking about it a lot. First, we need to expose them—gather as much proof as we can. Second, we need to free the kid—and whoever else they're experimenting on. And finally, we destroy as much of their HQ as possible. We need to make a scene so big that it forces people to wake up."

Sidric nods, determination sparking in his eyes. "Got it. And at least we know someone on the inside is looking out for us."

"That would be a *huge* help, honestly."

Under normal circumstances, Sidric would be unpacking his bags and indulging in a relaxing skincare routine right about now. Unfortunately, they left all their luggage at the airport. The only thing they have is a single carry-on with a few changes of clothes.

Deux notices Sidric pacing. "What's wrong, baby boy?"

"I need a little spa time! But all we have is a shower with zero water pressure and a bed covered in stranger pubes!" he cries dramatically.

Deux chuckles. "I got you. Sit back, relax, and let me take care of you."

His eyes scan the room. *Spa... spa... spa...*

Then, he spots it. The coffee station.

Jackpot.

Three packets of instant coffee. Two small cream packs. Two honey tubs. A couple of sugar packets. *This will do.*

He lays down a towel on the bed and, after some light convincing, gets Sidric to lie down.

Mixing the coffee with the cream, he carefully spreads it across Sidric's face. "We're starting with a *gentle* creamy coffee scrub," he announces, rubbing in slow circles.

Sitting this close, Deux inspects every inch of Sidric's face. He never noticed how Sid's nose tilted slightly to the left or how perfectly full his eyebrows were, he always assumed they were filled in.

After a few moments, Deux heats some water using the coffee maker, dunks in a small towel, and presses it to Sidric's face to remove the scrub.

Sidric sighs in relief. "You're good at this."

"Thank you. Now, we're following up with a—uhm—a honey and sugar face mask. This will... *purify all the impurities?*" Deux laughs.

He applies the golden mixture. Sidric's heartbeat speeds up beneath his fingertips, syncing with his own.

You're so gorgeous, Deux thinks.

As he smooths the last coat onto Sidric's skin, their eyes meet. For a moment, neither speaks. Sidric smiles, as if he can hear Deux's thoughts.

Deux's heart stutters. His fingers slip—and suddenly, a spark of energy zaps from his fingertips onto Sidric's cheek.

"Ow!" Sidric yelps.

"Oh *shit*—I'm so sorry!" Deux pulls back, eyes wide. "I promise I'm not a bad boyfriend!"

Silence.

Both of their eyes go even wider.

"Boyfriend?" Sidric repeats, his voice laced with surprise. "Is that what we are?"

Deux freezes. "I mean... would you *want* to be my boyfriend?"

Sidric grins. "Yes!"

Without hesitation, he launches forward, kissing Deux hard—smearing the sticky honey mask all over *both* their faces.

"I know it seems like an uphill battle with the long distance and having to fight this mega corporation but I think we can make it work." Deux says rapidly.

Sid stares deeply into his eyes, adoring how he fills every second of silence with his thoughts. For a moment, everything is quiet and still. The only sounds are the faint buzzing of the bathroom light and the distant bass thumping from outside.

"Do you hear that?" Deux pops his head up and rushes to the window, peeking just an inch through the blinds. "I know this song!"

Across the parking lot, the quiet diner has transformed into a makeshift disco. People filtering in and out, neon lights flashing, and music blasting every time the door swings open. If there's one thing Deux loves more than the Grinch, it's a chance to party.

He spins around to face Sidric, pointing at him with playful determination. "I dare you to come out dancing with me tonight!"

Sidric blinks. "What? Aren't we, I don't know, a little preoccupied with other things?"

"Come on! We can't even head to the headquarters until tomorrow night, Sunday's probably best for our mission. We could sit here, stressing out, letting our worries eat us alive... or—" Deux steps closer, eyes gleaming. "We could dance the night away!"

He stretches out his hand, waiting for Sid to take it.

Sidric's eyes dart around as he weighs his options. Finally, he exhales, closes his eyes, and reaches for Deux's hand. "Fine," he says, squeezing it lightly. "But you have to request at least one Taylor Swift song for me."

An hour later, they're dressed in their best, though, considering their limited wardrobe, it's more about making do than making a statement.

Hand in hand, they step out of the motel and cross the street, their matching purple eye-glitter catching the glow of the neon lights.

To keep their identities hidden, they wear their last remaining wigs. Sidric in neon green, Deux in neon pink. If anyone spotted them, they'd probably assume they were either lost from a bachelorette party or members of an ABBA-themed acapella group.

"Okay, if you feel your powers kicking in let me know and we will leave," Deux starts listing off some safety rules like a helicopter mom. "Also, avoid FiveLoko at all costs, don't talk to strangers and don't leave your drinks unsupervised at all."

"You're adorable," Sid chuckles, as he fixes Deux's wig and opens the door.

As they step inside, they realize the old diner has been completely transformed into a modern karaoke bar. Flashing lights bounce off every surface, and illuminated floor tiles guide guests from the entrance to the dance floor. At the back, a DJ booth sits beside a small stage where two women—probably in their forties—are butchering a country song, slurring their way through the lyrics with wild enthusiasm.

Just as Deux and Sidric take in the scene, a towering man dressed in all black steps in front of them, blocking their path.

"IDs," the bouncer says, his tone firm and impatient.

Deux startles slightly, catching Sidric reaching for his wallet. Thinking fast, he quickly grabs Sid's hand and steps forward.

"Oh, sorry!" he exclaims in an absolutely terrible Swedish accent. "We got lost from our party, ja? No IDs, but we can pay moolah?" He flashes a wide grin and pulls out a crumpled twenty-dollar bill.

The bouncer eyes them for a moment before snatching the bill. "Only for tonight."

"What the fuck was that?" Sid whispers holding in his laughter.

"We can't show our IDs we were just on national news!" He quickly replies, "Also nobody ever questions you when you're Swedish."

They weave their way through the dance floor, moving around each other, lost in the music. The crowd is an unusual mix—older folks reliving their glory days and younger professionals, still in their office attire, letting loose with heavy drinks in hand. Deux can't take his eyes off Sidric. Even in the ridiculous neon green wig, he's somehow the most attractive human Deux has ever laid eyes on.

The country song finally ends, and an extremely drunk woman stumbles onto the stage. A familiar guitar melody starts playing. Deux and Sidric glance at each other before turning toward the stage, both breaking into cheers as the woman launches into an off-pitch but passionate rendition of *Party in the U.S.A.*

As the song builds, Deux spins Sidric under his arm, pulling him close—so close their lips are just inches apart. Sidric's breath catches. Moves he'd only ever dreamed of sharing with a boy are happening right in front of his eyes. One song turns into one drink, and one drink turns into a quick peck on the lips.

Hours later, when Sidric is well past tipsy, he throws his arms around Deux's shoulders and yells over the music, "It's time! What are we singing?!"

"I got this," Deux smirks, making his way to the song request monitor. After a few taps, he turns back. "We're on next," he says, winking.

They take a quick shot for courage before heading toward the stage. Sidric still has no clue what they're about to sing—until the opening notes of *King of My Heart* by Taylor Swift fill the room. He chuckles, blushing as he watches Deux grab the mic and take the lead.

They trade verses effortlessly, their voices intertwining in the chorus. Deux barely notices the crowd—half of whom are too drunk to process what's happening, while the rest are either vibing to the song or staring at their neon wigs flailing to the beat. But it doesn't matter. Right now, there's only Sidric.

Deux points at him dramatically, blowing him a kiss across the stage.

As the song builds to the bridge, they jump around, letting the energy carry them. Deux suddenly grabs Sidric's hand. "Big finale," he grins— right before lifting Sidric into the air and spinning him around. Sid lands gracefully, laughing, and just as their eyes meet for a perfect, movie-worthy kiss—

Deux feels a jolt inside. His stomach tightens. His powers are flaring up. He panics for a second and quickly blurts out, "Show me your best *wigography* and I'll buy the next round!"

Sidric smirks and gives his head a dramatic swirl.

Immediately, his neon green wig flies off.

"Oh no!" Deux yells in fake horror. "Not your beautiful locks!"

Sidric bursts into laughter, stumbling offstage, and as Deux reaches out to help him up, Sidric grabs Deux's wig and yanks it clean off.

They both freeze.

Sidric, still slightly dazed, looks up at him with a lazy grin. "If you ask me," he slurs, tugging Deux closer, "you're hotter without it."

Deux barely has time to process those words before Sidric pulls him into a kiss, soft, warm, and full of something that feels too big for this little karaoke bar. The music swells around them, but at this moment, it feels like it's playing just for them.

Suddenly, a chilling stillness fills the air. The music cuts out. The lights flicker. A thick purple fog seeps into the room, curling around the dance floor like something alive.

Deux and Sidric freeze. They glance toward the bar—every employee is on the phone, speaking in hushed but urgent tones, their eyes locked onto them. Around the room, people casually pull gas masks over their faces, like this is just another Thursday night.

"Is that…?" Deux starts.

"A lavender haze heading straight for us?" Sidric finishes, gulping. "Yeah. Yeah, it is."

220

Deux looks up at him. "I think we should…"

"RUN," they both say at the same time. Then they burst into tipsy giggles until the realization hits them.

The fog is already in their lungs.

Sidric sways. His vision blurs.

"Quick!" A voice with a thick Southern drawl cuts through the haze. "This way if y'all wanna live."

A figure emerges from the hallway, shrouded in shadow and fog. Long black trench coat. Wide-brimmed cowboy hat. Their face is almost impossible to make out.

"You don't know me," the stranger says, "but I know you, Deux. Here." They toss a small bottle. "Vitamin C. It'll help counter the minor intoxication you're 'bout to feel. Now, breathe shallow and move fast. Whether y'all trust me or not—we gotta go."

Sidric stumbles. "How do we know this isn't a trap?"

"Sidric," the stranger hisses, "those men out there are hoping to find both of y'all *unconscious* on the dance floor so they can drag you straight to RainforesTec."

Deux hesitates. "I mean… they haven't *killed* us yet. That's something, right?"

But before they can argue, the stranger shoves open a door leading to a dimly lit garbage chute room. The stench is immediate. Deux's eyes water.

"Oh, *hell no*," he chokes.

"Yes," the stranger says flatly.

"I don't think we have a choice!" Sidric yells, voice slurring as he wobbles on his feet."The fog is coming!"

The stranger doesn't wait. They leap into the chute headfirst.

Sidric glances at Deux. "This is crazy, right?"

Deux nods. "Pray for me."

Sidric winks. "See you at the bottom." And then he's gone, sliding into darkness.

The fog creeps under the garbage room door.

Deux groans, tears streaming down his face. "I really don't like smelly things," he wails as he dives in after them, squishing his shoulders into the tiny vent, screaming all the way down.

"WATCH OUT BELOW!"

Dust flies everywhere as Deux crashes onto a dirty mattress. He coughs, shaking off the impact, and hears wet footsteps echoing ahead. Looking up, he spots Sidric following the trench-coated figure deeper into the sewer tunnel.

"Wait up!" he calls, scrambling to his feet.

The air is thick and damp, clinging to his lungs. Light is scarce, and the tunnels twist and turn like an endless labyrinth. After the third left turn, Deux gives up trying to keep track—he just hopes this person knows where they're going.

"So, do you plan on telling us who you are, or should we just call you *Mr. Trench coat*?" he asks, breaking the steady rhythm of dripping water.

The figure stops abruptly and turns around. "That would be *Miss* Trench coat, darling."

With a flourish, she removes her cowboy hat, revealing a sleek, high ponytail that glistens even in the dim light. Strands of green curls frame her face, coiling like tiny serpents. She steps forward into a faint glow, allowing them to take in her full visage—her eyes are framed by bold orange and purple eyeshadow that sweeps dramatically upward, and her glossy lips shimmer, reflecting the tunnel's scarce light.

"They call me *Lady Mars*," she says smoothly. "I used to perform at Grady's, back when it was a drag club. Back before the world was brainwashed."

Deux instinctively reaches for Sidric's hand, squeezing it tight. *She knows things.*

"What do you mean, brainwashed?" he asks cautiously.

Lady Mars scoffs. "Oh, please. I've been tracking you nonstop. I *know* you two have been snooping, and I *damn well* know about your little radioactive secret."

Sidric stiffens. "Huh? How do you know about that?" His voice wavers before he adds, "I mean, if we happened to be, uh, *somewhat* radioactive. Not saying we are."

Lady Mars smirks. "By day, darling, I'm not *Lady Mars*." She takes a deliberate step forward. "By day, I am Viktor Bessie, RainforesTec's *Head of Security*."

Deux's heart slams against his ribs.

"I've been in charge of your surveillance since you received that smartwatch at OnlineCon," she continues, her voice dripping with certainty.

"What?!"

Deux stumbles back, instinctively shielding Sidric behind him. His hands ignite with a flickering glow.

"Oh, relax, you two. I'm a spy, a rebel. One of the good ones," Lady Mars says with a smirk. "Y'all are *too damn cute*." She gives them an exaggerated once-over before strutting forward, the sharp clicks of her heels echoing through the damp tunnel.

Sidric and Deux exchange a wary glance before hurrying to catch up.

"I started the RainforesTec Resistance the moment they began *fucking up the world*," she continues. "I worked for them for *thirty-five years*, but I only discovered the *truth* about seven years ago."

She takes a sharp left turn, stopping at what looks like a dead end. Without hesitation, she presses her palm against the grimy wall. A soft *beep* echoes through the tunnel as blue light ripples outward, illuminating hidden circuitry beneath the surface. With a low mechanical hum, the wall splits open, revealing a dark corridor stretching further into the underground. Flickering lights barely illuminate the way.

Lady Mars steps inside without looking back.

"Their *first* subject, James Willow, was a volunteer for a medical trial. They were developing new contact lenses—ones that could eliminate the need for eye surgery." Her voice softens slightly. "Every day, my job was to check in on him, make sure he had everything he needed. And over time, we grew close. *Really* close." She lets out a small, nostalgic chuckle. "I *liked* him, and he liked me back. We snuck in a few dates. A few kisses. It had to stay a secret, of course—I would've lost my job if anyone found out."

She pauses for a second before continuing, her tone darkening.

"But after three months, everything changed. The tech team pushed an update to his lenses, and little by little, he *wasn't* the same. One moment, he'd be looking at me like I was the center of his world. The next, he'd scoot *away* from me. His expressions, his body language—something was *off*."

She exhales sharply, shaking her head.

"And then... suddenly, he was *head over heels* for the second subject they brought in. A girl." She clenches her jaw. "Now, when I tell you James was *gay gay*, I *mean* it. *No BS, honey.* First thing he ever told me was that he *only* liked men. But somehow, *RainforesTec changed him*."

A heavy silence lingers between them.

Deux grips Sidric's hand tightly.

Lady Mars presses forward. "Since that moment, I've been watching *everything* they do. I realized I could do more damage from the *inside*, so I stayed. I let them believe they'd stripped me down to *Viktor*—just another corporate drone." She tosses her hair back, her lips curling into a defiant smirk. "But *Lady Mars* never left."

Deux notices Lady Mars' eyes beginning to water. He can't imagine what it would be like to lose the love of your life to a *brainwashing* corporation, to watch them slip away, knowing it wasn't *their* choice.

Deux's grip on Sid's hand tightens.

"I'm so sorry they did that to you, Lady Mars," Deux says softly. "Is there any way to get him back? To bring back the *real* James?"

She exhales, her painted lips pressing into a tight line. "Until recently, I was losing hope, to be honest. But seeing you two?" She lets out a small, shaky laugh. "You've brought it all back."

Sidric and Deux exchange a cheeky look.

"We have a resistance," Lady Mars continues, standing taller now. "We're planning to come together, expose them, and *end* this. And maybe—*just maybe*—I can bring James back to me."

"So you'll help us?" Sidric asks. "We've been trying to come up with a plan to take them down."

Lady Mars smirks, her usual flair returning. "Oh, I *know* you've been scheming, Sid." She winks at him. "But first, we need to coordinate. If we merge your plan with *our* plan, we can make one *big ol' gay* plan together." She twirls a lock of her sleek green ponytail between her fingers. "And trust me, *wait* until you meet the other girls. Y'all are gonna love them."

22

i know places

Sidric

A bright light illuminates a steel door at the end of the tunnel. As they approach, Sidric spots at least seven security cameras discreetly hidden within the walls.

Lady Mars pulls out a compact mirror—the kind of vintage accessory a glamorous woman from the 1970s might carry. She flips it open and looks straight into the glass. A thin green laser scans her face from top to bottom.

"Access unlocked," a robotic voice announces as the steel door slides open with a soft hiss.

Sidric and Deux exchange looks of amazement.

"You like this lil' thing?" Lady Mars smirks, snapping the mirror shut. "Boys, I've got *so* many gadgets to show you. Come on in."

As the doors part, dust settles over the threshold, revealing a sprawling underground hideout. The space stretches like a massive cave but with sleek, industrial steel flooring. Their footsteps echo against the metal as they step inside.

At the far end of the lair, two drag queens practice a dance routine to an old Chappell Roan song, their sequins catching the dim, flickering lights. To the left, a lounge area beckons—plush pink couches wrapped in faux fur rugs, forming a perfect circle beneath a giant mirrored disco ball.

Sidric's eyes widen as he spots something truly miraculous.

A coffee genieeX.

He gasps audibly. The machine stands on four sleek stainless steel legs, its crystal bodice shaped like an old-fashioned tea kettle. Two blinking LED eyes scan the room, their movements eerily synchronized.

"What's your poison, honey?" Lady Mars teases. "Cotton Candy Latte? Tomato Espresso? Or—my personal favorite—Garlic Parmesan Cold Brew?"

"*Cotton Candy Latte!*" Sidric exclaims before she even finishes the sentence. He's been dreaming about it ever since RainforesTec discontinued the genieeX line.

"GenieeX, you heard him," Lady Mars commands with a flick of her wrist. "One Cotton Candy Latte."

The robot hums, processing the order, and within seconds, pink smoke billows from the top of its kettle-shaped body. A small compartment in the shape of a mouth slides open, and a steel tongue rolls out, gently presenting a pastel-pink coffee mug.

The scent is intoxicating. Sidric's mouth waters as he steps forward to claim his prize.

"Help yourself, Hun," Lady Mars says, waving him through.

She gestures around the lounge. "This is the *relax and untuck* area— the first hideout we ever built. Back in the day, before RainforesTec started hunting queers when everyone thought it was just another *boring* tech company, employees used to sneak in here. They'd take breaks, hide from managers, talk shit about their projects. But when things started getting *sinister,* we knew we had to turn this into something more. A revolution room.

Word spread. Soon, there were more than thirty of us. That's when we realized we needed our *own* lab, our *own* tech team. Two of my favorite engineers—absolute masterminds *and* lesbians—expanded this whole place into what you see now."

Before Deux or Sidric can respond, a thick, raspy voice calls out from the back.

"You talkin' shit about us again, Marsbar?"

Lady Mars grins. "Speak of the devil, and she shall be *nosy as hell*. Boys, meet Josannah and Taytish."

Descending the stairs is a short, sharp-eyed woman carrying a utility belt slung diagonally across her torso. She wears a printed bodysuit under black-and-white overalls, and her long black hair is styled into two space buns—each adorned with pencils poking out at odd angles.

Right behind her, an even *shorter* woman slides down the railing with practiced ease. She's dressed in all black, her long sleeves and pants covered in scattered mesh stars. Her short hair is styled upward in a soft, tousled look.

"Josannah," the space-bun woman says, extending her fist toward them. "And this is my wife, Taytish."

Taytish waves shyly from behind.

Deux spins in a slow circle, taking it all in. His eyes gleam with excitement.

"This place is marvelous!" he exclaims.

"Thanks, Deux! Now, over here is the operations center," Lady Mars announces, turning on her heel and speed-walking toward a room filled with glowing screens projected onto every wall.

Sidric and Deux exchange a glance before hurrying after her.

In one corner, two drag queens in fringe jackets are hunched over a data display, eyes locked on a rapidly flashing sequence of numbers—some green, some red. At the center of the room, a holographic 3D projection of RainforesTec headquarters hovers above a sleek metal table, rotating slowly.

"Star and Barb are tracking every smartwatch ever sold," Lady Mars explains. "We're working on a new code that could *divert* the entire system."

Sidric frowns. "Okay, but *how* does this even work? How can a *smartwatch* alter people's minds?"

"Taytish! Pull up the diagrams!" Josannah calls out, waving them over.

"*Diagrams!*" Taytish echoes in a sing-song voice. She whips out a tablet, tapping a few buttons before casting the projection onto one of the larger screens.

"This is the smartwatch," she begins, zooming in on the underside of the device. The detailed scan reveals an array of microscopic mechanisms embedded in the sleek design. "Now, underneath *this* part—" she gestures to the watch's back plate, "—Mr. Fugly-Bizous installed around one hundred thousand minuscule needles."

Deux shudders. "Needles?"

"Yep," Taytish confirms, enlarging the diagram further. "They attach directly to your central nervous system, allowing the watch to manipulate your brain—rewiring it however the code dictates. He could push an update *tomorrow* and make every single person wearing it do anything he pleases."

Sidric swallows. "Like what?"

"Oh, I don't know…" Taytish shrugs dramatically. "Become a tuna-obsessed dog? A circus monkey? Join a massive conga line on command?" She lets that sink in before lowering her voice. "*Anything.*"

"The more time you spend wearing the watch, the more it alters your body and mind," she continues. "We're not certain yet, but we fear there's a threshold. Once you pass it… the changes could become permanent."

Sidric's grip tightens around Deux's wrist. "You're saying people could be stuck like that?"

Taytish nods grimly.

"Do we know how many people have been brainwashed?" Deux asks, his voice laced with dread.

Josannah pulls up a world map, millions of tiny dots pulsing across every continent. "Our systems show around 1.55 billion active smartwatches. That number climbs every single day, and it's about to skyrocket with the next product drop."

Sid's stomach churns.

"We hacked into RainforesTec's system," Josannah continues, zooming in on different regions, "so we have exactly the same data they do. Every 'active' smartwatch represents a person actively being altered by their technology. And this didn't start with the latest models—" she swipes to a new screen displaying older devices, "—their previous RainVisions and Smartwatches were doing the same thing, just at a *slower* rate."

"Shit, it's bad," Deux mutters under his breath.

"Real fucking bad," Sid adds, louder.

"But we have a plan," Lady Mars interjects, flipping her ponytail. "Taytish has been working for years on a code that can deactivate the smartwatches and reverse the damage. And we think—" she glances at Taytish, who nods, "—we're finally close."

Sidric's heart pounds. "Okay, so... when does it go live?"

Josannah takes a deep breath. "This is where *you two* come in."

Sidric and Deux exchange a look.

"In order to infiltrate the main system and replace the old code with ours, we need a total RainforesTec HQ blackout." Josannah's voice wavers slightly, but there's hope in her eyes. She's lost too many people to this nightmare. "We had a few possible ways to do this, but after seeing your powers, we know now—you're the missing piece."

Sidric's jaw tightens. "Wait—*how do you know about our powers?!*"

Lady Mars dramatically tosses her hands in the air. "Hun, like I *said,* we've been tracking you." She smirks. "In the office, *I* oversee smartwatch deactivations for queer icons like yourselves. The moment Deux's watch malfunctioned, I was immediately intrigued. I checked the logs, saw abnormal electric currents, and knew something was up."

She steps closer, lowering her voice. "I have *never* seen a reaction like yours before. The power you both channel—out of thin air?!" She shakes her head. "Heavens to Betsy. You powered up a plane midair."

Deux and Sidric freeze.

"Oh, yeah." Lady Mars nods, reading their stunned expressions. "And by the way, *Mr. Nasty Bizous* himself was the one who nearly sent that plane *crashing* to the ground."

Sidric's breath catches.

"I tried to bury as much intel on you both as I could," she continues. "But for every undercover drag queen in the system, there are at *least* ten brainwashed straights." She sighs, then straightens her shoulders. "But I *swear* on my most prized human hair wig that I won't let that nasty man lay a single hand on either of you."

She pauses, studying them both.

"It's like… you were chosen to help us end this."

"The chosen ones by the FiveLoko gods," Sidric sighs, barely able to process the weight of it all. His brain is racing a thousand miles a minute.

The richest man in the world—the owner of *everything* tech—tried to murder them. That was *not* on his Bingo card.

And yet, rather than fear, a fire ignites in his chest. He's *ready* to fight.

Lady Mars claps her hands together. "Speaking of FiveLoko! Taytish! Josannah! Take them to the Cryptic and Machiavellian Lair!"

She sings out the words like a dramatic stage cue.

Taytish snorts. "You mean... the garage?"

Lady Mars gasps, placing a hand over her chest as if personally offended. "Yes... As I said, the Cryptic and Machiavellian Lair."

Taytish rolls her eyes and waves Sidric and Deux forward. "This way."

They all squeeze into a steel elevator, which hums softly as it moves. By now, Sidric has completely lost track of where they are. *Up, down, left, right?* It's all a blur. His chest tightens slightly at the disorientation.

Deux notices the shift in Sid's expression and gently takes his hand, squeezing it three times. A silent reassurance. Sidric exhales slowly, grounding himself in Deux's touch.

The elevator doors slide open, revealing a remodeled garage. The glossy green epoxy floors gleam under the overhead lights, contrasting sharply with the aged warehouse walls. Three large tables are scattered across the space, while a row of computer screens flicker at the far end.

"I guess I can *kind of* see how this could be a Cryptic and Machiavellian Lair," Josannah muses as they step inside.

"Don't get her started," Taytish chuckles, lightly elbowing Josannah.

Sidric smiles at their playful banter.

"Okay, we are *so* excited to show you these!" Josannah practically vibrates with excitement, weaving through the room. "Ever since Lady Mars told us about your radioactiveness from FiveLoko, our minds went *wild* with possibilities. We tested the ingredients with some RainforesTec electronics, and the results were *insane*." She starts grabbing objects from the tables. "We've got electrifiber gloves, vests, glasses, even panties!"

"Electrifiber?" Sid asks, raising an eyebrow.

"Yes! It's a textile we invented." Taytish steps in. "We got in touch with FiveLoko's offices, and they sent us all their leftover supplies of Gold FiveLoko. Up to the very last drop of L-ectiline+. That's the key ingredient. It helped us create your suits and all the gadgets you'll be using. Not only does it *amplify* the power inside you, but it also pulls energy from nearby sources."

"Wait, so… it's like a battery?" Deux tilts his head.

"Kind of. More like a *torrent* that gathers energy and stores it for you. That way, you don't exhaust yourself. But we haven't tested it on people yet." Taytish flashes a sheepish grin. "Which is why we'll be running a trial *tonight!* I'm about 89% sure it'll work perfectly."

Deux narrows his eyes. "And the other 11%?"

Taytish ignores him, grabbing their wrists and dragging them toward the corner of the room. "Ooooh, but this one? This one is *so fun.*"

They stop in front of what looks like a silver vending machine. Inside, multiple rows of tiny gold cans gleam behind the glass, each no bigger than a finger.

Sidric's eyes widen, his mouth practically watering. "No way. *Mini* FiveLokos?!" He presses both hands against the glass.

Taytish immediately yanks him back. *"No."* She punches a code into the vending machine, and a small can drops into the dispenser below. She holds it up with a grin. "For legal reasons, these are *SixLokos.*"

Deux snorts. "What's the sixth ingredient?"

"Forget that. Let me show you what it *does.*" Taytish winks, grabbing a handful of cans before making a beeline for the elevator. Josannah follows, her arms full of various gadgets.

Sid and Deux exchange a quick glance. *How much weirder can today get?*

"Where to now?" Sid asks as they step inside.

"We can't be indoors for this."

Taytish punches in a different code, and the elevator opens to a long hallway leading to a back door. The group walks down the corridor, stepping out into the open.

A vast desert stretches before them, mountains rising in the distance. The wind hums softly, carrying the scent of dry earth.

Sidric blinks, trying to make sense of his surroundings. He turns back, staring at the door they just exited—realizing it's built directly *into* the mountain. His mind scrambles to map out the entire drag queen resistance hideout inside the rocky terrain, but the scale of it all is impossible to grasp.

Everything about today feels like a dream.

"Okay, boys," Taytish's voice sharpens, claiming the space between them. "These SixLoko cans? Your new besties. Place them anywhere you want your powers to channel into. You can send power, take power, or annihilate. *You* decide." She struts toward an old, dust-covered pickup truck a few meters away, slapping five cans onto its sides. "Power it up."

Deux cracks his knuckles, taking a deep breath. He focuses on the rusted orange truck, raising both arms. A surge of energy ripples through his body, gathering at his palms. In less than a second—

BOOM.

The truck *explodes* into a fireball. Metal and debris shoot into the air like fireworks.

Silence.

Sidric stumbles back, slapping a hand over his mouth.

"Taytish," Josannah exhales, rubbing her temples. "We're gonna need to adjust those levels. Also… you're gonna need a new car."

"I am *so* sorry!" Deux whirls around, wide-eyed. "I tried to power it up, *not* obliterate it!"

"Deux, *don't* apologize!" Josannah grins. "If we're going up against RainforesTec, we *need* this much power." She tosses a look at Taytish.

"The truck was basically scrap metal anyway."

Taytish sighs. "Fine. But you owe me a ride after we save the world."

Josannah turns back to the boys, tossing them each a bundle of clothes. "Put these on. They should help your body *store* power instead of blasting everything in sight."

Sidric and Deux catch their outfits and jog off to separate rooms to change.

Sid pulls the suit on, adjusting the snug fit. It's a dark gray, high-tech material that hugs his body *just right*, making his already perky butt look borderline illegal. The light yellow gloves and boots add a striking contrast, and a structured vest piece fits snugly over his chest. He clenches his fist, feeling the electricity flow through his palm like water.

It's exhilarating.

A quick glance in the mirror, hair fixed, outfit settled, then he follows the sound of voices back to the lounge.

The moment he steps inside, he hears Lady Mars exclaim, "Deux, darling, you look *just* like a young Henry Cavill!"

Sidric stops in his tracks.

Deux stands in the center of the room, his suit stretching over every inch of muscle. The definition in his arms, his chest, his *everything*. Sid audibly gulps. He forces himself to *not* look lower. *Do not look lower.*

"Wow, Sid! You look sexy as fuck!" Deux grins, giving him an approving once-over. "Look at you! You're a super-cutie!"

Sidric flushes. "Look at you, Deux! Or should I say Muscle Man?" He playfully pokes Deux's bicep, barely denting it.

Deux flexes. "Admit it, you're impressed."

"Okay, enough, you two darling pies," Lady Mars interrupts, stepping forward. "Now that y'all are dressed like the *gay Avengers*, it's time we talk science."

She pulls out a pink lipstick and aims it at the wall. With a *click*, a holographic presentation titled *"Radioactiveness Realness"* beams across the room.

"So, as y'all know, wearing a smartwatch is like strapping a bunch of micro-needles to your wrist, injecting you constantly. Well, when you two spilled FiveLoko all over each other, things got interesting. Especially with the fifth element, L-ectiline+. Your DNA was permanently altered." She gestures dramatically.

The screen shifts to an animation, a cartoon Deux and Sidric *making out* before accidentally dumping FiveLoko everywhere. Little gold particles float from Deux's wrist, burrowing into his bloodstream.

Sidric blinks at the visuals, but his mind snags on one word:

"Permanently."

His stomach knots.

Up until now, they'd clung to the idea that this was temporary. That, one day, they could go back to being normal twenty-somethings with *normal* problems. But... *what even is normal anymore?*

He glances at Deux, who seems just as lost in thought.

There's no turning back now.

"The FiveLoko basically worked as a condom," Lady Mars announces, striking a pose. "It protected you from the smartwatch's malware. Once it reacted to the technology, it made your body immune to RainforesTec's virus and turned you into an electrifyingly gorgeous specimen."

She cackles at her own pun.

"Gorgeously electrifying," Josannah corrects without missing a beat.

Sidric raises a hand. "Okay, but what about me? I didn't have a smartwatch."

Lady Mars smirks. "Well, honey, we had a lot of questions about your case. But the only answer I've got? You had your tongue stuck down the wrong boy at the wrong time."

Sid's face burns.

"I'm guessing the lip-locking made y'all one entity for a brief second, letting the electrification spread. That's why you both have those marks on your hands."

On cue, the hologram shifts to an animation of Deux and Sidric making out, except now, tiny golden DNA strands pass from Deux's mouth to Sid's.

Sid groans. "Was that really necessary?"

"For science? *Absolutely.*"

Lady Mars claps her hands together. "Now, boys, we'll continue this little training session tomorrow morning. I need my beauty sleep."

Sidric hesitates, then blurts, "Wait! Before you go—can you help us find Naya? She was with us at the airport, but we haven't heard from her since."

Lady Mars's smile fades.

"Listen, honey-pie," she sighs, "if RainforesTec hasn't gotten her yet, we *might* be able to reach her. But I don't want to risk y'alls location—or our team's headquarters. RainforesTec can infiltrate almost any communication system in the world. They *know* we're up to something, which means they're extra vigilant right now."

Sidric's shoulders slump. "I just want to know she's okay."

Deux wraps an arm around him, pulling him close.

Lady Mars softens. "We'll do our best, darling. Now get to bed—you're gonna need your rest."

Taytish leads them down two floors to a sleek bedroom, then shuts the door behind them.

Sidric glances around, still completely disoriented. "I swear this place is a *giant maze.*" He whisper-yells.

Deux flops onto the bed. "I can't wrap my head around this."

Sidric nods. "I *know*, right? We arrived two floors *up*, then took an elevator *up* to the secret lab, *then* somehow ended up outside? It makes no sense."

Deux chuckles, shaking his head. "Not *that*, Sid."

He reaches out, taking Sidric's hands in his.

"We're *not* alone in this." His voice is quiet but firm. "There might actually be a chance we stop these fuckers."

Sidric sits down beside him. "Yeah."

Deux stares at his hands, flexing his fingers. "For the last couple of years, I really thought life was just gonna get worse for queer people. Like, permanently. I watched my family get brainwashed by RainforesTec, I thought they were gone forever. For a little I thought we were on to something. Maybe we could try to stop them. But deep down, I figured they'd catch us. That they'd reprogram us like everyone else. That one day, I'd wake up a stranger in some—some heterosexual relationship—"

"Okay, that's too depressing." Sidric cuts him off, throwing an arm around him.

Deux laughs, but his eyes are glassy. "I just— I felt like we were standing alone against this massive, evil monster. But tonight? I realized there are so many more of us than there are of them. We actually have a chance to take them down."

Sidric squeezes his shoulder. "We will take them down. And we'll get everyone's minds back—your family, Nate and Andre, every single queer person who lost who they are." He leans in, whispering, "Trust me. Nobody makes me radioactive and gets away with it."

23

homemade dynamIte

Deux

A sudden, insistent knocking shatters the cocoon of sleep wrapped around Deux and Sidric.

Deux shuffles, his senses slowly emerging from the depths of slumber. In the soft light filtering through the curtains, he realizes he's being spooned by Sidric. The warmth and steady rhythm of Sid's breathing makes him reluctant to move. Silently, they agree. *Twelve more hours like this wouldn't be the worst idea.*

But the knocking persists, more urgent now.

Then, a voice—smug, familiar, and brimming with mischief.

"You *twinks* really thought you could get rid of me that easy? Open up!"

Deux and Sidric jolt awake. They exchange wide-eyed glances before exclaiming in unison—

"Naya?!"

Sidric scrambles to the door and throws it open.

And there she is. Naya, standing in the hallway, looking completely unfazed in the same tie-dye shirt and plaid pajama pants she was wearing the last time they saw her.

"Come here, boys!" she declares, pulling them into a massive hug.

Sidric breaks away first, gripping her face with mock seriousness. "Bitch, I am pissed! Where the hell have you been?"

"Listen, bro, it has been a ride. You might wanna sit down for this one." She pushes them onto the bed with a dramatic flourish. Her eyes gleam with the thrill of storytelling.

"So, at the airport, I realized the phone was actively tracking us. No matter what we did, they'd know where we were headed. So, I made the executive decision to throw them off. I booked it, sprinted out of there, and saw a flight from Palm Springs had just landed."

Sidric leans in. "And?"

"And, well, Mawma knows best." Naya flicks her hair. "So I did what I do best, I socialized with the gays."

Deux raises an eyebrow. "Naturally."

"I found two gorgeous gays who looked *just* like you two. Same heights, similar haircuts—"

Deux scoffs. "I'm gonna need proof."

Naya rolls her eyes. "Anyway, I convinced them we were going to a sugar daddy's retirement party and took them on a little joyride. Rented a RainforesTec car, hit up brunch, went to the mall, grabbed coffee. Got some lavender rose muffins, to die for. All while these himbos thought they were about to meet a rich benefactor."

Sidric gasps. "Naya. *You decoy-gayed us?!*"

"Oh, full performance, babe." She grins. "And it *worked*. Black SUVs were tailing us all day. I ditched the fake yous in the lobby of the Ritz Hotel, and once RainforesTec realized they had the wrong gays, I got the hell out of there."

Deux stares at her, still processing. "You saved us."

Sidric clutches his chest. "We do not deserve you."

"Well, I thought I saved you, but then I saw you two all over my feed."

She smirks. "I was flabbergasted, to say the least. Also? You both are hot as hell as anti-heroes."

Deux groans. "Okay, just for the record, we did not try to crash the plane."

"I know. The people saying otherwise are literally being sponsored by RainforesTec." She scoffs. "They'd claim goat cheese cures aging if they were paid enough."

Deux tilts his head. "Wait, but how did you find us? Did Lady Mars contact you?"

Naya smirks. "Yes and no."

Sidric's eyes narrow. "Naya..."

"Okay, *remember* that summer I worked as a phone repair tech?"

Sidric gasps. "Oh my *God.*"

Deux frowns. "What?"

Sidric grabs Deux's arm. *"The Stallion."*

Deux's eyes widen. "Who's *The Stallion?*"

"This old RainforesTec Employee I used to date." Naya dramatically flips her hair. "And one time, we wanted a weekend away but couldn't afford a hotel. So he brought me *here.* Called it his 'secret hideaway.' Blindfolded me the whole way in—except, oops, he forgot my phone was tracking the entire route."

Sidric is *cackling.* "Wait. Hold on. Did you hook up in this exact room?"

Naya smirks. "Can't confirm. Can't *deny.*"

Sidric cackles and flops back onto the bed. "I *hate* how useful your hookups are."

"You're welcome."

"So then what?" Deux presses.

"So, yesterday, I knew you were in Nevada. Took the first flight I could find. Then, I get this *cryptic-ass* text from an unknown number: 'We have Sid and Deux. Our team is part of RainforesTec's rebellion.

Go home. -LM.'"

Sidric gasps. "Lady Mars tried sending you home?!"

"And I was like, *excuse me,* nobody tells me where to go. So, I made a list of possible places y'all could be, starting with the nearest hotel to RainforesTec HQ. When the manager told me two boys were running around last night in wigs, I knew it was you two idiots."

Sidric throws up his hands. "That is so fair."

Naya crosses her arms, smug. "And now, here I am. You're welcome."

A beat of silence. Then, all at once, Deux and Sidric tackle her into a hug.

"We *so* do not deserve you." Sidric mumbles into her shoulder.

"I *know,*" Naya says, grinning.

"You're forgetting the part where you nearly tackled me to *death,* sweetie."

Lady Mars bursts into the room, arms crossed.

"I step out for a smoke, and next thing I know, this *hoe* comes flying at me like a damn action movie."

Naya tosses her hair, unbothered. "I had to make sure you weren't hurting my gays."

The trio makes their way to the main room, where the inviting aroma of bacon and vanilla pancakes dances in the air. A delightful spread of breakfast foods awaits them on a long table just outside the computer lab. Josannah and Taytish emerge, dressed in matching chef outfits, their faces dusted with a generous sprinkle of flour.

"Dig in!" Josannah announces, her and Taytish's maternal instincts evident. Throughout their relationship, they had harbored dreams of parenthood. Unfortunately, the government's shutdown of adoption and surrogacy services for queer individuals had shattered those dreams. On the bright side, it had only fueled their determination to change the system and overthrow the oppressive reign of

RainforesTec—especially to take down the villainous Jacques P. Bizous.

In the middle of the brunch festivities, Lady Mars interjects, steering the conversation toward business. "Okay, so, I just got intel this morning. They're doing their yearly security system update tonight. During the update, all gates and access doors remain unlocked. That gives y'all the perfect opportunity to run in and out, freely wheely. You need to head straight to the Data Center, install this malware with our updated code, and then use your powers to shut it down and lock it up."

"How do we find the Data Center?" Deux asks.

"With these." Lady Mars tosses them two pairs of SmartGlasses. "These are Lady Mars originals, so no worries about being brainwashed, baby. We'll display maps, exits, alerts when people are nearby—everything you need."

"And you're sure destroying the Data Center will work? How will everyone be de-brainwashed?" Sidric asks, savoring a crispy strip of bacon.

"Yes. The Data Center is basically a room with the biggest computer you can imagine. It holds all of RainforesTec's software codes, updates, and system data. Once you install the malware, every RainforesTec gadget should immediately reverse any previous effects. Then, you two come in with your powers, shut the whole system down, and make the changes irreversible." Lady Mars grins, her excitement infectious.

"Jeez, Mars, you're *really* hyped about this," Taytish remarks, sipping her coffee.

"Well, duh! This has been a long time coming. The world needs to get back to treating everyone fairly." Lady Mars taps a button on the edge of the table, summoning a tall, slender robot carrying six champagne flutes. She distributes them with a flourish. "By this time tomorrow, RainforesTec will be gone! To *la résistance!*" She raises her glass, and the group joins in, their collective determination reflected in the clink of champagne flutes.

"La résistance!" they all cheer before taking a sip.

After breakfast, Taytish and Josannah retreat to their lab to perfect some of their inventions, while Sidric and Deux return to their room to suit up and mentally prepare. The air between them feels thick, the weight of the mission settling in.

Sidric heads to the bathroom. *Breathe. Breathe. Don't get in your head.*

A few minutes later, Deux knocks on the door. "You good in there, Sid?"

Sidric opens it, his eyes glassy, on the verge of tears.

"What if you don't actually like spending time with me?" he blurts out. "What if this is all just one big dopamine trip—some spontaneous blip in the universe that's going to come crashing down the second we stop distracting ourselves with... with this?" He gestures vaguely. "This madness consumes us because it happens at the expense of us— we're literally chained to it. If it's not the super-cyborg evil wristband coming to break down who we are, then it's the fear of losing the only person you care about by the time you finally find some kind of peace."

He exhales sharply, nearly breathless from the rush of words.

Deux grabs Sidric's shoulders and whispers, "Is this peace?" Leaning in, he kisses Sidric again. "Because peace is what you find when you search within yourself. Peace is knowing that everyone is too busy with their own problems, so you don't have to let yours consume you. Those are just problems—they come, they go, and they don't define us. I love you because somewhere along the way, shocking ourselves became the least interesting part of our story. When you smile, I feel a thousand surges of something more powerful than anything RainforesTec could ever do. I know what I feel for you is real. Here, I made you something with the help of Josannah."

He pulls out two metallic wristbands. One engraved with Deux's name and the other with Sidric's. Grinning, he takes the Deux bracelet and slides it onto Sidric's wrist.

"Whenever you feel like you're losing your power, let this remind you of all the things we have beyond our powers and beyond everything RainforesTec has put us through. There's something about being true to who you are and staying good in nature that protects you in ways you can't even imagine. Maybe these bracelets will shield us the way that kiss of light did."

They both laugh at his words.

"I know 'kiss of light' sounds cheesy," Deux continues, his voice softening, "but you are such a light in my life, Sidric, and you don't have to be afraid. I won't run at the first sign that our relationship seems ordinary. I'm excited to see everything you're going to do, that's why I'll fight so hard for us tonight. Truly, you make my days not just bearable, but a joy to live. I never thought I'd have this many great days, especially while facing some serious criminals. When we finally have the freedom to travel the world, I know we'll spark every town with our electric love, never letting this flame burn out."

"Damn. You are a true poet," Sidric says, smiling.

He looks down at the bracelet, running his fingers over the engraved letters. As he traces the name, he suddenly feels a slight pulsation. His eyes widen in shock as he looks up at Deux.

"L-ectiline+ baby," Deux says with a wink. "Whenever we touch it, it sends signals to each other's bracelet."

Sidric smiles, the warmth of the gesture settling deep in his chest. "I trust you," he says softly. "And I love you, Deux."

Two separate vehicles ease into the back entrance of the secret hideout, their engines humming softly. The air outside carries a dry, warm breeze, betraying the underlying tension that hangs in the atmosphere. The revolution is on the brink, and everyone within the resistance is preparing for the mission.

Lady Mars, a figure of authority and determination, steps into the fading daylight. She attentively inspects the vehicles, her keen eyes scanning for any potential flaws.

Inside each vehicle, Taytish and Josannah hunch over computers, their fingers dancing across the keyboards. Their mission is clear: strip the cars of any tracking devices, GPS systems, or technological breadcrumbs that might lead RainforesTec to their whereabouts. The corporation's insidious reach extends to almost any electronic device—phones, computers, and gadgets. But Taytish is undeterred; she installs her passionately crafted security system, a digital fortress guarding against unwanted surveillance.

Deux and Sidric, suited up in full superhero gear, complete with their new bracelets and SmartGlasses, step into the twilight. The synergy between them is palpable, evident in how Sidric's hand seamlessly intertwines with Deux's.

"Why are there two vehicles?" Deux asks, concern lacing his voice.

"We're splitting you up until we get there," Taytish replies, focused on dismantling an antenna. "Once we arrive, you'll meet at the Data Center. We can't risk having both of you in the same place."

"Uh, no," Deux retorts abruptly. He had spent the entire morning psyching himself up for battle, finding stability in the knowledge that he and Sidric would face it together. "We are sticking together."

"That's not possible, Deux," Josannah explains calmly, her attention on the second van. "We've tracked two different routes in case there are guards or drone cameras. If you were together and got caught, that would be it. RainforesTec would win."

"This is bullshit! We need to be together! What if our powers—" Deux begins, but Sidric interrupts with three reassuring squeezes of his hand.

"Deux, look at me. We got this. These bracelets will protect us like our kiss of light did," Sidric reassures him with a confident wink—a first for him.

"Kiss of light? Is that what we're calling it?" Lady Mars interjects. "I love it!"

"But—"

"Deux, everything will work out. Trust me."

Reluctantly, Deux agrees, acknowledging the detailed planning behind the mission. Lady Mars and the team have waited years for this, and now, with every detail accounted for, they stand ready to strike against tyranny.

As the sun dips below the horizon, casting an enchanting orange hue over the landscape, the signal to depart is clear. Deux and Sidric share a tender kiss, embracing for a few precious seconds.

"I'll see you soon, baby boy," Deux whispers into Sidric's ear.

The team splits into the two vehicles.

Inside the first vehicle are Lady Mars, Taytish, Naya, and Deux. The second vehicle carries Sidric, Josannah, and two drag queens, Miss LuLu Pita and Tyra Stanks. Both had once led the AI development sector at RainforesTec. Like many other queer employees, they had attempted to put an end to Jacques' secret mission against the LGBTQ+ community. However, the moment RainforesTec officials sensed their resistance, they were banned from the building and blacklisted across the entire tech industry. Since then, they had focused their talents on performing—and planning their take down.

Lady Mars retrieves an antiquated walkie-talkie from the cluttered console, its worn exterior hinting at years of use. She raises the device to her bright red lips, her piercing blue eyes locked on the road ahead.

"Lady Mars here," she announces, a faint grin appearing on her face. Despite her attempt at an official tone, her thick Southern accent asserts itself, adding warmth to the otherwise serious atmosphere. "We'll convoy until we crest the hill, then maneuver through the west side of the headquarters. BlueEagle, you take the east side. Over."

LuLu Pita, seated in the back of the second vehicle, furrows her brow. "Wait, I thought we were RedEagle?" she asks through the walkie-talkie. "Erh... Over."

"No, you're BlueEagle," Lady Mars clarifies. "We're RedEagle. Over."

LuLu opens her mouth to protest, but before she can speak, Josannah snatches the walkie-talkie from her grasp. "Yes, we'll follow your lead and then split up. Over and out."

The journey unfolds with a series of jarring bumps and sharp turns, the terrain shifting outside the windows. Sidric, seated behind the passenger seat, braces himself, gripping the handrail to steady his queasy stomach. Now is not the time to lose the battle against carsickness.

After ten minutes of twists and turns, Lady Mars's voice crackles through the walkie-talkie again.

"Okay, BlueEagle, ready to split up? Over."

"Confirmed. We'll connect once we reach the east wing. Over," Josannah replies.

RedEagle takes a sharp turn, and Deux's knee bumps into Naya's. He notices her shaking. They had offered her the chance to stay behind at the hideout, but she had refused, saying, "It wouldn't be right for you all to save the gays without me."

Deux takes her hand and gives her a reassuring wink. "We'll be alright."

Suddenly, static crackles through both vehicles' radios, followed by glitching sounds. The passengers exchange uneasy glances.

Then, a commanding low voice fills the cars.

"Hello, Viktor, I assume this is your formal resignation. Josannah, Taytish, haven't seen you in a while." A pause. "Deux and Sidric. I didn't forget about you."

Fear and confusion grip both teams. Lady Mars turns and mouths to

Taytish, *Break contact now!* Taytish immediately pulls out a sleek glass panel, her fingers flying across the interface as she codes a firewall.

"I'm going to ask you to stop whatever nonsense you're planning and turn yourselves in," the voice continues. "Nothing good will come from defying the technological advancements humanity can achieve. I'm giving you one last chance. Back off now, and no one gets hurt. Hand over Deux and Sidric. They are RainforesTec property."

"What do we do?" Deux whispers.

"He's contacting us through a radio station," Taytish whispers back, typing at an impossible speed. "So I don't think he can track us."

"You are so wrong, Taytish. Time's up. See you so—"

The radio cuts out as Taytish completes the firewall. But it's too late.

Drones flood toward RedEagle from all angles, opening fire.

"Deux! Overcharge the car! Make us go faster!" Lady Mars shouts, swerving to avoid the bullets.

Deux channels every ounce of power into his palms, sending a golden bolt of energy surging into the vehicle. RedEagle transforms, rocketing from 100 to 1,000 miles per hour, then into light speed. The drones are left far behind, the world outside blurring into a haze.

Lady Mars clutches the wheel, but the car is no longer under her control. Deux guides it as if it were an extension of himself. Everything moves in slow motion. Taytish and Naya grip whatever they can to stay steady.

Deux steers the car into a cave deep in the Nevada desert, then clenches his fists, cutting the power and bringing the vehicle to an abrupt stop.

"Holy fireball! We did that, girls!" Lady Mars exclaims, hands still gripping the wheel. The others nod in stunned silence. Naya clutches her chest.

"Taytish, did you cut off BlueEagle's tracking too? Are they safe?"

Taytish fights to keep her breakfast down before yanking the door open and puking onto the dirt. Finally, she gasps, "I *believe* so."

"Walkie-talkie them," Lady Mars orders.

******

Inside the dimly lit interior of BlueEagle, chaos reigns. Josannah grips the wheel with a mix of determination and desperation, her foot pressing harder on the accelerator as the menacing hum of drones grows louder behind them. Bullets spray from their metallic pursuers, punctuating the air with sharp, metallic shrieks.

Lady Mars's voice crackles through the walkie-talkie, urgent and edged with concern. "Josannah, Sidric needs to use his powers! Have him power up the motor—speed it up! It's incredible what they can do!"

Josannah glances at Sidric, her eyes pleading. "Sidric! You heard her!"

Sidric's wide-eyed gaze reflects the mounting pressure. A surge of panic threatens to engulf him, but he forces it down. The responsibility to save everyone now rests on his shoulders. His bracelet vibrates, pulsing against his wrist like a silent reminder.

He draws strength from it, his mind drifting to Deux—the warmth of his touch, the unwavering trust in his eyes, the shared moments of the day.

In the midst of the chaos, Sidric clenches his fists and channels the raw, untamed energy within him. Sparks crackle at his fingertips, light building like a storm ready to break.

Josannah's voice bursts through the walkie-talkie, "On it. Lady Mars, send your locatio—"

The call abruptly cuts off.

A deafening explosion erupts as two missiles collide with the car, one from each side.

Then—silence.

******

A sudden hush descends, broken only by the persistent crackle of static. The world inside the cave narrows to a tense, suffocating silence.

Deux's anguished scream shatters the stillness. "Sidric!" His voice, raw with desperation, echoes off the cave walls.

Lady Mars's frantic voice pierces through the airwaves. "Josannah, what's going on? Respond!"

Seconds stretch into an agonizing void of uncertainty. The weight of inaction presses down on them, thick and unbearable.

"We have to go back!" Deux insists, his voice sharp with urgency. But Lady Mars and Taytish exchange a grim glance, their silence heavy with unspoken truth.

"Deux, you know we can't," Lady Mars says, her voice steady but strained. "It's too dangerous."

"Too dangerous?" Deux's frustration ignites into fury. "They could be dead right now! We need to save them!"

He throws the car door open and slams it shut behind him, the sharp crack of metal ricocheting through the hollow cave. "You don't really care about them, do you?"

Lady Mars follows him out, her knee-high boots crunching against the gravel. "How dare you!" she snaps, her eyes blazing. "Do you know how long we've been fighting to take RainforesTec down? How many people I've lost to their brainwashing? Don't you dare stand there and question if I care."

Her breath shudders, but her voice stays firm. "I've spent the last twenty years researching, working, praying for any chance to end this.

I am demanding we stay here until it's safe *because* I care—about all of them. Not just Sid, not just Josannah, but every single queer person out there being controlled by that monster."

A single tear escapes down her cheek, carrying the weight of years of guilt, of loss, of helplessly witnessing Jacques Bizous' reign tighten its grip.

She steps closer, lowering her voice. "We *will* save them. And we *will* end this tyranny. But to do that, we have to stay alive."

24

buzzcut season

Sidric
Seconds before the explosion

The BlueEagle speeds down the desolate highway, the thunderous roar of its engine echoing against the barren landscape. Bullets rain from their pursuers, zipping perilously close as the vehicle weaves through the danger.

In the backseat, sweat beads on Sidric's forehead as he grits his teeth in concentration. The air is thick with tension. He can feel the impending threat, the weight of responsibility pressing down on him. His hands tremble as he channels energy, just as Josannah instructed. *Power up the car.*

Ahead, two ominous missiles streak toward them, leaving trails of smoke in their path. Time slows as Sidric focuses, his mind a maelstrom of calculations and electric currents.

With a surge of raw power, he directs the energy through his palms, sending it into the front of the car. His fingers move with precision, as if conducting an enigmatic symphony. A translucent shimmer materializes around the BlueEagle, forming an ethereal force field just in time.

Josannah's voice crackles through the walkie-talkie: "On it. Lady Mars, send your location!"

The missiles, now milliseconds away, collide with the barrier. A blinding flash erupts as the shield absorbs the impact. The shock wave rattles the car violently, the metallic groan of stressed steel filling the air as the BlueEagle is hurled into a chaotic ballet of flips and rolls.

Inside the tumbling vehicle, chaos reigns. Loose objects become projectiles. Josannah, Lulu Pita, and Sidric are tossed like rag dolls. The world outside blurs into a dizzying mix of sand and sky, each revolution amplifying the disorienting mayhem within.

Then—silence.

The BlueEagle screeches to a brutal stop, its mangled frame wedged between twisted wreckage. Smoke curls into the golden air, thick and acrid, stinging Sidric's lungs as he blinks through the haze. A heavy stillness settles, broken only by the distant hum of retreating drones. Sidric, battered but breathing, forces himself upright. His pulse pounds in his ears, adrenaline still thrumming through his veins. Sparks flicker across his fingertips—remnants of the desperate surge that saved them. He exhales sharply, watching the glow fade, but the weight of what just happened lingers.

We're not safe. Not yet.

His body strains against the seat belt, the only thing keeping him suspended in the wreckage. With measured movements, he reaches to unbuckle it, careful not to shift his weight too suddenly. But despite his efforts, the belt loosens—sending him plunging downward. Grimacing, he scrambles through the shattered window, dragging himself free. A shard of glass slices through his suit, clawing at his skin. Just as he pulls himself from the twisted wreckage, a sharp, dart-like bullet pierces the back of his neck.

Agony flares through him. His vision falters, the world tilting out of focus.

Through the haze, he discerns the whirring descent of a squadron of drones, their mechanical hum drowning out the fading echoes of the crash. They move with sinister precision, locking onto his battered body.

Sidric struggles, but it's futile. The drones lift him effortlessly, carrying him away from the wreckage.

Through the blur, he spots Josannah emerging from the driver's seat. Her silhouette stands against the backdrop of destruction, the harsh sunlight casting long, jagged shadows. She staggers forward, scanning the chaos, searching for him.

Their eyes meet.

Then everything goes dark.

******

After what feels like mere seconds to Sidric, the weight of time hanging heavily on him, he gradually opens his eyes. The world around him unfolds in a slow dance of consciousness. His initial perception is veiled by a disorienting fog, as if emerging from a dream.

The ambient light, an ethereal white glow, floods into his awareness, at first overwhelming his senses. Sidric blinks against the brilliance, his pupils contracting as they adjust. He squints, trying to make sense of his surroundings. The harshness of the light softens as he takes in his environment.

As his vision sharpens, he surveys the space around him with a mix of curiosity and apprehension. The air feels static, charged with an unspoken tension. The world outside his eyelids slowly comes into focus, revealing a sterile, clinical setting. White-silver floors and metallic walls stretch out before him, a horizontal cool light framing the entire room.

Attempting to rise, Sidric's body responds sluggishly, limbs weighed down by an unspoken fatigue. A hesitant hand reaches for support, only to encounter an unexpected barrier. A nearly invisible force halts his movement like a phantom wall. He winces as his forehead makes contact with the unseen obstruction, intensifying the residual haze in his vision.

With a restrained groan, Sidric massages his throbbing temples, the dull ache punctuating his disorientation. Determination sparks in his gaze as he extends his other hand forward, testing the limits of his unseen enclosure. The touch of an imperceptible barrier meets his outstretched fingers—a transparent shield trapping him within an enigmatic space.

As his vision steadies, Sidric examines his peculiar surroundings. A grid of radiant lights outlines the perimeter of his confinement, a surreal spectacle that captures his attention. He traces the pattern, following the interplay of light and shadow to reveal the contours of an invisible cage.

His heart races as full consciousness returns. Panic sets in, and his immediate instinct is to lash out in desperation. With a surge of adrenaline, he vigorously kicks at the cage walls while simultaneously shouting for help, his voice echoing through the enclosed space.

"Someone get me out of here!" he pleads, his cries bouncing off the metallic confines. But there is no response, only an eerie silence that amplifies his isolation.

Realizing the limitations of brute force, he shifts his focus to his unique abilities. Pressing his palms against the unforgiving walls, he summons his electric energy, hoping to break free. Bright bolts surge forth, dancing along the edges of the cage, only to fizzle out in impotence. The invisible force holding him captive remains unyielding.

Unswayed, he gathers his courage for another attempt. Concentrating with newfound determination, he channels more energy into his palms. A larger, more intense bolt erupts from his hands, tearing through the air before colliding with the barrier. But even this formidable display of power meets resistance. The energy disintegrates on contact, scattering sparks in all directions.

His breathing intensifies.

"That was sick!" a child's voice exclaims, breaking through the stifling silence. Startled, Sidric turns toward the source—a curious child watching from inside a cage across the room.

"Do it again!" the child urges with innocent excitement.

Shaved head. Sidric's sharp mind immediately recognizes him. The same kid from the airport, the very same one from the classified *Project Gamma VI* files. It all clicks into place. *This is the child subjected to their secretive experiments.* The files detailed the tests performed on him, and the implications send a shiver down Sidric's spine.

As the gravity of the situation sinks in, Sidric suppresses his shock, fearing any sign of alarm might terrify the boy. He takes a measured breath and forces a friendly tone into his voice.

"Hi!" he calls out, a smile plastered across his face. "What's your name?"

The kid smirks slightly before responding. "You want to know my real name or what they call me here? My name is Helios, but they don't like that. They call me *Subject 1023.*"

"Hi, Helios. I'm Sidric." He attempts to make it as normal an introduction as possible under the circumstances. "How long have you been here?"

"A couple of weeks. It all started when I asked my dad if he could call me Helios and get me boy clothes." His voice carries a mix of defiance and vulnerability. Helios absently traces hexagon patterns on the floor tiles with his finger, dressed in white clinical pants and a shirt. Sidric starts piecing everything together.

"But how did you get here? To this cage?"

"I'm getting there, Sidric!" he chuckles, a bitter edge to his laughter. "My dad put me here. He says they have medicine that can fix me. Medicine that can make me a girl. But I know I'm not sick. I know I'm not a girl. He says his work knows how to 'fix' people like me. To make them *normal*." Helios looks up. "My dad said it was kind of working for a while, but they need to make my next dose stronger."

Sidric's heart aches. "I don't think you need to be fixed, Helios."

"You should've been here last night—it was crazy! My hair was growing out, but I like it short, so I smeared some slime all over it, and they had no choice but to cut it off again."

"How mad were they?" Sidric asks, trying to gather information.

"Not too mad, they took my slime away though. Some guards are nice, but the ones with weapons can get really mean."

"Listen, Helios, we're getting out of here. We're going to make things better. For you, for me, for Deux, for everyone who's ever felt disregarded because of people like Jacques." Sidric clenches his fists, sending sparks crackling against the force field in frustration.

"Who's Deux?" Helios asks, intrigued.

"My boyfriend." Sidric smiles as the word escapes his lips, a warm sensation coursing through him. Until the chilling realization sets in: *If I don't get out, I may never see him again.*

Helios notices the sudden drop in his smile. "You'll see him again," he says as if reading Sidric's mind. "We just need to figure out an escape route."

A piercing alarm fills the room. The metal doors slide open.

"It's the guards! Pretend to be sleeping," Helios whispers, turning to the side.

"Good night, inmates," a sinister voice hisses. "Security check. Don't try anything—it won't end well, shockboy."

A towering seven-foot security guard stomps into the room, his black combat boots striking the ground aggressively. He approaches Sidric's cage first, taps a code on the console, and instantly, the force field vanishes.

It's now or never.

As the guard reaches down with a massive nine-inch syringe, Sidric reacts. Bolts surge from his palms, slamming the guard's body to the ground. Still breathing but unable to move, his body twitches as electricity courses through his limbs.

Sidric leaps free from his cage, pumping a fist in triumph. "Forgetting someone?" Helios yells.

"Oh, right!" Sidric rushes to Helios's force field. The console demands a code. He presses his hands against it, sending controlled shocks, but the screen flashes *ACCESS DENIED*.

Then, inspiration strikes.

"SixLoko!" he exclaims, retrieving a tiny drink can from the hidden pocket by his wrist.

Helios blinks. "Huh?"

Sidric attaches the can to the console. "Stay low. I don't know how strong these things are."

He takes cover behind a column, aims, and fires the tiniest bolt he can. The golden light arcs toward the can—

BOOM.

The explosion shatters the screen, deactivating the force field. Helios dashes free. "That was sick! You had me worried there for a second. I thought I was gonna blow up," he exclaims, his gratitude echoing through the room as they prepare for the next phase of their escape plan.

"What do we do with him?" Helios points down at the guard, whose eyes dart wildly, his body twitching with residual electricity every few seconds.

"Grab his other leg," Sidric instructs, already pulling. The guard's heavy frame resists at first, but after a few moments of effort, they manage to drag him toward the cage. With a final heave, they shove him inside.

Sidric steps back and sends a sharp jolt into the cage's control panel. Sparks dance across the screen before the force field flickers back to life, sealing the unconscious guard inside.

"We make a good team," Helios laughs. "Okay, let's go!"

They dart out of the room, finding themselves in an impossibly long hallway lined with doors on both sides—none offering an obvious escape.

A sudden *click* echoes behind them. A door opening.

Sidric yanks Helios behind a column, pressing a finger to his lips. Footsteps echo against the cold metal floor, growing fainter as whoever it is walks away.

"This way," Helios whispers, heading in the opposite direction.

At the hallway's end, he spots an air vent and quickly climbs up, gripping the edge.

"I don't know, kid," Sidric hesitates, eyeing the vent warily. "My last adventure in one of these didn't end well."

He exhales, acknowledging their lack of options. Just as he's about to hoist himself up, a surge of energy *slams* into the wall beside him, barely missing his head.

Sidric spins around.

A drone hovers in the air, its sleek frame reflecting the dim overhead lights. In its mechanical grip, a Freeze Foam IT gun, primed and locked onto him.

cold. With a single shot, it injects a dissolvable microchip into the attackers body, tricking their brain into believing their temperature is rapidly dropping to 32°F (0°C). Every second feels colder than the last.

As the freezing sensation intensifies, time distorts. Minutes stretch into what feels like an eternity. Then, at the peak of the experience—blackout.

After a few hours, the chip dissolves completely, leaving the attacker unharmed and feeling normal again.

"Not today, alien bitch!" Sidric yells, ducking as another shot narrowly misses him.

He slams the vent shut and fires a sharp bolt at the drone. The energy blast connects, sending the machine into a brief, erratic spin. Seizing the moment, he turns and bolts in the opposite direction.

The drone recovers fast. Sidric glances back, it's speeding up on him.

Then he's hit.

A sharp, freezing pulse detonates through his body. Agony spreads like wildfire, except instead of heat, it's ice—biting, suffocating. His muscles seize as he crashes to the floor. Each second feels colder, his nerves screaming in protest.

His eyes blur, the sensation like ice sculpting over his retinas every time he blinks. His skull pounds, his thoughts fracturing into frozen shards. He can't move. Can't fight back.

But at least Helios got away. That thought alone brings the smallest sense of peace.

A raspy voice breaks through the fog.

"No use trying your powers now, diva."

Footsteps. Heavy, deliberate.

A shadow looms over him. Cold metal presses against his forehead—a helmet, massive and unyielding. Suddenly, smoke billows out from it, swirling into his vision.

Sidric's last thought is of Deux. His lips, his warmth. The fear that he'll never feel them again.

25

broken kaleidoscopes

Deux

Minutes stretch into eternity as they wait for any news from the BlueEagle squad. Taytish, her heart a storm of desperation after realizing she may have just lost her soulmate, frantically tries to radio them every few seconds.

Drained of hope, Lady Mars gently takes the walkie-talkie from Taytish's hands and drops it onto the front car seat. "I don't think we'll get an answer anytime soon," she says calmly, placing a reassuring hand on Taytish's shoulder.

A gust of wind rushes into the cave, sending a chill down Deux's spine. He sees himself reflected in Taytish's despair.

Then, the suffocating silence is shattered.

The walkie-talkie crackles to life with a broken transmission.

"Tayti-… we're… alive… they have…" Josannah's voice cuts through bursts of static.

The room surges back to life. Laughter and smiles break across the squad like dawn after a storm. Lady Mars leaps into the car through the window, snatching the walkie-talkie.

"Josannah! Doll! I've never been happier to hear your voice! Where y'all at?"

The response drops like a bomb.

"They have Sidric."

Silence returns—heavy, unbearable.

Deux's breath catches. His eyes go wide as a tsunami of thoughts pulls him in and out of consciousness.

"What do you mean they have Sidric?!" He yells, grabbing the walkie-talkie from Lady Mars' hands.

"They took him, Deux. They bombed the car, we flipped over and over. Then I blacked out. When I woke up, the drone squad was flying him away." Josannah's voice is faint, buried in static.

Deux's jaw tightens. His fists clench.

"I'm going in. I need to save him."

He turns to face Lady Mars, Naya, and Taytish, his expression fierce with defiance.

"Deux, it's too dangerous right now," Lady Mars warns. "We weren't ready for them to know we were coming."

"If not now, when?" Deux snaps. "You just said you've been fighting for twenty years. Aren't you tired? There will never be a perfect moment."

"Deux, we don't know what they're going to do with Sidric! What if they capture you too? You'll both be gone forever."

"So what?" His voice rises. "Are we supposed to sit back and watch them take everyone we love? Watch them take over our lives while we do nothing? We deserve to fight. We deserve to put a stop to this."

He looks around the room, locking eyes with each of them.

"MarsBar," Taytish says, stepping forward, "the boy is right. We can't let this continue. We have the malware and the code ready. Deux can go in, rescue Sid, and install it."

"But you don't understand. It's too dangerous!" Lady Mars cries

264

out, pain laced in her voice.

Deux doesn't hesitate. "Wouldn't you do anything to get James back?" He softens, his voice steady but full of conviction. "I know you would risk your own life to set him free. So let me risk mine. I can't live with myself knowing we were this close and I didn't even try."

Lady Mars exhales sharply. Her eyes search his face, and then, finally, she nods.

It catches Deux by surprise.

"I'm not going to stop you from saving your love, Deux. I'm not going to stop you from trying to fix this broken kaleidoscope."

"Thank you." He takes a deep breath. "I just can't leave him in there. I can't risk losing him or anyone else."

Naya's wide eyes lock onto Deux, desperately trying to process the rapid-fire events unfolding before her.

With a determined stride, she steps forward and pulls him into a tight embrace. Her voice, thick with emotion, carries a plea. "Please be safe… and bring my bestie back."

Taytish, ever faithful and resourceful, nods in agreement as she swiftly puts on her VR glasses. "We'll do whatever it takes to help you," she declares, her focus already shifting to coordinating the retrieval of their stranded comrades. "Our queens are en route to pick up Josannah, Lulu, and Tyra from their crash. We'll regroup at the lair and establish a connection with you."

Lady Mars, always the steady presence, steps forward and holds out a pair of sleek, radiant boots. Their golden glow shimmers under the dim light, the translucent blue sole gleaming with an almost angelic energy.

"These will get you where you need to go, Hun," she says with a knowing smile.

Deux slides his feet in, and the moment the laces lock into place, magic ignites.

A surge of golden light spirals around him, wrapping his legs in a flash of dazzling, electric brilliance. He spins effortlessly, as if unseen wings have taken hold, lifting him into the air. His muscles pulse and expand, glowing with raw energy, the sensation tingling like static dancing across his skin.

With a sharp inhale, he crouches low—then launches skyward. His limbs stretch as if he's standing on stilts made of pure lightning. His soles flip outward, the structure shifting and morphing. Brilliant blue wheels materialize beneath him, thick and sturdy, humming with power. The golden accents on his rollerblades ignite, streams of radiant light racing up his calves and weaving together to form boots of shimmering leather, embossed with enormous, electrified golden wings.

He lands, weightless yet unstoppable.

Lady Mars smirks. "Now that's what I call an upgrade."

"I hope you know how to roller-blade," Naya chuckles.

His gaze lingers on the trio, gratitude, and determination flickering in his eyes. "I'll see you all soon," he promises, the weight of the world pressing into every word.

With a powerful push, he glides away, his strides quickening, the rhythm steady and precise. Soon, he's moving at an exhilarating speed, accelerating beyond earthly limits.

With calculated ease, he soars across the desert, the looming silhouette of RainforesTec HQ growing closer. Anticipating the security checkpoints ahead, he adjusts his trajectory, summoning a burst of energy to propel himself skyward. As he ascends, the world below shrinks into a mosaic of tiny details, the vast landscape reduced to a mere blur beneath him.

I'm flying.

At 130 feet above the ground, he hovers—a lone figure against the vast expanse of the desert night. His senses sharpen as he scans his surroundings, absorbing the panoramic view.

With controlled precision, he descends, landing effortlessly on a sleek electric line. The hum of energy pulses beneath his feet, resonating through his body in a rhythmic surge. The connection is instant. Tapping into the coursing electricity, he accelerates along the glowing pathway, the world blurring past in streaks of motion.

Above him, dark clouds gather, the scent of an impending storm thick in the air. A quiet irony settles in. *Of course, there would be a storm during a life-or-death mission.* But he remains focused, his resolve unwavering.

The RainforesTec building looms on the horizon, its ominous, rounded structure growing larger with each passing second. The sleek curvature of its walls, designed to be innovative, only amplifies the unease creeping up his spine. Shadows drape over its reflective surfaces, making the entire structure pulse with a transcendent energy.

As he nears the entrance, the finer details sharpen. Glass panels shimmer with an eerie radiance. On the outside, multiple drones and robots circle the perimeter. Inside, fragmented glimpses of futuristic technology flicker like silent ghosts. The sheer contrast, a flare of hyper-advanced industry standing in the midst of barren desert nothingness, makes the place feel all the more unnatural.

Now, if I were to kidnap Sidric, where would I put him?

His approach is seamless. He glides off the electric line onto a narrow rooftop ledge, barely a foot of space to stand. Carefully, he shuffles along, resisting the urge to glance down. No matter how many powers he has, heights still send him spiraling into panic mode.

The velvety night sky works in his favor, wrapping him in darkness as he moves like a shadow. He taps the sleek frame of his SmartGlasses, activating the augmented reality interface. With a soft command, he whispers, "Find an entry point."

A web of digital light flickers across the lenses, mapping the building's intricate structure. Seconds later, a robotic voice murmurs into his ear, its tone a mysterious harmony of artificial intelligence and mechanical precision.

"Entry point located. Northwest sector."

A vibrant green square highlights an open window.

Without hesitation, Deux slides toward it, his movements precise, his silhouette catching the faintest glint of moonlight. He grips the ledge, steadies himself, then leaps. The transition is flawless. A swift, silent entry.

As he lands inside, he straightens, barely exhaling. The air in the room is still, charged with an unseen tension. He has no idea what lies ahead.

But he's ready.

The room unfolds before him, a vast expanse of orderly desks stretching endlessly into the dimness. Each workstation is a carbon copy of the next – computers on the left, tablets neatly aligned beside the keyboards, and virtual reality glasses standing ready for use. The room is plunged into darkness, except for the faint light of the exit sign, casting an ethereal luminescence upon a door at the room's far end.

Deux attempts to remove his rollerblades but they extremely tight. In his struggle, he accidentally knocks over a stack of papers on the adjacent desk, sending them fluttering to the floor like whispered secrets in the silent room.

"Shit," he mutters under his breath, the gravity of the situation settling in as he grapples with the rollerblades. *How am I supposed to rescue Sidric if I can't even get these rollerblades off?!*

A familiar southern voice, warm and reassuring, emanates through the smartglasses, "Click the heels of the rollerblades together three times."

"Lady Mars?" Deux responds, surprise evident in his voice as he follows the instructions. The rollerblades respond to his touch, seamlessly transforming into regular shoes.

"That's sick!"

"Yes, Hun! We're back in the lair. Everyone's good, thank goodness! Taytish is tracking Sidric's suit. He's three floors down from you in the lab. I'm sending over a map now."

Her guidance steadies him, giving him exactly the support he needs.

"Okay I'm heading there! What do you see on your side?"

"We're hacking into the security cameras. There's drone security on all levels."

As he moves, the hallways stretch endlessly, forming a maze that threatens to engulf him.

With cautious steps, he approaches a door, the metallic handle cold against his fingertips. Slowly, he pushes it open, revealing yet another room filled with rows of computer labs. The soft glow of monitors and hum of electronic equipment adds an eerie soundtrack to the clandestine mission.

"Head right, and you'll find a stairwell," Lady Mars directs, her voice anchoring him against the creeping panic.

Following her instructions, Deux weaves through the labyrinth of corridors, each turn revealing a new potential threat. The air thickens with anticipation as he rounds a corner, spotting the stairwell bathed in muted light.

"Shit pancakes! They're coming toward you! Quick! Get in the room to your left!" Lady Mars shouts.

A heavy bang echoes down the hall. Deux's pulse spikes. A robot stomps into view at the far end of the corridor. He slips into the room, heart hammering.

"Stay in there, boy. I don't think it spotted you," Lady Mars says.

He presses against the wall, forcing himself to steady his breath. The room stretches ahead, leading to a narrow walkway and a set of stairs.

A massive window opens up along the walkway, revealing the floor below.

Cautiously, he peeks through the glass. His stomach knots.

The space is eerily familiar, like the surveillance room he and Sidric once snuck into, except this one is enormous. A colossal wall of screens dominates the far side, spanning both floors, each one flickering with live feeds.

At least fifteen different world leaders appear on the monitors. Hidden cameras stream their every move.

"Are you seeing this?" he whispers.

"Stay quiet. You're not alone," Lady Mars warns.

His gaze drops to the floor below. Rows of desks are arranged like a high-security control room, each labeled with a country's name. His breath catches.

Holy shit.

He scans the screens. The Japan feed shows the Prime Minister working late in his office. The Australia feed captures the Prime Minister stepping into a meeting, flanked by suited officials. The Mexican President is boarding a private jet.

Then—something feels off.

Several European leaders stand motionless in their bedrooms. Same rigid stance. Same blank, unblinking expressions.

A chill creeps down his spine.

"Shouldn't they be sleeping? It's the middle of the night over there," Deux murmurs.

"This is extremely weird," Lady Mars mutters. "Wait a minute! Look at the United States screen!"

Deux shifts, angling for a better view.

On-screen, the U.S. President steps up to a podium inside the White House conference room.

A voice echoes from below.

Deux's eyes snap to a man seated at the U.S. computer desk, speaking into a microphone. His lips barely move, but on-screen—

The President mimics every word.

A chill prickles down Deux's spine. He tunes in his super hearing, isolating the transmission.

"Welcome, everyone. Sorry for the last-minute summoning. However, I'm afraid this cannot wait," the man states.

Each syllable aligns perfectly with the President's mouth.

"It has come to my attention that we have been far too lenient with our nation's hostile enemies. Earlier this week, a terrorist attack targeted a flight to Nevada. The culprits? Members of the LGBTQ+ ring. Not a community, a dangerous ring. A network that thrives on destruction."

Deux's chest tightens. *No. No, no, no.*

"After careful deliberation, I have decided to outlaw any form of support for the LGBTQ+ ring. People may continue their personal choices in the privacy of their homes. However, in public none of it will be permitted. It is in the best interest of our nation."

A tremor of rage courses through Deux. Through his earpiece, Lady Mars's voice explodes.

"These motherfuckers. THESE MOTHERFUCKERS!" she screams from the lair. "They're controlling them! ALL of them! They're the reason for all these backward laws!"

On-screen, the President steps back from the podium. The man at the desk lowers his mic, then calmly reaches for a glowing button labeled **AUTOPILOT**.

He presses it.

And just like that—

The President walks off, expression blank.

Deux narrows his eyes at the screens, dissecting every frozen stance, every unnatural stillness. The eerie symmetry of the European leaders.

The identical posture, the lifeless eyes. It sends an ice-cold realization through his veins.

"I don't think they're being controlled," he says slowly. "I don't think they're real people, Lady Mars."

A moment of silence.

"If they're not," Lady Mars whispers, her voice tight with urgency, "then where the hell are the real world leaders?!"

Deux's jaw clenches. "We're finding out tonight. I'm getting Sidric. You guys scan the building. We are shutting RainforesTec down for good."

He peeks out the door. *Clear.*

Descending the stairs, he keeps his steps light, the hum of distant machinery swallowing the faint echo of his movements. Each step tightens the knot in his stomach. The air feels sterile, heavy with secrecy.

"Okay, two more floors," Lady Mars instructs. "You'll have to cross a large hallway. At the end, you'll see two big doors. He should be in there. But be careful. That floor is plagued with drones. Sending the map to your glasses now."

A detailed animation flickers into view, mapping out the entire level. Red dots, like a swarm of wasps guarding their queen, hover in the hallway, blocking his path.

I'm ready for this.

Deux keeps moving. LEVEL -2. A sign dangles over the last step. Without hesitation, he yanks two SixLoko cans from his pocket and tosses them toward the far end of the hall, right beneath a statue of RainforesTec's first public robot.

Seconds stretch into eternity. Then—

A metallic whisper slithers through the air, a symphony of motors and whirring propellers growing closer. Drones.

He ducks behind the wall as the shadows pass by. One, two… twenty.

They hover over the cans, scanning, inspecting.

Perfect.

Deux peeks out, raises his index finger, and fires. A direct hit.

BOOM.

The explosion rips through the hallway, sending shattered drone parts raining down like confetti.

"Get those fuckers!" Lady Mars whoops from the lair, giddy with adrenaline.

Deux doesn't waste a second. He speeds toward the examination room as the last remnants of the drones clatter to the ground.

Up ahead, two towering glass doors gleam under the cold fluorescent lights. Stamped across them in bold, sterile lettering:

TESTING LAB V.

His pulse hammers.

Without hesitation, without second-guessing, he shoves the doors open and steps into the unknown.

26

fearless

The expansive circular chamber stretches before him, an architectural marvel with three distinct rings of levels that draw Deux's attention like ripples on a tranquil pond. Each tier unfolds a new layer of intrigue. The room is completely dark, so Deux channels the power in his hands, using their vibrancy as a makeshift flashlight with every step he takes.

The outermost ring emerges as an observation deck, enclosed by seamless windows and glass panels that grant an unobstructed view of the enigmatic space within. His glowing hands bathe the area in a ghostly light, accentuating the sleek, minimalist decor. Computer monitors line the perimeter, their screens splurting out streams of data and graphs, providing a visual symphony of information that captivates Deux's curious mind.

Descending to the second ring, he steps onto a slender walkway suspended in mid-air. It acts as a precarious bridge linking the outer edge to the central floor. Its polished surface shimmers beneath him, the subtle hum of unseen machinery vibrating through the air. The sensation of floating intensifies as he glides forward, each step pulling him closer to the chamber's heart.

From the second ring, Deux directs his light downward, finally illuminating what lies at the room's center. His breath catches.

Sidric.

Laid bare on a sleek, metallic operation table.

Deux sprints down the stairs.

The inner sanctum reeks of antiseptic, sterile and suffocating. A tangle of electrodes clings to Sidric's torso like futuristic leeches, pulsing faintly with unreadable energy.

Colossal robotic arms loom overhead, their metallic limbs poised with an unsettling grace. Each of the eight appendages cradles a different instrument—blades, scalpels, syringes—tools of precision, or perhaps destruction. *If only this technology was used for good.* The entire room feels alive. The frequencies emitting from all around like old-school surround sound sets delivering an all-consuming, slow, sinister pulse.

Deux inches closer, his own body's rhythm pulsating against his ribs. Sidric's stillness is unnerving. Deux feels an intense nausea at the helpless sight.

For a split second, he flashes back to the first time they met.

He leans in, voice soft, hoping familiarity will pull Sidric back.

"Wake up, hot stuff," he whispers, half-joking.

Silence.

No teasing smile, no eye roll, no snarky comeback. Just Sidric, cold and motionless. Alone in his mind.

Panic grips Deux as he clutches Sidric's shoulders, shaking him lightly. "Sid, wake up! We have to go!"

His own heartbeat pounds in his ears, his grip tightening around Sidric's hand in a desperate attempt to reassure both himself and the boy he refuses to lose.

"I'm right here," he murmurs, voice raw with fear.

Then—

Lady Mars's voice slices through the tension, sharp and urgent through his transmitter.

"Deux! Behind you!"

A looming shadow creeps across the walls, and Deux whirls around just in time to see a metallic arm tipped with a menacing needle hurtling toward him. Reacting swiftly, he leaps sideways, narrowly avoiding the needle but taking a harsh blow from the metal structure. The impact sends him sprawling across the entirety of the floor against the wall. Gritting his teeth, he shakes off the pain and scans the dimly lit room, searching for the elusive appendage.

Through the darkness, another robotic limb emerges. This one is armed with a laser saw. It descends dangerously close to his right arm. A cold, calculating voice crackles through the speakers, every word dripping with malice.

"You dumb, dumb boy. Did you honestly think you could waltz in here and dismantle my empire? What was your plan? To shock me until I give in to your 'gay' demands?" Bizous chuckles mockingly.

Lady Mars's voice, a whisper in Deux's ear, urges him into action. "At the first chance you get, throw a SixLoko. Explode that sad excuse for a man! We're sending backup."

"Not before we install the code!" Deux fires back, his mind set. For too long, he's watched the world slide into hateful chaos. Now that he knows the root of the problem, he won't leave until it's all gone.

Moving stealthily, he ascends to the second level. The robotic arms continue their menacing dance, each movement punctuated by sharp, mechanical cracks. "Jacques!" he calls defiantly. "You'll need to try much harder if you want to erase us from existence."

The voice sneers. "I don't have to try, Deux. I will eradicate every single one of you. Lesbians, gays, trans, every letter of your stupid alphabet—gone! I will make our world great again."

The suspended walkway quivers as an arm strikes it, threatening to send Deux plummeting. He desperately grabs for the railing, but the ground beneath him gives way. He crashes to the lower level, his breath knocked from his lungs.

From the observation room, Bizous watches. Their eyes lock for a chilling moment.

The villain advances, unleashing two more robotic arms from different directions. Metallic pliers snap open, locking onto Deux's arms. Then, agonizingly, they begin to pull.

A scream rips from his throat as his limbs are stretched to their limits. His muscles strain against the relentless force, his body twisting in unnatural angles. The room fills with the clash of metal, his ragged cries, and the growling satisfaction of Bizous, reveling in his pain.

A blinding series of lights flash from the top floor, followed by a bloodcurdling scream from Bizous.

Through the haze of pain, Deux sees Jacques collapse. The tension in the robotic claws vanishes, and he drops to the ground, his body trembling from the aftershock.

Dazed and breathless, he forces himself to look up, trying to decipher what just happened. "There's someone else in the room." Lady Mars says.

He runs upstairs and sees Bizous' body lying on the ground at the feet of a seven-year-old boy, who stands still, gripping a taser in his hands.

"Helios!" Lady Mars gasps.

"Hi, Deux!" The boy beams. "I'm Helios!"

"How— Who — What are you doing here?!" Deux stares, his shock evident in his wide eyes. His body is still recovering from the painful stretching.

"I was trapped with your... boyfriend," Helios teases, chuckling.

He presses a few keys on the computer beside him, and the entire room floods with light. "I was hiding in the vent, and when I heard you screaming in pain, I jumped out and zapped him with this!" He proudly holds up the taser, pointing it straight at Deux.

"That was very brave of you!" Deux says, gently taking the taser from his hands. "Why don't I hold onto this so no one else gets zapped? And thank you for saving me. You're a true hero."

"No problem! Your... boyfriend." Helios grins. "He helped me escape from that mean security guard, so we're even. Now, what do we do with him?" He points to the tasered body.

Deux glances around before yanking a bundle of cords from the computer. He hands them to Helios. "Here, we'll tie him up with this. If he wakes up, I can shock him back to sleep in no time."

Helios eyes the cords with curiosity. "This is cool. So, you're like a superhero too, huh?"

Deux chuckles. "Not exactly, but close enough, I guess. Now, let's tie him up tight so we can get the hell out of here!"

With Jacques securely restrained in a chair, Deux descends the metal staircase. His eyes immediately land on Sidric, still sprawled motionless on the lab table. A knot tightens in his chest.

Standing beside him, Deux lays a hand on Sidric's chest, feeling the reassuring thud of his heartbeat against his palm. A mixture of worry and tenderness floods him.

"My sweet boy," he murmurs, his voice barely audible against the sterile silence.

Almost involuntarily, Deux leans in and presses a swift, protective kiss onto Sidric's lips. The moment their mouths connect, a sudden surge courses through Deux's body, reminiscent of the electric shock from their very first kiss. He jerks back, still tingling from the unexpected jolt.

The effect on Sidric is immediate. As if yanked from a slumber in the deepest waters of his unconscious, he gasps for air, eyes snapping open.

"Sidric!" Deux rushes forward, wrapping him in a fierce embrace. "I'm here, baby boy."

Sidric pulls back slightly, his hands gripping Deux's cheeks as if to reassure himself that this is real. They lock eyes, a silent acknowledgment passing between them. Sidric takes in the hazel hues of Deux's eyes—the same eyes he thought he'd never see again.

"The kiss of light," he whispers.

Then, with an urgency fueled by near loss, Sidric pulls Deux into a fervent kiss. It's a passionate collision of emotions, a celebration of reunion amid the shadows of danger. The world around them fades as they lose themselves in the warmth of their connection, the electricity that once threatened to divide them now a potent reminder of the strength of their bond.

"You two need to get a room!" Helios teases, breaking their moment. "Also, I think I found your stuff, Sid!" He points toward a drawer by the stairs, where Sidric's suit and SmartGlasses are neatly tucked away.

"Helios!" Sidric yells. "You're alive!"

"Yes! I literally just saved your boyfriend's life!" Helios chuckles.

"Okay, not to interrupt this cute moment, but y'all need to get out of there ASAP!" Lady Mars says to Deux.

"Got you, Queen!" Deux replies assertively. He helps Sidric off the table and helps him put his suit back on.

"Testing, one, two—testing. Sidric, can you hear me?" Naya's voice crackles through his SmartGlasses. "If you ever attempt to get kidnapped or murdered without telling me beforehand, I will hunt you down and kill you myself. You hear me?"

"Naya! Yes, 100%, I agree," Sidric laughs, savoring every moment. "Okay, where to now?"

"Y'all need to get out of the building. There are about two thousand drones swarming the perimeter. There's no way we can finish the mission," Lady Mars urgently declares, her voice heavy with tension.

"We can't leave, Lady Mars. You saw the other room. If we leave now, we can say goodbye to everyone in our community."

Sidric's eyes widen. "What did I miss?!"

"Not much. Just that multiple world leaders have been replaced with evil robots, and the U.S. robo-president just made it illegal to show any signs of queerness."

"Holy shit. We're not leaving, then," Sidric says, his voice unwavering with determination.

From the moment they met, an unspoken understanding has passed between Deux and Sidric, as if nothing was accidental. As if the universe had conspired to set them on a path destined to change everything. The FiveLoko was meant to spill during their make-out session. They were meant to get electrocuted and gain these powers. And now, here in the RainforesTec offices, surrounded by nefarious schemes and brainwashing technology, they stand on a battleground where they can finally right the wrongs they've witnessed for years.

Against overwhelming odds, they know that walking away isn't an option. Abandoning the mission would mean forsaking not just their own principles, but the chance to free innocent minds ensnared by RainforesTec's influence. Their decision is already made. They will fight. They will dismantle this oppressive infrastructure. A fire of purpose burns within them, and as they brace for the chaos ahead, the room itself feels like a crucible of determination and defiance.

"Here's what we're going to do," Sidric says, his voice now fearless. "Deux, you and I are going to find the Data Center. We'll attack from the inside. Helios, you have a very special task—you need to crawl back into the vent and find a way out of here. The queens will meet you outside."

"Wow, you're so hot when you take charge, Sid," Deux sighs,

admiring the transformation in him.

They head upstairs, decisive in their plan, ready to set it into motion. But just as they build momentum, nearing the top floor, they encounter their first setback.

Bizous groggily emerges from his taser-induced shutdown. The group halts as his eyes flutter open, adjusting to the ambient light. The tension in the stairwell thickens as they see him struggling, realizing he is still securely tied to the chair.

"Where the fuck do you three think you're going? Take one more step, and consider yourselves dead," he slurs angrily.

"Dad, you are not a nice person!" Helios cries out.

"Dad?!" Deux, Sidric, Naya, and Lady Mars yell in unison.

"That's your father?!" Sidric asks, disgusted, pointing at Jacques.

"Listen, Claire, you are not mentally well. You need help, and I am trying to get you that help," Bizous says firmly, his deadly stare locked onto Helios.

"My name is not Claire. My name is Helios, Dad."

"Then you're no child of mine, and you won't be until I set your mind right. Now, untie me." He thrashes against the restraints, trying to break free.

"I don't need fixing!" Helios steps forward, grabbing the taser once again. He connects its electricity to the cords. "My name is Helios. I am a boy, and I am proud of who I am!" Bizous' agonized screams echo as electricity surges through him.

"CODE RED—TESTING LAB V!" Bizous yells between shocks.

Powered by his voice, the entire room flashes red as alarms blare.

"CODE RED ACTIVATED," a robotic voice calls out. "INTRUDER DETECTED."

Deux and Sidric exchange frantic glances, their minds racing with a thousand plans. Without hesitation, Deux grabs Helios' hand, and they all sprint toward the exit, leaving behind the furious screams of

Bizous.

"I'm going to destroy you!" he yells as they shut the doors behind them.

The moment they leave the room, a frightening hum begins to build around them as thousands of drones approach from all directions. From upstairs, they hear an ominous banging on the floor.

"Lady Mars!" Deux screams while running for his life. "A little help here! We need to find the Data Center—STAT." He has no idea what 'stat' actually means but remembers watching *Grey's Anatomy* with his grandma and how they always used that word in extreme situations. This definitely feels like one of those moments.

"On it, Deux," Lady Mars replies almost instantly. "All the levels above are crawling with bots and drones heading straight for you. Your best bet is to head downstairs, then take a left, pass two doors, and go inside. As for the Data Center, it was moved after the last remodel. It's on the top floor."

With no other choice, the team abandons the upper levels and plunges down the stairs, each step echoing with a mix of urgency and tension. The dull hum of the pursuing drones reverberates—a constant reminder of the imminent danger.

They make a sharp left turn, moving like a well-rehearsed ballet, synchronized in their desperate flight. The vibrations of the drones intensify. Two doors blur past, and then they burst into the next room.

"This way!" Helios shouts, sprinting straight through and into the next chamber.

"Helios! Where are you going?!" Deux yells, chasing after him.

"I know this place like the back of my hand!" Helios calls back. "Follow me!"

He pulls out the taser and strikes an LED screen beside a set of large sliding doors. The screen crackles, then flickers as the doors begin to open. "Are these the ones you were looking for?"

Deux and Sidric storm into the room, their mouths falling open in shock.

All fifteen world leaders sit trapped in individual glass cells. The moment they see the trio, they begin pounding against the glass.

"Get us out of here!" one of them screams.

"Help! Please!"

"¡Por favor! ¡Sáquenos de aquí!"

Their voices are desperate, pleading. Who knows how long they've been imprisoned?

"Holy shit! Helios, you found them!"

"This was where my old cell was," Helios explains. "Then they switched me because Mr. Japan was teaching me Judo moves to use against the mean guards, and Miss Mexico taught me how to cuss them out in Spanish. *Hi, friends!*" He grins.

"Y'all, they're coming!" Lady Mars warns. "There's a vent at the back of the room that leads outside. Send Helios and all these people through there."

"How do we get them out of the cells?" Deux asks, scanning for an entry point.

"Oh my god! The cans!" Sidric exclaims. "I got this!"

He pulls out multiple tiny SixLoko cans and places them on the screens outside each of the cells.

"Turn toward the wall and cover your faces!" he instructs the prisoners.

He nods at Deux, and together they send electric bolts surging toward the cells. Within seconds, the glass shatters into a million tiny pieces. Shards fly everywhere as the fifteen leaders jump free, cheering.

"Thank you, thank you, thank you!" the Australian Prime Minister exclaims in a thick accent. "We've been trapped here for years!"

There's a brief exchange of relieved hugs before Deux interrupts.

"Okay! You all need to follow Helios *now!*" He pops open the vent. "Helios, lead them to safety. Lady Mars is sending someone to pick you up."

"Yes! We're on our way!" Lady Mars confirms.

Right before climbing into the vent, Helios turns back and pulls Sidric and Deux into a heartfelt embrace. Gratitude lingers in the air, the weight of the moment almost tangible. Sidric feels tears prickle at the corners of his eyes. When he glances at Deux, he finds him already shedding silent tears, their shared understanding unspoken but clear.

One by one, the world leaders crawl into the vent—a sight Deux never imagined he would see.

Just before the U.S. President disappears inside, he turns around and looks at Deux and Sidric. "History books will talk about this moment. Thank you."

Deux and Sidric stare in shock.

"Anytime!" Sidric quickly replies with a smile.

The vent door seals shut just as the sliding doors behind them burst open with a resounding *slam*. A swarm of airborne drones floods into the room, transforming it into an instant battleground.

Sidric and Deux dive behind an unused cell, seeking cover.

The ambient hum of the drones grows into a relentless buzz, their mechanical eyes scanning for movement. Holding their breath, Sidric and Deux navigate the dangerous waltz of evasion.

Within seconds, the drones' advanced heat-sensing cameras lock onto their targets. The air hums with tension before the room erupts in the deafening rattle of gunfire.

Panic flickers in Sidric's eyes, but instinct takes over. He summons a protective force field, enveloping himself and Deux in an iridescent barrier.

The force field crackles to life as a dazzling display of energy that absorbs the relentless onslaught of bullets. The metallic projectiles ricochet off the shield, filling the air with a chaotic symphony of pings and clinks.

Just as they make a break for the exit, the door within reach, a sudden movement disrupts their momentum.

Robot-crawlers.

With eerie precision, the mechanical creatures scuttle into the room. Their octopod-shaped bodies, reminiscent of robotic spiders, skitter across the floor before leaping straight at Deux's face.

Reacting in a heartbeat, Deux releases two precise blasts of electrowaves. The energy strikes the crawlers midair, sending them flying off-course, their circuits fried by the impact. The metallic intruders hit the ground, motionless.

In the midst of the chaos, Sid seizes the moment, hurling two SixLoko cans into the room. With practiced accuracy, he shoots at them just before they touch the ground. The cans explode upon impact with his electricity, unleashing a cascade of flames that engulfs every drone and bot in the room. Fire dances in the air, showcasing a mesmerizing yet deadly display that leaves destruction in its wake.

With no time to marvel at the damage, they surge forward, feeling a step closer to the Data Center.

Navigating the labyrinthine hallways, Deux consults the map displayed on his SmartGlasses, the light reflecting in his focused eyes. Sidric shadows him closely, their hands intertwined in a silent pact of solidarity.

As they speed through the corridor, the echoes of their footsteps blend with the fading sounds of combustion and destruction left in their trail.

"Boys, head south, then east. We're keeping the service elevator clear for you," Lady Mars relays, her instructions laced with urgency, though veiled in the confusion of the chaotic situation.

A bemused smile tugs at Sidric's lips, his laughter suppressed by the gravity of their near-death experience. "South, then east? What does that even mean?"

Naya's voice crackles over the comm, attempting to clarify Lady Mars' instructions. "Just keep going straight, then turn when you hit the wall. The elevator doors will swing open when you get there. All muscle, no brains bro." She teases.

A sudden, thunderous blast echoes behind them, and Sidric instinctively turns toward the source of the commotion. Emerging from the billowing smoke, an imposing figure materializes—an eight-foot-tall, gleaming white robot. Its metallic exterior gleams threateningly under the harsh lights. The robot's face shield slides open, revealing Jacques Bizous inside, controlling the mechanical suit.

In the daunting silence that follows, the robot springs into action. From its metallic arms, Jacques fires small spheres that hurtle toward them. Upon contact with any surface, the seemingly innocuous spheres morph into corrosive balls of acid, sizzling and eating away at everything in their path.

"How is he still alive?!" Sidric yells.

"Who?!" Deux shouts back.

The suit, a baroque creation of advanced technology, moves with an unsettling grace. Its elongated limbs extend at superhuman speed, almost reaching Sidric and Deux in the blink of an eye. The air crackles with tension as Deux struggles to comprehend the incoming projectiles.

"Just... don't look back!" Sidric's urgent scream cuts through the air.

But of course, Deux looks back. His eyes widen, shock and urgency mixing within them. Time stretches into an eternity as he absorbs the details of the approaching metallic menace. Jacques' evil red eyes lock onto Deux's, burning with intensity.

In one smooth motion, Deux propels Sidric onto his back, urgency etched into his every movement. His heels click together three times, activating the hidden rollerblades beneath them. With a sudden burst of acceleration, they shoot forward, swiftly escaping the impending threat.

"What?! I didn't get a pair of those!" Sidric exclaims, the wind tousling his hair. "I think Lady Mars has favorites," he teases, gripping Deux's back for dear life.

Glancing behind them, Sidric watches as the robot struggles to match their newfound speed. In a calculated move, he releases an electric wave that collides with the metallic monster, sending it crashing to the ground for a precious few seconds.

"Open the lift gates!" Deux's urgent command slices through the chaos as he rockets toward the elevator.

Lady Mars instantly responds, her fingers flying over the controls back at the secret lair. The two massive silver doors slide open just in time. Deux and Sidric soar into the lift, adrenaline coursing through their veins.

The colossal robotic Jacques Bizous, undeterred, clambers back onto its mechanical feet. Each step resonates with a thunderous stomp, echoing through the halls of RainforesTec.

Deux's fingers frantically dance over the elevator panel, repeatedly jabbing the button for the top floor. He can feel the threat looming closer with every passing second.

The silver doors begin their agonizingly slow closure, threatening to close just as the mechanical behemoth closes in. Deux's jaw tightens in determination as he wills them to shut faster, to confine the danger outside.

But the robot is relentless.

Just as the doors are about to slam shut, Sidric, in a last-second burst of energy, conjures a force field that ripples outward, creating a shimmering barrier. The electromagnetic sanctuary pulsates with an otherworldly glow.

For a split second, the colossal robot is frozen in place. Its systems violently short-circuiting as it thrashes within the electric field. Sparks burst from its joints, its mechanical limbs convulsing as if gripped by an invisible force.

With a final metallic clang, the elevator doors slam shut, sealing the duo away from the threat.

In the confined space, they catch their breath, their hearts pounding in synchrony with the hum of the ascending elevator.

"Okay, twinks," Naya's voice crackles through their headsets. "Time to learn how to install the malware and finish these fuckers off."

27

starliGHT

Sidric

The elevator doors jolt open with a sudden clang, revealing a sight that seizes Deux and Sidric's attention. The data center sprawls before them—enormous mainframe computers dominate the heart of the room, their sleek surfaces dimly illuminated by the ethereal glow of moonlight streaming through the glass dome rooftop above.

A soft, electronic hum drifts through the space, a mechanical whisper in the silence. Arrays of servers stand like silent sentinels, their metallic bodies reflecting the muted luminescence from the celestial orb overhead. Various lights flicker on and off in untraceable patterns across the computers, forming constellations of code and data.

The glass dome, a celestial skylight, adds an otherworldly touch to the scene, casting intricate patterns of shadows across the colossal computers. Moonlight dances upon the polished surfaces, heightening the room's eerie ambiance. Above, storm clouds gather around the moon, signaling an impending storm.

"We have to be quick. In simplified terms, tell us exactly what to do," Sid's voice echoes through the room as he steps forward, his eyes sweeping over the array of computers from a cautious distance.

"Alright, listen up, dumb and dumber. Hacking into a mainframe is like sneaking into a high-security club where the bouncers are literal lines of code trying to kick your ass out. Lucky for you, I'm the queen of backdoor entries—"

Sid and Deux exchange a look and immediately burst into laughter.

"—No, not that kind, you degenerates. Pay attention."

"Step one: You inject a little Trojan horse into the system—think of it as a regular guest pretending to be a celebrity manager. The mainframe won't even question it. While the system is busy giving the code the red carpet treatment, we slip in behind and start disabling the security layers one by one. Firewalls? Bypassed. Encryption? Cracked. Admin passwords? Stolen, baby. So go ahead and plug the malware into the huge machine in the middle of the room."

Deux pulls out a small microchip and heads toward the mainframe computer. He inspects all sides of the machine until he finally identifies the entry point. "Okay, I'm sticking it in now!"

Sidric chuckles.

"Perfect. Step two: The malware install. Now, imagine the mainframe is starting to send out the tabs for the shots everyone ordered. What I'm about to do is walk in, slap some fake credit card numbers on the bill, delete a few bottle orders, and replace them with my own promo codes. This malware is basically a virus with a God complex—it'll corrupt files, spread through the network like gossip at a high school party, and make sure no one can undo the damage without a total system collapse. To do this, look for a small round button—it should look like a little pimple. Press that one, then find a switch that's constantly flashing green and orange. This will open the gates for it all to go in."

Deux presses the red button, and seconds later, Sidric flips the switch.

"Step three: Distraction. While the system is busy freaking out over our little surprise, we'll cover our tracks so no one knows where this all came from."

"Beautifully done!" Lady Mars cheers. "We see it in our system. Once Josannah enters the code everyone brainwashed by RainforesTec should be getting their minds back! Get ready to blow this place up! How many SixLoko cans do y'all have left?"

"I have four," Deux replies, extracting them from his pocket. Sidric mirrors the gesture, displaying his own remaining stash. "So does Sid."

"Ah-mazing! Place these all around the room, form a circle around the machines."

As they meticulously set up the devices, the lift doors slam open, shattering the overpowering silence.

A gunshot pierces the air, prompting Sidric to dive behind one of the machines. His gaze frantically scans the room, ensuring Deux remains unharmed. In the shadows, Deux conceals himself beneath a spiral staircase leading right to the top of the dome.

"Where are you hiding?!" Jacques Bizous' voice, a rasp similar to nails on a chalkboard, pierces through the room as he limps out of the elevator. "Come on, show yourselves!" His face drips with blood.

Sid tries to retaliate with an electric shock, but as he focuses his energy nothing happens. No bolt, no spark. His powers are gone. Panic grips him as he strains to summon even a flicker of electricity, but it's useless. His breath quickens. Across the room, Bizous' shadow glides elegantly over the floor, twisting and shifting with each step. Like clockwork, Sidric moves in sync, mirroring his every motion, staying hidden in the shifting darkness.

"You know, nobody needs to get hurt," Bizous muses, his tone

291

deceptively amiable against the thick, suspenseful silence. "The people changed by RainforesTec are happy. They love their lives. They love being normal. That's all I want—for people to live normal lives. There's no need for all this gay, lesbian, trans nonsense. I've had power over the most powerful leaders for so long! No one has complained about it."

Sidric clenches his fists, anger building with every venomous word.

"This can end right now," Bizous continues. "I can turn you back into your old selves, fix your radioactivity, and send you home. How does that sound? I'm just trying to help."

Limping footsteps draw closer. In the brief moments between each step, Sidric meets Deux's gaze. Moving with practiced precision, he maneuvers toward him, unseen.

"My powers aren't working," he whispers.

"Mine neither," Deux murmurs, unease threading through his voice.

"We're scanning the room," Lady Mars reports through their SmartGlasses. "We're detecting an extreme amount of L-ectiline+. It's everywhere. It seems Bizous created some kind of force field using the same L-ectiline+ from the FiveLoko."

Deux scrunches his face in frustration. Sidric instantly deciphers his expression into two words.

We're fucked.

"Silence, huh?" Bizous sighs. "I take it you two don't want to be normal."

A gunshot cracks through the chamber. Glass explodes from the dome above.

"And I'm guessing you've realized you're powerless in here? It's just you two fags against me."

Shards of glass cascade from the shattered rooftop, catching the glimmers of the night sky. For a fleeting moment, Deux and Sid lock eyes, an unspoken realization passing between them. Time seems to slow as Bizous' limping steps echo through the cavernous space, weaving between the towering machines.

Sensing the perfect moment, Deux and Sid slip away, melting into the shadows of the staircase.

They ascend the metal steps cautiously, inching toward the apex of the dome. Just as they near the top, their shadows cross Bizous' path. He glances up and fires.

The silver bullet slices through the air, threading the needle between Deux's back and Sidric's face, missing them by mere milliliters. The air crackles with tension as it strikes the dome, shattering what little glass remains.

The fractured shards rain down in a crystalline cascade. The echoes of the gunshot linger as Deux and Sidric leap the final three steps, emerging onto the rooftop. A gust of wind whips through their hair, sharp and electric against the night.

The electricity reignites within them.

In seconds, Sidric, fueled by sheer determination, attempts to wield his powers once more. He feels the pulsing energy surge through him and releases an electric charge. Arcs of crackling lightning streak toward Bizous' face—

But the attack fizzles out right before entering the room, as if striking an invisible barrier.

Bizous' laughter reverberates through the space, low and sinister. "You are powerless in this room, Sidric! L-ectiline+ is *my* creation. I sold it to FiveLoko. I control everything in this world—don't you understand?" His wicked grin remains unwavering as he steps toward the staircase, gun now aimed right at him.

Sidric, quick on his feet, ducks just as another bullet whizzes past. His mind races, searching for a way out.

"Lady Mars!" Deux shouts over the comms. "Is there *anything* we can do to break the L-ectiline+ force field?"

293

"You're using the same power source. You need an alternate electric current to break through the force field. Something other than L-ectiline+," Lady Mars' voice crackles through the communication channel.

For an agonizing moment, darkness consumes Deux and Sidric—not just from the ominous stomps of Jacques closing in, but from an overwhelming sense of powerlessness. They stand at the precipice of victory, yet fate has tipped the odds against them.

Jacques hauls himself up the staircase, his bloodstained fingers gripping the railing. The gun in his hand stays trained on them, unwavering. Above, thunder rolls, weaving a sky of restless storm clouds.

A sharp tingling sensation surges through Sidric's body. Chills dance along his spine as he turns to Deux—and in that moment, he sees it. Deux's hair stands on end, charged with static. Sidric raises a trembling hand to his head, feeling his own strands lift in response. Their eyes lock. A silent understanding passes between them.

Sidric stumbles toward the far edge of the dome, hands raised. Deux mirrors his movement. They focus, drawing from the storm above. A golden shimmer ignites in their fingertips, spreading until their entire bodies radiate with divine brilliance.

From Sidric's perspective, Deux glows like a fallen star—a celestial beacon against the night. From Deux's view, Sidric is a burst of daylight, piercing through the dark.

Time stretches. The only sound is Jacques' ragged breathing, a stark contrast to the stillness before the storm.

Then—

A blinding flash. Two colossal lightning bolts split the heavens, striking their upturned palms with pinpoint precision. Energy crackles through their veins, raw power merging with human will.

With a synchronized thrust, Deux and Sidric hurl the lightning downward. The force field fractures. The mainframe computers below erupt in a surge of electricity. One by one, they explode in fiery brilliance, filling the air with smoke and metallic debris.

The room is consumed by chaos as computers explode one by one, their demise filling the air with fiery brilliance and metallic debris. In this explosive symphony, Jacques witnesses the destruction in slow motion, a surreal dance of the destruction of his darkest desires unfolding before his eyes. The staircase, once a sturdy lifeline, breaks off from the wall, tumbling gracefully into the chaos below. He gazes up at Sidric and Deux one last time, their figures etched against the backdrop of consuming fire and billowing smoke.

"You will pay for this!" He screams as he falls into the fiery pit.

Sidric and Deux sprint toward each other as the sky unleashes its fury. Rain pours in torrents, washing away the remnants of RainforesTec's wickedness.

Deux doesn't hesitate. Fueled by adrenaline, he grabs Sidric and lifts him off his feet. Their lips collide in a kiss—wild, interconnected, victorious.

"We did it!" Deux breathes against Sidric's lips. "I love you so much!"

A thunderous crash shatters the moment—the building is collapsing from the inside out.

"Let's get you out of there—NOW!" Lady Mars' voice commands through the SmartGlasses. The whir of helicopter blades cuts through the storm.

They don't think. They run.

Wind tears at their clothes as they leap from the rooftop, hands grasping onto the swaying ladder just as the ground crumbles beneath them.

Above, Naya grins from the helicopter, eyes alight with exhilaration. "Badass! You two are absolutely badass!"

Deux tightens his grip around Sidric's waist, holding him close as they dangle in midair. Below them, RainforesTec's headquarters is consumed by fire, its last remnants crumbling into the abyss.

Drones plummet like fallen birds, their mechanical wings silenced. The empire that once controlled them is no more.

The storm rages on—but now, it carries the promise of something new.

Something free.

28

iS it over now?

The secret lair has never been this packed before. Every queen is in full drag, shimmering under the neon lights, ready to celebrate the electric boys' return. World leaders lounge on velvet sofas, shoveling Josannah's famous peanut butter chicken wings into their mouths—their first proper meal in years.

As Deux and Sidric step through the door, the entire room erupts into a thunderous standing ovation. Deux jumps back, startled, but Sidric squeezes his hand three times.

"We did it, y'all!" Lady Mars barrels toward them and lifts them both clear off the ground. "Let this be the Second Big Bang—the collapse that sparks an opportunity to re-imagine the world!" She takes a deep breath. For years, she's dreamt of this moment.

"So it worked?" Deux asks, eyes wide with hope. "People aren't brainwashed anymore?"

"There's a full RainforesTec blackout, so that's a start," Naya replies. "As for whether people are waking up from their heterosexual hypnosis... guess we'll find ou—"

"Bessie." A voice bursts through the entrance.

The room fades around Lady Mars as she hears the name only one person ever dared to call her. Before she can think, James is in front of her, eyes filled with memories long buried. And then, suddenly, she's in his arms, years of longing crashing over her like waves.

"I remember everything," he whispers. "And I'm never losing you again."

For the first time in forever, Lady Mars lets her guard down. Tears streak through her makeup, and for once—she doesn't mind.

Across the room, Josannah and Taytish spot Helios, sitting alone, dipping peanut butter wings into his mint-chocolate milkshake.

"You know," Taytish leans in, smirking. "It drives Josannah crazy when I do that, but it makes the wings taste better. Don't tell her I said that."

"I won't." Helios winks.

Josannah chuckles, but the warmth in her eyes softens as she sits beside him. "I'm sorry about your dad, kid." She pulls him into a hug. "We'll find you a good family."

Helios hesitates, then looks up at them. "Can you be my good family?"

Taytish and Josannah exchange a glance before breaking into matching smiles.

"Yeah, kid," Taytish says. "We can."

The rest of the night is spent celebrating, laughing, and preparing for the unknown.

Twenty-one hours later, the world is in chaos.

RainforesTec's influence vanishes overnight. Flights are canceled. Banks freeze. Entire systems collapse. But amid the disorder, something else happens—long-lost lovers reunite. Families find their way back to each other. People rediscover parts of themselves they'd forgotten.

The team is flown to the White House, where world leaders scramble to repair the damage. In a surprising twist, they are rewarded with financial compensation beyond their wildest dreams.

"We're rich, baby!" Deux mouths to Sidric, who nearly chokes on his broccoli-flavored Cheetos.

The room buzzes with excitement—Naya envisions all the upgrades for her new management business, and Taytish and Josannah cling to Helios, knowing they can finally build the family they've always dreamed of.

But for Deux and Sidric, the real reward is waiting in another room.

As they make their way to the West Wing, Deux's heart pounds. He braces for judgment, for anger, for the sting of rejection he's spent years protecting himself against. But when the doors swing open, all of that disappears.

His entire family rushes toward him, tears in their eyes, love written across their faces. Sidric barely has a second to react before he's tackled by his own family. His mother clings to him tightly, cursing him in rapid-fire Spanish for scaring her half to death.

Laughter and joy ripple through the room as everyone embraces. Grandma twirls around with Sidric's dad, the moms effortlessly blend in with the queens, and Deux's dad chats animatedly with Josannah, soaking in her mechanical expertise. The once-divided families merge into one, celebrating not just a victory, but a new beginning.

Amid all the love and light, they steal a moment alone.

"So… we did it," Sidric chuckles. "Are you still going to want to date me now that you're a famous superhero?"

Deux smiles. "Sidric, being with you is like catching lightning in a bottle. A one-in-a-billion chance. I'm never letting you go. You complete me."

He leans in, capturing Sidric's lips in a kiss. Sparks fly around them, prismatic colors of pure energy pulsing through their bodies, amplifying the love they already feel.

"Maybe these powers won't be such a bad thing," Deux laughs, pulling away.

And in that moment, the past no longer matters.

They are here. *Together*.

In a world where love has won.

About the Author

Dion Yorkie and Sebb Argo are a dynamic creative duo whose shared passion for art and storytelling has driven them to create original music, videos and shorts that resonate with audiences worldwide. Their journey began in 2015 in the world of social media, where they initially garnered attention through engaging relationship content and glimpses into their life.

As a team, Dion and Sebb's creative synergy shines through in each of their projects. Their music, visuals and videos blend genre-defying styles with a deep commitment to crafting meaningful, authentic stories. Dion is currently producing his second studio album and Sebb's first EP.

Known for their genuine approach to social media, Dion and Sebb connect with fans through regular updates, behind-the-scenes peeks, and interactive content. This direct communication has fostered a loyal fan base who support their artistic endeavors, eagerly anticipating each new release. Their journey, built on authenticity and a love for creation, continues to inspire others.

With a focus on originality and an unwavering passion for pushing creative boundaries, they look eagerly to the future with their artistic legacy in focus - with the hope they uplift others in the industry as they go. Dion Yorkie and Sebb Argo are artists to watch in the ever-evolving creative landscape.

You can connect with me on:
- https://www.aryomedia.com
- https://instagram.com/sebbargo
- https://instagram.com/dionyorkie
- https://www.tiktok.com/@dionandsebb

Subscribe to my newsletter:
- https://www.aryomedia.com/newsletter

Also by Sebb Argo and Dion Yorkie

The Mess of it All

Raw, unfiltered, and unapologetically real—**The Mess of It All** is Dion Yorkie's boldest musical statement yet. This album dives headfirst into the chaos of love, betrayal, self-discovery, and finding your voice. With infectious beats, emotional lyrics, and genre-bending sounds, Dion invites listeners into his beautifully messy world.

From anthems that make you wanna dance to ballads that hit right in the feels, **The Mess of It All** is a soundtrack for anyone who's ever embraced the highs, the lows, and the beautifully chaotic journey of life. Stream now and embrace the mess of it all!

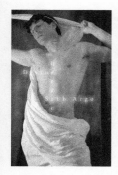

Divine Decree

Sebb Argo's debut EP is coming in summer 2025! This self-written collection explores what Sebb considers his Divine Decree—to make the world gay and fabulous.

Featuring six tracks produced by Dion Yorkie (Sebb's twink in shining armor), the EP showcases the couple's versatility in both genre and storytelling.

This ain't Sebb's first rodeo when it comes to making music. Join the Lost Boys and stream now!

So Rude! Podcast

Unfiltered. Hilarious. So Rude! Join Sebb Argo and Dion Yorkie as they spill the tea on pop culture, gay lifestyle, dating, romance, sex, and everything in between (and outside!). No topic is off-limits as they serve up laughs, hot takes, and a little bit of chaos. Whether you're here for the juicy stories, the unfiltered opinions, or just to feel like you're kiki-ing with besties, **So Rude!** is the podcast you didn't know you needed.

New episodes every Thursday! Stream now wherever you get your podcasts!

If you enjoyed this book, we'd love for
you to review and rate it wherever
you can!
Share it on your socials as well, let's
make this world gay again!

Sebb Argo & Dion Yorkie
HEART-STRUCK

www.ingramcontent.com/pod-product-compliance
Lightning Source LLC
LaVergne TN
LVHW040739190525
811641LV00006B/64